SUNDOWN ON TOP OF THE WORLD

A Hunter Rayne Highway Mystery

R.E. Donald

First print edition March 2015 by
Proud Horse Publishing,
British Columbia, Canada
ProudHorsePublishing@gmail.com

ISBN 978-1-7777510-0-5

Library and Archives Canada Cataloguing in Publication
Donald, R. E., author / Sundown on top of the world / R.E. Donald. (A Hunter Rayne highway mystery). I. Title. II. Series: Donald, R. E. Hunter Rayne highway mystery.
PS8607.O628S95 2015 C813'.6 C2015-901487-5

PUBLISHER'S NOTE:
This is a work of fiction. Names, characters, places and incidents either are the product of the author's imagination or used fictitiously and any resemblance to actual persons, business establishments, events or locales is entirely coincidental. This story is set in the year 1997.

For those hardy individuals who have chosen to live in the Yukon and Alaska, past and present.

You road I enter upon and look around,
I believe you are not all that is here,
I believe that much unseen is also here.

Walt Whitman
Song of the Open Road

CHAPTER ONE

Near Johnson's Crossing in the Yukon Territory, October 30, 1972

"I brought food for the dogs. Looks like they haven't been fed since before the snow fell. " The man gestured toward a sled behind his snowmobile. It held two tubs with frosted chunks. "Whitefish," he added.

Hunter could hear barking and howling, and saw the movement of grey and black fur between the tree trunks a hundred yards or so from the cabin. From the noise and movement, he could tell there were about half a dozen dogs in the dog yard, each tied to their own dog house with a chain. Whoever lived in the cabin used a dog team to get around in the winter.

"These your footprints, Mr. Klimmer?" he asked the man.

Fred Klimmer took a step backward, and RCMP Constable Hunter Rayne could see that the prints he had just stepped out of matched those leading to the front porch of the cabin. Klimmer's pant legs had ties at the ankle to keep the snow out of his boots, and he wore a thigh length grey parka which hung open due to the relative warmth of the mid-day sun. He was taller than Hunter, and big boned but lean like most creatures who subsist in the north, where fats are a rare luxury. His parka hood was off, a knitted black toque pulled down over his ears. A coarse black beard concealed his lips and chin, revealing only his dark eyes above the ruddy skin of his cheeks and nose.

"Did you touch anything inside?"

Klimmer shook his head. He looked as if he hadn't trimmed his beard in a couple of years, a contrast to Hunter himself, who always felt uncomfortable going more than a day or two without shaving. "I hollered, but there was no answer. I could tell by the snow and the open door that no one had been in or out since the snow fell last Monday and I figured it wasn't my place to go inside. That's why I called you guys. With the door open and no heat, not likely there's anybody in there alive."

Hunter nodded. It had dropped to several degrees below freezing during the night, and even now in the early afternoon was below freezing unless in direct sun. Klimmer had radioed the Whitehorse RCMP detachment who in turn had dispatched Hunter to investigate a likely death at the scene. Hunter found it odd that way out here, far from any emergency services, Klimmer had hesitated to go inside himself, but then again, he did the right thing in not contaminating the scene with his presence. From Hunter's perspective, it had been a good decision.

It had been a relatively heavy snowfall for so early in the year, leaving over six inches of powdery snow on the frozen ground, with drifts over a foot deep. The isolated trapper's cabin was not far from the small community of Johnson's Crossing, on the bank of a creek leading to the Teslin River. The nearest vehicle access was a narrow, rutted dirt track off a gravel road that started at the Alaska Highway. Hunter had left his Suburban where the gravel road ended, and hitched a ride the last few miles with Klimmer on the back of Klimmer's snow machine, carrying a pack slung over his back.

He dropped his pack beside the snow-covered steps and opened the flap to pull out a flashlight and his Polaroid camera. If there was death involved, he wanted to document the scene just as it looked when he arrived.

"Go feed the dogs," he told Klimmer, before pulling his right glove off with his teeth and stuffing it in his jacket pocket. "They sound pretty hungry."

The man just stood there until Hunter turned around and aimed the Polaroid at him, taking in the man's Ski-Doo and the sled full of frozen fish. Klimmer shrugged, then straddled the snow machine and revved its engine before slipping away through the trees.

The Polaroid captured the rough wooden porch, the wisps of snow that had drifted through the open door into the cabin. The interior of the cabin was dim, the only light coming from the doorway and a small window above the sink in the kitchen. The remaining windows were shuttered. The shutters were designed to keep in heat, not to conceal the inhabitants from non-existent neighbors. Flashlight in hand, Hunter took a cautious tour of the cabin's main room. It was an open space with a kitchen to the right of the door and a sitting area with a free-standing woodstove on the left. It was a cut above the usual trapper's cabin and it might have been cozy and attractive at one time, but not anymore.

There was no question that there had been violence here, violence that could have ended in death. It wasn't Hunter's first such encounter since his posting to Whitehorse as a rookie in the spring, but the hair stood up on the back of his neck and his heart began to race. He stuck a four-sided flashcube in the camera and began to take photos, starting with fresh scratches on the wooden door. He opened the shutters, and as each of the first few photos slid out of the Polaroid, Hunter placed it face up on the windowsill. His breath created small vapor clouds in the frozen air, so he took care not to exhale before a shot.

It was a chaotic scene. There were plates and kitchen utensils strewn across the floor. The small kitchen table had been overturned and one leg was broken off. Shelves and a small cabinet had been partially ripped off the wall. There were two metal pails, one upright on top of the woodstove and half full of ice, the other tipped on its side with a thin film of ice on the floor in front of it.

Hunter was pretty sure that the culprit who had ransacked the cabin had left no fingerprints. He did, however, leave his mark. On what was probably a trap door to a cache under the floor and on the planks that served as a kitchen counter, there were the unmistakable parallel scratches of a giant set of claws. In the sitting area, chairs were upended and a sofa's cushions were scattered with their fabric shredded.

Hunter sensed the presence of Klimmer in the doorway. "Grizz, looks like," the man said. "Any sign of bodies?"

"Please remain outside," said Hunter. He didn't like being distracted from his current task, but talking to Klimmer was also part of his job. "Still have to enter the back room, but I agree with you about the grizzly. How were the dogs?"

"Listen."

Hunter realized the earlier yapping had subsided into the occasional snarl or growl. He nodded. They were occupied with the frozen fish. He walked back to the front door and bent to find a new package of blank Polaroids in his bag. "What prompted you to come by here?"

Klimmer was leaning against the door frame, lighting up a hand-rolled cigarette. He waved the match out and inhaled deeply. Hunter held out his hand for the spent match but Klimmer smirked and tucked it into his own pocket. "I was out hunting. I ran across Blake's trap line, and I could tell it'd been a long time since he'd cleared it. Remains of a fox in the trap. Scavengers took most of it. Thought I should come check on him."

"Were you and Martin Blake friends?"

The man snorted. "He was an idiot, but his woman was nice. Pretty, too." He ran his tongue over chapped lips, then spat over his shoulder into the snow. "Don't know why she shacked up with him, except maybe it's not a bad cabin to winter in."

"Abusive?"

"Unfriendly. Paranoid. Suspicious and probably jealous. Crazy son of a bitch, far as I could tell. You figure it out."

"But you came to check on him."

Klimmer shrugged. "Unwritten law up here, kid. Nobody ever told you that? You gotta watch out for your neighbors."

Hunter turned away, walked back into the center of the cabin.

There were dark smears on the plank floor leading from the door at the back of the room. Hunter suspected they were a sign of something bloody being dragged to the front door. A grizzly likes to bury its kill and keep the site clearly marked as its own for a later meal. Hunter clenched his jaw, preparing for what he might encounter in the bedroom. Flashlight in one hand, camera in the other, he followed the smears to the back room's doorway and stepped inside.

There was no door, just a ragged grey blanket hanging from the frame. Shutters on the single small window were closed; the only slivers of light seeped through their cracks. The bedding was in a dirty tangled mess half on the floor, the mattress askew, its blue and white ticking exhibiting several large dark stains that Hunter knew were blood. There was smeared blood on the floor of the small room as well as a trail of it leading to the door, and an area of the log wall beside the bed was visibly spattered and streaked with blood as well.

Hunter's flashlight played over a photo on one wall, hanging straight, looking untouched by whatever violence had taken place inside the room. He caught his breath. He knew her. She was young and pretty, a self-professed hippie chick from Michigan who got stalled in Whitehorse on her way to Alaska. In the photograph she was grinning and cuddling a Malamute pup against her right shoulder, her long dark hair draped like a curtain on the left. He'd met her in a Whitehorse bar during his first few months in the Yukon. Her name was April and she was waiting tables as a temporary job. They had flirted a little across pints of beer once or twice and he had decided that next time he saw her he would ask her out, but then she was gone. "Cashed her last check here and moved on," said the bartender. "Free spirit, eh?"

Hunter swung the flashlight away from the photo and back to the bloody bed. "Not her," he whispered, looking at the blood. "God help me, it can't be her." He swallowed hard and pushed the thought out of his mind. Just because her photo was on Blake's wall, it didn't mean she'd been in the man's bed. He played the light over the other walls but there was no sign of other pictures. Only the one.

By the time he was finished, he had used up all of the Polaroid film he had brought with him and his fingers were nearly numb from the cold. He collected up the photos – about ten of them – and those that had developed he wrapped in a clean rag and tucked into a pocket in his pack. He stood on the front porch and looked for Klimmer, saw the man walking through the trees beyond the outhouse, about forty yards away, his eyes scanning the snow around him, in places nudging the snow with his boot. Hunter whistled sharply, and when the man looked up, waved him in.

"What were you looking for?"

"Anything," said the man.

Hunter assumed he'd been looking for signs of a body, or what was left of one.

"What did you find in the back room?" the man asked.

"Nothing," said Hunter. "Just a mess, like the rest of the cabin." He paused. "The woman. What was her name?"

"April," the man answered, squinting as he searched Hunter's face. "Like I said, she was pretty. Pretty and nice." He licked his lips. "It's too bad."

"What's too bad?" asked Hunter, although he already knew.

"What do you think, kid?" The man's face expressed his scorn. "A grizzly doesn't take prisoners."

CHAPTER TWO

A cabin near Eagle, Alaska – June 1997

Betty Salmon brushed a mosquito off her cheek and tucked another bean seedling into the sun-warmed dirt. The growing season in Alaska was short, and she had to make the best of it. The joints of her fingers were swollen and stiff from arthritis, but never mind the pain. There were two more rows to plant in the cold frame before she would go in for tea. The more food she could can or freeze, the less she had to buy over the winter and the less money they would need to survive. Betty's crippled fingers made it hard to hold a needle, so her income from selling beaded deerskin purses and moccasins had fallen sharply the last two years. Goldie was talking about going outside to work, and Betty didn't want to lose her. "It would be the death of me," she said aloud, with only her aged Malamute to hear, if he were able. She'd begun to suspect he was going deaf. Hootie lay flat in the sun, flicking a mosquito off his ear from time to time.

Sometimes Betty would lie awake at night imagining her life without Goldie. Left alone here in Eagle she would die, she was sure of it. It wasn't a physical thing. Physically Betty was tough as an old grizzly sow. But Goldie was her only reason to stay alive, except for Hootie, and he wasn't long for this world. Once he left it, she would surely follow right behind him if Goldie wasn't here. Many of the people who lived in Eagle and Eagle Village were nice enough, and some of them had tried to be her friends, but she'd been gruff and unfriendly for so long, intentionally keeping them at a distance, that now they mostly left her alone.

She knew they called her the Salmon woman, instead of Betty. She imagined the woman at the post office wondering why that old Salmon woman hadn't come for her mail and sending someone to check on her. They would find her frozen – of course she would die during the dark days of winter – frozen solid. Maybe they would find her sitting in her chair with a frozen cup of tea on the table beside her, her beadwork on her lap; if the generator hadn't run out of fuel, maybe the television would still be going. Hootie would be curled up at her feet, frozen, too. Or maybe they would find her frozen under the covers in her bed, the woodstove long dead from no one to add another log. She would just go to bed one dark winter afternoon and find no good reason to get back up again.

"Come with me, Gran. When I find a job, we could get a little house in Fairbanks, or maybe even Anchorage," Goldie had said. "You could still have a garden, and Hootie can come, too."

Goldie had said it more than once, and more than once, Betty had made a sour face and shook her head. She had wanted Goldie to get an education – as much of an education as a kid can get in a one room school – so she had moved from the old, remote trapper's cabin up the river to this one just a few miles from Eagle Village, and this was what had come of it. Betty herself was happy enough seeing the world through the videos Goldie borrowed from the library and the educational programs the Alaska government beamed out to villages in the bush; those same videos and TV programs had made Goldie want to go Outside to see it for herself.

"I can't live in a city," Betty would reply. "My soul needs to be somewhere wild and quiet and uncrowded. It's half Indian, my soul. You know that."

"There's lots of houses near town where you can't even see your neighbors, Gran. It's not like you'd be living in New York or Chicago or somewhere, where it's all concrete and glass."

Betty would grunt, toss her long grey braid back over her shoulder and say, "You go ahead, child. Don't stay here for my sake. I'm old and it's about time I died anyway." She said that, knowing that Goldie couldn't bear to think of her dying, because she was all Goldie had, too. Or so she liked to believe.

"Please, Gran. Life would be easier for us both. Give it a try for my sake. I've got no life here in Eagle. I want to take courses at a university. I want to stretch my wings. I want a family one day." She would sigh and look so unhappy that Betty felt guilty, but then she would think about what might happen if they moved to a city.

What if 'they' – nameless, faceless people in government, people Betty had never seen or wanted to see – found out that Betty wasn't really Goldie's grandmother, wasn't even related in any way to the only family she had? Goldie was in her twenties now, so it's not like she would be taken away, but that's not what worried Betty. If 'they' found out, then Goldie herself would know. She would learn the truth about her mother, and maybe even find out about her father, and worst of all, she would lose faith in her Gran, and she might turn against the brittle old woman who loved her more than life itself.

Betty straightened her aching back and rubbed her eye with the back of her hand. Her fingernails, even her fingers themselves, were black with the dirt from her garden plot, made richer than the poor Alaskan soil around it from years of composted leaves and chicken manure. The half a dozen chickens she bought each spring were a major indulgence on her part – almost her only indulgence – as feeding them properly wasn't cheap, plus they required a good deal of care, and protection from predators. She'd developed a taste for eggs many years before, and powdered eggs just weren't the same. She was able to sell or barter some during the summer, and the least productive chickens that survived until the fall were killed, boiled and canned to provide meat for winter. Any leftover fruit or vegetables that wouldn't be boiled for soups and jams went to the chickens. It was in her genes to make use of every last bit of food, just like the Athapascan people on her mother's side had always made use of every scrap from the barren-ground caribou, from its eyes to its four-toed hooves.

Where was Goldie? Betty looked toward the narrow dirt driveway that led to Eagle Road. Goldie was supposed to be home by now. She helped out with the cleaning and cooking at Yukon Sally's Lodge in the busy season, got paid in cash, or sometimes in groceries if there were more leftover supplies than cash at the end of the week. You had to take what you could get. Betty listened for the sound of the old Mercury pickup coming up the road toward the cabin. Neither she nor Goldie had a driver's license, but nobody seemed to care since they never drove anywhere but the five or six miles between the cabin and Eagle. The Merc – a robin's egg blue speckled with rust spots where the paint had chipped away – was parked after the snow came, usually by mid-October or early November, when you only needed a snow machine to get around.

Goldie was spending more time in Eagle or at the Lodge these days, less time home at the cabin. That didn't bode well. Betty wiped her hands on her pant legs, slapped and killed a mosquito on her neck, then bent down to lift another bean seedling from the tray to plant. "We have to live in the moment, don't we, Hootie? Right here in the sunshine." She smiled fondly in the direction of the old dog, who was panting from the heat of the sun. "The future's gotten to be a scary place for old creatures like us."

"You need help with that?" Goldie smiled at the new guy at Yukon Sally's Lodge. She figured him for mid-twenties – about her own age, maybe younger – and too tidy to be a bush Alaskan. He was clean shaven, his hair a glossy brown, a wavy lock of it falling over his right eye. He wore work jeans and a black tee shirt, sleeves tight around his biceps. It looked like Yukon Sally had started him with an easy job – splitting firewood for the lodge's big fireplace or the outdoor fire pit – but he was swinging a light double-bladed axe. "You're from Outside, aren't you?" she said. "From someplace warm, where you don't burn wood?"

The young man's smile was more like a grimace as he picked up the log, still intact, that he'd just managed to shake off the axe blade. He replaced the log on the stump and straightened up. "I'm okay," he said with a quick glance in her direction. He tossed his head to get the hair out of his eye and was preparing to swing the axe again.

She shook her head. "You'd do better with the maul," she said. "It must be in the shed."

The young man swung the axe and, not surprisingly, it embedded itself in the log again and he struggled to work it loose. A flush rose up his neck into his face. Goldie ducked into the shed before he could see her smile, then emerged with the maul just as he managed to free up the axe.

Goldie strode forward dragging the maul behind her. "Here. Let me show you," she said, grabbing another log and setting it upright on the stump. "This sucker weighs about five pounds more than that axe, and it does the work for you." She wiped her palms quickly on the thighs of her jeans, then picked up the maul, raised it above her head and let it fall right in the center of the log, sending two halves of it flying in opposite directions. "See? Even a girl can do it."

The young man didn't appear to be impressed. He looked away, his jaw clenched.

Goldie laughed. "I've been splitting wood since I was ten," she said, leaning the maul against the stump. "I'm Goldie. Who are you?"

The young man turned to look at her. He narrowed his eyes and seemed to be seeing her for the first time. She saw his eyes open wider and a smile play at the corners of his mouth, and she knew he liked what he saw. It was her turn to blush, so she dropped her head and kicked at the split log beside her foot.

"Mark," he said. "Sally's my mom's cousin."

"Where are you from?" Goldie asked all the outsiders the same question. She'd never been anywhere farther than Fairbanks, and that only a couple of times with a friend from school and her friend's mother. Gran didn't believe in travelling. Goldie wanted so much to go Outside and see it all. All of the United States, all of North America, all of the places she'd only read about.

"Somewhere warm," he answered, nodding. "Santa Barbara, California."

"Nice. I'd love to visit California sometime. I want to see all the states."

"You've always lived here?" He sounded incredulous, as if he couldn't understand how anyone could live in this part of Alaska for their whole life.

"What's wrong with that?" Goldie raised her chin. "This is one of the most beautiful places on earth. Everybody who comes here says that."

He snorted. "Sure," he said, picking up the maul. "If you like the cold and don't care much for civilization. You don't even have TV here. Stand back."

"You call television civilization? The opiate of the people? Most of us have better things to do." She raised her chin and looked down her nose at him. "Besides, we do have TV. Free satellite TV. I bet you don't have that in Santa Barbara."

"Oh, I guess you figure watching ice break up on the river in the spring is a better way to spend your time? I hear that's the biggest show of the year here in Eagle. C'mon, get a life."

"So being glued to the boob tube watching the Simpsons and Seinfeld is better than watching nature? If you've never seen breakup, you wouldn't understand." Although a voice inside of her told her to ignore the insult, Goldie couldn't help herself. She and Gran had a satellite dish and often watched TV during the long winter nights, taking advantage of the four rural channels supplied courtesy of the Alaskan state government. "Soap operas and sitcoms. Yuck," she said, making a sour face.

"Who said anything about soap operas and sitcoms? I'm talking about real live concerts, live theater, sporting events. When's the last time you saw a good band?"

Goldie couldn't think of an answer. A few guys from school had put together a rock band, but she would have a hard time calling it good.

"See? What'd I tell you? In the past year I've been to see Bruce Springsteen, Garth Brooks and the Allman Brothers – live –, watched the L.A. Dodgers beat the New York Mets, and attended the Professional Bull Riding finals in Las Vegas." He brought down the maul and split another log with an immediate ease that Goldie couldn't help but admire. "And that's just for starters."

"Well, I've seen several grizzlies – live – and shot a bull moose in the past year." She couldn't think of anything else to add.

He just looked at her and shook his head, as if to say, "How pathetic."

"I've got to get back to work," she said stiffly, and walked off toward the lodge. She heard the thwack of the maul hitting the log again, and resisted the temptation to look back.

"Hey, thanks," she heard him say. "You were right. This thing works like a damn."

"Bull riding finals, big deal," she said under her breath. She took a quick look behind her as she rounded the corner of the lodge. He was standing still, watching her. She felt heat rise up her neck. He was as handsome a man as she'd ever seen, and she hoped she would see him again.

And she would, for sure. As long as he stayed at Yukon Sally's, she would be able to see him almost every time she came to work. She knew that Gran was upset with her for spending so much time away from home, but as much as she loved Gran and was grateful to her for all she had done, for the past few years Goldie had felt like a caged bird. It was all very well for someone like Gran, or Yukon Sally for that matter, who had already had a chance to live in other places and experience the world outside of bush Alaska, to say that they wouldn't want to live anywhere else. Goldie couldn't say that. Life in the bush was all she had ever known.

"I wouldn't even have known that some people live in houses with running water and an indoor toilet, if we hadn't moved to Eagle," she had said to her school friend, Tessa Charlie. "We lived upriver until I was eight. I thought everybody hauled water from a creek in summer, and chopped a hole through the river ice every day for water in the winter. I thought it was normal to freeze your ass off using the outhouse at forty below, not that we ever knew for sure that's how cold it was because Gran didn't have a thermometer. We still don't have running water or an indoor toilet, but at least now I've met people who do, and seen how people live on the Outside. Upriver we had no TV, no radio. It was just me and Gran most of the time."

She and Tessa had been sitting on a log in the woods not far from the Eagle school, sharing a cigarette that Tessa had stolen from the glove box in her uncle's truck. It was the final year of school, and both of them dreamed of going outside to college, doing some travelling and seeing the world, but neither of them knew how they were going to pay for it.

"What'd you eat, way off in the bush alone like that? Long way to buy groceries, wasn't it?"

"A lot of salmon, smoked mostly. Caribou and moose meat. Two or three old guys in the area – hunters and trappers – used to stop by and sleep by the stove once in a while; they'd usually give Gran some of the meat from what they'd killed or trapped. Gran had enough dogs to pull a sled then, so sometimes we would make a trip to Carmacks on the frozen river in the winter. Gran fished and trapped and hunted herself, too. I was helping her skin animals when I was just a few years old. She would sell some of the furs, but all the caribou and moose hides she would tan and then sew stuff."

"Like what stuff?"

"Little purses. Moccasins. Vests and jackets sometimes. A guy would meet her in Carmacks in the spring and buy all the stuff, then she'd have cash to buy supplies and we'd go back to the bush."

"How come she didn't have a husband? She doesn't like men, or what?"

Goldie shrugged. "She was married before I came into the picture."

"She must have been if she's your Gran. What happened to your mom?"

"Died, I guess."

"You guess? You don't know?"

"Gran always said, 'Best you don't know now, child' and promised to tell me when I grew up."

"How old is grown up? Like, you're not old enough now?"

"Now she says she'll tell me before she dies."

"I wouldn't put up with that." Tessa crushed the cigarette butt against the heel of her boot, then spat on it before burying it under the dirt. "Make her tell you."

"How? Twist her arm behind her back? Threaten her with a rifle? How do you make a granny tell you something she doesn't want you to know?"

They had both laughed, it sounded so absurd.

Goldie entered the lodge's laundry room, thinking about Tessa. They had been close friends at that time, told each other everything and could almost read each other's minds. Living upriver in the Yukon Territory, Goldie's only companions had been Gran and her dogs. On Gran's orders, she barely spoke to the occasional visitors – the smelly, bewhiskered trappers or hunters – that showed up at the cabin, since Gran somehow never let her be alone with them and would often give her a quiet chore to do when they were around. So becoming friends with Tessa had been precious to her, akin to a first love. They exchanged whispers before class, passed furtive notes during school hours, and found secret places to sit and talk during breaks and after school. Then school was over and Gran kept Goldie busy all summer: fishing, bringing home firewood, helping with the tanning, cutting and sewing of skins, tending to the dogs or chickens and working in the vegetable garden. She only saw Tessa once or twice that last summer, and that's when Tessa announced she had a boyfriend.

Her old friend now had two children and lived with her husband, Sam, in a two bedroom house in Eagle Village. She and Tessa didn't have much to talk about when they ran into each other at the post office. College was never mentioned, nor was travelling. It was usually just, "How're the kids?" and "How's your gran?" and "Friggin' cold today, isn't it?" Funny how people could grow apart. Maybe if Goldie had a husband and children, they would have more in common and be close friends again. But if living here with Gran was a cage, having a husband and children here would be like a prison, a life sentence. Goldie shivered at the thought, then opened the clothes dryer to check if the bed sheets for Yukon Sally's 'Caribou Cabin' were dry.

CHAPTER THREE

New Westminster, BC - June 1997

Hunter was scrubbing at dried white and grey seagull shit, splattered like Rorschach inkblots on the hood of his navy blue Freightliner, when he heard his dispatcher yell across the yard at him from an open door on the loading dock. With the back of his hand, he wiped the sweat from under his brows, but not in time to keep it from stinging his eyes as he raised his head. It was early afternoon on an unusually hot day in June and he was washing his truck in full sun behind the Watson Transportation warehouse.

"Get in here!" Elspeth Watson had a very loud voice, and she wasn't afraid to use it. "Now!" she bellowed over her shoulder as she walked back into the warehouse, out of Hunter's sight.

He sighed and tossed the torn tee shirt he was using as a rag into a plastic bucket beside the Freightliner's front tire. He turned on the hose, rinsed off his hands and splashed cold water on his face, then ran his wet hands over his hair to get it back off his forehead before heading around the building to El's office in the front. She was on the phone when he walked in the door. There was an oscillating fan on the front counter, so he stopped it from turning and aimed it straight at his face and neck while he waited for her to finish the call.

"I've got a load for you tonight," she said as she slammed down the receiver. "Good one."

"Tonight? You told me this morning I was leaving for San Jose tomorrow morning." He tried to remember if he had a clean pair of jeans, and hoped he'd have time to do his laundry before the pickup.

"That's not your fuckin' fan, it's mine. Turn it loose, would you."

Hunter frowned. "The load? Tell me about the load and I'll give your fan back." The breeze on his face was a relief from the afternoon heat and he was loath to give it up.

El growled and raised a sheet of paper off her desk. "Pays good. Good weight. Good client. Could be the start of something profitable, you know what I mean?" She raised her eyebrows and nodded, as if waiting for him to agree.

"What's the catch?"

She cleared her throat. "Alaska," she said.

Hunter moved closer to the fan. The Alaska Highway was hard on trucks. Hard on trucks and on truck drivers.

"Haven't you got anyone else for that run?"

"Like I said, Hunter, this client could be a money maker. I need an experienced, reliable driver with a reliable truck. You're not only reliable, you're the most respectable looking driver I've got. Besides, you told me once that you used to live up there. You'll know your way around."

"What is it? The load?"

"Some kind of mining machinery. Guess there's still gold up there." El raised her eyebrows again, her mouth frozen in a hopeful little smile.

It had been over twenty years since Hunter had been north of the 60th parallel. He didn't think of those days often, but when he did, he felt real affection for the Yukon and a cautious nostalgia for the time he'd spent there in his first years with the Royal Canadian Mounted Police. How would it feel to go back? he wondered. It might be a mistake. "Where in Alaska?"

El's smile widened. "He said it was somewhere around Fairbanks. You know the area?"

"Yes, I know Fairbanks." He had done a lot of exploring during his years in the Yukon. Those were the days – the early 70s – when 'going for a drive' was still a common form of recreation. The best drives were those that he and a fellow RCMP rookie took together.

He and Ken Marsh had been through the depot in Regina together – the Mounties' boot camp – and became close friends. Some of the 'drives' up north lasted for days. Whitehorse to Dawson was over 300 miles, Dawson to Fairbanks was almost 400 miles, Whitehorse to Skagway a mere 100 miles or so. And there weren't a whole lot of towns in between, just miles of unpaved road, trees stunted by the long cold winters, limitless wild vistas fashioned out of earth, rock and water that took your breath away and were sparsely inhabited by tough, sometimes dangerous creatures, both animal and human.

"You'll take it?" asked El.

Hunter took a deep breath and gazed out the front window toward the street. The air above the asphalt shimmered in the heat. The north had been good to him. He had been young and strong and they felt they would live forever, he and Ken. The north must have changed in the past twenty-five years, and he wondered how much. He'd like to see it again, and now was as good a time as any.

He nodded.

"Good man," said El. "Go home and pack, and be back here by four thirty."

"You betcha," he said, and headed out the door.

"Wait," she hollered. "Wait, you shithead."

He turned and glared at her. She was half way out of her chair, glaring back at him.

"Please," she said, with a phony smile that lasted less than a second. "Release the fuckin' fan."

Hunter knocked on the front door of the house he lived in, on a residential slope below Grouse Mountain in North Vancouver. He rented a suite in the basement – a modest but comfortable one-bedroom suite with a bachelor's kitchen and back door entrance – from a retired medical doctor named Gord Young. Gord was a widower, and shared the upstairs with his bachelor brother, John, who spent most of the summer at Eagle Bay on Shuswap Lake. Hunter had seen his landlord's Siamese cat sunning itself in the backyard so he knew Gord was home.

The old man opened the door and invited Hunter in. He was barefoot and wearing baggy denim shorts and a white tee shirt with blue bicycles silhouetted across the chest.

"Can't stay," said Hunter. "Just wanted to let you know I'll be out on the road again for a couple of weeks, if you could bring in my mail."

"Where are you off to now? Back to California?"

"Heading north this time. Through B.C. and up the Alaska highway, then across the Yukon into Alaska."

The old man raised his eyebrows above the rims of his glasses. Hunter noticed a fingerprint smudge on one lens. "That'll be quite the trip. You used to live there, didn't you?"

"Back in the seventies. It was a wild place then, with wild people. Be interesting to see how it's changed."

The old man nodded thoughtfully. "You were one of the wild ones? You must've changed since then yourself. I'm sure it will look different through older and wiser eyes."

"Older, for sure. But wiser?" Hunter smiled at his landlord, then turned and walked to his car. He threw his duffle bag on the back seat.

"Have a safe trip," said the landlord, waving from the doorway.

Hunter thought about what Gord had said as he headed east on the Upper Levels highway. The midday traffic was light, scattered with summer travelers in motor homes and pickup trucks with campers. Was he so different now, from the idealistic young police constable who'd moved to the Yukon? There he'd met the girl who would become his wife. He'd left the Yukon, married, raised two daughters – although his ex-wife Christine would dispute how much he'd contributed to their raising – worked in investigations with the RCMP and become a seasoned homicide investigator, been through a painful divorce and lost his best friend to suicide. Yes, he had to be different now.

The traffic bottlenecked briefly at the Second Narrows Bridge, and as he inched forward, it occurred to him that the idealistic young police constable he used to be would never have believed that he would one day walk away from his dream career in law enforcement to become a long haul trucker. It was the solitude of the job that had appealed to him, the solitude and simplicity of life on the road, something that his wounded psyche had craved then, when he resigned from the force, and still needed now, some five years later.

A young girl in a VW Cabriolet cut him off, then turned and smiled sheepishly at him when traffic brought them both to an immediate stop. She had a bouncy blond pony tail, and reminded him of his youngest daughter, Lesley, who hoped to one day join the RCMP herself. He truly wished she wouldn't – it was a hard road for a young man to travel, and no doubt even harder for a girl – but at the same time, he was proud of her choice, and it touched him deeply that she wanted to follow in his footsteps.

He reminded himself to call and let her and her sister know he would be away again, for a couple of weeks at least. Summer in the north. Everyone should experience it at least once in their life. Would Lesley be free to go with him? Would it be wise to even ask her? There was always the risk that she would fall in love with the North and want to stay, like other young girls with adventurous spirits had done before her.

Unbidden, he saw in his mind's eye the image of just such a young woman he'd known briefly during his first year in Whitehorse. He saw her waving to him with a cheerful smile from behind the wheel of a 1964 Volkswagen bug, strands of her dark hair blowing around her face. The bug was a dull white, with hand-painted pink and yellow daisies on each side. The memory was tinged with grief, and accompanied by a sense of unfinished business. She had disappeared – presumed dead, although there was no way to know for sure. He had never wanted to accept that such a vibrant spirit had been extinguished, so he had looked for her as long as he was in the North, and even after.

He decided not to call his daughters until he was on the road.

"You cannot just quit a job because it's boring to you, mon cher. You have two young children. They need clothing and shoes, and they want things like their friends have. You promised we would save up to buy a house – our own house. I don't want to live every month worrying if we can pay just the rent. Daniel!" Simone Beliveau Sorenson stamped her foot. "Are you hearing me?"

Dan Sorenson couldn't help admiring his wife's pretty foot, which was right in his line of vision given his head was bowed and his eyes were trained on the scuffed linoleum of the kitchen floor. She should have been a ballet dancer, the way she moved. Her toes were perfect, her toenails a hot pink, the skin of her foot smooth and tanned, bare except for a delicate leather sandal. "I'm sorry, Mo," he mumbled.

"You are always sorry."

Sorenson wondered briefly if she was referring to his nickname, but decided Mo wasn't in a joking mood. Her voice, which normally reminded him of a sweet French melody, was as unmusical as he'd ever heard it.

"I'm sorry doesn't pay the bills, you know." She turned away and crossed her arms over her chest, her shoulders stiff. She was looking out the kitchen window at the back yard, where Bruno and little Sasha took turns chasing each other with water pistols while Doobie the Doberman kept trying to catch the spray in his mouth.

Sorry felt like a real shit, as he did every time he lost a job.

Mo turned to face him again. "Go ask your boss to give you back the job."

Sorry looked up at her, then dropped his eyes to the floor again, where a fly was exploring a crumb of cheese that Doobie had somehow missed. "I can't." He had hoped this wouldn't come out. "He yelled at me because I didn't give him notice so I gave him the finger." The look on her face made him tell the whole truth. "And I took off the company hat and pretended to wipe my ass with it and he told me to fuck off and never come back."

"Daniel!"

The look on her face made him take a step backwards. He'd never seen her eyes flash like that before.

"I think I could learn something from your boss," she said. "Fuck off and never come back!"

Sorry almost gasped. He'd never heard her talk like that either. "Mo… I…"

She turned away again and stomped – gracefully, as always – out of the kitchen into the yard, slamming the door behind her. Through the window, Sorry saw the two kids stop their playing, startled. "What happened, Maman?" asked Bruno.

Sorry was about to follow her out when he heard her answer.

"Daddy is going away for awhile. He has some thinking to do."

"Can't Daddy think at home?"

"No, Bruno. It seems that he can't."

"Where's he going?"

"Away."

"For how long?"

Sorry saw her shrug.

"Will he be back for my birthday?" Sasha would be eight – Sorry did a quick calculation – in about three weeks.

"Maybe," said Mo, and Sorry's mouth fell open.

He was shocked. Shocked and confused. Mo had never been angry like this with him before. She couldn't mean it, could she? Was she kicking him out? How could she do that? Yes, he'd screwed up yet again, but she loved him, didn't she? She was his woman. He had even married her.

Sorry took a few deep breaths, debating whether to go out after her. He knew if he did something stupid, like maybe roughed her up, he would lose her and the kids forever. But she was his woman. *His woman.* He wasn't a 'yes, dear' type of guy, and besides, he'd already said he was sorry. He began to think about what his biker buddies would say if they saw him crawling to her. Worse yet, if they knew he'd gone crawling back to his old boss.

"Fuck it," he said aloud, but not too loud. Then, "Fuck it!" loud enough that he saw her shoulders stiffen again. Then, "I'm outa here, bitch," and he turned on his heel and headed for the garage. He grabbed some clean clothes from the laundry room as he passed by, and stuffed them in a canvas duffle bag that he hurriedly strapped behind the seat of his Harley.

Moments later, he was heading for Highway 1, trying to feel nothing but the wind on his face, to think of nothing but the road beneath his wheels.

CHAPTER FOUR

Hunter was just pulling his rig into the Petro Canada station south of Kamloops when his cell phone rang. He frowned as he picked it up and flipped it open. Not many people used this number. Just El and his two daughters, and because of them, his ex-wife. "Hello," he said, wondering which one it was, and chiding himself for always expecting bad news.

"Hey, man. Where ya at?"

Hunter shook his head. He'd forgotten that Sorry had this number, too. "On my way to Alaska. Where are you?"

"Alaska? What a fuckin' great idea. That's where I'm heading, too."

"You're joking, right?"

"Where are you now, man?"

Hunter paused. Would Sorry want to meet up with him or what? If he did, would that be such a bad thing? "Kamloops."

"Perfect. I'm just outside of Savona, came up the Canyon. Wait for me, okay?"

"I'll be in the restaurant at the Petro Canada station–" Hunter was about to say he'd probably be finished dinner by the time Sorry got there, but Sorry cut him off.

"Another fuckin' great idea. Order me a steak and fries, I'll be there in twenty minutes."

He wasn't kidding. He must have opened up the throttle on his Harley, because he slid into the booth seat opposite Hunter exactly twenty minutes later, almost knocking over Hunter's water glass with his German army helmet. Hunter had managed to snag a booth where he could just manage to keep an eye on The Blue Knight, as El Watson sometimes called his Freightliner, which he had fueled up and parked in the blistering sun. Although the waitress had breezed by with water and coffee, she had not been back to take his order.

"Put that beanie on the bench," said Hunter.

"What's the matter? Is it being seen with a biker or being seen with a Nazi helmet that's got your shorts in a knot?"

Hunter glowered and Sorry moved the helmet.

"It's a fake, if that makes you feel any better. Some asshole lifted my old one."

"What's this about you going to Alaska?" Hunter asked.

"I could ask you the same thing. Why's Big Mother Trucker sending you so far north?"

"Why not?"

Sorry shrugged, batting a salt shaker from hand to hand along the tabletop like a hockey puck. "Can I go with you?"

"I don't need another driver. I'm doing just fine with single hours."

"Yeah, but for company. Or just in case you need help or something." Sorry kept his eyes on the salt shaker, but Hunter could read tension in the way the biker's lips worked under his blond mustache.

"Why? What's up with you? You lose another job?"

Sorry's broad chest rose and fell with a massive sigh. "Yeah, but it's worse than that. Mo kind of kicked me out."

Hunter raised his eyebrows and waited for Sorry to elaborate.

The biker swiped hand across his mouth a few times, then straightened his mustache with the tip of an index finger, as if he were debating how much to say. "I lost the job for being an insolent jerk, as usual, and Mo was really pissed at me. This thing with Mo, it's been building for quite a while. Remember I took her and the kids down to see my folks in Yreka at Easter?"

Hunter nodded. He'd been pleased to hear about it, knowing that Sorry and his dad had barely spoken to each other for over a decade until Sorry took an hours-of-service break in Yreka with Hunter's truck back in February and the two started talking again.

"Things got a little tense again between me and my old man, and the only thing that seemed to keep us comfortable with each other was if we downed a few beers together." Sorry shrugged, as if to say, 'what choice did I have?'

"You've been drinking again?"

"Yeah. Beer. Only beer. But that got me doing more weed, too. I kind of got back in the habit and Mo's been warning me for weeks that I had to get my shit together or else." Sorry's mouth and eyes got hard. He slammed the salt shaker down on the table. "Never thought she could be such a bitch."

"Don't get mad at her, chief," said Hunter.

"Who the fuck else then? Me?"

Hunter paused before he answered, watching Sorry go back to sliding the salt shaker up and down the table. "Give your wife a break. Give yourself a break. Your trip to Alaska might be just the right thing for you two right now."

Sorry's mouth relaxed and his eyes brightened as he sat forward, elbows on the table, salt shaker forgotten. "It's not about the money, you know. Maybe with you and me both driving, we can take a few days up there, be tourists, like. It's a win for you, too."

"And your bike?"

"Got room for it behind your load? Surely you can spare a few feet in the back of the trailer, strap it down safe-like. What do you say?"

Hunter was of two minds. A few days' break in Alaska and the Yukon might be worth having to put up with the chatty biker, although he was sure Sorry didn't have much cash on him and dreaded having to stop and feed the big man four or five times a day. If he could help Sorry find a resolution to his family problem, however, it would certainly be worth the investment. Mo was a wonderful woman with a gentle and generous spirit. Sorry couldn't do better, and without Mo or someone like her – and it was highly unlikely Sorry would ever find another woman like Mo – his life was destined to go off the rails.

"You're on," he said, just as the waitress arrived at their table.

"Steak and fries," said Sorry, grinning through his mustache, "with a chocolate shake and a big piece of pecan pie."

Hunter drove as far as Prince George. Sleepy after a big dinner, Sorry crawled into the bunk half an hour after they left Kamloops and Hunter had to shake him awake to take over at about one thirty Friday morning. They both got out to stretch their legs and take a leak at the Husky truck stop off the Cariboo Highway. "Wake me in Dawson Creek," Hunter told Sorry, handing him a take-out coffee from the truck stop restaurant before climbing into the sleeper. "We can fuel up at the Petro Canada cardlock, then grab some breakfast before hitting the Alaska Highway."

Two hundred and fifty miles later they arrived in Dawson Creek at the southern terminus of the Alaska Highway. By nine o'clock, even Dawson Creek, north of the 55th parallel – farther north than Ketchikan, Alaska – was warm for the time of year, and Hunter felt the morning sun's heat penetrate the fabric of his denim shirt as he climbed down from the passenger side of the cab and walked around the trailer to stretch his legs. The cardlock was smaller than any of those he'd normally pull into along his usual route up and down the I-5; it was an asphalt lot with a row of diesel pumps under a high canopy, smaller and without the usual lineup of big rigs waiting to fuel up. The only other customer was a dirty red Kenworth pulling a load of logs.

Before heading to the fuel pumps, Hunter did a quick visual check of his Freightliner tractor. It had been running well for over a year without requiring much input of cash, other than regular maintenance. He knew his luck wouldn't last, because it was six years old and had eaten up over three quarters of a million miles of North American highways, more than half of them since he'd bought it used from a trucker who was fed up with eking out a living in a cutthroat business.

Hunter heard a hawk and spit from the other side of the truck, and seconds later Sorry joined him, stretched his back with a grunt and scratched his belly. "Are we there yet?" His eyes were squinted to slits against the sun. He pulled a cigarette out from behind his ear.

Hunter frowned and motioned at the fuel hose with his head. He was filling up the tank on the right side of the truck with 120 gallons of diesel fuel using Watson Transportation's card. El wouldn't pay for the fuel, though. She'd deduct it from his percentage for the job when the time came. After filling both tanks, the cost of the fill would be over $300 but he wouldn't have to fuel up again until he reached Whitehorse.

"You think I'm stupid? It's not even lit." Sorry wagged the cigarette in front of Hunter's nose. "Where can I get a coffee?" He spun around and took in the dusty yard, unmanned fuel pumps, and what appeared to be a locked up office building. "Isn't there a phone here? Where can we get breakfast?"

"Alaska is still some 1200 miles away. You sure you want to go there? It's not too late to unload your bike and head back home." Hunter tried to keep the irritation out of his voice. He had to remind himself that his old friend was going through a hard time with his wife and could use some support, and that much of the trip they'd be separated by sleep and Hunter would still get hours of the solitude he was accustomed to.

Sorry shook his head. "If I wasn't with you last night, man, I'd probably have gotten stinkin' drunk wherever I'd stopped for the night and picked a fight, ended up 'detained'" – his face and voice expressed a certain scorn for the word – "in 100 Mile or Barriere. And that would've been just for starters."

"Go have your smoke. We can look for a restaurant when I've finished fueling up."

Ten minutes later, they reached the sign in Dawson Creek that proclaimed the start of the Alaska Highway. Sorry gave a loud whoop that made Hunter wince, then broke into a booming chorus of Johnny Horton's "North to Alaska", the sound erupting from deep inside his massive chest, although the first three words were followed by "duh duh dum, the rush is on".

A few blocks later, they pulled in at a small motel that not only had a café where they could get breakfast, it also had a parking lot large enough to accommodate an eighteen wheeler. "Order me a breakfast special," said Sorry, heading toward a payphone outside near the front entrance. He hesitated, then turned back to Hunter, saying, "Got any change on you?" and holding out an open hand as if he already knew the answer.

Hunter found a seat at a small table by the window and turned over the two cups that sat upside down on their saucers, then motioned to the waitress for coffee. He watched Sorry through the window. The big biker held the phone to his ear for a couple of minutes, didn't appear to say very much, then hung up so hard Hunter could hear it from inside the café. He could also hear Sorry swear loudly as he yanked open the door.

Hunter let his friend be the first one to speak.

"I never thought she could be such a fuckin' bitch," he said, slamming an open hand against the table on the last word. His mouth was working under his blond mustache, his eyes narrowed to slits and directed unfocussed at the table. "Fuck her," he said, uncharacteristically softly.

"She's worth working for, Dan," said Hunter. "Don't let your cowboy pride make you do something you'll regret."

The big biker was quiet for a moment, mouth still working, then he sighed deeply and leaned back against the bench. "You know something? Mo and the kids are the reason I'm here right now" – he stabbed at the tabletop with an oil-stained index finger – "and not in jail or five feet under. If I can't hang on to them, I'm nothing but a fuck up."

"Don't sell yourself short," said Hunter. "You can do it. Take a break, lay off the booze and get your head straight, then go back and take care of your family."

"It's not like I screw up at work, at least not usually. It's more like I always end up working for some idiot asshole I got no respect for." He shrugged. "Then my big mouth gets me in trouble. I can't help myself."

A skinny woman with dark hair in a pony tail approached the table, a full coffee pot in one hand, a bowl of small creamers in the other, and menus tucked under her elbow. She wore jeans and a yellow tee shirt. "Morning, boys," she said. "I'll be back to take your order in a minute." She filled up their coffee mugs and handed them each a menu. Hunter nodded his thanks and looked at the menu briefly as the waitress walked away.

"You don't have to respect a man to treat him with respect," he said to Sorry. "It's like singing a song. Just sing the words the way they were written; they don't necessarily have to be true for you."

"Huh?"

"I've never known you to have any trouble lying if it gets you what you want."

"Yeah. Doesn't everybody? You've caught me a few times. So?"

"So, like I said. Make your boss, whoever he is, believe that you respect him – and you can disagree with someone without being disrespectful, don't forget – and keep your eye on the prize, which would be a good relationship with Simone and your children. Make sense to you?"

Sorry sighed again. "Thinking about it makes my head hurt," he said as the waitress approached the table again, her pen poised over a small order pad.

"What's your pleasure, boys?" she said, smiling in Sorry's direction.

"It's not on the menu," said Sorry, pushing the menu across the table without looking up.

"A Denver omelette, please," said Hunter, "and my sad, young friend here will have the special."

"I'm coming with you."

Goldie was just reaching for the key to the Merc where it hung on a nail by the cabin door. They used to keep the key in the truck, but one of the kids from Eagle Village 'borrowed' it and didn't bring it back for three days, so they now had to keep the key inside. She turned to stare at her grandmother, pausing briefly before asking, "Why?"

"Because I want to see if my order has arrived at the post office yet, that's why." The old woman sounded annoyed.

"I can check the post office for you, Gran." Goldie wondered if her grandmother was still upset that she hadn't come home for dinner the night before. Yukon Sally had invited her to stay and join the lodge staff for a barbecue, as an introduction and welcome for her cousin's son, Mark. Goldie had even had a glass of wine – Mark offered it to her himself, and she felt she couldn't refuse – although the last time she'd had anything to drink she'd sampled Tessa's brother's moonshine with Tessa after school. That time, Gran had smelled the alcohol on her breath and gave her a stern lecture on the dangers of drink. "Remember Ellie Thomas? Froze to death in her own outhouse, passed out drunk," was one of the examples. Last night, Gran hadn't mentioned alcohol, but she'd been angry that Goldie was so inconsiderate. The old woman refused to have a telephone, so what was Goldie supposed to do to let her know she'd be late? Send smoke signals?

"Sure you can check the post office, but then you won't be back here until you're finished at the lodge – whenever that might be." Goldie had no trouble picking up the sarcasm in her grandmother's voice. "I'm expecting a package on the mail plane today."

"So will you pick me up after I'm finished at the lodge?"

Gran smiled a lop-sided smile and gave her a faint nod. Goldie didn't like the look of it. Was the old woman planning some kind of payback for her being late last night? "Are you ready?" she asked. I don't want to be late–" She stopped mid-sentence when she saw Gran's face.

"Yes, we don't want you to be late," said Gran, shrugging into a padded vest. "You don't want to keep Sally waiting." Gran held out her hand for the keys.

It was only five or six miles to Eagle and another couple of miles to the lodge, but it was slow going on the rutted spring road. The old Merc needed new shocks, among other things. Gran was silent on the way, and Goldie found herself thinking about how her grandmother had changed. She'd always been a little crusty, but now there was a bitter edge to her crankiness.

She had been strict with Goldie as a child, and Goldie realized as she grew older that she had to be. Life in the wilderness doesn't leave much room for mistakes. How to handle the dogs, for example. Sled dogs could be trouble if you didn't treat them right; they could kill each other, or they could even turn on you, or they could run off and leave you stranded miles from home. You had to know how to hunt efficiently so you didn't starve over the winter. How to kill and not just wound a large animal; not only was it kinder, it was important in case the wounded animal charged and hurt you back. How to make sure the river ice was thick enough to walk or run a sled on, or you could fall through the ice and never be seen again. How to protect your winter food supply from bears. How to safely tend your stove so you didn't burn down your cabin. It was basic survival, and some lessons had to be learned well the first time or you could pay with your life.

Goldie thought she knew the reason why the old woman was changing; it was fear. Betty Salmon had been self-sufficient and independent for so long, she wasn't adapting well to aging. She didn't want to have to give up her independence; she hated to have to ask for help, even from Goldie. She knew the old woman tried to be as active as ever, but now her finger joints were swollen and Goldie frequently saw her massage them with warm oil distilled from juniper berries; as her strength was slowly being sapped by age, she had to rest longer and more often. Gran probably felt that her body was turning against her and she was helpless to stop it. It had to be making her fearful, and it had to be making her angry.

Goldie was afraid, too. She was afraid that she was trapped with an angry old woman who needed her. She felt such a powerful yearning – it must be in her heart, for it seemed to be deep in her chest – a yearning for a new life, a much different life than she'd experienced so far. She wanted to see the world, she wanted to go to school, to learn new and interesting things, to accomplish something important, and she wanted to fall in love. But she owed her grandmother so much, and her grandmother had no one else in the world to look after her as she aged and lost her independence.

She studied her grandmother's lined brown face, bright and alert as she looked ahead through the windshield. I couldn't bear to hurt her, Goldie thought to herself. Oh, God. Please show me the way. "What are you waiting for from the post office?" she asked. "Something for the garden?"

Her grandmother smiled a tight little smile that had an air of mischief. "Maybe," she said.

"Don't be such a tease, Gran. Give me a hint."

"Guess, then."

Goldie inhaled deeply and looked at the ceiling of the old Merc while she thought. The cloth lining was torn and drooping above the rearview mirror. "Seeds? Some special kind of seeds like Jack's beanstalk seeds? I'll come home and find a giant beanstalk in your garden, and no trace of you, just Hootie snoozing at the bottom waiting for you to climb back down." She grinned at her grandmother, but there was no reciprocal smile.

"I won't leave my Hootie behind." The old woman spoke with such grim resolve that Goldie's grin disappeared and she spent the rest of the drive in silence, wondering what she really was going to come home to.

Hunter first heard the noise several miles north of Prophet River. It was a faint kunk-kunk-kunk that he hadn't heard before, at least not in the thousands of miles he'd driven the Blue Knight so far this year. At first he wasn't sure if it was a result of the road surface or if it came from under the hood. When the sound subsided on a smoother patch of pavement, he decided it must have been the road and was relieved. The last thing he needed was a mechanical breakdown on a long, lonely stretch of the Alaska Highway. Well, maybe not so lonely. Every five or ten minutes, they passed a vehicle going the opposite direction on the two-lane highway, either a southbound tractor-trailer, a loaded RV, or a dirty pickup truck.

Sorry was still driving, and Hunter was enjoying the chance to concentrate on the scenery instead of the road, watching for wildlife along the edges of the highway. The highway wound around gentle hills in wide curves, flanked on either side by stands of white spruce, lodgepole pine and subalpine fir, with a wide margin of low scrub between the trees and the road that allowed drivers to see a bear or moose approach the highway before it darted across the asphalt. Signs of human habitation were long distances apart, giving Hunter a sense of just how vast the northern wilderness could be.

Sorry had been chatty after breakfast in Dawson Creek. There were sarcastic comments about every passing vehicle and driver, especially if the driver was a woman, and his sentences were peppered with expletives if the driver did something that didn't meet with his approval. In between, he delivered colorful recollections of the best and worst breakfasts and breakfast stops he'd had on the road, and eventually he settled into an analysis of his problems in life.

"My old man wanted me to be just like him, you know what I mean? Settle down and marry a local girl, have kids, work in a hardware store nine or ten hours every fuckin' day of my dreary fuckin' life and come home to meat and potatoes on the table and a couple hours of boring chores around the house and then fall asleep in front of the fuckin' depressing national news at the end of every day." He turned and looked at Hunter with raised eyebrows and an intense stare. "What the fuck was he thinking?"

Hunter pointed urgently at the road and Sorry reacted in time to avoid running the right front wheel onto the gravel shoulder. "Everybody's different," was all he said, although he found himself thinking that a quiet, orderly life with his wife and two daughters might not have been a bad thing. There was a familiar ache in his chest, thinking about his wife and daughters as they'd been ten years and more ago. He'd loved each of them more than his own life, and yet he'd spent so many hours working that his wife had felt neglected, and as his daughters grew older they often seemed like strangers to him. Would Christine still have divorced him if he'd worked in a hardware store?

"I mean, what kind of life is that? Every day the same thing. Yes, Bob, you can have ten percent off this bag of screws. No, Fred, we don't stock that brand of paint. Sorry, Chuck, you can't have any more credit with us until you pay your bill. Can you imagine me behind the counter in a hardware store six days a week?" Sorry shook his head but kept his eyes on the road. "Or you? Could you imagine yourself putting in ten hours a day selling plumbing parts and screwdrivers to Joe Q. Public?"

Hunter was doing just that, trying to imagine himself working nine to five, Monday to Friday, and coming home to spend time with his young family. Going to PTA meetings, taking the girls to swimming lessons, watching their soccer games and taking Chris out for a nice dinner once a week. Would that have saved his marriage? Or was he just like Sorry, needing to be on the move every day, whether in a police cruiser or on the seat of a Harley, just on the move? He snorted softly. On the move, like a long haul trucker. Maybe that's just who he was.

"Well, can you?"

"Maybe not, Dan," he said. "But then again, maybe you get used to it. Maybe there are tradeoffs that make it worthwhile."

"Like?"

"Coming home every night to a good woman who loves you. Watching your children grow up, hearing about their day at school, their new friends, their heartaches and fears. Listening to them practice playing piano..."

"Whoa! What fuckin' piano?"

Hunter frowned. "I hope you don't swear like that in front of customers when you're driving my rig."

"Jesus! What's your problem?" Sorry sighed, paused a moment, then said, "My kids don't have no fu..., I mean, no goddamn piano. Where the hell did that come from?"

It came from Hunter's past, but he didn't say so. "Maybe not a piano, but some kind of keyboard. Every kid wants to be a musician. Doesn't Bruno have a drum set yet? Does Sasha play a flutophone or whatever?" His own girls took piano lessons. It had been Chris's idea, but Hunter was supportive, even if he wasn't around much in the evenings to hear them play. Hunter's parents had made him take violin lessons. That was okay until he hit his teens, began listening to rock and roll, and his friends started playing guitars and drums. Did his girls still play? It had been a long time since he'd even thought about it.

A dirty white pickup truck passed them – a Ford diesel – doing ninety miles an hour and spewing smoke from its exhaust. Sorry held up a finger, but there was no way the driver could have seen it, nor could he hear Sorry call him a fuckin' asshole, then apologize to Hunter. Sorry pressed the pedal down and again Hunter heard that kunk-kunk-kunk, accompanied by a noticeable vibration. It was his turn to swear, silently to himself.

"Slow down," he said. "This isn't a Harley."

"Yes, boss."

Sorry let the Freightliner slow to sixty miles an hour and the noise went away.

CHAPTER FIVE

The package Betty was waiting for – kale seeds in spite of how she had teased her granddaughter – was not on the mail plane. There was nothing at all at the post office this week, neither for her nor Goldie. Betty waved a vague thanks to the postmaster, who also happened to be the town's mayor, and got back in the old blue pickup. It was warm inside from the sun, and she just sat a moment, savoring the comfort of that warmth, thinking about all the work ahead of her. It seemed like there was precious little time to enjoy easy living during the north's short summer, because there was always so much to do to get ready for the next winter. Stocking up on food and firewood, smoking and canning fish, meat and vegetables, making jam, repairs to the cabin, obtaining supplies for her sewing and beadwork; it never seemed to end. It had been that way ever since she could remember, but this was the first time she dreaded the work ahead.

"I'm tired," she said to herself, or perhaps to God, whoever he was and if he listened to aging half-Athapascan women feeling sorry for themselves. Even if he did, she didn't expect God to answer, nor help her out. Perhaps a tonic would help. As she often did, she thought out loud. "Maybe I should brew up some swamp tea."

"I beg your pardon?"

Betty looked up, startled. The voice came from a man she'd never seen before. Or had she? She peered at the face looking back at her through the Merc's open window, but it was mostly hidden behind a tousled grey beard, unevenly streaked with brown and white, and a mustache that hid the man's upper lip. He wore what once might have been a grey cowboy hat, sweat-stained around a hatband of braided horsehair which sported a single raven's feather. His grease-splotched shirt and dirty blue jeans were at odds with his British accent.

Normally Betty would have said, "I wasn't talking to you", rolled up the window and fired up the engine. For some reason she didn't understand – did some small part of her want to believe this old man was God's answer to her unsaid prayers? – she said instead, "I thought I might brew up a tonic. I'm in need of a little pick me up."

"What a lovely thought." By the way the corners of his mustache moved, he must have smiled broadly. "May I join you?"

"It's just swamp tea," she said, realizing that he probably thought she meant something alcoholic.

He pointed to an old brown and yellow pickup truck parked beside the post office. "I could contribute a little something to sweeten it up." Again the mustache rose at both ends. He had a gentle voice, and right then Betty felt in need of some gentleness. "I'm Orville, by the way." He stuck out a hand that matched his face, weathered and creased. "Orville Barstow."

"I live out of town," she said, not taking his hand.

If her rudeness was meant to discourage him, and she wasn't sure that's what she meant to do, it didn't work. Less than twenty minutes later, his old truck pulled up beside her own at the cabin. There was an old Arctic Cat snowmobile in the bed of his pickup, and tucked around it were several oil-stained canvas sacks. She noticed that he had a Yukon license plate. As soon as the man's feet were on the ground, Hootie trotted up and sniffed at the old man's boots, then offered his head for a pat.

"Lovely old Mercury you have," he said before slamming the door of his truck. "About a '68, if I'm not mistaken. I have a distinct fondness for earlier Ford products, as you may have noticed." He indicated his own vehicle with a wave of his hand. "I call her Tinkerbell. She is currently carrying everything I own."

Now that they were standing side by side, his physical presence made Betty extremely uncomfortable and she could barely contain the urge to ask him to leave. She imagined herself reaching inside the cabin door for her rifle and pointing it at him until he drove away. What if he refused to go? Would she really shoot this stranger? If she did, what would she do then? Hide his body? Drive his truck into the Yukon River after dark? She held her breath, and he seemed to be watching her intently, and as far as she could tell, sympathetically. Was he so different from the trappers she used to welcome to stay the night in the cabin upriver not that many years ago? It wasn't that she feared him physically, she told herself, it was that this odd old man from Canada threatened her privacy, something she had guarded from the people of Eagle and Eagle Village ever since she'd arrived here.

"Oh yes," he said. "The sweetener for the tea." He reached in behind the seat of his truck and pulled out a brown paper bag. "My one indulgence, an infrequent one at that." His mustache tilted up at the corners again, and he motioned toward the cabin door. "Shall we?"

Betty didn't want this man inside her cabin, so she led him around the cabin to the two frayed lawn chairs that Goldie had brought home from the lodge, left behind by tourists with a big RV. They faced a campfire littered with lumps of charred wood over a pile of ash long since gone cold. "Here, have a seat," she said. "I'll bring out the tea." She felt suddenly ashamed being so inhospitable, so she added. "Hootie here will keep you company."

She went inside and made sure there was enough hot water in the kettle that sat perpetually on top of the woodstove. She tried to keep live coals in the stove at all times, both for cooking during the day and for heat at night, when the temperature sometimes dropped to freezing, even in June. Then she tossed what breakfast tea was left in the aluminum pot out the cabin door and took a jar of dried Labrador tea leaves down from the shelf, tossed a handful of leaves into the teapot and filled it from the kettle. Teapot in one hand and two mismatched mugs in the other, she went back outside.

"It has to steep some," she said to her visitor. He was leaning back in the chair, one hand on Hootie's head, the other resting on his stomach, and his eyes were closed. She saw that he had removed his hat and his boots, and was wiggling his toes inside grey wool socks.

He opened his eyes and nodded. "This is a lovely, peaceful place," he said. "You are a lucky woman, Miss –?"

"Betty. Just call me Betty." She put the mugs and teapot on a block of spruce between the two chairs.

"How lovely that we are on a first name basis right at the start." His eyes sparkled and she found herself admiring how brown and clear they were. They looked kind. "You are a lucky woman to have found such a peaceful place to settle. You weren't always here near town, though, were you? I see by the traps and snowshoes hanging on your cabin, assuming they're yours, that you've led a more adventurous life."

"I still do," she said. It rankled that he also assumed she was no longer trapping. "I still trap and hunt, just not so much and closer to home."

"Ah, yes. That's the advantage to trapping here in Alaska. No exclusive concessions like they have across the border. I have just said a poignant goodbye to my trap line concession near Stewart Crossing," he said. "A young couple from Manitoba has taken it over, and I wish them well." He nodded and took a couple of slow deep breaths before continuing. "I came very close to death on my trap line this past winter; my strength failed me and I didn't make it back to shelter during a storm. At the ripe old age of seventy three, I was forced to admit that unless I was ready to become wolf bait, it was time to retire." He smiled, his eyes wistful. "Dust to dust. A cycle we all face, and I've had to accept that I'm nearing the end of it."

A cycle we all face. Betty drew some unexpected comfort from his admission, a sense of relief that she was not alone in facing her increasing debility and eventual mortality. She nodded, mirroring his wistful expression.

"I feel that you and I are kindred spirits, Betty. I was very close to a woman much like yourself for many years. We are two denizens of the northern bush, our spirits forged in the wilderness. We're peas in a pod, much of a muchness. Don't you feel it, too, Betty?"

Betty was still waging an internal battle against feeling any kind of a personal relationship with the man, but what he said described just what she felt herself struggling against. It was as though this man, this odd little Englishman who appeared out of the blue this morning, was in a way her counterpart, her male equivalent. It appeared that both had been forced to emerge from the northern wilderness, almost against their will, by the ravages of age.

"Why didn't you just stay in the bush and face your fate, like the old bear and caribou?" she found herself asking him. She had wondered the same thing about herself. Wasn't that the way of the wilderness? You get old, you get eaten by younger and stronger creatures. Wasn't that a more honorable way to leave this earth than allowing yourself to get weak and lazy? But she had Goldie to think of and care for, hadn't she? Goldie needed her, or at least she used to.

"Because ultimately we're survivors, my dear. We have spent our lives being cautious to avoid being frozen to death, or drowned, or eaten by bears. We have had to know and respect our physical limitations in order to stay alive, and now we have had to adjust to the depletion of our physical vigor. We can no longer trek for days or weeks to obtain supplies, our arms and shoulders can no longer maneuver our canoes through the river rapids nor can our fading hearing and eyesight detect the approach of predators through the underbrush." He sighed and looked as if he were scanning the surrounding tree line for bears and wolves.

Betty took the lid off the teapot and peered inside. The spicy aroma told her it was ready to drink, so she arranged the mugs and prepared to pour.

"To continue being the survivors we are, we must adapt to this thing called age." He scratched his bearded chin with thick, uneven fingernails. "I suppose I should have married. If I had some grown children somewhere I could move in with them, but it's too late now, isn't it?" As he said this, he pulled a bottle of Southern Comfort out of his paper bag. "But age and civilization have their perks."

She watched the edges of his mustache turn up again, and this time she smiled back at him. She surprised herself by saying, "It could be you are right." She settled herself into the other lawn chair and watched him pour some liquor into each mug of tea. "Perhaps it's time I try to find the advantages of getting old."

"Yes, indeed. Why try to hold on to a lifestyle that no longer suits your life? You wouldn't keep wearing your parka in the summer, would you? The bull moose doesn't keep carrying his antlers around when the rut is over, does he? He doesn't need to be a show off for the ladies during the winter, he just needs to feed himself well and survive." He blew on his tea and took a cautious sip. "Mmmm. Delightful. You make the best swamp tea in Alaska, my dear Betty. I'm sure of it."

Since when did she become his dear Betty? She didn't totally approve of it, but she felt a warm little thrill in her chest when he said it. She didn't dare look at him, afraid it would betray her pleasure at this unexpected intimacy, so she blew on her own tea and inhaled the sweet and spicy combination of Labrador tea and the syrupy liqueur. She tried a sip, and tasted the sweetness of it on her tongue and felt the warmth of it as it slid down her throat.

"Good, isn't it?" Orville was smiling again, and there was a twinkle in his gentle eyes.

Betty coughed, then nodded. "I guess I could learn to like this." In fact, there was no learning required. Why had she not wanted to like it? Why did she feel guilty for enjoying it as much as she did?

"Wonderful! Perhaps you'll let me camp in your yard for a day or two until I decide where I'm headed, if I promise to repay you with some Southern Comfort in this northern home of yours. I could cut some firewood for you …" He indicated jumble of logs near the edge of the clearing, some of them pulled from the Yukon after breakup, now awaiting splitting and stacking. "… or perhaps do some odd jobs around the cabin?"

He was terribly bold, and in most men, it would have angered her and she would have sent them packing immediately for presuming that she would welcome their intrusion into her life. But Betty realized she was tired of trying to hold on to her old way of life, with Goldie trying to wiggle out from underneath it. It would be so easy just to embrace the presence of this old fellow – although he was only a couple of years older than Betty herself – and let him entertain her and help with the work here, at least for a day or two. She had no doubt that he would soon be ready to move on, and that she would soon be impatient to see him go.

"Are you hungry, Betty? I have some bear jerky in my truck. Would you care for some?"

Over a picnic lunch of Orville's bear jerky and some of Betty's homemade bread, spread with goose fat and sprinkled with salt, Orville told Betty more about himself and she found herself listening with great interest in spite of herself. Like many men in Alaska and the Yukon, he had come in pursuit of gold. Surely there were unexplored streams or undiscovered deposits waiting for him to find. To support his quest, he trapped and hunted in the winter, trading mostly marten and fox, but also the occasional wolf and lynx pelt for supplies. Like Betty and Goldie, he tanned the hides of any caribou or moose he shot for meat. He was close enough to Stewart to obtain other supplies every few months.

"I have a particular fondness for potatoes," he admitted, "and I sometimes treat myself to carrots, cabbage and beets when they're available. I see you have chickens. A rare bird indeed in this part of the world! I love a good English breakfast of scrambled eggs, sausage and toast." He leaned his head back and closed his eyes, the sun full in his face. There was a long comfortable silence between them, then, eyes still closed, he said, "How about you, Betty? You must have led an interesting life. Tell me about yourself."

After another hour or so on the Alaska Highway, Sorry parked the eighteen wheeler on a side road across from a Petro Canada station in Fort Nelson and they went into a pub for lunch. Hunter had coffee and a Ruben sandwich and Sorry had a coke and a beef dip with extra au jus for dipping plus gravy on his mountain of fries. Fortunately, the heavy meal put Sorry to sleep in the bunk almost immediately after Hunter got behind the wheel. Unfortunately, Sorry began to snore loudly from the sleeper, interfering with the quiet reveries Hunter usually enjoyed during daylight driving.

Reveries and snores both soon faded, eclipsed by what he saw beyond the windshield. The scenery was spectacular on the winding two lane highway – the lanes a little narrow for comfort in places when passing oncoming trucks – as it snaked through the Northern Rockies, along the Tetsa River with forests dressed in a hundred shades of spring green, often backed by snow-dappled mountains, and past Summit Lake at an elevation of over four thousand feet. The road then descended to the shores of Muncho Lake, which on this sunny afternoon was a breathtaking blue, and on into the Liard River Valley through a diverse landscape of forest, meadows, wetlands, sand dunes, hills, and lakes. He slowed the Freightliner as he passed a herd of bison grazing beside the highway.

Sorry must have turned over in his sleep miles before, because the snoring had stopped somewhere around Toad River. "I'd forgotten just how amazing the north can be," Hunter whispered quietly so as not to wake his co-driver, and he was grateful to El, at least for a while, for sending him in this direction.

The Blue Knight was making that clunking noise consistently by the time they reached the Yukon border so Hunter's first thought was to find a mechanic in Watson Lake. By then it was late evening and Sorry had woken up hungry as a bear coming out of hibernation. He told Hunter if he didn't get something to eat right away, he was likely to pass out, so they stopped at a restaurant in a nice log building just as they entered Watson Lake.

"I feel like a beer." Sorry put his menu down on the table and scanned the room for a waitress.

"Too bad," said Hunter.

"What do you mean? Why can't I have a beer?"

"You're working."

"Not yet, I'm not. I haven't had my ten hours off yet."

"If you're riding in my truck, you're working."

Sorry stroked his big mustache. By the set of his jaw, Hunter could see that the big biker wasn't ready to give in.

"You realize that's the sign of an addict, don't you? At this moment, drinking that one beer is more important to you than making your boss happy and keeping your job." Hunter cocked an eyebrow at him. "Am I right?"

Sorry closed his eyes and exhaled, his jaw muscles working. Then he dropped his chin and sighed.

"I thought you were my friend, not my boss."

"I'm your boss, and your friend. If I was just your boss, I wouldn't care if you had a beer or not."

A young woman came by and took their orders. They both ordered the special of steak and home fries. Sorry ordered a coke, looking Hunter straight in the eyes as he did so.

"Gimme a break, would you. I lost my job and my wife kicked me out and I'm feeling fuckin' depressed. Let me indulge myself a little on this trip, okay?" Sorry picked a fork up off the table and began playing with it, drumming it double-time against his palm.

"You hadn't had a drink for years until that visit to Yreka a few months ago. Just how much good did going back to drinking do you?"

"It's just a lousy beer, for fuck's sake." He threw the fork down on the table with a clatter.

"And Simone's just a good wife, you big dope." When Sorry rolled his eyes, Hunter continued. "Thin edge of the wedge, chief. Thin edge of the wedge."

The waitress appeared with a coffee for Hunter and Sorry's Coke.

"Thanks, sweetheart," said Sorry. "That's just what I needed to save my marriage."

The girl smiled uncertainly, looking from Sorry to Hunter and back again, then nodded slightly and walked quickly away, Sorry's booming laugh following behind her.

Forty minutes later they were topping up the fuel tanks at the Petro Canada, making inquiries about a mechanic who might be available in Watson Lake after nine o'clock on a Saturday night.

"I'll bet dollars to donuts it's your U-joint," said the driver of a southbound flatbed who was fueling up at the same time. "Had the same thing happen to my Mack last year. Good luck finding a mechanic here over the weekend. You'll have better luck in Whitehorse." As the driver headed back to his cab, he shot back over his shoulder, "I'd take it easy on the speed though, if I were you."

Hunter smiled grimly in Sorry's direction as he settled in behind the wheel again. It was almost two hundred and seventy five miles to Whitehorse with few services in between and it wouldn't be a great stretch of highway for an eighteen wheeler to break down on.

Sorry was in the passenger seat, poring over a travel guide he'd picked up at the restaurant. "Can we stop at the signpost forest? It's on the way out of town. It says here that since 1942 people from all over the world have put up tens of thousands of signposts. I want to see if I can find one from Yreka."

Hunter fired up the big Cummins. It was June, cooling off some but still bright daylight, and the sun wouldn't set until almost eleven. Whether or not they stopped, they'd be arriving in Whitehorse in the wee small hours of Sunday morning.

"Sure," he said. "Why the heck not?"

He wondered if the hand-lettered sign that he and his friend Ken had put up in 1972 would still be there. It had said 'RCMP DEPOT, REGINA - 1475 MILES'.

Goldie waited half an hour past her quitting time but there was no sign of Betty and the truck. She had walked up the long unpaved driveway and was sitting on a log with a view of the road. It was a pleasant enough spot to sit, but she had nothing to read or otherwise occupy her attention, so she kept her eyes focused on the road and her mind on the fact that her grandmother hadn't yet come to pick her up. "I can't believe she'd be so vindictive. She's got to show up soon."

She couldn't help worrying that her grandmother's behavior today was due to something more sinister than just teaching her granddaughter a lesson about being late. Once when Goldie was in the town clinic there'd been an old woman swearing a blue streak at the receptionist and berating her son. The man had apologized to the receptionist, explaining that his mother had Alzheimer's and sometimes got angry for no reason. Could something like that be happening to Gran? Had the truck broken down or had she just lost track of time?

She heard the crunch of tires on gravel from the direction of the lodge and soon a red Jeep soft-top slid to a stop beside her. "What are you still doing here?" It was Sally's nephew, Mark. He was wearing a straw cowboy hat, which he pushed back on his head as if to improve his view of her.

"Waiting for my ride. My gran took the truck today."

"Hop in. I'll take you home."

Goldie hesitated briefly, then stood up and brushed bits of bark off the seat of her jeans before climbing into the Jeep. "Sure. Thanks. Just be prepared to stop if I see my ride coming, okay?"

He grinned at her, and she felt as if she had butterflies inside her ribcage. Before he put the Jeep in gear, he pulled his hat down further on his forehead to shade his eyes from the afternoon sun. She noticed how tanned and strong his fingers looked as he changed gears, and she was uncomfortably aware of his hand so close to her knee.

"Where are you going?" she asked, raising her voice to be heard over the crunch of gravel and fluttering of the vinyl rear window.

"You tell me." He grinned at her again. Again, the butterflies.

"I mean, where were you going before you picked me up?"

"For a drive. There's not much happening at the lodge, so I thought I'd do some exploring. Want to show me around?"

Goldie looked away. Wouldn't it be nice to be free enough to just say, 'Sure' and spend the entire evening showing him around Eagle? They could go for a walk down by the river, maybe pick up something for a picnic and eat it on the bluff. What if she just did that and didn't go home?

"My grandmother would worry," she said.

"About me?"

"No. I mean, if I didn't show up at home."

"Well, let's go tell her where you'll be."

Goldie was at a loss for words. Her grandmother had always been strict, and had been so angry about things lately, she tried to imagine how she would react if Goldie showed up with this young man from Outside and told her they were going out for the evening. It seemed like an impossible situation but...

"Well?"

Goldie told him there was no reason why they couldn't try, if her grandmother didn't need her for something. She directed him through town and down the road past Eagle Village, pointing out some of the landmarks on the way, although she realized that the beauty of Eagle wasn't where the roads and houses were. The beauty was the Yukon River, the big sky, the wildlife and the plants and trees in the vast wilderness that surrounded the town. The closer they got to her home, the more she worried about what her grandmother's reaction would be. She pictured the old woman she'd seen at the clinic, screeching like an angry eagle, hate on her face and in her eyes, and suddenly the old woman had her grandmother's face.

Goldie shivered and wondered if it was too late to ask Mark to stop the Jeep and let her walk the rest of the way home.

It was only a hundred yards or so off the main road that Mark's jeep came nose to nose with the old blue Merc. There was no room to pass, so Mark backed the jeep up to the road to let the Merc come ahead, and Goldie found herself face to face with her grandmother. The old woman was leaning out the pickup's window, peering around Goldie to see who was driving. Goldie held her breath, bracing herself for whatever caustic remark would come out of her grandmother's mouth.

"Who's that?" was all she said.

"Gran, I'd like you to meet Mark. He's Yukon Sally's cousin's son." She turned to Mark. "I heard you call her Aunt Sally." Goldie felt flustered, worrying about what her grandmother would say to Mark, or more likely, to her, so she kept talking. "But I think she's your second cousin." Back to Gran. "Mark is working at the lodge for the summer and when he saw me sitting at the end of the driveway waiting for you, he offered to give me a ride. You know, just in case you got delayed somewhere, or the truck broke down, or …"

The old woman nodded at Mark, said a terse, "Nice to meet you," then ground the old Merc into reverse, turned around on the road, and headed back down the bumpy dirt driveway toward the cabin.

Her grandmother had been civil, almost polite. Was the worst still in store? Goldie glanced at Mark.

"Why do you look so shocked?" he asked with a little laugh.

She stammered, not sure what to say. "It's just that my gran – she's a bit– she can be a little abrupt."

"You didn't finish the introduction, you know." He put the Jeep into gear and began to follow the Merc. "What am I supposed to call her? Goldie's Granny? Ma'am? What does everybody else call her?"

Goldie had to think a few seconds. They seldom had visitors at the cabin, almost never, in fact, and everyone from Eagle already knew them both, so introductions were rare. "People in town call her Betty mostly, I guess. She's not real friendly. I'm not sure if–" There was a strange truck. They had come out of the woods into the clearing around the cabin, and Goldie saw her grandmother pull the Merc in beside another old pickup. She was trying to make sense of it when she noticed Mark looking toward the other side of the cabin.

"You never said anything about your grandfather."

"My grandfather?" Goldie stared open-mouthed at the bearded old man standing at the woodpile. He wiped his forehead with the sleeve of his shirt, then waved cheerfully and started walking in their direction.

"There's that look again," said Mark, pointing a finger at Goldie's face. "You weren't expecting to see him?"

"Sorry," was all she could say. "I don't know who that is." She slid out of the jeep and walked away, toward her grandmother and the stranger.

"Hello, you must be Goldie," said the bearded man as she approached. He was quite short, and she saw the smile in his eyes as he stepped forward and extended a hand, still dragging the maul behind him in the other. His voice reminded her of Kris Kringle in that black and white Christmas movie with Maureen O'Hara and young Natalie Wood. "I'm Orville. Your grandmother has been kind enough to let me camp here a few days."

Goldie looked at her grandmother, who nodded curtly and turned away. "I've got to get back to my baking. Is your young friend leaving or not?"

Mark was standing in front of the jeep, his hands in his pockets.

"Do you want him to go, Gran?"

"Why would he stay?"

Goldie licked her lips. "Actually, we talked about me showing him around the area a little. He's only been in Eagle a couple of days and hasn't had a chance to explore. I wanted to see you first, make sure you knew so you wouldn't be worried."

"Fine," said Gran. Goldie followed her over to the outdoor kitchen, an area with four peeled logs as corner posts and a slanted tin roof. It housed a long wooden counter, half a 55-gallon drum, split the long way, with a hole in the bottom for a sink, a big wood stove and a brick oven for bread. Besides cooking and baking in all but the coldest weather, they used it for messy jobs like skinning animals, tanning hides and cleaning fish. Next to it there were south-facing drying racks for hanging fish and stretching skins, and another 55-gallon drum that served as a smoker. Under the shelter of the roof there was also a roughly constructed wooden table with plank benches where they frequently ate their meals in nice weather if the mosquitoes weren't too bad.

"Who is that man, Gran? Are you okay? When you didn't come to pick me up, I began to worry."

"Everything is fine, child. He's an old trapper I just met in town." She pulled a big lard tin with a cloth draped over it down from a shelf above the stove. She removed the cloth to reveal a white mound, like a bubble of bleached skin, and thrust her fist down into it. "You go on. Supper will be ready in an hour. Will you be back?"

Goldie nodded as she inhaled the smell of yeasty dough, watched her grandmother pull out the flaccid mass, throw it on a flour-dusted board and begin to knead. She obsequiously waved some flies away from the counter as she watched the old woman's knobby hands press and pull and spin the elastic ball.

"Is it okay with you, Gran? Sorry I'm not helping in the kitchen. I'll clean up after supper."

Her grandmother snorted softly. "We won't wait for you if you're late," she said, waving Goldie away with a puff of flour.

We? Her grandmother and that man had become *we*?

As she and Mark drove away, Goldie felt as if she were in a dream. Since they'd come to live near Eagle, her grandmother had been fiercely protective of their privacy at the cabin. She'd managed to rent them a small and isolated homestead on the far side of Eagle Village where there were few passers-by. She did all her business – buying, selling and bartering – in town and discouraged Goldie from inviting school friends over. Now here she was, all in the same day, not only had she not scolded Goldie for bringing a young man to the cabin, but Gran was entertaining a stranger she met in town. It was peculiar enough for Goldie that she found herself in the company of an attractive young Outsider, but her grandmother's uncharacteristic behavior eclipsed even that.

Betty Salmon had changed. She was becoming unpredictable. The change was sudden, it was drastic, and to Goldie, it was cause for alarm.

CHAPTER SIX

According to the hours of service regulations, Hunter shouldn't have been driving when they arrived in Whitehorse, but he was. Sorry had dozed off in the passenger seat, then retired to the sleeper around midnight and hadn't yet emerged. Hunter wanted to baby The Blue Knight to help forestall any further deterioration of the U-joint, so he was happy to do the driving himself. The road was good, a few twisty, hilly stretches but for the most part the curves were gentle and the horizon clear and distant. Besides, it was June north of the 60th parallel so it was still dusk around midnight, and the sun had already risen when he pulled into a Petro Canada just south of Whitehorse that looked like it had a machine shop. It was about four-thirty a.m.

The service station was closed, and the bunk behind him was occupied by his co-driver, so he had no choice but to try and catch some sleep sitting almost upright in the driver's seat. Usually he could sleep almost anywhere, but not so now. It was partly due to the daylight, and partly because he kept looking out the truck windows at the two lane highway lined with skinny trees, remembering what it was like to live and work in the north. It had been over twenty years since he'd left, and he'd never been back – until now.

Faces he hadn't pictured in his mind for many years kept coming, uninvited. The face of the man who'd owned the service station he was parked in; Hunter judged that he'd been over fifty then, could he still be here? The faces of the staff and regulars at the restaurant he and Ken used to frequent in the Edgewater Hotel. Would it still be the same?

They'd stayed at the Edgewater briefly on their arrival in Whitehorse in 1972 until they'd found a small house to rent on Jarvis Street, a walkable ten or eleven blocks from both the old G-division RCMP building and the Edgewater Hotel, whose bar and grill remained one of their favorite haunts. Not that they didn't sometimes drive – Hunter had a '63 Nova and Ken a '65 Rambler – but in the summer especially they enjoyed the walk and the small town feel of Whitehorse, seeing familiar faces on a daily basis, checking out the fresh-faced girls who'd come to town for summer work.

The traffic was picking up as the sun climbed in the sky. He watched a small convoy of RVs lumber by, then closed his eyes and returned to his reminiscences.

He pictured the face of one girl in particular, the dark-haired flower child who had been a waitress that first summer at a watering hole called the Sluice Box Pub. Again he saw her waving to him from the window of her VW Beetle, her long hair windblown, a wide smile lighting up her face. April. Did she die in that isolated cabin near the Teslin River? He thought so, but they hadn't found a body by the time he left the Yukon. Maybe he could hunt up the detectives here, and ask if the case was ever solved.

He tried to remember the names and faces of his colleagues in G-division, and later M-division. Several he recalled fondly, others not so much. Some of them might still be here, maybe retired, maybe still with the force. How would he feel about seeing them again? He knew they would ask about Ken, although he had no doubt that the news of Ken's death would have made it to his old detachment. Thinking about Ken still hurt; it hurt a lot. He knew he couldn't tell any of his old colleagues how he had seen his best friend's body, and found the suicide note that Ken had written to his wife, but that she had never seen. He couldn't tell them what he did with the note, how he staged the scene so it wouldn't look like anything but an accident. It was something he hadn't told anyone, and never would.

But Helen had known anyway. He had seen it in her eyes that first day, after he told her to go make coffee while he stayed with Ken's body and called the police. He had seen it again a few months ago when he'd driven Helen and her son, Adam, to the Vancouver airport after Adam was released from hospital. The secret had created a wall between them that neither one had the courage to breach, each unsure and afraid of what damage the truth could do. Funny how little secrets could be fun, but this big secret wasn't fun at all.

He pictured Helen, her hair, her face, her eyes. He could recall the scent of her, the softness of her skin when her lips brushed his cheek as they said goodbye in February. They hadn't seen each other for years, and they'd had no more than two hours together, in the company of young Adam, who only knew the official story, that his father had accidentally shot himself while cleaning his gun. Conversation had been sparse and superficial. Their eyes seldom met, but when they did, they only telegraphed pain and sympathy, on both sides. On his side, sympathy for Adam's growing up without a father, troubled and rebellious; sympathy for Helen being a widowed single mother trying to steer her son through adolescence whole and unbroken; sympathy for the nightmares that must haunt the widow of a man who had been unmistakably suicidal in spite of the coroner's verdict of accidental gunshot.

On her side, Hunter suspected she felt sympathy for him because of his divorce and the resulting separation from his two daughters – although he did see them now and then – and like many others, she probably didn't understand why he left a good career as a homicide investigator for a solitary life as a long-haul trucker. So many people thought it was a come-down, a disappointment, an admission of failure on his part. In truth, it had been a blessed relief; it was like therapy for his wounded psyche after the twin tragedies of his wife's demand for a divorce and his best friend's death. Both events he had no choice but to attribute to him and Ken being police officers. He'd had to stop; he wasn't sure if it was forever, but he had to stop.

Ken's face came to him, startlingly clear, in a scene from the past, about a year before Ken's death. Ken sitting across from him in the bar at the Villa Hotel in Burnaby, just after they'd come from court. A case had just been dismissed. They'd worked for months to find enough evidence for an arrest. He could remember Ken's voice, slurring slightly after a couple of double vodkas. "What the fuck is wrong with the system. You think what you're doing is important.

You think you're making the world a safer place. You bust your ass trying to put these scumbags behind bars and then some slick lawyer in Gucci loafers has 'em back on the street before you can spit." Another slug of vodka, then, "Well, fuck it, Hunter. Just fuck it! Don't you get tired of being a fuckin' retriever? You bring your handler the stick, and then he throws it back for you to go fetch again. You've accomplished fuck all. You complain about it, and the big shots pat you on the head and tell you to go lie down, like some kind of idiot Irish Setter."

Hunter shook off the image and settled deeper into the truck seat. He finally dozed off, soon to be awakened by the sound of the roll-up door on the mechanic's shed. He looked across the cab at the building, and saw a figure retreating into the dim interior. Hunter rubbed the sleep out of his eyes and opened the cab door. Time to find out what this clunking sound was going to cost him. He hoped it wasn't going to cost him his entire paycheck for the trip, or even more.

The news wasn't good. Parts needed ordering and would have to be shipped, so Hunter's Freightliner wasn't going anywhere for at least three days. Hunter called El. Even on a Sunday she was in her office catching up on paperwork and chewing the fat with any drivers who happened by. Her work was her life. Hunter understood her. Days without work could bring you face to face with yourself. They could feel as empty as an abandoned warehouse and leave you examining the crumpled scraps of yesterday that littered the cold concrete floor.

"Damn it, Hunter. Don't screw up this account for me. Hold on, would ya." He heard some yapping and rustling, then from a distance but still loud, "Pete! Get back here you little shit. Come. Sit." Hunter couldn't help but smile, imagining El's little black dog, Peterbilt, blissfully unabashed, with his pink tongue hanging out and his dark eyes glittering with mischief. When El was back on the line, she said, "You've got a few days yet before the deadline. How far is it to Fairbanks from where you are?"

"About six hundred miles. I'd say twelve hours or so once we're on the road."

"Good thing you've got Sorenson on board. You won't have an hours-of-service stop before you get there. Then again, he's probably the one who fucked up your truck."

"I've thought of that, but it was probably just a matter of time. Wear and tear."

"Or it could just be some kind of Alaska Highway curse. I haven't sent many loads that far north, but it seems to me every time, there's some kind of mechanical on the trip." She sighed. "Call me when you're back on the road, sweet cheeks." She hung up before he could reply.

The trailer was tucked in beside the building, secured with a pin lock. "It'll be fine there," said the mechanic, who also happened to own the shop. "I live just out back."

Sorry came back from the convenience store at the Petro Canada, munching on a prefab sandwich and carrying a coffee. "Good thing we got spare wheels," he said, pointing to the trailer. "Open up the back and let's wheel 'er out so we can go somewhere good to eat."

"Somewhere nearby where I can rent a car?" Hunter asked the mechanic.

The man shrugged. "Airport?"

"What for, man?" said Sorry, sounding aggrieved. "Let's just use my bike."

Hunter made a face.

"What?"

"I don't relish the thought of snuggling up behind you every time we want to go somewhere. Besides, I don't have a helmet."

"Fuck the helmet." Sorry turned to the mechanic. "The cops stop you without a helmet up here?"

"'Fraid so," the man threw over his shoulder as he walked back to his shop. "If they catch you. See you in a few days."

Hunter opened the back doors of the trailer and hooked in a ramp so they could wheel Sorry's Harley out. He was relieved to see that the straps and dunnage had held it firmly so there was no visible damage to the bike. At least something had gone right.

A few minutes later, duffel bags roped securely behind him, he was seated behind Sorry as the bike roared down the highway into Whitehorse. The wind ballooned his jacket and whistled past his ears, but it felt seductively free to be bareheaded and unbelted at that speed. He only wished he had control of the brakes and throttle himself, as being a passenger made him feel disturbingly vulnerable.

He tapped Sorry on the shoulder and pointed when it was time to veer right off the highway, and they ended up cruising down 2nd Avenue into the heart of town. The early birds out on the street turned their heads at the sound of the Harley, no doubt concerned or at least curious about the arrival of an outlaw biker from the south. By this time they were at a speed that allowed Hunter to relax, but it was still a relief when Sorry finally slowed to a stop in front of a Tim Horton's, one of the few places open at that time of day, which was just before seven-thirty.

"Now what?" Sorry sipped at his coffee, keeping an eye on the counter for a signal that their breakfast sandwiches were ready for pick up.

Hunter couldn't help yawning as he stirred some sugar into his coffee. "I need some sleep. I should have stayed with the truck."

"You would've had to eat cold cardboard sandwiches wrapped in plastic if you had."

"Right. I'll probably feel better after I eat." He blew on his coffee, then took a sip. "I'd like to look up some old friends while I'm here."

Sorry snorted. "Cops, no doubt."

Hunter just smiled.

"Well, I want to check out the town," said Sorry. "On my bike."

"You do that."

So after breakfast, Sorry revved up his Harley and roared up 2nd Street while Hunter, duffel bag hiked up over his shoulder, set out on foot for the RCMP detachment on 4th. He needed wheels, and was hoping he'd find an old colleague with some to borrow.

"You old son of a gun." Bartholomew Sam grabbed Hunter's right hand in both of his and shook it vigorously. "I thought I'd never see you again."

Hunter took a step forward, and his old friend took that as a cue to grab him and lift him off his feet in a big bear hug.

"Damn, but it's good to see you," said Staff Sergeant Sam as he released Hunter momentarily, then lifted him off his feet again. "You've hardly changed. If I didn't know better, I'd think you were still a cop."

"Good to see you, too, Bart," grunted Hunter. "Real good," he said as Bart released him.

"Come to my office. We've got some catching up to do."

Bartholomew Sam had been one of the first Native Special Constables in the Yukon in the mid-seventies, and he and Hunter had worked together on a number of investigations during Hunter's time in Whitehorse. Bart was born the son of a shaman of the Tr'ondëk Hwëch'in First Nation, and after several years serving as a Special Constable, became a regular member of the RCMP. He was smart, and fair, and Hunter had found him intriguing, right from the first time they'd met.

"Congratulations on the stripes. You still in investigations?" he asked as he dropped his duffel bag on the floor and pulled a chair around to face the one Bart had settled into. Homicides in the Yukon were rare, but there were enough assaults and property crimes to keep investigators working.

"Yep." He tapped a folder on the desk beside him. "Just had a homicide in town early yesterday, in fact. The owner of a strip joint on the north side of Whitehorse was found dead in the parking lot of his club, just outside his truck. Knife under the ribs. Only weapon at the scene was his own hunting rifle behind the back seat of his truck. Door was open, seat forward, like he'd been going for his gun."

"Got a suspect?"

"Hah. You got your nose in the air like a wolf picking up the scent of a cariboo. I hear you left the force. Want to talk about it?"

Bart always did have a way of getting right to the heart of things. Hunter had frequently had the impression that Bart saw, or sensed, things that normal people had no access to. Did he really possess some spiritual or psychic connection? Hunter couldn't explain it, but sometimes he almost felt that Bart disappeared from his body. He'd be standing in front of you with his eyes wide open, but he would be gone. It would only last seconds – maybe half a minute – at a time, and when he came back, he would often seem to have received a new insight into their investigation. Where did that come from? Hunter didn't know, and he found it a little spooky.

Hunter inhaled and held it, then let his breath out slowly. If it were anyone else, he probably wouldn't talk about it, but he almost got the sense that Bart knew anyway. "You heard about Ken?"

Bart nodded, his face solemn. "Not your fault," he said.

Hunter just stared. He had never told anyone. He barely acknowledged it to himself. After his wife asked for a divorce, Hunter lost his patience with Ken, with Ken's drinking, with Ken's depression. Hunter was preoccupied with his own problems and stopped commiserating with his best friend. Soon after, Ken had killed himself. Officially, it had been labelled an accidental death, but Hunter had been haunted by guilt ever since. How did Bart know?

"I mean it. Ken chose his path. You were not meant to stop him from following it to the end."

Hunter looked into Bart's eyes. "How do you do that?" he asked, then shook his head. He didn't really want to know. "Back to your murder. Any suspects?"

"Everyone's a suspect, remember? We do have two persons of interest. The bartender there – the place was called 'Lost Mine'; no 'The', which leads me to believe the reference was to virginity and not a gold claim – said there were a couple of guys he'd never seen before in the club earlier that evening. He didn't know who they were, but seemed to be someone from Colin's past. He said Colin wasn't exactly happy to see them."

"Colin been around long?"

"Showed up in town about ten years ago with enough money to buy the club. Except for the fact that he made his living off of liquor and naked girls, he seemed to be a nice enough guy. He married a local girl and they had two young boys. She was pretty much a basket case when I told her."

Hunter could picture it. He'd had to do enough next-of-kin notifications himself, and it was always the worst part of the job. It reminded him that it wasn't his job to hunt down killers any more. "I have faith in you, chief. I have no doubt you'll find the killer."

"Even without your help?"

"Even without my help."

"Maybe." Bart smiled one of his spooky smiles. "Or maybe not. So tell me, what are you doing now?"

Hunter almost laughed. So the shaman's son didn't know everything about him after all. "I'm a long haul trucker," he said. "I drive an eighteen-wheeler – up and down the west coast, mostly. BC to California and back, but sometimes across Canada and elsewhere in the States."

"Good on you, man. That's something I've always wanted to do myself. Did you drive up here? Where's your truck?"

They spent another ten minutes catching up, with lots more yet to say. Bart's phone buzzed, and he told the caller he'd get back to them in a few minutes, so Hunter took that as his cue to ask if Bart knew anyone with a spare vehicle he could borrow for a couple of days.

Bart leaned back and tapped his lips with a forefinger. "Not mine, but my wife's brother took his new girlfriend to Las Vegas for a week. I'll see if I can reach him and get back to you."

Hunter met up with Sorry back at the Tim Horton's at noon.

"Where'd you go?" he asked the biker.

"I did some exploring. Somebody sent me to Miles Canyon, another guy said I should maybe go see Takhini Hot Springs. I didn't want to leave my bike and gear where I couldn't keep an eye on it so it was mostly just a fuckin' road tour. I saw some guys on bikes stopped at a gas station further up the highway there, so pulled in to shoot the shit and ask about where's good to ride. They said there's so fuckin' much road construction, and unless you stay on the main drag, most of the roads are dirt or gravel. The dirt roads are a real bitch if it rains. One of the guys blew a tire, another one trashed his rear sprocket and had to have his bike loaded on a flatbed to get it back to Whitehorse."

"You still want to ride to Dawson?"

"You comin'?"

"Not on your bike, I'm not. I think I've found a car, though."

Sorry sighed; his mouth worked beneath his blond mustache. "I really want to ride."

Hunter shrugged. "No guarantee we can find – or afford – a hotel room wherever we go. At least with a car, we've got somewhere to sleep." He saw Sorry's eyes widen and knew that was something he hadn't considered. "I don't know about you, but I'm too old to sleep under the stars without even a ground sheet or a sleeping bag."

"Right," said Sorry. "So when do you get this car?"

Late that afternoon, they parked the Harley in Bart's garage and he handed over the keys to his brother-in-law's 1978 Chevy Blazer. The aging SUV was a dark brown or red with one grey front fender on the passenger side and a badly dented rear bumper. "You can see why he was willing to lend his car to a complete stranger. He's hoping you total it so he can make you buy him a new one," said Bart. "Where do you plan on going?"

"Dawson City," said Hunter, opening the hatch above the tailgate to throw in their gear. The space behind the back seat was strewn with belongings, including unidentifiable articles of clothing, mud-caked boots, a red metal gas can and pair of snow shoes. It smelled of motor oil. He briefly considered asking Bart if they could dump everything from the back of the Blazer in his garage, but decided against it.

"Alaska," said Sorry.

As usual, Bart seemed to read Hunter's mind. "Here. Unload all that stuff out of the back. It'll be okay here in the garage 'til you get back."

Sorry pulled everything out of the SUV while Hunter piled it as neatly as possible beside a stack of winter tires.

"If you're heading for the border," said Bart, "keep an eye out for those persons of interest I was telling you about. One's an old guy with a grey beard in an ancient Ford truck." He smiled as he scratched his belly and Hunter noticed that he'd put on a little weight, like most men Hunter knew who had entered their forties. "The other one's a younger man, looks like a native, maybe thirty-five or so. He had longish hair, scrawny beard, with grease under his fingernails."

"Those descriptions apply to five out of every ten men up here," said Hunter.

"Very funny. Evidently the older man was overheard saying something about heading to Alaska. We've asked the Troopers to watch for him as well. The two may or may not be travelling together. The witness said the younger one sounded like a local, but the old guy had some kind of English accent."

Sorry snorted. "So if we see these guys, then what? My buddy the ex-cop here is supposed to arrest them?" He poked Hunter in the shoulder. "You getting paid for this, Hunter? We're just being tourists for a couple days, right?"

Hunter shot him a look. "Sure," he said to Bart. "Got a couple of your business cards handy?"

Sorry shook his head and tossed his gear into the back of the Blazer, then slammed the back shut. "You driving?"

Hunter thought about it. He'd had almost no sleep since Fort Nelson at lunch time the day before. It was about three hundred miles from Whitehorse to Dawson.

"I'm bagged. I'd rather find a place to stay here in Whitehorse for the night and leave for Dawson in the morning. I could show you around town and we could get a good meal before we call it a night." He turned to Bart. "Any suggestions on a clean, cheap place to get a room?"

"It's my wife's quilting club night," he said. "How about I join you for dinner instead of eating leftovers out of the fridge, then you can both come back here for the night. There's a pull-out in the den and a nice big sofa in the living room."

Hunter looked at Sorry, who shrugged as if to say, "Why not?"

"Sounds good to me," said Hunter. "I'll take my friend here to see the S.S. Klondike and tour the town a bit more, then we could meet in the restaurant at the Klondike Inn at, say, seven o'clock?" He had thought about suggesting the restaurant he and Ken used to frequent at the Edgewater, but something stopped him. Just in case. "We can catch up some more," he added, nodding in Bart's direction.

He caught Sorry rolling his eyes, and figured listening to two cops catch up wasn't high on the biker's list of favorite ways to spend time.

He was still thinking about the Edgewater as they drove away, asking himself 'just in case' of what? In case it hurt to remember being there with Ken? In case someone there recognized him and asked about Ken? Buck up, he told himself. You're a grown man, an ex-police officer, a trucker, for God's sake. Your friend's dead but you're not. Life goes on.

The next morning they were on the road before seven thirty. The sleeping accommodations at Bart's hadn't been the best – the pull-out in the den was too hard for Sorry, and the sofa in the living room was too soft for Hunter – but the price was right, the shower was decent, and the morning coffee was fresh, hot and free.

"So what's the plan, boss?" Sorry had lit up a cigarette and was slouched comfortably in the passenger seat.

Hunter waved the smoke away.

"Wha-a-a-t," said Sorry. "Dude here's a smoker. He won't give a shit. Look at the fuckin' ashtray." He'd already rolled down his window, but now positioned his cigarette closer to it.

Hunter rolled his own window down. "The plan was to drive to Dawson, wasn't it?"

"How far is that?"

"About three hundred and fifty miles, give or take, heading north on the Klondike Highway. Eight hours or so, depending on stops."

"What stops?"

"There aren't many, that I know of. Braeburn Lodge for a coffee refill and one of their big cinnamon buns. Carmacks is maybe an hour or so further. There's a hotel there with a restaurant, if I'm not mistaken. Then not much until we reach Dawson."

"So we'll eat before we get out of town, won't we, Hunter?"

And they did. They were back on the road again after a big breakfast, with a couple of fresh coffees to go. Sorry's coffee cooled in the cupholder as he nodded off just outside of Whitehorse. Hunter was happy to have some time without the distraction of Sorry's running commentary on the scenery and other drivers, so he could continue contemplating the case he'd discussed with Bartholomew Sam the night before.

In spite of how tired he'd been, Hunter had lain awake much of the night thinking about the conversation he'd had with Bart over dinner, and having flashbacks to his years in Whitehorse as a young

Mountie. He'd asked his old colleague about the case of the blood-smeared trapper's cabin he'd worked his first year in the RCMP, whether they'd ever found a body, or whether they'd ever concluded there was foul play involved.

"Refresh my memory," Bart had said.

"A man named Fred Klimmer called it in." Hunter paused, recalling details he hadn't thought about for years. "Klimmer was a trapper with a concession close to the missing man's, roughly north of Johnson's Crossing on the Teslin River. I didn't like the man – Klimmer, I mean. What bugged me the most was how he seemed to be lusting after the man's girlfriend, April. What was the man's name?" With the objectivity of the elapsed twenty-odd years he suspected that his own feelings for April had fostered that dislike. He looked up at the ceiling, searching his memory. "Blake. Martin Blake. Although his name might as well have been John Doe, as it turned out."

Bartholomew Sam was leaning back in his chair, his beer almost untouched, his eyes never leaving Hunter's face. Perhaps in spite of himself, Sorry seemed to be listening with interest. He had ordered a pint of draft beer – averting his eyes from Hunter as he did so – and drank half of it the first time he put the glass to his lips, then pushed it away as if to keep himself from drinking it all at once.

"It was late October or early November. The cabin door was open, snow drifting in. The missing man kept a trap line and had a dog team. The dogs hadn't been fed for days, so Klimmer brought some fish for them." Hunter described the blood, damage and scratches that made it clear there had been violence, probably death, possibly the work of a grizzly. "Evidently a young woman from Michigan named April Corbett had been living there with Blake for several months. According to Fred Klimmer, Blake wasn't such a nice guy and he didn't know why she stayed with him. There was no sign of either one of them, alive or dead, except the blood."

"So what was the theory?"

"In spite of the grizzly, there was no way to rule out murder or murder-suicide. We were looking for evidence, either way."

"Was it a woman's blood or a man's or both?" asked Sorry.

"Back in the 70's, all we had was ABO testing. All the lab could tell us was blood type, which was type A. Given almost half the population was type A and almost half was type B, it wasn't much help." Hunter turned to his former colleague. "Ring any bells yet?"

"Starting to. It wasn't a case that I got actively involved in, but I can recall hearing about it. Was there a vehicle belonging to one of them?"

"No vehicle found at the scene, or nearby, which was suspicious in itself. The road to the cabin was almost non-existent, so it's entirely possible that a vehicle could have been parked off site for the winter, but none was ever reported. A British Columbia driver's license was found in Blake's belongings, but it was a fake. Klimmer thought he'd seen Blake driving a Ford truck, but we found no record of any vehicles registered in the name of Martin Blake in British Columbia or the Yukon. April was known to have had a 1964 Volkswagen." Hunter took a long pull on his beer. "It was white, with flowers painted on it. A hippie car." He pictured April and her hippie clothing: loose, flowing dresses and tunics, bell-bottom pants, leather sandals, colorful bandanas.

"Maybe Blake drove off in her car?"

"No reported sightings of the Volkswagen since then, as far as I know."

"No tracks?" Sorry must have been finding the discussion more interesting than he'd expected.

"Fresh snow since it happened. No sign of tracks except for Fred Klimmer's from his first time on the scene before he called it in."

"Maybe the woman killed Martin and took off in her own car. Women do kill. It's been known to happen."

"You can't rule that out. We contacted the girl's family in Michigan – she'd held a job in Whitehorse that summer and had given her employer information on her next of kin – and talked to her father. It wasn't a notification, since there was no way to really say she was dead. All we had to go on was her picture on the wall and Klimmer's word for it that she had even been living there – so we just asked if anyone had heard from her. Her father basically told us to take a hike, that she'd been dead to them – his word – since she ran off with a 'damned hippie' a few years before. All we could do was request that he contact us if he ever heard from her. Might be worth looking for her again, or checking to see if her family ever did report her missing."

Bart leaned forward, centered his beer glass on its coaster, his face thoughtful. "Then again," he said, "at that time of year especially, it could be the grizzly, or grizzlies – could be a mother and yearling cub trying to fatten up before denning – broke into the cabin while they were sleeping and killed them both before they could get to a rifle. Grizzlies drag their kill off and bury them in leaves and dirt."

Hunter nodded slowly. "Of course, we considered that. We searched the adjacent land, with no success. But if neither one of them left the cabin alive, what happened to April's car? Or Blake's truck, if there was one?"

"If there was one," repeated Bart.

Sorry took a slug of beer, wiped drops off his mustache with the back of his hand. "Maybe the fucker hid the car on her so she couldn't leave him, if he was the asshole that trapper guy thought he was."

"Also possible."

"When was that again?"

"1972. Early November, I think. Around the first snowfall."

"So we're talkin' almost twenty-five years ago. What're the chances you'd ever solve this now?" When neither Hunter nor Bart answered, Sorry continued. "Would there still be blood for testing? They can test the DNA now, can't they?"

Hunter shrugged. He thought it unlikely.

"If the girl was living there, wouldn't there have been clothes and stuff. You know, female stuff left behind?" asked Sorry. "Or ID? A wallet?"

"No ID or wallet. There was some women's clothing. We assumed it belonged to April, but there was no way to prove it."

"Was there a rifle left at the scene?" asked Bart.

"Under the bed. Loaded."

"Just one?"

"Just the one."

"Loaded for bear?" Sorry laughed at his own suggestion. Hunter half smiled.

Bart didn't smile at all. "Not like a trapper or hunter to have just one, but always possible. Lends a little weight to the theory that Blake killed the girl, took his other gun – or guns – and went on the run."

"Plus, if it had been a murder-suicide, the rifle would have been out in the open," Hunter said.

"Any reason why you'd suspect a murder-suicide?"

Hunter shrugged. "Looking at all the possibilities, the usual suspects."

"How about the guy who called it in?" asked Sorry.

"If he did it, there was no reason for him to call it in. Killers do that if there's a reason for suspicion to fall on them, in order to divert suspicion elsewhere. He had no prior record, neither here nor in Manitoba where he was from. Also he had no obvious motive and there's no way we would ever have connected him to it if he hadn't called us."

"Were there any forensic clues?"

"Bears eat everything they can get that time of year," said Bart. "What they don't finish, the wolverines will clean up, bones and all. Pretty safe there wouldn't be much left to autopsy, even if we'd found some remains." He shrugged. "If Fred Klimmer hadn't called it in, and the bears hadn't been there, could be no one would've found the bodies for months."

Hunter had to concede that he was right. Who knows how long it could have been before anyone else had happened by the cabin.

"You said there were dogs. Wouldn't bears stay away with a bunch of dogs around?" Sorry asked.

"Sled dogs are kept chained up. I've known a bear to kill a chained dog and make a meal of it. They can yank them right off their chains and drag them away. Besides, there was no question that a bear had been there. I saw the scene myself, remember?" He paused before musing, "If it had been Fred Klimmer, he might've called it in for the sake of the dogs. Funny how some men think nothing of killing a fellow human, but don't like to see an animal suffer."

Bart countered with, "If that were the case, he could have just taken the dogs. No one would've been the wiser."

Hunter saw the scene again in his mind: the blood on the bed and the floor, the scratches and destruction throughout the cabin, and

April's photograph on the wall. And he recalled how he and his colleague and friend, Ken, had shared similar discussions over and over again that winter and for years afterward. The last time they'd rehashed the case was in the year before Ken's death. Ken remembered seeing Blake in Whitehorse previously. Ken's theory had always been that April couldn't have been living with a 'loser' like Blake, at least not for long. "Wouldn't matter to her more than a week or two that he was a good fuck, if that's what attracted her in the first place. The guy was probably looking for a drudge to cook and clean for him, as well as keep his bed warm. April was a free bird, remember? She never would've stood for it."

Hunter had found part of Ken's speculation offensive, but still fervently hoped that he was right. It had been an intriguing case, but was now as cold as a January night in Old Crow, and Hunter had accepted that he would never know the answer.

Before they'd left this morning, Bart had made them coffee and seen them off. "So you keep an eye out for my person of interest, and I'll see what I can do about finding the Martin Blake file," he'd said. "The case is so cold it's probably iced over, but you never know."

Hunter had smiled sadly and shook his head. "I'm not holding out much hope."

Bart just smiled that spooky smile, as if he knew something Hunter didn't.

"You never know," he said again.

CHAPTER SEVEN

Betty took pains not to wake Goldie, walking as quietly as she could from the alcove that contained her bed across the cabin floor. She opened the cabin door and stepped outside. The air was crisp and imbued with smells of spring: the subtle spice of new growth and the earthy smell of newly turned soil. She heard a raven croak in the distance. She could see around the corner of the cabin to where her visitor had tied a canvas tarp between two trees at the edge of the clearing, making a lean-to shelter from wind and damp. The bulk to the sleeping bag told her that Orville was still asleep, or at least still stretched out on the ground under the tarp. She watched until she could make out the slight swell of his torso with each breath.

There was a movement beside him, and she recognized the grey mound as her dog. Hootie raised his head to look at her but made no move to get up. Betty tried to be annoyed, but found herself more amused by the fact that Hootie had chosen to sleep beside the stranger instead of at his usual post near the cabin door. Her smile lingered as she made a quick trip to the outhouse, up a well-worn dirt path on the opposite side of the cabin. By the time she returned to the kitchen, Hootie had joined her and settled down in his customary spot outside the door. Leaving the solid door open to the early morning sun with the screen door closed against mosquitoes, she took a couple of sticks from the kindling pile and lay them on top of the embers in the woodstove.

Once the sticks had caught, she gently laid a couple of splits across and left the damper wide open while she went outside again. She had a dozen eggs or more stored in the cold room, but fresher was better, and she always liked to check the chicken coop first thing. It was solidly built and the hens were locked in at night, but foxes and weasels were clever, sneaky creatures and Hootie was sleeping more soundly these days, so she liked to reassure herself that her flock was intact. They were. Cradling half a dozen eggs in a shirt-tail sling, she headed back to the cabin to check the fire and heat up the kettle for morning tea. By the time the kettle boiled, she had begun preparations for breakfast.

"You opened the bacon?"

It was Goldie; pushing aside the curtain, she stopped just outside the alcove that passed for her bedroom to tuck in her tee shirt and fasten her jeans. She raised her nose and sniffed enthusiastically. "Smells great. What's the occasion?"

Betty just shrugged.

"Trying to impress your gentleman friend?" Goldie's voice held a smile.

Betty could feel herself begin to blush. "That would be stupid," she said. "We don't get many visitors. I don't like to open a whole can of bacon for just you and me, so I thought we should take advantage of another mouth to feed."

"If you say so." Goldie shot her a worried look – feigned or not, Betty wasn't sure – as she passed by on her way out the door. "And potatoes, too?" she added over her shoulder. "What a treat."

Betty huffed, but she had to admit she was enjoying the pleasures she had just begun to allow herself, and looking forward to Orville's reaction when he sat down to breakfast. She wasn't surprised that Goldie seemed concerned. This was a departure from her usual frugal summer breakfasts of fried bread and eggs, and even more of a departure from her usual attitude toward extravagance, not to mention her attitude toward visitors. The sudden change in her outlook was a source of confusion even for her. Lately she'd been feeling increasingly irritable about Goldie's threatened defection, and now in a total about-face, she felt herself beginning to not care. In fact, she felt herself sliding down a slippery slope towards some kind of carefree self-indulgence.

Was it just the arrival of that man?

Betty picked out two potatoes and began to peel them with a small paring knife. It was difficult to hold the skinny handle of the knife with her arthritic fingers, so it took her longer than it used to. As she worked, she wondered: what was happening to her? She pictured an ice jam on the Yukon River. After the first ice floes blocked the river from bank to bank, pushed relentlessly from upstream, the mass of ice built up one frozen chunk at a time, ice piling on ice in a jagged patchwork until it blocked the river. The river built itself up behind it, only a fraction of its mass moving beneath and around the jammed ice, the dammed water rising higher and wider. When the ice began to thaw and weaken, with the relentless water pressure, small chunks would start to give way, then bigger ones, and before you knew it, all the jammed ice would start to shift and bob, and soon there would be a mighty flood of ice and water rushing downstream, sweeping away everything in its path.

Had she created an ice jam in her life, in her very soul? Had Orville's arrival been what finally breached the dam and started the flood? Would it be impossible for her to go back to the simple, ascetic life she'd been living ever since–. Ever since what? What had started this ice jam in her soul?

Betty's life had always been about hard work and self-sacrifice and making do. No one had ever given her anything; no one had ever volunteered to make her life easier or more pleasant. Even her mother had been too preoccupied with her own survival to give Bitty (as her mother called her) more than basic care, except for an occasional brief glimpse of tenderness when her father was out of sight. Betty had learned to work at her mother's side as soon as she could walk. Except for the gifts that nature bestows on all her creatures – gifts like the warmth of the sun, the freshness of a breeze, a cool swallow of clear water from the creek, the smell of newly picked herbs and the taste of wild blueberries – pleasure to Betty and her mother was nothing more than the absence of pain, usually just the oblivion of sleep. Her father had worked her Athapascan mother into an early grave, then worked his daughter just as hard until he traded Betty to a fellow trapper for a new rifle when she was only fourteen.

Her first husband, if you could call him that, was a taciturn, grey haired French Canadian with a cabin near Hootalinqua who had treated her much like he did his sled dogs. She was told to call him 'patron', which she assumed was his name. He took care of her because she was useful to him, but there was no tenderness or affection. He came to her bed frequently at first, and she was grateful that sex for him was primitive and quick; the less fondling there was, the faster it was over, the sooner he left her alone. She had been with him for two years when she became pregnant. He scowled and grunted when he realized in May that her belly had begun to grow. Soon after, he took her on a three day journey on foot, and left her sitting on a log with her few possessions and a small bundle of tea and dried moose meat at her feet beside the Yukon River. Betty sat on that log for hours, before it sank in that he had no intention of coming back for her.

Up to that day, Betty had spent her lifetime living in what could be considered the Yukon wilderness. She had often gone hunting small game, setting rabbit snares or picking herbs and berries, sometimes walking for many miles alone in the vicinity of her camp or cabin. Her trapper father and her husband had often left her for days and weeks at a time as they checked their traps or took their skins to sell, so being alone was not unusual or uncomfortable for her. What was different that time on the bank of the Yukon was the knowledge that her future was hers alone to decide, her path hers alone to choose. No one was waiting for her to return, and no one would come looking for her if she didn't. She knew that she didn't want to go back to where she'd come from, but she had no idea where to go or how to get somewhere she would be safe.

Once she had accepted and begun to relish the thought that she was now in control of her life, her first instinct was to move a good distance from where Patron had left her, in case he did come back for her. She took care not to leave a trail as she made her way along the bank, following the flow of the river downstream. After walking for two hours or more, she made herself a bed of tree boughs and sat there, her back against the rough bark of the sturdy spruce that had provided most of them. She felt as if she were hidden, yet she could still see the roiling brown surface of the river, swollen with spring runoff, from where she sat.

Although she was hungry and tempted to eat the moose jerky, she remembered stories her Gwich'in mother had told her as they worked side by side, and decided to fast and ask for a sign to guide her path. She realized that the direction she chose could determine not only her happiness, but her very survival, and she did not want to let fear rush her into a decision she might regret. Perhaps her mother's spirit would know of her plight and send her a sign. She tried to clear her mind of idle thoughts and leave it free for some kind of message, but her stomach growled and she began to think about what she could eat. She pushed those thoughts away, but then found herself thinking about the point of a spruce twig that was pricking the skin of her thigh. Emptying her mind was not so easy. It was no wonder that she had never been able to receive messages from her mother before.

When darkness finally fell, the night was clear and cold. She moved closer to the river so her head and heart were open to the night sky and the stars strewn across its surface, shining like the silver scales of a big salmon. Her hunger had passed. The cold almost numbed her cheeks. She pulled a worn wool blanket from her bundle and wrapped it around her, then made herself small, huddling against the root end of a tree that had been deposited by the ice jam after breakup. Again she tried to clear her mind. Instead she fell asleep.

When Betty was sixteen, the Yukon River was still the only highway between Whitehorse and Dawson City, and when the sun woke her a few hours later, she saw a plume of smoke and heard the chug of a massive engine from upriver. Was this the sign she had been waiting for? Or should she gather her belongings and slip into the trees to hide? Her fear of the noisy, smoking machine dissipated as a great sense of peace came over her, and she knew that she was meant to wait here on the shore. Soon a massive white boat appeared from behind the bend.

Betty walked to the bank of the river and raised a hand to shield her eyes against the sun as she watched the boat draw closer. She could make out someone on the deck gesturing toward her and heard men's voices, raised to carry over the noise of the engines. The sound of the engine changed and the sternwheeler seemed to almost float in place as a small boat was launched from its side. The motorboat headed slightly upriver to come ashore just twenty feet from where she stood quietly waiting. The next day she was in Dawson City at the home of a couple who had befriended her on the boat and so began more years on a path that was not of her own choosing, more seasons of ice packed into her soul.

Betty's wonderings were interrupted by the sound of voices outside the cabin.

"Am I in heaven?"

"If you are, then Gran and I must be in heaven, too."

"Last time I woke up to the smell of bacon frying must be twenty years ago or more." Orville scuffed his boots on the mat outside and stepped into the cabin. "Good morning, my fair Elizabeth," he said, "and what a lovely morning it is." His grin was so big she could almost see his teeth under the grey bush of his mustache.

After one brief glance at her visitor, Betty turned her back to him and busied herself at the stove. Her lips quivered with the effort of holding back a smile, and she was surprised how light her heart felt. She felt years melting off her age and thought that she surely must be ill. Perhaps she was experiencing a stroke, or had accidentally included some strange herb in yesterday's tea.

"Fix Orville and yourself some tea," she said sternly to Goldie, who had appeared at her elbow.

She felt Goldie's arms slip around her shoulders from behind, and the girl gave her a quick hug and glancing kiss on her cheek, like a hit and run, before Betty had a chance to protest. "Are we in heaven, Gran?" she heard her whisper.

Betty's only answer was a smile.

Without consulting his travelling companion, Hunter took a right off the Klondike Highway and drove the borrowed Chevy down a gravel road. They weren't much more than half an hour out of Whitehorse.

"There are strange things done in the midnight sun, by the men who moil for gold," he recited. Hunter paused, momentarily at a loss for the next line, then, lowering his voice, resumed with *"The Arctic trails have their secret tales that would make your blood run cold. The Northern Lights have seen queer sights, but the queerest they ever did see, was that night on the marge of Lake Lebarge, when I cremated Sam McGee."*

"I didn't know you were a poet." Sorry punched Hunter on his right shoulder.

Hunter frowned at him as he pulled into a gravel lot beside a vacant campground picnic area and put the gear shift into park. "It's a Robert Service poem, dummy. I can't help thinking of it every time I pass Lake Laberge."

The big lake, a widening of the Yukon River, lay in front of them. The poem was probably more famous than the lake itself, but looking out over a natural body of water always held an attraction for Hunter, no matter whether the lake was glassy and quiet or lashed with white capped waves.

"Okay, let's hear the rest of it." Sorry had already rolled down the window and lit a fresh cigarette.

"I don't know more than one or two other verses." Hunter frowned, then cleared his throat. *"I came to the marge of Lake Lebarge, and a derelict hulk there lay. It was jammed in the ice, but I saw in a trice it was called the 'Alice May.' And I looked at it, and I thought a bit, and I looked at my frozen chum, then 'Here,' said I, with a sudden cry, 'is my cre-ma-tor-eum.'*

"And the last verse or so goes, *'I was sick with dread, but I bravely said, I'll just take a peep inside. I guess he's cooked, and it's time I looked, then the door I opened wide. And there sat Sam, looking cool and calm, in the heart of the furnace roar, and he wore a smile you could see a mile, and he said, 'Please close that door. It's fine in here, but I greatly fear you'll let in the cold and storm. Since I left Plumtree, down in Tennessee, it's the first time I've been warm.'"*

"Haw, haw," said Sorry, opening the door of the Blazer and stepping out onto the gravel. He looked around, then sauntered over to a tree and unzipped his fly. He held his cigarette in his lips as he urinated.

Hunter shook his head and walked closer to the lake, taking a deep breath as he surveyed the wide expanse of water, backed by rocky lumps of low hills. Limpid waves licked at the pebbly shore, and a breeze off the lake tickled his forehead with a lock of his hair. Although the sky was clear, it was still cool enough that he was glad he'd kept his jacket on.

Sorry walked over to join him, tossing his cigarette butt on the rocky beach, where its smoke continued to spiral upwards. "What's our next stop, boss?"

"You're tired of this view already?"

Sorry shrugged. "It's a big fuckin' lake. We drove past dozens of them the last couple of days. How long do we have to look at this one?"

Hunter sighed. "Let's go then." As Sorry walked back to the truck, Hunter picked up the now dead cigarette butt and threw it in a bear-proof trash container. He thought again how he missed his solitude.

"We've got another seven hours or so of driving ahead of us," he told Sorry as the Blazer wound its way back toward the highway, tires crunching on gravel. "Like I said earlier, I figure we can take a coffee break in about half an hour at Braeburn Lodge, maybe pick up a burger or something in Carmacks and grab something to snack on until we reach Dawson. There might not be anywhere else to get a meal until we get there." He glanced sideways at his passenger. "I assume that your main interest is in where do we eat next."

"You know me well, man. I'm hungry already."

They drove in silence for several minutes. Hunter looked over at Sorry a few times, seeing the look on his face change from worried to sullen to worried again.

"Want to talk about it?"

"No." The big biker sniffed, his jaw working. Then, "Yes. Maybe." He rubbed some dust off the dash with his fingers. "One minute I'm sure she's missing me, and two minutes later I picture her sucking face with some guy in the neighborhood who's just been waiting for us to split, you know?" He slammed his fist against the dash. "It's driving me fuckin' crazy, thinking about it."

"You know this guy?"

"Not a real guy, you idiot. I mean, some guy maybe she talks to sometimes when she's picking the kids up at the school or picking out kumquats at Safeway or whatever."

"An imaginary guy, then."

"Well, no. A real guy. Just not one particular guy, if you know what I mean."

"I think I know your wife well enough to know that she doesn't take relationships lightly. I expect you know that yourself. I'm pretty sure she wouldn't take up with another man unless it was permanently over between you."

"Maybe she thinks it is." Now he was hitting the palm of one hand with the fist of the other, like a boxer warming up for a fight.

"If it was your idea to leave, she might. Do *you* think it is? Do you want it to be?"

"No. Of course not. You think I'm an idiot? We're a family. I love those kids, and I thought we loved each other until she kicked me out." He exhaled loudly and pulled another cigarette out of his jacket pocket, then began searching his pockets for a lighter.

"Console," said Hunter.

Sorry lit his cigarette and took a deep drag, holding the smoke in his lungs until he'd rolled down the window halfway, then letting it out in a rush.

"I'd say Simone wanted you to decide just how important she and the kids are to you, and whether they're worth giving up some of your selfish indulgences for."

"What the fuck is that supposed to mean? Selfish indulgences." He almost spat out the last two words. "That's a load of crap."

"Think about it. Since I've known you, you've quit every job you've ever had because you got pissed off at your boss, or else you lost your temper and did something impulsive that got you fired. Like the time you were working as a bouncer at the King George and threw some poor customer through the stained glass window."

"He started it."

"You can't tell me you didn't know what you were about to do was wrong and would get you fired."

Sorry stared out the window and took another drag on his cigarette.

"That's an indulgence, chief. You indulge yourself in destructive behavior because you feel like it at the time, without regard for your family's well-being."

Sorry snorted in Hunter's direction, threw his cigarette butt out on the road, and rolled up the window. "Wake me when it's time for coffee," he said, then crossed his arms across his belly, snugged his chin into his chest and closed his eyes.

They did what most tourists in Dawson City do. They arrived just after four o'clock and after an early dinner (which Hunter somehow knew wasn't going to be their last meal of the day), they visited the cabins of Robert W. Service and Jack London on Eighth Street – although Sorry claimed never to have heard of either writer except for what Hunter had told him during the drive – and did quick tours of the Dawson City Museum and the S.S. Keno paddle wheeler down by the water.

In their quest for a hotel room, they walked the unpaved streets of town and ended up at the Sourdough Saloon. Even Sorry passed on the famous Sour Toe cocktail, opting instead for a draft beer while Hunter ordered his usual Labatt's Blue. And of course, they had something to eat. They managed to get tickets for the second show at Diamond Tooth Gertie's, and came out of the theatre twenty minutes before midnight and marveled that the sun had still not set.

"What now?" Sorry stretched, his biceps bulging then relaxing as he brought his hands over his head, then straightened his arms in front of him. A grey-haired woman walking past raised her eyebrows at the sight of the cobra tattoo on the big biker's forearm.

Hunter was wearing a blue cotton shirt with the sleeves rolled up. They had left their jackets in the borrowed Chevy but the temperature had fallen by a good fifteen degrees since then, so Hunter rolled down his sleeves and suggested they head back to the SUV.

"Where else we gonna go?" Sorry pulled his cigarette pack out from where he'd stashed it in the sleeve of his tee shirt. "We struck out on finding a hotel room. Unless you want to try sleeping on the beach or under a fuckin' tree."

The combination of daylight and Sorry's loud snoring made it impossible for Hunter to sleep in the close confines of the Blazer. The back seats folded down so the two of them lay side-by-side in the back of the vehicle, each wrapped in a twin-sized blanket, the only bedding they had, and using their duffle bags for pillows. Sorry couldn't stretch out his full six-foot-something length, so parts of him – one arm and two legs to be exact – were encroaching on Hunter's side of the make-do bed.

At about 1:30, Hunter crawled out of the back of the SUV, trying not to wake his friend. The big man snorted and stirred, but quickly resumed his loud snoring. Hunter had parked in a little alcove of trees across the road not far from the ferry dock, so he walked up and over the dike to the beach, then along the beach until he found a log that had been deposited by high water. He sat on the rocky shore with his back snugged against the log and wrapped his blanket around his shoulders. In spite of the hour, the river, ferry and opposite shore were easily visible in the northern twilight.

The ferry ran through the night, if you could call it that at this season of continuous daylight, taking cars and trucks across the Yukon River to West Dawson. There was a small intrepid community in West Dawson, he knew – although to his way of thinking, all the year-round residents this far north were intrepid –who lived off the grid in semi-isolation. Once the car ferry shut down for the winter, they had to risk taking a small boat across the half-frozen river or wait until the river ice was solid enough to support themselves or their vehicles before they could come into town for supplies. The ferry was part of the highway system that linked the northern terminus of the Klondike Highway to the Top of the World highway, which led to the Yukon-Alaska border crossing.

Hunter watched the ferry leave its gravel dock across the river, drift briefly downstream, then power up to fight against the current in order to reach the Dawson side. There were three cars and two motor homes on the ferry; two pickups with campers and several motorcycles waited on the near side to load. The motorcycles made him think of Dan Sorenson, sleeping like an innocent in the borrowed Blazer. He could tell that Sorry wasn't going to want to spend another day in Dawson. He was a restless soul who would no doubt find some trouble to get into, like a hyperactive child, if he was bored for very long.

Ken had been a lot like that. His enthusiasm for life had energized Hunter, who liked to be productive himself, but happily spent time alone in quiet contemplation, especially outdoors. Ken liked to be around people; more, he needed to be around people, needed their feedback and approval. Whenever Hunter heard the Barbra Streisand song about 'people who need people', he had always thought of Ken, and envied him his outgoing nature. Yet in the end, Ken was the unlucky one. He had suffered from that need, suffered unbearably.

Hunter sighed. Last time he'd been to Dawson City, it had been with Ken. When they had served here in the Yukon, they had hailed the North as an almost magical place. They were proud to be here, be part of this community of audacious souls who put up with the long dark winters, the blood-thirsty mosquitoes, the lack of civilized amenities in order to have the freedom of living in a vast, sparsely populated territory where individualism and eccentricity were celebrated instead of frowned upon or ridiculed.

They had talked about staying here for life, or at the very least, retiring to the north when they eventually left the RCMP. Then Hunter had met Christine and moved back to B.C. to keep her happy, and Ken had followed him to Kamloops and married Helen, and their priorities had shifted to making homes for their families and advancing their careers, which was what good providers were supposed to do. Somewhere along the way, they had gotten confused about their priorities, somehow lost sight of the meaning of life, if they'd ever known what it was. Too much work, too much pressure, not enough peace, not enough joy. Hunter took a deep breath and let it out again, slowly.

"We should've come back here, Ken. We should've chucked it all and come back here when things started to go sour, at least long enough to get our heads straight again."

Hunter watched the ferry leave again, watched the mighty Yukon River carry it downstream toward the landing on the opposite bank, then fixed his eyes on the surface of the river with its swells and whorls and riffles and furrows, signs of the enormous force of the current beneath its liquid skin. In spite of its terrible power, watching the river somehow gave him a sense of peace. He slouched lower so his head rested against the log, and eventually he dozed off.

"No body."

"Ken?" Weird. Ken was wearing red serge – the RCMP dress uniform – but instead of the regulation Stetson, he had a muskrat fur hat with ear flaps, the kind he and Hunter used to wear in the Yukon winters. "What are you doing here?"

Hunter looked around and didn't know where he was until he saw the dogs. He and Ken were back at Martin Blake's cabin, standing side by side in deep snow, up to their knees. Hunter tried to move his legs but couldn't. He might as well have been standing in cement.

Ken had a bottle of Everclear in one hand. He lifted it to his lips and took a long pull. Through the clear glass of the bottle, Hunter saw a severed toe, brown and wrinkled, tumbling through the overproof alcohol. Ken wiped his mouth with his red serge sleeve and grinned at Hunter.

"All that blood," Ken continued, "two people missing from that bloody cabin and no bodies. Why didn't we ever find either body, bro? We searched all around here that first week, then we searched again after the snow was gone in the spring. No body. No skull. No bones. No scraps of clothing. Nothing."

"The grizzly. That's why."

"We never found the grizzly either, bro." Ken turned and grinned at him again. Hunter felt immeasurably sad.

"Why have you come back? Have you got something to tell me?" Ken was dead, wasn't he? If a dead man could come back, why would he come back to discuss an old case? Weren't there more important things to talk about?

"We always get our man, remember? Don't let me down, bro. Don't let me down."

Hunter felt something cold and hard against the back of his skull, felt the cold, uneven ground beneath his butt and legs. He opened his eyes and saw the shifting surface of the river, saw the sun gilding the tops of the trees on the other side. Feeling disoriented, he sat up straighter with an effort, his muscles stiff, feeling clumsy from the cold. The back of his head felt bruised from his hard wooden pillow.

He hadn't dreamed about Ken for years. Even now, awake, he couldn't throw off an overwhelming sense of sadness. It took a conscious effort to hold back tears, a situation that almost shocked him. At the very least, it made him extremely uncomfortable.

"What the hell …?" He ran a hand over his face. His mouth felt stale. Had he been drinking? Just a couple of beers, he remembered. "What was that all about?" he said aloud, looking around him. He could see no one on the beach, except a raven pecking at something in the rocks near the water. The ferry was on the other side of the river. He guessed from the sunrise it wasn't much later than three o'clock.

He had to move. If sleeping here on the beach meant he risked another disturbing dream, he wasn't going to stay. He stood and adjusted the blanket around his shoulders, then made his way back to the SUV. Sorry had turned on his side and the loud snore had been reduced to a soft snuffle. Hunter crawled back in over the tailgate and made himself as comfortable as he could, flipping the blanket up over his head to block out the light, and with any luck, the noise.

Ten minutes later he was asleep.

"Where to now?"

They were sitting at a restaurant table littered with the empty cups and plates from breakfast, and as Hunter had predicted, his biker friend had seen enough of Dawson and was ready to move on.

"You want to go to Alaska?" Hunter answered Sorry with a question of his own.

"Hell, yeah. How far is it?"

Hunter smiled and took a deep breath. The state of Alaska was not much more than a hundred miles from Dawson City, but he was curious what his friend expected to see when they crossed the border. "What in Alaska do you particularly want to see?"

Sorry shrugged. "I've heard it's beautiful in Alaska. Nature, I mean. Maybe we can see a grizzly or something."

"Nature doesn't really recognize political boundaries. I'm not sure how far you want to go into Alaska, but we don't have more than a day or two before my truck is ready, remember?"

The waitress – a young woman with the dark hair, brown skin and round face typical of Northern natives – came by and offered coffee refills. She wore jeans and a lime green tee shirt, and had a short black apron with pockets tied around her waist. Sorry shook his head. Hunter asked for half a cup, but she filled it up instead. He nodded his thanks.

"How long will it take us to find a lunch stop if we're heading west from here?" he asked.

The young woman laughed, showing even white teeth in an engaging smile. "That would be Chicken. There's one bar and one café. Take you anywhere from three to six hours, depending on road conditions. "

Sorry's eyebrows went up, and he looked distressed.

"Want to order lunch to go?" The waitress used her free hand to pull the order pad out of an apron pocket, held it above the table. "If you're looking for something else, that'd be Fairbanks, in which case you'd better order dinner, too." Again the smile.

They ordered sandwiches to go, and she was back ten minutes later with a brown bag and the check.

"Sounds like there's not much in Chicken. Can we get to Fairbanks and back in the time we've got before your truck is ready?" Sorry ignored the check.

Hunter made a wry face. "Fairbanks is another three hundred miles, give or take."

"What's in Fairbanks?"

"It's been years since I've been there." Hunter flipped the check over and looked at the total.

"I've *never* been there, dude."

Hunter shrugged. "Pretty much the same kind of things that are in Whitehorse and Dawson, just it's in Alaska instead of the Yukon."

"Like?"

"Museums. Historical things, mainly to do with native culture or the gold rush. Exhibits or whatever of wild animals that live in the north: bears, caribou…" He had pulled his wallet out and looked at what was left of his cash. If they were going to stop in any small towns, he might need it, so he pulled out his Visa card instead.

"Okay, okay. I get it." Sorry glanced at the Visa card and made no move for his own wallet.

"So you want to go to Fairbanks?"

Sorry stroked his mustache. "I want to go to Alaska. Let's start with that and see where we get."

"Sounds good to me," said Hunter. He motioned at the check with his chin. "You going to pick up your share?"

Sorry reached over and took a leftover orange slice from Hunter's plate. He bit the pulp off the rind with his front teeth. "I'm a little short of cash," he said. "Just put it on my tab."

Hunter was behind the wheel as they left Dawson on the ferry across the Yukon River, but he was already feeling the effects of his lack of sleep and the heavy breakfast, so he pulled over on the incline just the other side of the river and let the biker take over.

"The tires on this jalopy are pretty worn," he cautioned. "Take it easy on this gravel."

They hadn't gone more than a mile when Sorry said, "This is a highway?"

"The Top of the World highway."

"Where are we going again?"

"Alaska."

"Right." Sorry snorted and kept driving. A few miles further along, he jolted Hunter awake with a long whistle. "I see why."

"Huh? What?"

"I see why they call it the Top of the World. Will you look at that. You can see for-fucking-ever in all directions."

The highway ran on top of a ridge that afforded a three hundred and sixty degree view that stretched to a distant horizon on both sides, as well as ahead of them. Fresh spring growth of a hundred shades of green, mostly ground cover and low bushes, was strewn with stunted evergreens in places, almost devoid of them in others. Line upon line of gentle hills receded ever further toward the horizon like dunes in a green Sahara.

Hunter enjoyed the views whenever he could keep his eyes open. Mostly he dozed. The road had been chip sealed, but with frost heaves, pot holes and getting stuck behind dusty motorhomes, even Sorry didn't dare go faster than thirty miles an hour, slower at sharp turns with no guard rail, steep drops and sometimes oncoming traffic. It took them almost three hours to reach the border, which from far away was visible as a few tiny manmade structures huddled together in a vast expanse of northern wilderness. The border was marked only by a sawhorse sign and an Atco trailer on the Yukon side, and an American flag beside a log cabin on the Alaska side. There was a lineup of two motorhomes with Illinois plates ahead of them at the U.S. border. The passengers were standing in the middle of the road, chatting amiably with the customs officer.

"I'm getting hungry," said Sorry.

"Where's your sandwich?"

"Ate it while you were sleeping. You hungry?"

"Don't touch my lunch." Hunter hoped it wasn't already gone.

"That sandwich was pretty small."

"It'll have to hold you until Chicken."

The group of tourists ahead climbed back into their respective motorhomes and Sorry drove forward until the customs officer was beside his window.

"You both Canadians?"

The lonesome customs officer looked out of place here. Hunter was used to seeing the American customs officers surrounded by concrete and glass, backed up by large buildings and dozens of fellow staff members. The man looked fit and tanned, and Hunter reflected that any man willing to be posted up here had to love life in the outdoors. Hunter passed his driver's license to Sorry, who passed both of their driver's licenses to the officer.

"You both Canadian citizens?" he asked.

"I live in Canada but I'm an American," said Sorry, then jerked a thumb in Hunter's direction. "He's a Canuck."

"Where in the States are you from?" The officer barely glanced at Hunter, and turned his attention back to Sorry.

"Yreka, if you know where that is. California. Where you from?"

"Wisconsin. Green Bay." The man smiled for the first time since he'd approached the car.

"A cheesehead, huh?"

The officer looked sideways at Sorry, his brief smile had evaporated. “How long you been in Canada?”

Sorry made a show of counting on the fingers of one hand, then said, “About a quarter century.”

The officer ran his tongue around inside his cheek before saying, “Ever been in the military?”

Hunter realized the officer may have mistakenly pegged Sorry as a draft dodger or deserter, and that the man was probably a Vietnam veteran himself.

“Do I look like a military man?” said Sorry before Hunter could interrupt.

“I think the officer is trying to find out if you came to Canada to avoid military service,” Hunter said to Sorry. “You were too young to hit the draft, Dan. Tell him when you moved to Canada.”

The officer glared at Hunter, as if to shut him up.

Sorry rolled his eyes. “Look, I was never drafted, if that’s what you’re getting at. I left the States in ‘73, and I’ve been back and forth dozens of times since then.”

The officer’s jaw was still set, and Hunter figured it was time to change the subject.

“Say, chief.” Hunter leaned forward to interrupt. He could do his friend Bart a favor and head off any potential conflict between Sorry and the officer at the same time. He asked the officer if he’d seen an older, bearded man in a beat-up pickup cross the border in the last few days. “He’s got an English accent,” he added.

The officer paused, appraising Hunter with narrowed eyes. “Where exactly are you boys headed and how long do you plan to be in Alaska?”

Sorry looked at Hunter, who said,”We haven’t decided whether to go to Chicken or Eagle, or maybe both. We’ll probably stay the night at one of them, then turn around and head back to Whitehorse. My truck’s in the shop there, waiting for parts.”

“We had a couple of days to kill, wanted to do some sightseeing,” Sorry added, nodding.

“Who’s this man you’re looking for?” The officer leaned a forearm on the Blazer’s window frame and squinted over at Hunter when he said it.

Sorry kept his head out of the way and stared straight ahead, letting Hunter decide what to say. Hunter wasn't surprised. The biker had had more than his share of trouble from men with badges for saying the wrong thing. Hunter himself had been one of those men the first time they'd met. He noticed the officer's eyes drift to the cobra tattoo that snaked around Sorry's wrist.

"A friend in Whitehorse asked us to keep an eye out for him." Hunter shrugged, smiling vaguely. He wasn't looking for the old man in any kind of official capacity, and knew that if he mentioned a murder he'd be opening a can of worms that could see them refused entry to Alaska. "Maybe he was afraid that old truck would break down on this lonesome highway."

The customs officer looked thoughtful for several seconds, then handed their driver's licenses back. He slapped the window frame with one hand as he said, "Enjoy your stay in Alaska," and stepped back from the vehicle. Hunter looked in the Blazer's side mirror as they drove away, and he noticed the officer looking at their rear license plate and writing something down in a small notebook.

"So where *are* we going," asked Sorry when they were out of earshot, "Chicken or Eagle?" When Hunter didn't answer immediately, he added,"Don't forget, we need to eat soon, okay?"

The highway wound up and down along a ridge toward a distant horizon, nothing but scrub covered hills in variegated waves in every direction. Hunter stuck his head out of the window to look behind them and saw essentially the same landscape, with the insignificant and isolated customs posts getting smaller by the second.

"Chicken is closer," said Hunter, unwrapping his sandwich. "By about forty miles, if I remember right."

"Chicken it is."

CHAPTER EIGHT

"Have you ever wondered what your life would be like if you had done one thing – just one important thing – differently?"

Orville and Betty were having a tea break. Betty had been back at work in her garden and Orville had been busy with the firewood again, using the chainsaw to buck some of the windfall logs Betty and Goldie had dragged back to the cabin with the snow machine during the winter. He had then split and stacked them in orderly piles in the woodshed. The smell of freshly turned earth mingled with the smell of his sweat. Betty raised her mug of tea – a more familiar, safer scent – and inhaled deeply.

"Like what?" she asked.

"Just imagine," said Orville, squinting into the sun, "that you and I had met and got to know each other when I first came to the north in 1958. I was a young Englishman, jilted at the altar by my first love and disillusioned with the workaday world. I wanted to strike it rich by finding gold in the colonies to make my sweetheart regret she'd thrown me over for a rich man's son." He turned his gaze on Betty with an impish smile. "What about you, Betty? Where were you then? Could we have met?"

"We didn't meet. We are who we are. Things are how they are." She didn't look at him as she spoke.

"Come on, Betty. It can't hurt to play a little with your imagination. Your imagination can create a little joy in your heart, even if it's for just a little while." He tapped her gently on the knee. "Where were you in 1958? Could we have crossed paths then?"

Betty closed her eyes and tried to remember. An involuntary shiver went up her spine. 1958 was one of the worst years of her life. It had been 1945 when she'd been abandoned, pregnant, on the river and had ended up living with that family in Dawson. After her baby was stillborn, she'd met a prospector friend of the family's named Monroe James. She had it in her mind that if she could get to her mother's people in Old Crow, she would feel like she was with family, like she belonged. Monroe had promised to take her there, to Old Crow, but on the way, he took her to his remote cabin on the Fortymile River northwest of Dawson – just until breakup, he'd said – and there she stayed.

Monroe was a quiet American from Georgia, and reasonably kind. Life at his cabin was full of hard work, but not unpleasant. With Monroe, she felt secure and comfortable, but it never occurred to her to love him. Her period stopped twice in the seven years they were together, and each time she brewed herself a strong yarrow tea – something she'd seen her mother do –to end the pregnancy. In early April of 1954, he left to check his trap line and hunt for badly needed fresh meat, but he never came back. After three weeks had gone by, Betty had a vision of him going through the river ice with his dogsled. By snaring rabbits and boiling up the rest of the lost dogs' frozen whitefish for herself, she managed to survive until breakup. He never returned.

After breakup, she took the gold poke Monroe had hidden beneath the cabin floor and launched his canoe in the Fortymile River. That was the first time she'd seen Eagle, because that's where the river had taken her. She stayed with a native family in Eagle Village, helping with chores, until the river froze over again and she caught a dogsled ride back upriver to Dawson. She'd decided to give up on getting to Old Crow, but she didn't want to depend on another man, so she started asking around for a cabin and trap line she could take over herself. A Dutchman named Wim Reinder said he knew just the place for her.

Reinder took her to his cabin on the Stewart River, but once they were there, he stole her gold poke and essentially made her his slave; unlike Monroe James, he was not a kind man. Once she tried to sneak away while he was out on the trap line, but he followed her tracks in the snow and caught up with her early the next morning. He dragged her back to the cabin and beat her until she was sure she would die. She even *hoped* she would die. But she survived, and in fear of his anger, committed herself to serving his wants, while praying that he would meet the same fate as Monroe. Then early in 1959, Reinder got sick. At first he complained of a persistent belly ache; a few days later he was doubled over in pain, clutching at his abdomen. "Help me, woman," he roared. "Surely you goddamn Indians got some medicine for a gut ache."

Betty nodded submissively. "I will help relieve your pain," she told him.

She walked downriver about a quarter mile from the cabin and searched in the woods under the snow for the frozen remains of the monkshood she knew to be growing there. Although her mother had told her about its powers, she'd never seen it used and wasn't sure how much would have the effect she was looking for. To be on the safe side, she chipped away at the frozen soil beneath it until she was able to free the roots. Back at the cabin, she chopped them fine and stirred them into a small pot of wild blueberry preserves, which she fed to Reinder with a spoon. After a few spoonfuls, he roughly brushed her hand away, and the spoon fell to the floor. One of the dogs rushed to lick it up but Betty kicked the dog's head away. She had never kicked a dog before. Reinder knew it.

"What did you feed me, woman?" he said, suspicion in his eyes.

"The pain will be gone soon," she told him, kneeling to clean up the spilled jam, then quickly walking to the door and taking her parka down off its hook.

"My tongue is tingling," he said. "What have you done to me, woman?"

"I've given you medicine for your pain. I'll go get some fresh water and make some tea for you," she said, as she stepped outside.

She grabbed the axe and bucket and headed down toward the river. She had only gone half way, when she heard him bellow out the door. "You goddamn devil squaw." He was shrugging into his parka. "I'll kill you. If it's the last thing I do, I'll kill you, you goddamn witch."

She hurried toward the river, glancing back to see him stumbling along in her footsteps, one hand still clutching at his belly. The two dogs from the house were running beside him, leaping at his flailing arm. The outside dogs began to bark furiously and pull against their chains. She didn't see a rifle in his hand, but as she ran she could feel his hatred aiming at her back. Could she outrun him? No. He was gaining on her.

She ran out on to the river ice and turned to face him. As he drew closer, his face contorted with pain and rage, she dropped the axe and with all her strength, threw the bucket at his head. As he dodged it, he lost his balance and fell sideways on the snow-covered ice. "You witch," he roared again. He rolled onto his hands and knees, struggling to get to his feet, the pain or the poison sapping his strength. Betty grabbed the axe and raised it over her head, then brought it down as hard as she could on the back of his neck. It stuck there, blood leaking around the blade as Reinder collapsed to the ice and his body began to convulse. The house dogs crouched on their bellies a few feet away.

Breathing heavily, Betty watched the body twitch, then turned away and vomited into the snow. When it was clear he was no longer going to move, she sank to her knees and sobbed. She was still racked with dry, spasmodic sobs as she yanked the axe from his neck and began to chop away at the ice. When the hole was wide enough, she dragged the heavy body by its feet until the head and shoulders were level with the hole, then struggled to maneuver it headfirst into the hole. She pushed on the legs until what was left of Wim Reinder disappeared under the ice, into the swift current of the Stewart River.

"Well, Betty," said Orville, bringing her back to the present. "Can you imagine how different our lives could have been?"

Betty swallowed hard and nodded. She couldn't imagine having any opportunity to meet the Englishman in 1958 when Reinder was alive. He had not been very hospitable to the few trappers who had happened across the remote cabin. "Very different, Orville," she said, but she would never tell him how.

"You going to finish those fries?"

Hunter pushed his plate across the table to his friend, leaned back in the chair and gazed out the window at the main street of Chicken, Alaska. They were in a café, which was next door to Chicken's saloon, which was next door to a small store. That was pretty much the extent of downtown Chicken. The woman who served their chicken pies had told them the winter population was usually less than ten, given there was no road access at that time of year.

Sorry dunked one of Hunter's cast-off potato wedges in ketchup and popped it in his mouth. "Where to next?" he asked, picking up a second fried potato. He waved it toward the street. "Seems we can see most of Chicken right from here."

"I think we should head on up to Eagle, unless we want to stay the night here. That couple," he motioned toward the next table, which was now empty, "said they'd stayed in a lodge up there." He finished off his coffee. "I really don't want to spend another night in the back of the Blazer."

After gassing up and buying a couple of souvenirs at the Mercantile, they were back in the Blazer, heading back toward Canada. Feeling somewhat rested, Hunter was in the driver's seat. They were told it would take them about three hours to get to Eagle. Hunter hoped there would be room at the lodge, since their only other option, except for sleeping in the Blazer, would be the long drive back to Dawson City.

"Did you see that chick in the Mercantile?" Sorry had a cigarette going again. Hunter coughed pointedly and the biker rolled his window right down. "I think she was ripe for the pickin', if you know what I mean."

Hunter looked sideways at his friend. "You're an ass."

"Wha-a-a-t?" Sorry snorted and took a deep drag of his cigarette, then blew the smoke at Hunter. "We made eye contact, dude. I didn't do nothin' to encourage her. She walked right past me and brushed her tit against my arm."

Hunter sighed but said nothing.

"Look. Mo booted my ass out of the house. Who knows if she'll even let me come back. You're so fuckin' prissy." He looked out the window for thirty seconds, then said, "Don't tell me you didn't mess around some after Chris kicked you out."

It wasn't a subject Hunter wanted to discuss. "Chris filed for divorce, Dan. I never even dated another woman for two years, until after the divorce was final."

"Well, that's you. It's not me."

"Do you want Simone to take you back?"

"Of course I do." Sorry sounded indignant, then said, "Or maybe I don't. Maybe I'll just show her I don't give a flying fuck whether I see her again or not."

"And Sasha? And Bruno?"

"There you go again. You're such an old woman sometimes." He spit on the ash end of his cigarette and threw it out the window. "You had kids, too. Did you want Chris to take *you* back?"

Hunter took a deep breath and shrugged. He knew it would never happen, so he hadn't even considered the question, not for years. "Very different situation. My girls were already in their teens when we split up, and now they're both in college." Jan was twenty-one and studying marketing, Lesley was nineteen and taking criminology courses. She wanted to become a Mountie, like Hunter had been.

Sorry yawned and sniffed. "Whatever," he said. "Wake me when we get there." He slouched down lower in his seat and Hunter could soon hear the steady snuffling noises that indicated he was asleep.

Hunter's mind wandered back to the first year of his marriage, when his first daughter was born. He and Christine still lived in Whitehorse at the time. They'd met when Chris was in Whitehorse one summer, kept in touch during the winter, and resumed their relationship the following spring. The next year they were married. Even before Janice was born, Chris made it clear she hated the Yukon winter. It wasn't the cold so much as it was the dark, she said.

Hunter remembered coming home from a long day at work, stamping the snow off his boots on the wood planks of the back porch of their rented house, and entering to find all the lights in the house burning, his pregnant young wife curled up in bed, crumpled tissues on the nightstand, her eyes red and swollen from crying.

"I can't live here, honey," she whispered as he bent to kiss her. "I miss my family, I miss the ocean, I miss the daylight, I even miss the damn rain."

"You'll get used to it," he'd told her, but she hadn't. He'd had to put in for a transfer back to B.C., ended up accepting a posting to Kamloops and even that wasn't good enough for Chris. Eventually he got a transfer to the coast, and it wasn't until years later that he finally realized it wasn't where they lived that had distressed her, it was how. No matter where they lived, she felt alone and neglected because of the hours he spent on the job. Irregular hours, unpredictable hours, late hours, long hours. Things he wouldn't, and couldn't, talk to her about. That was the life of a homicide investigator with the RCMP.

By the time he fully recognized the real issues, the divorce was final and it was too late. He probably wouldn't have quit the force anyway, if she'd given him an ultimatum. His work had been his passion. Then after the divorce and Ken's suicide, that passion evaporated and he was left feeling drained, sucked dry. Like a truck with an empty fuel tank, he had stalled and drifted to a stop on the side of the road.

He was too preoccupied to notice a pothole and the Blazer jolted into it on the passenger side. Sorry stirred, muttered a drowsy "fu-uck" and nodded off again. Hunter scratched the stubble on his cheek and again hoped that they would find decent accommodation for the night. He slowed when they reached Jack Wade, not much more than the intersection of two gravel roads, then turned north toward Eagle.

Goldie didn't usually bother taking a break at work, but as she walked between the lodge and one of the cabins, she saw Mark sitting beside the woodpile with a can of Coke in his hand and wandered over to join him.

"How's it going?" he asked. "Your grandmother kicked the old guy out yet?" He was sitting on a big upended log, but got up and stood another big log upright beside him. He brushed the dust and woodchips off it and invited her to sit. She did, and her knee was just inches away from his.

She laughed. "Shocking, but no. When I left today she was still being uncharacteristically friendly."

"Sip?" He offered her his Coke, but she shook her head. "I still can't believe you grew up out in the woods with crusty old Betty, and look at you now." He gestured toward her. "How did you turn out so – so – I don't know, smart looking and articulate? I would've expected a bush baby to speak in monosyllables and wear gunnysacks."

Goldie could feel her cheeks begin to burn. She vacillated between being flattered and offended, so stalled for time by asking, "What on earth is a gunnysack?"

He shrugged. "I don't know, but it sounded like something a bush baby would wear." He slapped at a mosquito on his neck. "Thank god there's a breeze this afternoon. I thought they would eat me alive this morning."

"Bush baby?" She decided it was more humorous than offensive. "It's not like we were living in the Amazon jungle. We moved to Eagle so I could go to school, and we've had public satellite TV here in Alaska since forever, although Gran didn't get a TV until we moved here. The cabin came with a generator. Bush baby." She said it with a smile and gave his shoulder a little push. "Give me a break. You Outsiders can be so ignorant."

He pushed her back, gently, and she could smell the Deep Woods Off on his arm.

"Were your mom and dad both from up here?"

Her smile faded. "I guess so. I was too young to remember them, and Gran's a little secretive."

"Yeah? About what?"

Goldie shrugged. "Her past. My past. The past in general."

"What happened to your parents?" he asked, frowning as if what she had told him was worrisome.

She shrugged again. "I don't really know," she said. She didn't tell him that the same question had been burning inside her ever since she started school and realized most other kids had a mother and father, not just a grandmother.

"Okay, tell me something you do know. Like, where did you live before you moved to Eagle?"

Goldie took a deep breath and blew it out between her lips. "Until I was about six, we lived in a cabin near a river. We call it the moose cabin, because there was a big moose rack over the front door. I once heard Gran refer to it as the Stewart cabin, so I assume it was the Stewart River." She half smiled, remembering. "She said something like, 'I wish I hadn't left that big kettle behind at Stewart.' I asked her to tell me about the cabin at Stewart and she pretended she hadn't said any such thing.

"Before that," she said, "we lived in the snowshoe cabin. It had a pair of big, broken down snowshoes hanging on the wall. I was only two or three, so I don't actually remember it, only what Gran has told me." She picked up a piece of bark and began breaking it into little pieces and throwing them into a clump of weeds. "Gran's old dog team came from Hootalinqua – that's why she called her dog Hootie – so I always figured she lived there when she got the team. It makes me wonder if that's where the first cabin was."

Mark crumpled the Coke can in one hand, grunting like a caveman, then tossed it up over his shoulder. "You're weird, kid."

"Why?"

"You're the only person I've ever met who doesn't know where she lived or what happened to her parents. At least adopted kids have their adopted parents. Orphans usually know that their parents are dead. You're an enigma to yourself, Goldie, not just to me. By the way," he raised his eyebrows as he peered into her face, "what's your real name? You can't tell me your name is just Goldie."

She compressed her lips together, sighed and answered him in a quiet voice. "Don't laugh, okay?"

"Uh-oh. You don't know your real name either?"

She frowned and made a 'tsk' sound with her tongue.

"Okay. I'm sorry. What?"

"Golden Dawn Salmon."

He smiled but he didn't laugh. "Golden Dawn sounds like a hippie name."

"I suppose."

"It's pretty though." His voice was gentle and his eyes searching. "It suits you."

She looked down, away from him, and brushed some sawdust off the calf of her jeans. The way he'd looked at her gave her a fluttery feeling under her breastbone.

"Your grandma's name is Betty Salmon, right?"

She nodded.

"So she must be your dad's mother, right?"

She smiled weakly. She wished she could say it was true. The truth was, she didn't even know that.

When she didn't answer, he shook his head. "Okay. Here's something I know you can answer. Have you ever had a boyfriend?" He was looking sideways at her, a crooked little smile on his face.

It was her turn to shake her head. "I *could* answer that, but I won't. I better get back to work," she said. She wanted to get away before he noticed her cheeks get red. "See you later."

Goldie was just coming down the stairs of the front porch when a beat-up old SUV with Yukon plates pulled up in front of the big log lodge at Yukon Sally's. Two men got out. One was a big man with longish blond hair and a mustache; he made her think of Hulk Hogan. The other was more compact, probably a little older, and looked tidy, although he wore jeans and obviously hadn't shaved for a couple of days. He gave the impression of being very self-contained, almost wary, much like the State Troopers she'd occasionally seen in town.

The big blond guy wasted no time in spotting her. "Hey, sweetheart," he called out, his voice louder than it needed to be. "Do you work here? Where's the office? Can we get a room for the night? I hope they got a restaurant here," he said over his shoulder to the other man, who seemed mildly irritated.

"We just ate a few hours ago."

"Yeah, but road trips always make me hungry. Don't ask me why." He took a deep drag on a freshly lit cigarette. "What do you say, sweetheart? You think we can get a room here for the night?" The smoke trailed out of his mouth as he spoke.

Goldie had cleaned and changed the bedding in a couple of rooms that afternoon, so she said, "Right now we do have a couple of empty rooms, but they might be booked. I don't do the reservations, so I don't know."

"You do work here, though?" asked the older man. He had a pleasant voice, unexpectedly deep. He'd been staring at her since she first began to speak. His eyes were so intense, it was a little uncomfortable. She nodded, her smile uncertain.

As if he could read her thoughts, he said, "Sorry to stare, but I thought at first you were someone I knew." He looked a little sheepish as he added, "Except the last time I saw her was more than twenty years ago. She'd be old enough to be your mother, if she were still alive."

Goldie's heart began to thump so hard, she thought she would pass out. She found the man a little intimidating, but she had to know more. "A woman who looked like me? Here in Alaska?"

His eyes never left her face as he said, "In Whitehorse, actually, but she told me she was on her way to Alaska." Again, as if he'd read her mind, he added, "Her name was April."

Goldie backed up a few steps and sank to a sitting position on the bottom stair.

"Are you alright?" the man asked. He sat down beside her, leaning forward with his elbows on his knees.

She nodded, unable to speak right away. Her thoughts were racing. Who was this man? Had this man known her mother? Could he tell her something about her mother? Why did he say 'if she were still alive'? Was she dead? Did he know when and how she died? Was it possible that he also knew her father? Could he even *be* her father? A dizzying parade of possibilities ran through her mind.

"I never knew my mother," she finally managed to say, then swallowed hard. "But I think her name was April." She tried to remember what the picture had looked like, the one with a note on the back. It had been a small square photograph with a white border, the image washed out and a bit blurry, of a black bear crossing a road, a cub right behind her. On the back was a note, written with a ballpoint pen:

Betty - See you next spring!
Thanks for everything! April

It had fallen out of a book that she found under her grandmother's bed when helping Gran with spring cleaning. When she went to look for it again, the book was gone. Seeking for any connection to the mother she couldn't remember, Goldie had always imagined that the book – a paperback book of poetry with a painting of a bearded man on the front – and the note had come from her mother. Was April her mother? Had she never returned in the spring? She asked Gran who April was, and Gran got so angry with her for snooping that she'd never dared to mention it again.

The big man with the blond mustache clomped up the stairs, saying, "Hey, Hunter, I'll go see if they've got a room" as he passed by.

"I'm sorry if I've upset you," the man called Hunter said quietly. "The April I knew had no children, at least not when I knew her. It could be just a coincidence that you look like her."

Goldie took a deep breath. "Yes, of course. It's just that it took me by surprise."

He asked her what her name was, and she told him. "Do you have a family, Goldie?" he asked then.

"I have my grandmother. She's been both mother and father to me, I guess. Her name is Betty Salmon. Do you know her?" She looked at him hopefully. If he knew her grandmother, then the April he knew must have been her mother.

He shook his head, sadly it seemed. "You grew up here in Eagle?"

"We lived a couple of other places first, but Gran moved us here when I was old enough to go to school. She never had much education herself – she can just barely read and write – but she thought it was important for me to finish school." Goldie had picked up a stick and now she started tracing circles in the dry earth at the bottom of the stairs. "She's lived in the bush all her life."

"So your grandmother is on your father's side?"

Goldie thought it was spooky how she'd been asked that question twice on the same day. The first time, she'd just ignored it. She thought now it didn't make sense that she would refuse to answer Mark, but discuss it with this stranger. She gave a weak laugh. "Really, truly," she began. "This is going to sound pretty strange, but I honestly don't know for sure how I'm related to my grandmother. She's the only family I've ever known, and I use her last name. She has never once mentioned my father." She pressed her lips together and stole a glance at the man, then turned her attention back to the circles in the dirt. "I always assumed my mother was her daughter, but now that I'm older, I'm not sure, because for some reason she won't tell me anything about her."

He was quiet for a long time. She didn't look directly at him but she could still feel his eyes on her face. "I wish I knew more about her," she said, hoping with all her heart that this man would be the answer to that wish.

The man took a deep breath and got to his feet. "I'd like to meet your grandmother. Will you take me to her?"

Hunter couldn't stop thinking about the girl. She looked so much like the April he'd known, and she had been told her mother's name was April. Was it possible that April had survived whatever bloody thing had taken place at the trapper's cabin near the Teslin River almost twenty-five years ago? *I should have asked the girl how old she was*, he thought. He wondered why the girl didn't know the name of her mother. Had her grandmother hidden her birth certificate, or did she even have one? He wondered if perhaps it wasn't unusual for a child born in bush Alaska – in a remote cabin with no access to a hospital or even to a doctor or midwife – to have an undocumented birth.

And Betty Salmon, the woman who was – or perhaps wasn't – the girl's grandmother. Where was she from? Had she known that same free-spirited young woman Hunter had known briefly during his first summer in Whitehorse?

He was on his back, hands behind his head, eyes fixed on the ceiling, lying on one of two twin beds in a small but comfortable log cabin at Yukon Sally's Lodge. In spite of the window curtains designed to keep out the midnight sun, it was almost bright enough to read a book. Sorry was snoring softly in the other bed. Hunter envied him the ability to put the cares of the day out of his mind and sleep soundly whenever he was tired.

The girl, Goldie, had seemed uncomfortable when he'd asked to meet her grandmother. After a few false starts, obviously unsure of how to answer, she had told him that her grandmother was a bit of a recluse and it wouldn't be wise to spring a surprise visit on her. "I'll talk to her tonight," she'd said, then quickly ended the conversation by excusing herself and walking away.

Hunter had watched her fire up an old blue Mercury pickup and rattle off down the rutted driveway. He briefly considered tailing her so he could catch the grandmother unprepared, but knew it would be impossible. How could anyone not be aware of being followed when there were no other cars on the only road through town? Besides, he wasn't about to use police interrogation techniques just to satisfy his curiosity.

He and Sorry had been lucky enough to get a cabin for the night, and a hearty moose stew for dinner as well. The meal was followed by a blueberry cobbler, made with local berries that had been picked and frozen the summer before. At the same table in the lodge dining area, which was just off the kitchen, were two women from Florida who had driven the Top of the World Highway that day on their motorcycles, a fact that made Sorry cranky at first.

"What the fuck was I thinking?" he said. "I let this bozo talk me into leaving my bike in Whitehorse and driving here in that stinkin' Blazer. He said it would make a good place to sleep, and turns out he fuckin' don't want to sleep in it anyway. I should've rode my bike."

Hunter ignored him and asked one of the women what made them want to ride to Alaska.

"It was on our bucket list," said one, and the other one nodded.

Hunter watched as they grinned at each other and slapped hands in a high five. One had short dark hair flecked with grey, the other was blond with her hair pulled back into a lopsided braid. Neither wore makeup. He guessed that the two women were a couple and wondered if that was partly why Sorenson had suddenly become so grumpy. He was surprised after they'd finished dinner to see his friend accompany the women to their cabin while Hunter was on the porch talking to Yukon Sally about the town of Eagle.

"I followed the love of my life up here almost twenty years ago and it wasn't long before he stopped being the love of my life and left town. Me, I fell in love with the lifestyle here in Eagle and decided to make it my home." Yukon Sally was surprisingly tiny – probably just over a hundred pounds – and dressed like the outdoorswoman she was, in jeans, hiking boots and a man's plaid shirt over an Eagle City souvenir tee shirt.

"Pretty impressive building for a town like this." Hunter nodded toward the lodge behind them. He'd been surprised when they drove up to the lodge. It hadn't been here when he'd visited Eagle in the seventies, and he couldn't imagine there was enough tourist traffic to justify the building costs.

Yukon Sally shrugged. "Our place isn't as big or as fancy as the ones closer to Fairbanks. Just four guest rooms in the lodge and the three cabins. We can put up a couple of wall tents if we need to accommodate a big group."

"You get enough business to pay the bills?" he asked.

"You mean, is it just an expensive hobby?"

"I'm sorry. I guess that's none of my business. It's a nice place, but I've never thought of Eagle as a tourism hotspot."

She didn't seem to mind. "My dad would turn over in his grave if he knew what I'd spent my inheritance on." Her eyes narrowed to slits as she laughed; her laugh was loud for such a small person. "He was horrified when I told him I was going to live here. He spent his whole life in Texas and thought it was the only place in the world worth living in."

"Get many visitors in the winter?"

"We're full to overflowing at Yukon Quest time, but otherwise it's pretty quiet. You can't get here by road in the winter, you know, and not many tourists travel by dog sled. Just the Questers." She laughed again and Hunter couldn't help laughing with her. "Me and my husband live like most everyone else up here in the winter. We close off the rooms in the lodge we don't use and fire up the big wood stove, hunker down on the coldest days, run the dogs out on the river and check our traps when the weather's good. Most winters we'll fly out for a vacation somewhere warm and sunny when the SAD kicks in."

"Husband? I thought the love of your life ran off."

"I found a new one. Or he found me." Another laugh.

Hunter felt a trace of envy. He couldn't help wondering if the same thing would ever happen to him. An image of Helen Marsh the last time he'd seen her flashed and quickly disappeared from his mind's eye. He'd had a nice note from her in March, but no phone calls or any indication that he would see her again soon. He hadn't tried to call her either. He didn't know if he was ready to be anything but alone, but how would he know when he was?

"You've been here before?" Sally's question brought him back to the here and now.

"In the early seventies," he told her. "I visited here with a friend."

"Before my time." She sniffed a few times and looked in the direction Sorry and the two women had disappeared. "Wood smoke. They must've got the campfire going. I guess I'd better go spend some time in the kitchen."

"Mind if I tag along?" he said. "I wanted to ask you a few questions about the town."

There wasn't much she could tell him about Betty Salmon. She said that Goldie always seemed well cared for when she was younger, and now she seemed to be a happy, well-adjusted young woman. "I hope she gets a chance to go Outside," she said with a frown. "It's all very well for those of us who have made our own choice to live here in Eagle, but I don't feel it's fair that a young person like her never has a chance to experience life outside of a bush town."

Betty, she told him, seemed to be very distrustful of everyone in Eagle. "I suspect she'd be most at home living all alone out in the bush somewhere and only coming into town for supplies. She's not real friendly. I think she only moved to Eagle because of Goldie."

Hunter asked her if she knew anything about Betty's background. She shook her head, a look that bordered on astonishment on her face. "Nobody does," she said. "Nobody." She said it had been a source of gossip and conjecture soon after Betty's arrival, once the locals realized Betty had no intention of making friends in town. Was she crazy? Was she running from the police? Was she in hiding from an abusive partner? Had she kidnapped the kid?

"But you know, half the people who come to Alaska are running from something in their past, so pretty soon most of the people around here stopped speculating and kind of accepted her just the way she is. She does awesome leather and beadwork. I saw her in town once wearing a beaded caribou skin jacket I'd kill for. I asked her if she'd sell it and she turned me down flat, but I've bought a few things from her over the years. Some I've kept, others I've resold to tourists here at the lodge." She added thoughtfully, "Betty may be a prickly old recluse, but Goldie is a sweetheart. She's very protective of her grandmother's privacy."

After talking to Sally, he'd wandered over to the campfire. Sorry and the two women from Florida were sitting on logs, passing around a joint. They each had a sweating can of beer nestled in the grass at their feet.

"Want a toke?" asked the blond woman, inhaling as she spoke.

"He doesn't smoke," said Sorry.

"I'll take a beer, though."

He sat with them for the better part of an hour, finally got tired of the biker stories and the feeling of being an outsider, so he excused himself to go for a walk. Yukon Sally's was situated on the north side of town, in a wooded area more than half a mile from the river. He wandered down a trail and found himself in a clearing with some old buildings. He recognized it as Fort Egbert, a historic site from gold rush days that he'd visited with Ken on his first trip to Eagle. He recalled that Fort Egbert was where Norwegian explorer Roald Amundsen had first telegraphed news of his successful crossing from the Atlantic to the Pacific along the north coast of America in 1905. Hunter remembered reading that Amundsen's journey had taken three years, and reflected on how much the world had changed in the last hundred years. The Concorde could fly around the entire world in less than thirty-six hours.

From the fort he made his way down to the bank of the Yukon River. He sat on a grassy spot on the bank and watched the river below, wondering how long it would take to float downriver from Dawson instead of driving overland. When would the water he'd seen in Dawson this morning be passing by this spot? There were two eagles drifting in silent circles high above the river, and he watched a weather-beaten motorboat with a single occupant fight its way against the current to Eagle City.

His thoughts eventually turned again to the disappearance of whoever the inhabitants of that cabin near Johnson's Crossing were, and the endless discussions about it he'd had with Ken over the years. Most of the others at the detachment had written the bloody cabin off as a grizzly attack – rare but not unheard of – and if Hunter hadn't known April, he imagined he'd have done the same. As he'd headed back to Yukon Sally's, he chided himself for always dwelling on the past, but as much as he tried, he couldn't envision a future for himself, other than what he was doing now: driving a truck, preferably alone, for a living, and hoping he would soon feel motivated to do something more with his life. By the time he got back to the cabin, Sorry was asleep, surrounded by the smell of beer, marijuana and wood smoke.

As he lay on his bed at Yukon Sally's staring at the ceiling, he decided he would drive out to the home of Goldie and Betty Salmon before leaving Eagle. He knew he'd regret it the rest of his life if he didn't do his best to find out if Goldie was April's daughter, and follow up on this possible chance to solve the mystery behind the bloody cabin near the Teslin River. Betty Salmon might not want to see him, but he had to try.

When Goldie got back to her cabin, her grandmother was just putting two pans of bread dough in the oven of the summer kitchen and Orville was over by the cabin, tinkering with an old bicycle her grandmother had once brought home from the town dump. She gave Gran a quick hug and stood watching the old man from a distance.

"What's he doing?"

"He says he can fix that bicycle. It'll be handy for you going to work, save on buying gas for the truck." Gran started scraping the skin off a carrot. She nodded at a pot that was simmering on the stove. "Fresh rabbit stew tonight. I hope you're hungry."

"Nice, Gran." A good hunting day always put her Gran in a good mood.

"Orville shot it, just up the hill where we got that bear last fall." The old woman spoke matter-of-factly, but Goldie knew her well enough to recognize a note of satisfaction in her voice, as if she herself were responsible.

Goldie watched her grandmother reach for another carrot – wilted after spending months in the root cellar – then turned and watched Orville bent over the bike. He began whistling an unfamiliar but catchy melody. When she turned back to her Gran, the old woman was trying to conceal a satisfied smile. "I'll go wash up, then I'll come help with dinner," Goldie told her.

On her way home, Goldie had debated how to approach her grandmother about the man at the lodge. She decided she would wait until the time was exactly right, just mention it as an aside as if it weren't really important. Because, she felt, it was *too* important. This might be her only chance to find out about her mother from someone who had actually known her. How else could she learn more about a woman whose first name she wasn't sure of, and whose last name she didn't know, and who her Gran wasn't willing to talk about?

Maybe now that her grandmother seemed to be a little more open to change, she might finally be ready to talk to Goldie about her mother. Was it time to ask her? Would she agree to see the man who the big blond guy had called Hunter? If Goldie asked at the wrong time, when her grandmother was in the wrong mood, the answer was sure to be no, and once Gran said no to something, she wasn't likely to change her mind.

When she got back to the outdoor kitchen, Gran told her everything was done. If she wanted to help, she could put plates and cutlery on the table while Gran took down the washing that was drying on the clothesline, she said. Goldie glanced over at the clothesline, and saw some unfamiliar clothing. A man's clothing. Had Gran been doing Orville's laundry?

"You did his washing?"

"There was room in the machine," Gran answered, almost defensively.

Goldie wondered if Orville had helped by catching the clothes Gran fed through the wringer so they wouldn't fall onto the ground, the way Goldie usually did. The washer was outside, parked beside the gas generator in a little shed built on the back of the cabin.

"That was nice of you, Gran," she said to her grandmother's back as she walked away.

Orville did most of the talking over dinner, in his cheerful and pleasant voice. "How was your day at work then, Goldie?" he asked, reaching for a sourdough bun.

Goldie almost mentioned the man who thought she looked like someone named April, but she glanced at her grandmother's face and lost her nerve. Would her grandmother refuse to talk about something so personal in front of Orville? "Good," she said instead, and went on to describe her job at the lodge. "So I only work in the summer, when the lodge is busy. Mostly I clean the guest rooms, but I do pretty much anything Sally needs me to do."

Orville asked her grandmother whether she had ever worked for someone else, and Gran answered, "A long time ago in Dawson, when I was very young."

"You're a strong and independent woman, Betty. Your husband was a very lucky man."

Goldie couldn't conceal her surprise. What had these two talked about when she wasn't present? Why had her grandmother, who had always been so secretive about her past, told this man things that even Goldie didn't know?

Gran looked somber. "I don't know about that," was all she said, and Orville just smiled at her.

It was surreal. After years of just the two of them, here was a third person at the table, chatting away as if they were good friends. No one could ever call her grandmother talkative, but she was answering his questions, nodding at his observations, and even cracking a smile now and then, much as she did when she and Goldie were alone.

"I hope you don't mind my asking," he said, "but I'm finding your company so very pleasant that I would love to stay on a few more days. Would either of you mind terribly if I did?"

Goldie looked at her grandmother, waiting for her response. She knew from experience that what she herself thought wouldn't matter.

"You've certainly made yourself useful here," Gran said, wiping a spot of gravy off her chin with the back of her hand. "The rabbit you brought back this morning made a good stew."

“Ah, but I just brought home the rabbit. You’re the one who made it into such a tasty stew, my dear.”

Watching her try so hard not to smile, Goldie felt a rush of affection for her grandmother. Her heart almost ached, she was wishing so hard that Gran would allow herself to be happy.

“I don’t see any reason why you can’t stay another day or two.” Gran didn’t sound enthusiastic, but at least she didn’t say no.

“Thank you, Betty. Goldie?” Orville turned to her.

“Of course,” she said. “It’s been nice having you here.”

Goldie volunteered to clean up after the meal, and to make tea for them all.

“Later, perhaps. I’d fancy a walk after dinner. How about you, Betty?”

Goldie watched the two of them walk away, following the trail that led down toward the river. Orville pointed at something in a tree; Goldie saw her grandmother’s gaze turn in that direction and caught a glimpse of a smile before her face disappeared from Goldie’s view. Although her first instinct had been to celebrate the fact that her grandmother had found a new friend, she couldn’t shake an uneasy feeling. What was Orville doing here? Why was he working so hard to befriend an old and unfriendly bush woman? How much did her grandmother know about him? Was there some past connection that Goldie hadn’t been told about?

She had half-filled the wash pan with water from the barrel they kept beside the summer kitchen, then warmed it up with water that had been heating on top of the woodstove. As she washed the plates and put them on a towel to dry, her thoughts turned again to the mystery of her mother, and to Mark’s comment: ‘You are an enigma to yourself.’ She felt a flutter of excitement. Meeting Mark, her grandmother meeting Orville, now the appearance of a man who may have known her mother: suddenly her life was opening up like a flower and her future was now as big a mystery as her past.

In the cool evening that followed the seniors’ walk, the three of them sat around the fire pit, the old Englishman entertaining them by playing songs on a battered guitar he’d pulled out from behind the seat of his truck. One of the songs he sang went, “Cockles and mussels, alive, alive, oh,” and Goldie recognized it as the tune he’d been whistling earlier. At Orville's urging, even Gran chimed in on the chorus, "Alive, alive, o-oh, alive, alive, o-oh, singing cockles and mussels, alive, alive, oh."

After some moments of silence, as they all stared into the orange flames dancing around the evening's last log, Orville picked up his guitar again. "This one's for you, Betty," he said. "I learned it from an old partner of mine." He fiddled with the tuning on a couple of strings of his guitar and apologized for the sound, saying he hadn't replaced the strings for ten years or more, then began to play.

Goldie had heard the song before, but she wasn't sure if Gran had. The way Orville played it, strumming gently on the strings, the words were clear. Gran seemed to be listening intently. As the old man sang the final words, "May you stay-ay-ay-ay-ay, forever yo-o-ung," her grandmother nodded, said a curt goodnight, then got up and walked away. By the time Goldie had thanked Orville and excused herself, Gran was in her bed, behind the alcove's curtain.

Goldie drew back the curtain and sat on the bed for a moment to see if her grandmother would stir, but she didn't. She seemed to be holding her breath, as if she wanted Goldie to think she was asleep and to go away. Goldie took the hint, but rested her hand softly on her grandmother's shoulder for a few seconds before leaving.

Tomorrow, she thought, as she brushed her hair, getting ready for bed. Tomorrow I'll tell her about the man called Hunter.

CHAPTER NINE

Elspeth Watson took a deep breath, leaned her elbows on her desk, and lowered her face into her open hands. "Oh, shit," she said. "Shit, shit, shit."

She had just gotten off the phone with Hunter Rayne, and he'd told her that the delivery to the mine outside of Fairbanks was going to be late. His truck was in Whitehorse waiting for parts; he said he'd just talked to the mechanic and the parts weren't expected for another two days. Now it was her job to call the customer, and she wasn't looking forward to it.

"Why me?" she wailed, addressing the small black dog curled up in a basket beside the photo copier. He tucked his nose back under his tail, evidently unmoved by her despair.

She had tried to extract the promise of a guaranteed ETA, but Hunter's response had been, "This far north, there's no such thing as a guaranteed delivery date." The call was short but not very sweet. He told her he was on a satellite phone from some godforsaken place in Alaska and that it was costing him a fortune, plus the connection was less than perfect. She wanted him to tell her something more so she'd be equipped with details for the purchaser at the mining company, but he hung up on her before she could even yell at him. It crossed her mind that she was usually the one hanging up on him, but decided that was her right, as his dispatcher.

Wally, her warehouseman, walked in from the warehouse with paperwork from a delivery. "What's up?"

"Where in hell is Eagle, Alaska?" she asked him.

"Sorry," he said. He dumped the papers in her in-basket and beat a retreat.

She pulled her beat up copy of the Motor Carrier's Road Atlas across the desk and opened it up at the Alaska page, noting that the Hawaii page opposite it had a map of Oahu that was almost as big as the map of Alaska, plus contained ten times as many orange lines denoting highways. "Good God! Eagle is at the end of the road." The nearest dot was for a town named Chicken. "What the hell is he doing there?"

Her phone buzzed and line one flashed. "Watson," she barked into the mouthpiece.

"I'm looking for Hunter Rayne." It was a man's voice, kind of official sounding.

"So am I," she said. "Who's calling?" Realizing it could be a prospective customer, she added a quick, "please."

"This is Staff Sergeant Bartholomew Sam from the Whitehorse RCMP Detachment. Do you know how I can reach Mr. Rayne?"

El knew that Hunter had friends in the RCMP, that he'd worked in the Yukon at one time and might still have friends there, but the voice was so official sounding, she was pretty sure it wasn't a social call. "What's this about?" she asked.

"I'm not at liberty to say."

Was Hunter in some kind of trouble? Why would the cops be calling him on official business? She ran through a few scenarios: his truck was stolen, a tragic or suspicious death in his family, he was wanted for questioning. Less than six months earlier, he'd been the prime suspect in a murder; did they want to talk to him about that again? But this guy was calling from Whitehorse, so it had to be something new.

"He's on the road and I'm not sure if I can reach him, but I can try to get a message to him and have him call you." She took down the Sergeant's number and put the receiver back in its cradle, then sat drumming her fingers on the desk, thinking. Hunter was up to something, she decided, and reached for the phone again.

Hunter was just walking out to the Blazer after a quick breakfast when Sally hailed him from the front porch of the lodge. "Phone's for you," she yelled.

It was El. "What's going on? Why do the police want to talk to you?" She sounded excited, just shy of angry.

He refused to tell her anything until she explained. "Briefly," he added.

"Staff Sergeant Barth–"

"Got it," he said. "I'll give him a call."

"Whoa! What the hell is it about?" she asked. "And don't hang up on me again."

"A murder."

"Who? Where? Is it something I should know about?"

Hunter knew she'd be on his case until he gave her at least some information. "It's one of two things. Either he has some information for me about a cold case I asked him about, or he wants to talk about a knifing that occurred in Whitehorse the day before we arrived there."

"A murder? Does he want you to be part of the investigation? How will you have time for that? You've got a delivery to make."

Hunter sighed. "No, El, I don't know what he wants, but the Yukon RCMP detachment has no need for my help. Look, this is a pretty expensive call."

"Goddamn it, Hunter. I'll pay for the fuckin' call. What's this about a cold case?"

"I just asked him to look up the file on a case from the seventies. A girl I knew, she disappeared along with the man she was living with. I wanted to know if they'd ever found her."

He heard a grunt. "The seventies? Cold is right. Good luck. So if you're not helping the RCMP, why would he call you about this knifing?"

"He asked me to keep an eye out for a person of interest. Maybe he wants to know if I have anything to tell him."

"And do you?"

"No, and I probably never will. Can I go now?"

Her tone changed. "Listen, Hunter. You know I'm here for you if you need anything. If there's information I can get for you related to that cold case, or whatever."

He groaned inwardly. El found his involvement in murder investigations fascinating and frequently tried to help, sometimes with disastrous results.

"If you need me to make some phone calls, look things up, whatever. You just let me know."

What could it hurt? "There is one thing you can do," he said. "That girl who disappeared in 1972, her name was April Corbett. She was from a town called Hastings in Michigan. Maybe just see if you can find any current phone listings there under the name of Corbett. You never know, she could have left the Yukon by choice and ended up back in her home town. Or maybe her parents are still there and they've heard from her."

"I'm on it," she said.

He could hear the scratching of a pen on paper. She must be taking notes. "Just look for numbers, that's all, okay? We can let the RCMP make any phone calls that may or may not be necessary. I'll call you as soon as I hear about my truck," he said, but there was no reply. As usual, his boss had hung up without saying goodbye.

He tried calling Bart, but the call went to the receptionist, who told him the Staff Sergeant was on another call. He left a message that he'd called and would call again later.

An unusual smell drifted into the cabin and prompted Goldie to roll over and sit up in bed. Fresh coffee. Her grandmother habitually drank tea in the morning, and Goldie had never picked up a coffee habit, although she enjoyed the occasional cup with Sally at the lodge. She sniffed again to be sure. Yes, it was coffee. A cup in the morning would be a nice treat. She pulled on her jeans and a tee shirt, grabbed her Yukon Sally's sweatshirt and headed for the outhouse.

She found her grandmother and Orville sitting at the table in the outdoor kitchen, a tin percolator shuddering with each perk on top of the woodstove. A thin line of smoke, barely visible, rose from a green mosquito coil at the edge of the table. Hootie lay snoozing in a bowl he'd carved out of the dirt just outside the kitchen, frequently flicking an ear to dislodge a mosquito.

"Ah, here's our girl," said Orville. "Just in time for coffee."

Goldie nodded a good morning. "You too, Gran?" she asked, as she watched the old man pick up the pot and start pouring coffee into the first of three mismatched mugs lined up along the planking that served as a counter. "No tea this morning?"

"Had my tea," she said. "Orville wanted to make coffee."

He smiled and spoke without turning around. "Betty thinks all Englishmen should drink tea in the morning. I may still speak like an Englishman, but I'm a Yukoner at heart." He put the pot on the back of the stovetop to stay warm. "I enjoy a good cup of tea, but I love a fresh coffee to start my day. Here you go, Betty."

Goldie pushed a can of evaporated milk across the vinyl tablecloth to her grandmother and unscrewed the lid on the sugar jar. She remembered that she wanted to talk to Gran about the man at the lodge, and hoped that Orville would leave them alone. Or perhaps that was the wrong strategy? On a sudden impulse, she found herself saying, "Have you told Orville about my mother?"

Gran was stirring sugar into her coffee but stopped suddenly, staring straight ahead with unfocussed eyes, holding the spoon upright in the mug.

Orville set his mug down on the table and slid onto the bench beside her, raising his eyebrows, obviously curious. When she didn't speak, he said, "No, she hasn't. She must have been beautiful, though, to have such a beautiful daughter." His voice was low and gentle when he addressed the stone-faced woman beside him. "And a beautiful mother? Was she your daughter then, Betty? Goldie's mother?"

Gran finished stirring her coffee and passed the spoon to Goldie. "You know I don't like to talk about her," she said sternly. Then to Orville, "Goldie knows I don't like to talk about her."

There was half a minute of uncomfortable silence before Orville cleared his throat and said, "What would you like me to do today, Betty? I noticed that you have a broken shutter on that side window. Perhaps I can find a new hinge at the Mercantile in town, what do you think?"

Goldie sipped at her coffee, regretting her impulse to broach the subject of her mother in Orville's presence. "I'm sorry, Gran."

She half expected her grandmother to leave the table, but instead she remained sitting quietly, her hands wrapped around the mug in front of her, and suggested that Orville check out the remains of an old cabin near the airport. Early in the winter a fire had burned most of it up, she told him, but she thought there might still be a usable hinge in the rubble, maybe even a whole shutter.

Goldie decided it wouldn't hurt to push a little. If she had already blown her chance, what difference would it make? "I met a man at the lodge yesterday who said I looked like someone he used to know." She stared down into her coffee as she spoke, then raised her eyes to her grandmother's face.

Her grandmother said nothing, just stared back at Goldie, her expression unreadable.

"They say we've all got a doppelganger somewhere," said Orville. "I'm sure you're curious to meet whoever it is that looks like you. As for myself, I wouldn't be. I don't even like to see my reflection in the mirror."

"Who was this man?" Her grandmother's tone was almost belligerent.

"His name is Hunter, and his car had Yukon plates. That's all I can really tell you." She frowned. "Except he drove up with a big guy who looks like Hulk Hogan, and that he seemed like a nice man. Hunter, I mean."

Orville stood up and retrieved a pan of buns from the warming oven. "A little jam, a boiled egg. These buns of yours will make a fine breakfast." He set the buns down on the table, then resumed his spot on the bench. "Tourists, these men?"

Goldie shrugged. "I guess so. They had no reservations at the lodge, just showed up." She tapped an egg on the tabletop to crack the shell, picked the peel off it before reaching for a bun. Hootie raised his head to watch as the food appeared, panting softly.

Her grandmother had been silent, frowning as she watched Goldie pick a small piece of shell off her egg.

"She wasn't my daughter," she said.

Goldie was momentarily stunned. "Then – my father was your son"

Gran shook her head, her eyes on the table between them. "I'm sorry, Goldie."

Goldie said nothing as she tried to process what her grandmother had just said. *She is not my real grandmother. She is not a blood relation.* "Then, how –?"

Orville cleared his throat. "I think I should go for a walk." He had torn a bun in half and spread each side with cranberry jam. He squashed the two halves together and got to his feet, looked from Gran to Goldie and back again. Goldie turned to look at him and he smiled, then picked up his half-empty coffee mug and walked away. Gran watched him leave.

"I've been afraid to tell you."

"Afraid?"

"Afraid to lose you, child."

Lately, Gran seldom called her 'child'. Goldie swallowed hard.

"You are the reason I live in Eagle, the reason I trap and skin and sew, the reason I plant a garden. If I lost you –" Her voice trailed off.

The conversation was moving into familiar territory. Gran didn't want her to leave. Gran's secret had been another way to keep her here. Goldie wanted to say, *How could you? How could you lie to me all these years?* It had been a lie, hadn't it? Not telling the whole truth was a type of lie, wasn't it? She didn't know whether to scream or cry. The why of the old woman's secret was clear, but what about the how, and the who, and the where?

"But who then, Gran? Who is my mother? What happened to her?"

"I don't know."

"You don't know? Why am I here? Tell me that, Gran. How did I come to be with you?"

Gran lifted up her chin, listening. Alerted by her movement, Hootie growled. Then Goldie heard it, too. The sound of a vehicle, slowing to navigate the ruts and potholes as it approached.

Hunter found out from Yukon Sally's young nephew where the girl and her grandmother lived. It wasn't hard to find, given there weren't many roads in Eagle, so it wasn't even possible to take the wrong one.

"Her grandmother's not real friendly," said the young man, "but Goldie's easy to talk to."

Hunter pulled in beside two vintage pickup trucks, one of which was a brown and cream colored Ford with Yukon plates. He did a double take, but told himself it would be too much of a coincidence to run across the person of interest Bart was looking for here.

The girl named Goldie and an older woman, presumably her grandmother, were watching him walk toward them, the girl on her feet, the woman seated at a plank table in an outdoor kitchen. A dog – possibly a Malamute – approached cautiously and sniffed at his ankles. He must have passed the sniff test, as the dog turned around twice and, with a low grunt, dropped into a slight depression in the dirt.

"You found us," said Goldie. "Gran, this is that man I was telling you about, the one from the lodge."

"You must be Betty Salmon." Hunter entered the kitchen and extended his hand to the grey-haired woman seated at the table. Her hair was pulled back into a long braid. The woman hesitated, then put a limp hand into his before pulling it away again. The skin on her hand was rough and dry. "My name is Hunter Rayne. Please excuse me for interrupting your breakfast."

"Coffee?" said the girl. "I think there's some left."

"That would be nice. Thank you." Hunter hoped that him sharing their table would help to put the older woman at ease. She appeared to be in her late sixties, maybe older, thin and muscular, with an appealing albeit stern face that had obviously spent many years in the sun and wind. "You've got a nice little hideaway here." He nodded at the garden on the south side of the house. "Making the most of the long days, I see. What grows well for you here?" He thanked Goldie as she set down a tin mug half full of black coffee. He saw an open tin of evaporated milk and opted to drink it black.

Betty Salmon seemed to warm up a little during several minutes of small talk, but he could see it wouldn't be easy to get a smile out of her. She spoke with the minimal inflection typical of northern natives, a low, nearly monotone pitch with a distinct and abrupt ending to each word.

Since talking to Goldie, he had debated what the best approach would be. Sometimes it helped to mention his association with the RCMP, and sometimes it didn't. Not everybody felt comfortable with the police. For some reason – perhaps her guarded expression – he felt the woman would be more likely to talk to a harmless Cheechako than a former cop.

"I was telling your granddaughter that years ago, while I was living in Whitehorse, I met a young woman named April. Goldie here is the spitting image of her and I just had to find out if they were related." When she didn't respond, he continued, "Goldie said she doesn't know much about her mother, but she thought her name might have been April. Could it possibly be the same April I knew from Whitehorse?"

Hunter sensed that Goldie beside him was holding her breath. There was no response, so he continued. "Her last name was Corbett, and she had driven up here from Michigan in a Volkswagen Beetle with flowers painted on it, sort of a hippie car."

Betty bit her lip and looked away, then took a deep breath and nodded.

"That's her?"

She nodded again. "April Corbett," she whispered.

"April Corbett." Goldie echoed her grandmother's whisper, then louder, "My mother's name is April Corbett."

"Yes," said Betty. "I only knew your mother, never your father."

"What happened to her, Gran? Where is she?"

"I don't know, child. I told you. I just don't know."

Hunter sipped at his coffee and hoped he could find out more just by listening. When he realized it wasn't going to happen, he said, "Where did you meet April, Betty? Last time I saw her was in the summer of 1972 in Whitehorse, but I'd heard she went to stay with a fellow around Johnson's Crossing."

There was the hint of a sad smile on Betty's face as she kept her eyes on Goldie.

"Gran? Where did you meet my mother? Where did she go? Did she tell you anything about my father?"

Hunter could feel the girl's desperation and briefly regretted creating what was obviously a very painful situation for both of the women. He reminded himself that, as a homicide investigator, he'd had to ask much tougher questions than these when interviewing family members of murder victims. "When did you last see April? It must have been after 1972. When I knew her, she didn't have a daughter." Or had she? He had to admit she may not have wanted him – or anyone in Whitehorse – to know.

"I was born in 1973." Goldie turned to Hunter. "On the first day of the year."

Betty shook her head.

"I wasn't?"

"I don't know your real birthday, but it was early that winter, weeks before the shortest day. After you started school, you wanted to know when your birthday was. I picked January first because I thought the first day of the year would be lucky for you."

"No birth certificate?" asked Hunter. "She'd have needed one to start school."

"They let her start school in Eagle without one. I never had a birth certificate myself. I told them that her mother had taken it, and I was trying to get a copy, then everyone forgot."

"Did her mother really have it?"

"How could she? Goldie was born in the bush." Again that sad smile at Goldie. "Did you ever wonder why I've never left Eagle? Outside you need government papers."

"Tell me more about my mother."

The older woman took a deep breath. "It will be hard for you to hear, child."

"Please, Gran. I have to know."

"I was living in that cabin not far from Hootalinqua. You know," she said to Goldie, "the one we call the snowshoe cabin. It's upriver in Canada, north of Lake Laberge. I was down at the river getting water – it was before freeze-up – and I heard a woman's voice cry out. She was calling 'Help me, please, help me'. I put in my canoe, and I let it drift with the current until I came to where she was. She was huddled against a spruce tree beside the river, shivering and crying, with a tiny baby – you, child – under her coat.

"She had big purple bruises on her face, one eye swollen almost shut, and a lip like a balloon. She started to cry when she saw me. She said she didn't think anyone would hear her, and she thought she would die there, and her baby with her. She said she was trying to reach Whitehorse, but she had taken a canoe down the Teslin River from somewhere near Johnson's Crossing. I don't know how she survived. It's an easy river, but it must have taken her days. And it wasn't taking her anywhere near Whitehorse. When she saw she'd reached the Yukon River, she knew she was done for. She was cold and dead tired and had nothing left to eat. She would have died. You would have died, if I hadn't come for water just when she cried out."

Betty Salmon took another deep breath before continuing. Hunter didn't move, trying not to distract her from her story, afraid she would change her mind.

"You look so much like her, that when I see her bruised face in my mind, it turns into you." She reached for Goldie, and the young woman grasped her hand in both of hers and squeezed it. Both women now had tears spilling down their cheeks.

"With what strength she had left, she helped me get my canoe upriver to where the trail to my cabin was. First I carried the baby – you – to the cabin and wrapped you in a blanket. You were very cold and weak, but strong enough to cry like a lost pup." This brought a rare smile from Betty. "Then I helped your mother up the trail. She had a sack of her things tied around her middle, and I took it from her and tied it around myself. She couldn't walk without my help, but I got her to the cabin. I stripped her down, and tucked her in beside you. She had bruises everywhere." She shook her head, as if to shake the image out of her mind. "You tried to suck on her but she had run out of milk, so you began to cry again. I fed the fire to heat the cabin, gave her warm tea and soup, just a little at a time, and by night time she was able to feed you again." Her voice cracked as she said, "You were so tiny, but such a fighter even then."

Hunter was surprised that this woman, who appeared tough as an old boot on the surface, showed so much emotion in relating this story. "You saved their lives," he said. She was right. The fact that this young woman, Goldie, was here today depended on Betty being at the river at exactly the right time. Not for the first time, he reflected that a 'mere' coincidence was anything but 'mere'. He'd seen many supposed coincidences create major triumphs, or sometimes tragedies. Hunter wouldn't call himself a religious man, but he often had a gut feeling that something, or someone, god-like had a hand in creating such events.

He knew he could have rushed the conversation, gotten into interrogation mode and asked where April Corbett had gone and when. In spite of his strong desire to find out what had happened to April, he was beginning to feel like a voyeur. What these two women were experiencing was intensely personal as well as highly emotional; there was no urgency to him finding out, and he didn't belong here at this moment. What Betty Salmon had to say could very well be relevant to the cold case from the bloody cabin on the Teslin River, but it was almost twenty-five years ago and another day would make no difference. He would wait until Goldie had gone to work at the lodge, and return to speak with Betty alone.

He stood, and the two women looked at him, surprised, almost as if they had forgotten he was there. "May I come see you again later?" He addressed his question to the older woman. She nodded almost imperceptibly, her face without expression. He smiled gently, nodded his thanks and walked away.

Betty felt wrung out. She had kept the secret of Goldie's mother, and their arrival in her life, for so long, it had been like dredging gold nuggets from the rocky river bottom to bring those memories back to the surface. Yet now she felt strangely peaceful. She had always known that this day would come. She had promised herself to tell Goldie the story before she – Betty – was no longer able. She was relieved that it was over, but had to ask herself if the spirits had sent the man from the lodge to make it happen because it would soon be that time, because soon Betty would no longer be able to tell the story. That thought did not disturb her peace. Maybe it was time.

Goldie had listened intently, holding Betty's hand in both of her own young hands, their smooth skin a contrast to Betty's veined and wrinkled skin, the slender perfect fingers so unlike her knobby, crooked, arthritic ones. She didn't ask any questions until the end, when she asked about the photograph she'd found in the book of poetry. Betty had never read the book. Her evenings were spent on useful things like beadwork and sewing. But that book had been important enough to Goldie's mother that the poor girl had kept it with her even as she struggled along the banks of the Yukon, trying to save her baby.

Betty rose silently and went to the cabin where she pulled up a board in the floor near her bed. There, wrapped in old newspaper, she had hidden the book and the photograph April had left for her so many years ago. A mother bear and her baby. It was somehow not right that the note on the back was from a mother who was abandoning her baby, something a mother bear would never do. Any mother who would abandon her baby had no right to expect that baby back. Betty felt a pang of guilt. What wasn't in the book was a letter, with a return address of Seaside, Oregon, postmarked in the spring of 1974.

As much as she tried to pretend it had never existed, she could still remember the way her gut twisted when she first picked the letter up at General Delivery in Carmacks. Goldie, then about eighteen months old, had been snug in a carrier strapped to her back. Betty felt the baby's little fingers playing with her long braid. She had taken the letter back to her cabin, afraid to open and read it. That evening, watching little Goldie sitting on the bed, playing with a rabbit skin doll Betty had sewn for her, she'd grabbed the letter and opened the door of the stove, prepared to throw it in unopened. Instead she hid it beneath the cabin floor. She had never read it.

"This was your mother's," she said, handing the book to Goldie, who stood up as she approached.

Goldie held the book with both hands, as though she were afraid it would break if she dropped it. "Walt Whitman. Leaves of Grass," she read aloud.

Betty nodded. "She would read it from time to time. The picture's inside."

Goldie sank slowly back to the bench and opened the book, almost reverently, to look for the picture.

A good mother doesn't leave her baby, Betty thought again. "I've got more planting to do," she said as she walked away. She still wasn't sure if she was sorry she'd shared information about April with Goldie. She still had secrets, and she always would.

She picked up a wooden box of garden tools from the lean-to beside the house and was about to go into the cabin for the old biscuit tin that held her collection of seeds when she saw Orville emerge from the shadows of the tree-lined trail. He motioned to her to come closer.

"Was that the man asking questions about Goldie's mother? Is he with the police?" There was an intensity in his eyes that seemed out of keeping with the nonchalance of his voice. She realized he must have been watching them from the shelter of the woods.

She shook her head. Now that he mentioned it, there had been something in the way he carried himself that reminded her of some policemen she'd seen over the years.

"Did he ask about me?"

"Why would you think he would ask about you?"

He shrugged. "Perhaps he saw my truck?"

She frowned. "Of course he saw it. He parked right beside it. Why would it matter?"

His mustache moved in what passed for a grin. "I might have stolen it in Canada and the Mounties are after me."

"It's almost as old as my truck. If you stole it you were doing someone a favor."

He put his hands on her shoulders, his eyes kind. "My dear Betty, you've made a joke. I think that's the first time I've heard you say something that was meant to be funny."

She could feel her face get hot. She really hadn't meant to be funny, but she liked it that he thought so. And she liked the feeling of his hands on her shoulders. He gave her shoulders a squeeze before dropping his arms to his side.

"In any case, I'm glad I wasn't here when he arrived. I'm not a big fan of the police."

"He wasn't the police."

"Of course. All the same, I'm sure it was a private matter between you and Goldie."

She realized he'd been watching the whole time she'd been talking to Goldie as well. "He's coming back again," she told him. "To speak to me later."

His brows came together in a slight frown. "Later today?"

She was just about to ask him why he cared, when he reached for her again, his smile so broad she could see the edge of his teeth under his mustache.

As if he had a sudden inspiration, he grabbed one of her hands and said, "Come with me, Betty. Let's go to Fairbanks, and we can have a few days of fun. I've got a bit of money put aside. We can stay in a hotel and go out to dinner and maybe see a movie or something. It would be a fun, madcap thing to do, don't you think?"

"But Goldie… "

"Goldie will be fine. She's a big girl. You've told her about her mother today for the first time and she has a lot to think about right now." He gave her hand a little squeeze. "Let's do it, Betty. You've worked so hard for so many years. Isn't it about time you let yourself have a little fun?"

Betty felt like her head was spinning. Grave and grumpy Betty Salmon who hadn't been anywhere bigger than Eagle City for over a decade, going to a city – Fairbanks, a place she'd never been – for nothing but fun. Fun! If anyone had told her a few days ago that she'd even be considering the idea, she'd have said they were crazy. This would be a huge, dizzying plunge down that slippery slope of self-indulgence. The idea suddenly made her almost giddy with excitement. She would have to change into her best clothes for the trip, and pack up a few things to take along if they were going to stay overnight.

"Don't think about it, Betty. Just say yes."

"Okay," she said, feeling as if she were in a dream. "I guess… Yes."

Goldie was on auto-pilot driving to the lodge. In the past few days, her life had been turned upside down and she was trying to make sense of it. First it was meeting Mark at the lodge. She'd had a couple of schoolgirl crushes on boys in Eagle, but Mark was the first boy – man, really – she'd ever met who had the potential to fulfill her dreams of going Outside and seeing the world. It was an intoxicating thought, that if Mark wanted her to – and she thought he liked her more than just a little – she would go with him to California and a whole new life. She chided herself for letting herself even dream about it; she would only be disappointed, she decided.

Second was the arrival of Orville, and how he seemed to be sweeping Gran off her feet. While Goldie was cleaning up after this morning's late breakfast, her grandmother had hastened to feed the chickens and the dog while Orville puttered around his truck. Soon Gran had appeared wearing her new jeans, a clean shirt and her beaded vest, and announced to Goldie that she and Orville were going for a drive and to please make sure Hootie and the chickens were fed until they got back. Goldie had never known her grandmother to go driving for pleasure, but that's sure what it looked like when she joined Orville in waving a cheerful good-bye as he turned the Ford around before heading down the road.

The change in her grandmother represented the biggest revolution in Goldie's situation. Instead of maintaining the strict, reclusive existence they had led for so long she had inexplicably opened up their world to Orville; she was the closest to being friendly that Goldie had ever seen her. In addition to, or maybe because of that, she had finally revealed the secret that had kept Goldie tethered to the little homestead in Eagle by giving her information about a mother who might still be alive, somewhere.

"She left," Gran had said. "After you were weaned, and before the snow fell, she said she had to go, and she left."

"But she meant to come back," said Goldie. "The note. It said, see you in the spring."

"She must have changed her mind." Gran looked away. Goldie sensed that Gran was lying, or at least not telling the whole truth, and wondered which part of what she said was the lie. How could her mother have abandoned her? Had something happened to her mother? What was Gran hiding? She thought about a recent news story where a woman had kidnapped a baby right out of the hospital because she couldn't have a child of her own. Was it possible?

"Do you know where she went?"

“Michigan, maybe. That’s where she was from.”

“Where in Michigan?”

“She didn’t say.” At this point, her grandmother had almost clamped her lips shut, and Goldie knew the conversation was over. She knew that the man from the lodge, Hunter, was planning to go back and talk to Gran later, and perhaps she would be more forthright with him.

Goldie braked to a stop in the middle of the road, struck by a sudden insight into why Gran and Orville had gone ‘for a drive’. Gran had no intention of talking to Hunter later today. She had talked Orville into taking her away from the homestead to avoid seeing him again.

Goldie made a growling sound in her throat and smacked the steering wheel with her hand. She watched in the rearview mirror as the dust raised by her sudden stop began to settle before easing the old Merc back up to speed. So much for finding out more from Hunter. She would just have to see what she could find out on her own. Or, she thought with a sudden burst of optimism, it just might be possible that Mark would be willing to help.

At least, Goldie thought, although her grandmother was acting out of character, she didn’t seem to be losing her mind. She was still sharp as a needle and not on a fast track to senility.

CHAPTER TEN

"What can I do for you, Bart?"

Hunter was on Yukon Sally's satellite phone again. At almost five dollars a minute, he needed to keep the conversation short.

"Picked up my murder suspects yet?"

"I didn't know you had any." Hunter recalled the old Ford pickup with Yukon plates parked at the cabin past Eagle Village. He hadn't had a chance to even ask about it, but when he went back to interview Betty Salmon this afternoon, he'd remedy that. "Are you talking about your persons of interest? I haven't seen anyone fitting those descriptions, if that's what you were hoping for."

"Just kidding; I'm sure we'll get that under control without your help, but I do have something for you. I looked for the Martin Blake file, since that was the name of the missing trapper, as far as we knew. There was a note in the otherwise empty folder cross-referencing the name Grant Sanford, and someone had moved everything to a separate file. I wondered how they had come up with that information until I found the note."

"What note?"

"In a newer file under the name Grant Sanford, along with the case notes and the fingerprints lifted from two of the few items in the cabin suitable for dusting ¬– seems the only clear prints came from a tin mug found in the sink and the corner of Martin Blake's drivers license – was a handwritten note, evidently received at the detachment from an anonymous source. All it says is, 'Murder near Johnson's Crossing last October. Real name Grant Sanford. From military base in Leesville, Louisiana. Wanted for murder.' You remember that note?"

Hunter frowned. "I never heard about a note. I wasn't officially in investigations in Whitehorse, so I guess that's not surprising. Tell me more about the note."

"It's written on a page of lined paper, the kind with holes in the side that students use. Cheap ballpoint pen, kind of blobby. Looks like it was written in a hurry."

"Come in an envelope?"

"No envelope with it. Folded up, on the back side is scrawled 'Whitehorse RCMP'. Nothing in the file to say who or where it came from, but someone noted that it was left at the reception desk on October 3, 1973. The note led them to check the fingerprints against the military records at Fort Polk in Louisiana, which probably took months, if not years. Sure enough, they were a match. Turns out the guy, Sanford, was wanted for the murder of his estranged wife and her brother. He deserted immediately after the killings, never reported back to his unit."

"Is there a photo?"

"Usual military ID photo circa 1964. Clean shaven, short hair. Looks close enough to the photo on Blake's forged driver's license where the fingerprint came from, allowing for the hair and beard difference and Blake's John Lennon glasses."

Hunter rubbed his chin. "Kind of opens up the suspect list, doesn't it?"

"Meaning?"

"Revenge. Did someone from the wife's family find out where he was? But who would have left the note? If the note was dropped off at the Whitehorse detachment almost a year later, it's more likely it was left by someone from here."

"Whoever it was wanted to make sure the dead man's real identity was discovered," said Bart. "No sign in the file of any follow up calls regarding the Louisiana case, but –."

Hunter looked at his watch. "Look, I'm sorry, Bart. I'd love to discuss this in more depth but I've got to get off this phone unless Her Majesty wants to pick up the tab."

Hunter told Bart he expected to be back in Whitehorse in two days and would try to find the time to talk before he got back on the road. He almost mentioned Betty Salmon's story about April, but he didn't want to get into it over the phone.

After he hung up, he went looking for Sorry and found him in the big lodge kitchen with Yukon Sally and the two women from Florida. The kitchen was full of the yeasty odor of fresh baking.

"Have one of these," Sorry said, gesturing at a plate of cinnamon buns in the middle of the table.

Sally pushed back her chair. "I'll get you a coffee," she said.

Hunter's mouth began to water. He pulled up a chair and reached for a cinnamon bun.

"What's next, boss?" said Sorry. He was spreading butter on a still-steaming bun. "Aren't we leaving today? No offense, Sally, but this isn't exactly a happening place."

"Want to go back to Dawson?"

Sorry made a face.

Hunter heard footsteps behind him, and saw Yukon Sally look up as she was setting a mug of coffee in front of him. He swung around in his chair, and saw young Goldie. He was struck again by her resemblance to April Corbett.

"You're early. Join us for coffee?"

Goldie thanked Sally, but shook her head and remained standing. "I was hoping we could talk," she said to Hunter, so shyly that she reminded him of a child. When he nodded, she added, "I'll be down by the creek." She excused herself and left again.

Sorry raised his eyebrows. "Isn't she a little young for you, boss?"

Hunter scowled at him, surprised at how irritated he felt. "Get your mind out of the gutter. She's almost as young as my daughter."

"Whoa! Just jokin'." He reached for another cinnamon bun. "A little touchy, are we?"

Hunter saw the two Florida women exchange glances. He punched Sorry lightly on the arm. "If you don't want to go back to

Dawson, I think we'll stay here another day, if Sally's still got room for us."

She nodded.

He put milk and sugar in his coffee, wolfed down what remained of the cinnamon bun, then excused himself. "I'll take a rain check on a second cinnamon bun, if that's okay," he said. "They're fantastic." As he walked, he licked the sticky sugar glaze off his fingers, then wiped his fingers on his jeans.

He found Goldie sitting on a rough log bench – just a plank supported on two upright rounds – beside the creek. He straddled the bench facing her and set his coffee down in front of him. "Your grandmother told you what you wanted to know?"

"Yes and no." She smiled, almost mournfully. "So now I know who my mother is. Or was." She bent down and picked up a coarse stalk of grass and began rolling it between her fingers. "But I have almost as many questions as I did before. I still don't know if my mother is alive or dead, or why she left me. Or if –." She didn't finish the sentence, just stared at the creek with her mouth slightly open, as if lost in thought.

"What did your grandmother say?" Hunter prompted gently.

"It's what she didn't say. What she didn't say for so long." She turned to face him. "Why did she keep this from me for so long? I can't help but wonder what the reason was. It's like she was hiding something, maybe something that she did. My grandmother, I mean. What do you think? Can you understand why she would keep it such a secret from everybody?"

Hunter shook his head. He had his own suspicions. He tried to imagine what it had been like for Goldie, growing up with a woman who was hiding such important information from her. How much affection had the sullen bush woman shown to Goldie when she was a child?

"Was she good to you?"

"Gran? Betty, you mean?" A smile played over her lips as she nodded. "She was strict about some things, and there were the secrets, but yes, she was good to me. She worked very hard to provide for us and she taught me so much about living in the bush. She always let me know that she was proud of me, and in spite of her being sort of crusty, I always felt loved. I guess I'm much luckier than a lot of girls Outside."

"More than you'll ever know," he said. During his years on the force, he'd seen girls who were forced to endure appalling childhoods. Many hadn't survived unscathed, some hadn't survived at all. On that spectrum, yes, she was lucky.

A raven began to squawk in the woods behind them, and they both turned to see who or what he was complaining about. Nothing appeared, and soon the raven flew out of the trees and away, following the creek toward the river.

Betty Salmon hadn't told her much more after he had left them alone, Goldie said. Her grandmother described how she had taken care of April until the young mother had recovered from being beaten, and from the exposure she'd suffered trying to carry her baby to safety. April stayed with Betty at the Hootalinqua cabin until after the baby was weaned, then told Betty that she couldn't stand to spend another winter in the north and wanted to go back south to make a home for herself and the baby. She was afraid the journey would be too hard with the baby, and asked Betty if she would be able to take care of Goldie until she came back to take her home in the spring.

"My mother came along on Gran's annual fall trip to Carmacks to sell her furs and beadwork and pick up winter supplies. That's a hundred mile trip down the Yukon by boat. She found someone who would give her a ride to Whitehorse, kissed me goodbye, and Gran said she never heard from her again." She emphasized the word 'said'.

"You don't believe her?"

Goldie sighed. "I don't *not* believe her. Not totally. Something could have happened to my mother so she was never able to come back, I guess."

"But?"

"If she cared enough about me to struggle along the river bank carrying me in her arms as a baby, wouldn't she care enough to come back for me in the spring?"

He said what he thought any daughter would need to hear. "I'm sure she loved you very much."

They were both silent for a few moments, watching the water boil and ripple across the creek bed, listening to its liquid music in counterpoint to a series of raspy tsik-a-dees from a boreal chickadee before Goldie spoke again.

"I love Gran, but I feel somehow incomplete, not knowing anything about my parents. I need to know who they are, and if they're still alive." She looked straight at Hunter as she said it, and her expression, if not her words, seemed to be pleading with him for help.

His heart, almost literally, ached for her. He had not been in love with her mother, but he had been captivated by April's ingenuousness and fascinated by her enthusiasm for life. The thought that April's bright light might have been extinguished in that bloody cabin had haunted him ever since he'd seen her picture on the wall. And now to see her daughter – much the same age as his own two girls – suffering through no fault of her own, touched him deeply. And how could she, with no telephone and few or no connections outside of Eagle, even begin to find information about her parents?

"I'll see what I can find out for you," he said. "Maybe your grandmother will be more forthcoming with me this afternoon."

"She's gone."

"Gone?"

"She and Orville left before I did. They didn't say where they were going or when they'd be back, but it looks like they're gone for the day."

"And Orville is –?" He thought about the old pickup he'd seen.

"Oh, that's right. He wasn't there when you arrived. He's just retired from trapping and prospecting, from what I gather. Gran seems to like having him around." She stood up. "I'm sorry. I really should get to work. How can I get in touch with you again, in case you find something out?"

He told her he'd leave his phone number with Yukon Sally.

She suddenly stepped forward and bent to hug him where he sat, then stepped back. "Thank you so much. I was feeling so – so helpless, I guess. And hopeless."

Hunter felt the strength of her lean forearm, however briefly, on his neck. "I can't promise anything, but I'll do my best. I can see how much this means to you."

"Like you just said." She smiled briefly. "More than you'll ever know."

A breeze swept her long dark hair across her face as she turned away, and for a moment, she was April. April in that photograph on the bloody cabin wall.

Betty began to second guess her decision as soon as Orville pulled out of the cabin's driveway onto Eagle Village Road. What was she thinking? How could she let herself be talked into this crazy drive with a man she hardly knew? She had avoided male company most of her life, and for a good reason, she thought. After Wim Reinder went under the ice in 1959, she had sworn never to lose her independence again, and in the case of an abusive man – one like Reinder had been – that meant never allowing herself to be alone in a man's company without suitable protection.

Over the years, she'd had trappers and travelers stop at her cabin seeking refuge from the elements, and like any responsible northerner, she had let those who needed shelter spend the night. But she had never encouraged visitors and always slept with her rifle, loaded, by her side. She made sure there was a securely fastened curtain, if not a door, between the main room and the place where she slept. It might not keep them out, but it would keep them out long enough for her to wake and grab her gun. Fortunately, it had never come to that, and over the years she had become less wary of her own safety. After Goldie became a part of her life, her main concern had become to protect the girl.

The thought of Wim Reinder made her shudder involuntarily. After his body had disappeared under the ice, she had run back to the cabin, the two dogs at her heels. She had barred the cabin door behind her – as if Reinder might have survived both the axe and the frigid river – and sat near the stove with a rifle at her feet. She was shivering uncontrollably, and put as much wood as she dared in the stove; the heat didn't help as much as the passage of time. An hour or so later, she had stopped shaking and the feeling of panic had abated. She had gone outside to the burning barrel and lit a fire inside it. Then she had thrown all of Reinder's clothing and blankets –

everything of his that might carry any trace of his scent, a scent that had become abhorrent to her –into the burning barrel. She watched the flames, stirred the embers, added fuel to the fire if she had to, and didn't go inside for the night until there was nothing left of his belongings but ash.

After a few days of meditation and deliberation, she had then decided what to do. She loaded the dog sled with as many supplies as she could fit, and made sure to remove any traces of herself from Reinder's cabin. What she couldn't burn followed the same route Reinder himself had gone, beneath the ice and into the river. When all was ready, she hitched up the dogs and headed south on the frozen river to see if she could find the cabin she and the French Canadian trapper had previously occupied near Hootalinqua.

The beard of the man she knew as 'Patron' was already grey and his skin was slack when he abandoned her, sixteen and pregnant, beside the river, so she felt there was a good chance he would be gone by now. If he was there, she would carry on to Whitehorse. If he was gone, she would make the cabin hers. It was a long and potentially dangerous trip, but the late winter weather was good, the dogs healthy and energetic, and the river was a solid highway of ice. She prayed that the trapper had gone but the cabin was still standing and no one else had taken possession of it in the intervening years, and was relieved to find it so.

So she and the dog team had made Hootalinqua their home. As 'Patron' had done, she made two or three trips a year into Carmacks taking furs and any articles that she'd sewn and beaded, exchanging them for several months' worth of supplies. She trapped and fished, snared rabbits and grouse, shot the occasional caribou or moose, stacked firewood from the surrounding forest, and started a small kitchen garden. Like her mother and her Gwich'in ancestors, she tanned skins and hung meat and fish to dry in the sun. She allowed her lead dog to breed with her best bitch, and was also able to sell a few puppies every fall. Living alone was hard at first, but better than life with Reinder had been. She loved her dogs, and suffered terribly when she was forced to shoot one that had become sick or injured. She loved the puppies above all; they seemed to fill an empty place in her heart. She would sometimes sit with them in the whelping box when the bitch was taking a break, and she would feel a great sense of peace and belonging.

She had felt that same sense of peace and belonging the first time she held the baby, Goldie, and she knew right away that she didn't ever want to lose that feeling. But now, Goldie would soon be gone. That being the case, what did it matter if this man beside her in the truck beat her or even took her life – not that she seriously thought he would – because without Goldie her life wouldn't be much use to her any more.

Orville was uncharacteristically silent; she noticed that he took his eyes off the road from time to time and glanced over at her with a look of concern.

"The door won't fall off, Betty," he said finally. "Are you feeling terribly frightened of my driving?"

She hadn't been aware of holding so tightly to the armrest on the door. She relaxed her grip, but rounding the next bend, she realized that she was again clutching the door. They weren't going particularly fast – it was impossible on the road out of Eagle with its potholes and tortuous curves – but she was unused to travelling anywhere but back and forth between Eagle and the cabin. The old truck's shock absorbers creaked as the truck lurched over the worst of the potholes, and sometimes Betty felt herself bounce clear off the seat. That she was used to. The steep drops off the edge of the road she was not.

"We're not making very good time, my dear," said Orville. "Looks like getting to Fairbanks will take a lot longer than I thought."

When she wasn't worrying about their destination and feeling uncomfortable about allowing herself to leave Eagle, Betty found herself enjoying the ride. They passed a herd of caribou grazing beside the road, and saw a mother bear hustle her cub up a slope as the truck approached. It almost took her breath away to see the rows of mountains stretching away to the horizon, some of them still pocked with irregular patches of snow. Orville made a point of reading the license plates on the few tourist vehicles that they encountered heading in the opposite direction, a few of them bigger than bush cabins.

"California again," he said as a truck and camper jolted past. Not far behind it was one of the larger vehicles, like a cabin on wheels with an engine in front. "That one's from Oregon."

Her stomach did a little flip, like it did every time she saw a vehicle with Oregon license plates in Eagle. She normally ducked away when she saw one, but this time she let herself peer into the big front windows as it passed. The driver was a man with white hair; the woman beside him had short dark hair and was wearing big sunglasses. Neither of them looked in any way familiar.

It was around noon when they arrived in Chicken. Orville said they had better stop for fuel and lunch, and getting down from the cab of the truck, she found that she had stiffened up from sitting still for so long. Her right hip ached, and it took a few seconds for her to straighten out her back. She glanced over at Orville, and he must have been feeling the same, for he screwed up his face as he stretched his arms and back.

They sat at a table in the cafe. The woman who asked them what they wanted for lunch wasn't very friendly, but Orville smiled and chatted with her as if she were. Betty realized he had done the same with her, and for some reason it made her angry, at the woman more than at Orville. *Am I being jealous?* she asked herself, and felt a little silly. The only time she'd felt jealous before was when April was nursing the baby, little Goldie. Betty had always looked for something to do so she didn't have to watch. Her jealousy had been unexpected then – after all, she'd drunk yarrow tea to keep from having a baby of her own – and was even more of a surprise now. *Orville? At my age, jealous of that old goat?* The woman who took their order responded to Orville's charm by scowling and walking away, and Betty covered her mouth to hide an involuntary smile.

They were half way through their sandwiches when the door opened and an Alaska State Trooper in his blue uniform stepped inside. Betty watched him scan the faces in the restaurant, but Orville had his back to the door and his attention was on the potato salad that came with his sandwich. The trooper stood at the door with his hand on the butt of his holstered gun as he asked who owned the Ford truck with a Yukon license plate.

Orville froze for a second, a forkful of potato salad halfway to his mouth. Then he calmly put down the fork and began to get to his feet.

"Sit! Put your hands on your head," said the trooper, drawing his gun and moving quickly toward the center of the room, a spot that would give him a better view of Orville.

"What seems to be the problem, officer?" said Orville, slowly raising his hands and placing them on his head. "The truck is mine. It's not stolen, if that's what you're thinking."

"Stand up nice and slow. Keep your hands on your head." The trooper approached without taking his eyes, or his gun, off Orville. When Orville was on his feet, he gave him a quick one-handed pat down, then grabbed Orville's elbow and propelled him toward the exit.

"Finish your lunch, Betty," Orville said over his shoulder as he was escorted out the door. "I'm sure I'll be right back."

Betty's mouth had gone dry, and it was all she could do to finish chewing the mouthful of sandwich she'd bitten off just when the trooper opened the door. She stood up to follow them outside, but the woman from the restaurant called out from behind the counter. "Hey! Where do you think you're going? You haven't paid for your lunch."

Betty scowled at her and walked toward the door.

"Hold on there. I don't care if you two are a geriatric Bonnie and Clyde. You're not leaving without paying for your lunch."

"Calm down, stupid woman. We'll be back to finish the lunch," she said, continuing to the door. It suddenly occurred to her that they might not be. What if the trooper took Orville away? Where would that leave her? Would she be able to drive his truck back to Eagle? Would she be stranded here in Chicken? Why *would* they take Orville away? He'd wanted to go on this drive to avoid seeing a man he thought might be with the Yukon police, and here he was, being led away by an Alaska trooper.

The trooper, his gun back in his holster, was standing with Orville beside the trooper's car, talking. Orville handed the trooper something from his wallet; the trooper examined it briefly, then motioned for Orville to get into the back seat of the car. After closing the door on Orville, the trooper glanced over at her, frowned, then seated himself in the front seat and picked up some kind of radio microphone.

Betty was afraid to get closer. Common sense told her they would never connect her with the disappearance of Wim Reinder, but she had lived in fear of his death being discovered for so many years. The thought of him brought back the sickening sound of the axe sinking into the back of his neck, the sight of his blood on the snow. She wished she could somehow erase that moment from her memory.

She could see that the trooper was talking into his microphone, and now and then asking Orville a question. Now they were both looking in her direction. A few moments later, the trooper got out of his car and came over to her. He wasn't smiling, but she thought she could see a trace of sympathy on his face. She backed up against the log railing of the restaurant's porch, wrapping her arms around the upright log post as if it could keep him from taking her, too.

"I'm sorry, ma'am. Your friend is wanted in Whitehorse, Canada for questioning and the RCMP are sending a plane to pick him up. His truck will be towed back to Whitehorse. He tells me you have no other means of getting home. Is there someone you can call for a ride?"

"I don't understand. Is he under arrest?"

"He will be if he doesn't cooperate."

"Can I talk to him?"

"They must have me mixed up with someone else," Orville told her, the trooper beside him, listening and watching closely. Orville apologized to Betty, then handed the trooper two hundred dollars in wrinkled Canadian bills for him to pass on to her, and apologized again. "Maybe the kind officer will call your granddaughter where she works. If she can't make the trip in that old rust bucket of yours, then perhaps that nice young man who drove her home the other night?"

Betty was now more convinced than ever that contact with authorities always led to no good, and that leaving the safety of her cabin near Eagle Village with Orville had been a mistake. "I shouldn't have listened to you," she said. "I should have stayed home." She turned her back on Orville and began to walk away. She wondered how long it would take to walk the hundred miles back to Eagle, and how to get there without exposing herself to traffic on that road. Was there a trail?

She heard Orville asked the trooper if Betty could get her belongings from the truck. The trooper got them himself, looked inside Betty's little sack, where she had a change of clothes and a nightgown plus a few toiletries, then handed it to her. In spite of Betty's objections, he called Yukon Sally's Lodge and asked them to send someone for Betty.

"If that young man can't do it," Orville piped up, "I'm sure they'll find someone who can."

"What the fuck am I supposed to do while you're gone?" Dan Sorenson kicked at a dry branch that hadn't made it into last night's campfire. "Why don't you let her pick up her own fuckin' grandmother."

"Look, Dan. You're the one who wanted to come with me on this trip. You've got no job, which means you probably have no money, you've been kicked out by your wife. I don't think you're in any position to call the shots."

Sorry glowered in Hunter's direction without making eye contact.

"Besides, you were in a hurry to leave Whitehorse, you don't want to go back to Dawson, you don't want to stay here. What exactly is it that you want to do?"

"Exactly? I'll tell you exactly. I want to go home and see my wife and kids."

"That's out of my hands. Call Simone when we get back to somewhere with a regular phone. She's probably cooled off by now." Hunter pulled the keys to the Blazer out of his jeans pocket and checked to make sure he was carrying his wallet.

"I'm also out of smokes."

Hunter got the hint. He pulled out his wallet, took out a twenty and handed it to Sorry. On second thought, he took out another ten. "In case you need to buy something to eat. The drive could take up to three hours each way, so I should be back before eight."

Sorry nodded his thanks, his face still sullen.

"In the meantime, why don't you talk to Sally. Maybe she can put you to work here since you've got nothing better to do."

Just under three hours later, Hunter picked up Betty Salmon in Chicken. She was standing at the intersection of the Taylor Highway and the road to Chicken, a lone figure looking rather small, a bundle at her feet, preoccupied with something on the ground in front of her until he eased to a stop beside her on the gravel. She then straightened up and peered suspiciously inside the Blazer.

"You," was all she said.

Hunter opened his door and was about to come around to pick up her belongings and help her into the passenger seat, but she pulled the door open herself, threw her bundle behind the seat, and climbed in.

Although he would have liked to get out and stretch, maybe take a coffee break, Hunter sensed that Betty Salmon had already had all she could take of Chicken. He decided that if he couldn't take another three hours on that bone-jarring road, he wasn't much of a trucker, so he did a U-turn and headed back up the highway.

He said nothing for over fifteen minutes, curious whether Betty Salmon would be the first one to break the silence. He wasn't surprised when she didn't.

"Let me know if you need a break," he said.

No reply.

"What happened back there?" Hunter had already talked to Bart again, but he thought if he pretended not to know the story, perhaps she would be more inclined to talk about it. "Sally said your friend was being flown back to Whitehorse. Was it some kind of emergency?"

"I never should've left Eagle," she said. "I never met a man I could trust."

"He lied to you?"

"No. Yes. He made me think it would be good for me, going with him."

"Maybe he thought it was." Hunter swerved quickly to avoid a pothole and he noticed Betty clutching at the door handle so he slowed down. He had always considered himself a trustworthy man, although he knew his ex-wife would debate that, and obviously Betty Salmon would, too. "I never met Orville. What's he like?"

She hesitated, then said, "Orville is the only man who wanted to take care of me, instead of wanting me to take care of him."

The personal nature of that revelation took Hunter by surprise. "He's a good man, then?"

"That's what I *thought*." Her voice faded so he could barely make out what she said next above the noise of the engine. "But maybe he's like all the rest."

"We're not all bad, Betty." He smiled in her direction and was happy to see her glance at him long enough to notice.

"I guess not. I never met a lot of people, living in the bush." She stared off at the horizon, a wistful smile on her face. "Sunshine. Orville was like sunshine on a warm day after a long winter."

"I hope he'll be back, then."

"I don't know." A sigh. "Sometimes I feel so tired."

He felt a pang of sympathy, and a sense that Betty Salmon's life had been a continual struggle for survival in a very harsh landscape, both physical and emotional. If her relationships with others, men in particular, had been mostly cold and hurtful, it would certainly explain her taciturn and reclusive nature. To open up, she needed stroking, not prodding.

"Tell me about April."

"Why should I?"

"Because I care. I've worried about April ever since she went missing in 1972. I was relieved to hear that you had nursed her back to health, and that because of you she didn't have to watch her baby die, then die herself of starvation and exposure. Thank you." He glanced over at her, but Betty was staring out the side window and all he could see was the back of her head, wisps of grey and black hair escaping the irregular braid that hung down her back. "And don't forget that I cared enough about you and Goldie to spend over six hours on this godforsaken potholed highway to bring you back to Eagle." She still wasn't looking at him, so he hoped she could hear the smile in his voice.

"I'm sorry," she said softly. "I guess I stopped trusting other people a long, long time ago. What happened with Orville today didn't help."

She sighed, seemed to hold her breath, then sighed deeply again. "April left before the first snow. She said goodbye in Carmacks, said she found a ride to Tagish to pick up her car."

Hunter had wondered where she'd left her car, and thought about the note Bart mentioned, the one that identified Blake as Sanford. The note had been found by the RCMP receptionist on October 3, 1973. Tagish was about sixty miles south of Whitehorse, just off the Alaska Highway. Could April have dropped the note off on her way through Whitehorse?

Betty continued, "She told me many times that she loved her baby, although she wasn't a very patient mother. I am sure she meant to come pick Goldie up in the spring." Betty sniffed; nervously, Hunter thought. "But she didn't."

"It was good of you to look after her baby when she left."

"I never held a live baby before Goldie."

Hunter sensed that what she had just said held more than a superficial meaning. "Did April tell you what had happened to her before you found her?"

"She was beat up bad. I was beat up many times in my life, but never so bad as that. They always wanted me to be fit enough to work after, but it looked like who beat her up wanted her to die. It's just lucky the places she got hit that hard wasn't where it would've killed her."

"Did the man who beat her kill himself?"

"Why would he do that?"

"The man went missing, too."

"Good," she said. "He deserved to die."

Hunter tried to process that. Did Blake kill himself, or did April kill him? "Did she fight back?"

"When you fight back, they hit you harder." She said it matter-of-factly, and Hunter thought not for the first time that he was lucky not to know what it felt like to be a woman at the mercy of an abusive man.

"Did she know his name wasn't really Blake?"

Her tone turned angry. "How am I supposed to know these things? I told her I didn't want to hear about her men."

"Her men? More than one?"

Betty Salmon snorted. "Why do you think she left her easy life Outside to move to the northern bush? She was running away from the baby's father."

Goldie had fed Hootie and the chickens, collected the day's eggs, wiped them off and stashed them in the cool of the root cellar, then sat down in the outdoor kitchen with a mug of tea to wait for Betty's arrival home. It had clouded over, and a cold breeze slid across the back of her neck. She pulled up the collar of her jacket and circled the mug with her hands for warmth.

Yukon Sally didn't have any answers to the questions that troubled her; as much as she tried not to, Goldie was left to speculate and worry. She'd been so happy for Gran, that she and Orville were enjoying each other's company, and now this. How would Gran be feeling when she got back home? Would this be the end of Orville's presence in their lives? If Orville was just wanted for questioning, why would the Mounties send someone to get him? Why wouldn't they come talk to him in Chicken and then let him go?

Early that afternoon, Sally had come to find her in the Caribou Cabin where she was cleaning the bathroom and changing the bed sheets. "You don't have current tags on that old rattletrap of yours, do you." It was a statement, rather than a question.

Goldie shrugged, feeling a little guilty. She and Gran only used the old Merc on the local roads, and so far everyone seemed to turn a blind eye to the fact that it wasn't insured. Gran wouldn't even consider licensing it properly. Some old guy she barely knew had given it to her before he left town, at least that's what she said. She said that was why she didn't have proper papers for it.

"Your grandmother needs a ride home from Chicken. I don't think Mark's jeep is right for that road; too open. Your poor gran would be windblown and covered in road dust. Maybe that fellow from Canada will go get her. He seems like a nice enough guy. You want me to go ask him?"

Goldie had asked her about Orville's truck, and she said Orville and his truck were both being taken to Whitehorse; something about questioning in a serious crime, but the trooper wouldn't say what.

"You mean Hunter, the man from Canada, don't you? I'll ask him myself. Where is he?"

She found Hunter and the big guy playing horseshoes on the pitch behind the lodge. It was Hunter's turn to throw, and she waited for him to finish before she approached. He got a ringer. Goldie clapped, and both men turned to look at her.

"Dumb luck, boss," said Sorry, walking toward the stake to pick up the horseshoes. "My turn."

"What can we do for you, Goldie?" said Hunter.

"I need a huge, huge favor, if you have time." She began to explain, and he drew her away from the pitch and his partner as if to give her more privacy. When she'd finished, he nodded his head slowly, as if he was trying to think something through.

"I have to make a phone call," he said, "but we'll be staying here another night so I can certainly take the time for it." He asked her a couple of questions that she couldn't answer, then told his friend he had to go.

"Where you goin'?" the big guy called out.

Hunter said he'd be back in a few minutes. "You could use the time to practice."

She'd followed Hunter, and from a discreet distance, listened in as he spoke to someone he called Bart on the satellite phone. Hunter's end of the conversation didn't tell her anything she didn't already know, but it had to do with Orville and it sounded as if what happened had been no surprise to Hunter. It made her wonder if Hunter was somehow involved with the Mounties.

"Was that the police?" she asked when he'd hung up.

His frown at the question made her uncomfortable, and made her more certain he'd been talking to the police, or maybe was a police officer himself. He did have that look about him, clean cut, almost military in appearance, like a State Trooper.

Instead of answering her question, he said, "I'll go pick up your grandmother."

"Why can't Orville drive her back?"

He frowned again. "How long have you known Orville?"

"Just a few days."

"Did he say anything about where he was or what he was doing just before he came to Eagle?"

She shook her head dumbly.

"Don't worry about your grandmother. She'll be home safely by tonight."

She hadn't been too worried about Gran until he'd said that. It was the first indication that perhaps her going off alone with Orville had been something worth worrying about. Goldie sipped her tea, then checked the position of the sun. She didn't expect Hunter to be back with Gran for at least an hour, maybe more, and she knew she couldn't relax until she'd had a chance to talk to her grandmother about what had happened.

Hootie's head went up, his ears pricked forward. Someone was on the road heading toward the cabin. She stood up, feeling an unfamiliar shiver of fear. Life had been so predictable until recently. Violence hadn't been a part of her personal experience, but hearing about the abuse her mother had suffered, and now with the implication that Orville could have harmed her grandmother, Goldie was suddenly feeling a vague uneasiness, with fear hovering on the horizon like a storm cloud.

The sound of a motor drew closer, and Mark's jeep emerged from the trees. A sense of relief made her want to run to him, but instead she forced herself to stand beside the summer kitchen and wait for him to come to her. He approached with his head down, watching the ground as he walked, carrying a grocery sack with something heavy in the bottom. As he got close, he lifted his head, tossing his hair off his forehead and breaking into a lopsided grin. She felt a tickle under her rib cage and couldn't help but smile back.

"What's up?" she asked.

"I come bearing gifts," he said, holding out the grocery sack. He'd brought beer, he said. "I knew you were on your own, and thought we could just hang out together until your grandmother gets home." He cocked his head to one side, his eyebrows raised, as if asking for her okay.

"I could sure use the company," she told him. "I'm used to being alone out here, but it's not every day a girl's grandmother gets stranded in Chicken after her travelling companion gets picked up by the police."

He grinned again as he popped the top on one of the beer cans and offered it to her.

"Where'd you get these?" she asked, taking it from his hand. Her fingers brushed his for an instant; it gave her a sensation almost like an electric shock.

"Those tourists from Oregon who arrived today brought a stash of booze. They took Sally's advice in a big way." There were no bars or liquor stores in Eagle, so Yukon Sally always suggested to her clients that they bring their own favorite alcoholic beverages when they came to stay. "I bought a six-pack off them and had these two chilling in the freezer."

"You're one of those bad influences everybody warned me about," she said with a laugh. "First wine, now beer. You trying to get me drunk?"

"If you manage to get yourself drunk on one can of beer, you deserve it." He popped the top on his own beer and held it out toward her.

"A toast?" she said.

"Yeah, a toast."

"Okay, what are we toasting?"

"Why not us?"

"Us?" The thought gave her a thrill, but what exactly did he mean?

"Yeah. To us – you and me – having a fun summer." His eyes seemed to be searching hers for a reaction.

She could feel heat rising up her neck. "A fun summer," she repeated, doubtfully. What was he expecting from her? There'd been a couple of older girls she knew from Eagle Village who'd let themselves get involved with outsiders during the summer. They thought they were in love and believed the feeling was mutual, but the outsiders went away and never looked back. Adding to the girls' heartbreak, the local boys made fun of them and called them sluts.

"Well, yeah. I thought you liked me."

"Maybe I do." She liked him at lot. She would have loved to touch him, brush that hair back off his forehead, lay her cheek against his chest, feel his arms around her. She felt an almost magnetic pull toward him, but she fought against it. Instead, she sat down on the bench behind the table, giving him no choice but to sit down opposite her.

"So what do you suppose the cops nabbed that old guy for?"

Goldie shrugged. "I wish I knew more about it. He seemed like such a nice man. Harmless. Hard working. He certainly wasn't looking for a free ride here. He was always asking Gran how he could make himself useful."

"They say psychopaths are like that." Mark took a pull on his beer. "They can be charming as hell, but they really don't give a damn about anybody but themselves."

"That doesn't mean just because someone is nice, he's a psychopath."

"I didn't say that."

"Like you, for example," she interrupted him to add, with a smile.

"Haw haw." He said, scowling, then immediately breaking into one of those cute grins.

It took her half an hour to drink half her beer. It wasn't as tasty as pop. He offered to finish it for her, while she told him more about growing up in the bush and going to school in Eagle. She learned a lot about him, too. How he liked to spend his time, what his family was like, that he didn't much care for school but managed to get reasonably good marks.

"I loved school," she told him. "I wish I could go to college."

"Why don't you?"

"On what I make working part time at Sally's during tourist season? Fat chance."

"You could work your way through school. Lots of students do."

"Yeah? Where? It's not that easy to apply for a job thousands of miles away when you live in the bush without a phone."

She was about to tell him about her search for her mother when Hootie's ears perked up again, and seconds later, Goldie heard the sound of a vehicle approaching. Soon the nose of that reddish SUV emerged from the trees, and moments later, Hunter and her grandmother had joined them at the outdoor kitchen. Gran slid onto the bench, but Hunter remained standing.

"If you don't need me for anything," he said, "I'll be on my way."

Goldie began to thank him, in case Gran was her usual sour self, but her grandmother turned and smiled up at the man. "Thank you very much," she said. Goldie was surprised to see her grandmother's smile remain as the man put his hand briefly on her shoulder, and told her to take care.

Hunter pointed at Mark's beer can and said, "I hope you left a couple of those at the lodge for me." He smiled as he turned to walk back to the SUV. Mark picked up on some invisible cue – perhaps the awkward silence that followed Gran's arrival – and excused himself, driving away from the cabin soon after Hunter.

"Are you okay, Gran? Can I make you some tea?" Gran hadn't even blinked at Mark's presence. She looked tired, but not unhappy, and Goldie was dying to hear all about her day.

"Yeah. Tea. And something to eat."

While Goldie put together a quick supper for them both, she asked Gran to tell her what had happened. Gran sketched the events of her day, then said, "Nobody says Orville is guilty of anything. I really don't understand why they would have to take him to Whitehorse, and even tow his truck back there. Hunter – the man who gave me a ride – he said not to touch Orville's belongings, if he left anything here. He said they will probably be sending someone from the Mounties to take it to Whitehorse as well." She shook her head. "I don't like police coming here."

"Why does it scare you so much, Gran?" She left the moose sausage sizzling on the stove to sit beside her grandmother. She winked at her and added, "You never killed anybody, did you?"

Her Gran's face froze, and Goldie reached for the old woman's hand. "Gran? Are you okay?"

"I'm fine, child," she said. "Don't you worry about me, child. I'll be fine."

Elspeth Watson arrived at the office much earlier than her usual six thirty. Hunter had asked her for help – well, to be honest, she had asked him if she could do something to help get some information related to that cold case he was interested in – and she wanted to show him that he could count on her when he needed assistance with an investigation. Michigan was three hours ahead of the west coast, in case she had to make any calls.

Of course, Hunter didn't want her calling the relatives of the missing woman. That was certainly understandable. What could she possibly say? 'Hi, I'm a freight dispatcher in New Westminster, British Columbia. Can you tell me where your daughter is?' What good excuse could she possibly give?

That got her thinking, as she scooped some dog kibble into Peterbilt's food dish and put fresh water in his water bowl. He looked up at her expectantly. "Is that all?" he seemed to say. "No roast chicken? No filet mignon?"

"Eat," she said.

Not that she planned to call anybody, but what *would* be a legitimate excuse to be looking for someone who might have been missing for – she tried to recall the notes she'd made, while she spooned ground coffee into a filter in the coffee machine – twenty-five years? An old school friend? No. She didn't even know what school the woman had attended. Could she have found something belonging to the woman? Something at least twenty-five years old? *Oh, hell*, she thought, *screw that.* She was only looking for a phone number. Someone named Corbett, in or around Hastings, Michigan.

Hastings was a familiar name to anyone who'd spent much time in Vancouver. El thought of Hastings Street, which ran from Coal Harbor on the west side of Vancouver – close to the entrance to Stanley Park – through downtown Vancouver, across East Vancouver, all the way to the northeast corner of Burnaby. The intersection of Hastings and Main had at one time been the downtown hub of Vancouver, the site of the Carnegie Library and the once elegant Balmoral Hotel. Now the neighborhood was referred to as the Downtown East Side, and that mile of Hastings Street was a skid road populated by the homeless, addicted and destitute. But Hastings, to El, still had an aristocratic ring to it, and made her think of the thoroughbred races at Hastings Park – the sport of kings – and the Battle of Hastings in 1066.

El looked up the coordinates for Hastings, Michigan in the back of the road atlas, then turned to the page with the map of Michigan. There it was, a relatively small dot almost in the center of a skewed rectangle with Grand Rapids, Lansing, Battle Creek and Kalamazoo at the corners, each anywhere from twenty to thirty miles away. What did people do in Hastings, she wondered. What's the weather like in June? What kind of talk would she hear if she sat down at the corner table in a coffee shop? That was one of the things that she loved about her job, and also hated about her job. She got to travel to towns all over North America in her imagination, but never for real. She sent her drivers out on the road, and sometimes they came back with stories, but mostly they came back with a shrug and a blank look. "What was Hastings like?" she might ask. "Any other town in the Midwest," might be the reply.

Sometimes El wished she were still a driver, just so she could see all of these places with her own eyes, but life was much more comfortable with a phone and a desk in front of her, a lunch room and washroom just a few steps away. She'd paid her dues on the road, sitting behind a steering wheel, watching for a place to buy a decent meal, and trying to time her need to pee with her arrival at a parking lot that could accommodate an eighteen wheeler.

The gurgling of the coffee machine told her coffee was ready, and she was soon back at her desk with a big mug full of it – two spoons of sugar and a hefty splash of real cream – ready to make her calls. She got hold of directory assistance and soon had a list of Corbetts in the 616 area code. There were twenty-six of them, none of them April. Now what?

She couldn't very well give Hunter twenty-six telephone numbers that *might* belong to a relative of April Corbett. She wondered if perhaps she could call a few, just to see if she could weed out the ones that had never heard of an April. If they said yes, they knew April, she could always hang up. The first two numbers she called just rang and rang, the third one went to an answering machine, but she didn't leave a message. She was about to try the fourth number when the front door opened and her friend, Marilyn Jenkins, dropped a pile of paperwork on the front counter with a big sigh.

"You're early," they said to each other at the same time.

"Whatcha doin'?" said MJ. "Want to go to Edna's for breakfast?"

El dropped the receiver back in its place and decided the remaining phone calls could wait.

Edna's Kitchen was a small, bare restaurant that catered to workers in the industrial complex where Watson Transportation's warehouse was situated. The tables were cheap and plain, the chairs small and uncomfortable, especially for big women like El and MJ, but the service was fast and the food edible.

"That's new," said MJ, pointing at a framed print on the wall.

El looked around and saw a total of six prints, three on each of the side walls. They were all scenes of dogs playing poker.

Susan, the proprietor of Edna's, appeared at the table, arriving swiftly and not quite silently in her white Reeboks. She and her husband, Walter, were Chinese-Canadians. They owned and worked at Edna's, she waiting tables and manning the cash register, he doing double duty as short order cook and dishwasher. Walter was seldom seen outside the kitchen, and only communicated to the clientele with smiles and nods from behind the kitchen's pass-through. El suspected he didn't speak English, because Susan always shouted her orders in Chinese, or what sounded like Chinese.

"Coffee?" Susan, always in a hurry, filled both cups at the speed of light. "What you want to eat?"

"Nice addition to the décor," said El, nodding at the print.

"Junk shop. Five dollar. Nice, eh?"

MJ congratulated Susan on the find. El ordered a fried egg sandwich and MJ ordered scrambled eggs and sausages with toast.

"That all you're having?" she asked El.

"I stopped at MacDonald's on my way in."

"So what are you doing in so early?"

"Trying to find a woman named April Corbett."

"You got a shipment with no address and phone number?"

"I'm helping Hunter…"

"Not again." MJ rolled her eyes. "You planning to open the Watson Detective Agency?"

El didn't know why she bothered talking to MJ about this kind of thing. She could count on MJ for some smart remark, making fun of her attempts at helping Hunter with an investigation.

"Forget it. What about you?"

"Rush shipment for some outfit in Boston Bar. River rafters near Hell's Gate rapids. I guess they've got a big group booked for tomorrow and one of their rafts got trashed."

"You ever done that?" asked El. "River rafting?"

"Are you kidding?" MJ made a face as if El had suggested she body surf through Hell's Gate. "I'd probably sink the raft. Besides, I'm not crazy about the idea of white water. I'm even scared to get close enough to the edge of the Fraser Canyon to throw rocks in the river."

Susan arrived with their orders, deposited them on the table and was gone again in less than three seconds.

"Why would you even *want* to throw rocks in the river?" El asked, shaking ketchup into her fried egg sandwich.

"I wouldn't. But it might be cool to throw a bottle in the river, you know, with a message inside. Your name and the date and something like, call me if you get this note. Who knows, it could end up in San Francisco." She waved a sausage in the air. "Or even Japan."

A message in a bottle? El's chewing slowed as an idea began to take shape. That was possible, wasn't it? A bottle found floating where? Why not the mighty Fraser? Anyone heading for the Yukon would have driven through B.C. and was sure to have reached the Fraser River at some point in their journey, anywhere along its eight hundred and fifty mile length, from a spring high in the northern Rockies to its ultimate destination near Vancouver. Entirely possible…

Not only that, but Watson Transportation's warehouse was on an island – Annacis Island – in between the two main arms of the Fraser as it widened at its delta, so it made perfect sense that a bottle could wash ashore near here, maybe be buried for years in the silt of the delta. What a creative excuse to be looking for a girl from Hastings, Michigan, thought El. Not that she would use the excuse, of course. She was only looking for a phone number after all.

"Thanks, MJ," she said, but refrained from mentioning why.

"No way," said MJ. "You're paying for your own damn sandwich."

CHAPTER ELEVEN

Hunter was back at Betty Salmon's cabin again, early on the morning after he'd picked her up in Chicken. He found Betty Salmon working in her kitchen garden, and Goldie chopping kindling over at the woodpile. Betty got to her feet when she saw him, holding a stick she'd been using to poke holes in the dirt. The dog met him at the Blazer, sniffed his pant legs, then trotted behind him.

"Why are you here?" Betty asked, demanded almost. "Is it about Orville?"

"Good morning to you, too, Betty," he said cheerfully. He'd seen a softer side of her yesterday, and was determined not to let her put that wall back up. "I come bearing gifts." He held up a thermos of coffee he'd brought from the lodge. "Can I tempt you with hot coffee? I've even brought cream." He dug in his jacket pocket and pulled out a handful of little creamers.

She maintained a stern face, but dropped the stick and walked toward him, wiping one hand against the other, then both against the denim on her thighs. "Real cream?"

By the time he'd poured the coffee, Goldie had joined them. "Any news?" she asked.

He passed each of them a mug of coffee across the plank table before pouring what was left into the thermos lid for himself. "Sort of," he said, sitting down opposite them.

"I haven't been totally honest with you," he said. "I told you I knew April on a personal level when she worked in Whitehorse." He didn't want them to think the relationship had been more than it was, so he added, "She was waiting tables in a bar my friend and I used to go to and we used to talk. What I didn't tell you was that at the time, I was a member of the Whitehorse RCMP, and was the first officer on the scene at the cabin near Johnson's Crossing where she was living with a man named Martin Blake. At least, that was what he called himself."

"On the scene? Like, the scene of a crime?" Goldie asked.

He nodded. "There was no one in the cabin, but there was a lot of blood, and evidence that a grizzly had been there. The man, and your mother, of course, were missing."

The girl shuddered visibly. Betty Salmon just stared at him, her face like stone.

"The grizzly killed him?" Goldie asked.

"Nobody knows. No body was ever found. The man's dog team was still there, five dogs, chained to their houses."

"Do you think my mother killed him?" Her voice was almost a whisper.

"I was afraid the man – or someone, or something – had killed your mother, until I saw you."

"What happened to the dogs?" There was a note of accusation in Betty Salmon's voice, and Hunter wasn't surprised that she was more concerned about the dogs than the man.

"One of our dog men took charge of them." He didn't know the details, and didn't want to speculate.

"Are you still with the police, then?" asked Goldie.

"No." He took a deep breath. "And yes. I still have friends at the Whitehorse detachment." He addressed Betty. "You remember I told you yesterday that the RCMP will probably want to see any personal belongings that Orville may have left here? Well, given I'm heading back to Whitehorse today, Staff Sergeant Bart Sam of the RCMP has asked me to collect those belongings and deliver them to the detachment." He and Bart had discussed the pros and cons of this, knowing that anything a civilian brought might not have any value in court if it came to a prosecution for murder. However, at present there wasn't enough evidence against Orville to justify sending an officer of the law to Eagle for them, but having access to his personal effects might make the difference.

He noticed both women turn to look at a makeshift tent near the edge of the clearing. "Is everything of his over there?" he asked.

The two women accompanied him to Orville's campsite. Like many travelers prepared for the unpredictable on northern highways, Orville had evidently packed up much of his gear and taken it in the truck. Consequently, there was no bedroll or sleeping bag, nor any cooking supplies, but it was clear he had intended to return, for the overhead tarp was still in place, secured to trees, and there was some miscellaneous gear stacked underneath it, including a rusty gold pan, a tangle of steel chain, an old chainsaw, a small gas can, an axe and a shovel, plus two coils of dirty rope. A tarp covered another pile of goods. Hunter lifted up the edge of it.

"Is any of this yours?"

The women peered at what was there, but didn't touch anything until Betty nudged a grime-stained canvas bag with her foot. "Winter clothes, maybe," she said. "It's all Orville's. That old snow machine, too." Her face still stone, she turned and walked away.

Hunter felt uncomfortable. Loading the man's possessions – worth nothing to most people, but treasured implements of survival for their owner – in the back of the Blazer, it was almost like going through the belongings of the dead, and a better picture of Orville – a man he had still not met – took shape in his mind. A resourceful outdoorsman, a dreamer with low income and high hopes, used to surviving in the bush. A man who had been kind to Betty Salmon and given her hope. Hunter looked forward to meeting him, if circumstances permitted it, and also found himself hoping that Orville wasn't guilty of the murder Bart was investigating.

When he walked into the summer kitchen to say goodbye, Goldie was finishing her coffee, a paperback book open on the table in front of her.

"Where's your grandmother?"

"In the cabin. She's upset you didn't tell her yesterday you were with the police."

"I'm not." Why did it feel like a lie? He might not be on their payroll, but he had to acknowledge to himself that sometimes he still felt like a member of the force. He'd told Betty yesterday that she could trust him. Irrational as it was, he felt like he'd let her down.

"This was my mother's." Goldie held up the book, interrupting his train of thought. "Walt Whitman. Do you like poetry?"

"Not something I read, as a rule."

"Me neither." She pulled out what looked like a Polaroid picture. "This was in it, a note that she left for Gran."

He took it from her. It was a typical tourist photo of that decade from the north. Bears seen from the highway. He turned it over and read the note.

"Can I take this?" he asked. "It could be important in helping find your mom."

She reached for it. "These things are all I have of my mother's," she said. "There's no way I can let you take it. Besides, I don't see how it could help."

He let her take it from him. "Is there a photocopier anywhere in town?" He'd rather have the original, but a copy would be better than nothing. "The RCMP will want to compare the handwriting to a note they received around the same time."

"Do you think the other note was from my mother?"

"It's possible. The timing was right."

"Does this mean the Mounties are actively looking for my mother?"

Hunter didn't want to give her false hope, but at the same time, it didn't seem fair to keep her in the dark. "Last I heard, they were considering reopening the unsolved disappearance I just told you about. Now that I know she survived, I expect they'll try to locate her."

She reached out as if to touch his arm. "Please, please, help me find my mother."

"I'll do what I can."

"Will you call me after you talk to the Mounties in Whitehorse? Call me at Yukon Sally's. You'll be in Whitehorse tomorrow?"

"I can't promise you we'll find her."

"But you can promise to call me, can't you? I won't rest until I know what's happening."

He gave her a gentle smile. "It may take them a while, Goldie."

"But I don't want to believe they're working on it if they're not. Will you let me know?"

"Yes. I will. I'll let you know."

As usual, when El got back to the office her phone had already started ringing. Drivers, shippers, receivers.

Can you get me a trip back home? I've been on the road four weeks already.

Where's my freight? It was supposed to be here yesterday.

How much will it cost to get a load shipped to San Jose? Can you pick it before four thirty?

Things quieted down around five o'clock. El ordered a delivery from the local pizza joint, put on a fresh pot of coffee, and pulled out the list of numbers she'd got from the Michigan operator. Peterbilt growled – a sound much like marbles rolling over hardwood – and punctuated his growl with a couple of sharp barks. El scowled at the little black dog; his glittery little eyes were fixed on her face and his curled up tail jerked back and forth. She sighed and hoisted herself out of her big captain's chair.

"Okay, Pete. We'll walk around the yard until the pizza guy gets here."

Pete got to the door before she did and put his little paws on it, as if his twenty pounds were enough to push it open. They strolled the yard between a couple of parked eighteen wheelers and a few empty trailers. Pete lifted his leg on a broken wood pallet, and sniffed at an old Subway wrapper that lay flattened on the asphalt. El followed him around until the pizza guy pulled up in a VW Rabbit that had seen better days.

Ten minutes later, two slices of pizza under her belt and a fresh coffee beside the phone, El began dialing, trying to find a woman named April Corbett for Hunter. No luck the first few calls. When anyone answered, she simply asked, "Is April Corbett there?" If they said 'no', she would ask, "Do you know April? Is this the right number?" If they said, something like 'there's no April at this number', she would ask, "Are you related to April? Do you know how I could reach her?" After half a dozen calls, she took a break for another slice of pizza. Peterbilt's pitiful but hopeful expression moved her to share a couple slices of salami with him.

Three calls later, she got a response that she wasn't totally prepared for.

"Who wants to know?" It was a man's voice, confident but not belligerent.

El cleared her throat. "Uh. I – I guess that means you know April?"

"Who are you, and why are you looking for April?" Well, maybe a little belligerent.

"I live in British Columbia," she began, knowing that anyone with caller ID would have her number anyway. She couldn't very well just hang up at this point. "I – uh – found a note in a bottle."

"Huh? What kind of idiotic story is that?"

"There's nothing idiotic about it!"

She heard a woman's voice in the background. "Who is it, Cal?"

His voice, muted, "Some broad in South America looking for an April Corbett. Ever heard of her?" A pause. "Me neither."

"So just hang up."

El beat him to it.

She slid her fingers under a fourth slice of pizza and lifted it out of the box, absently pulling off a small piece of salami for Pete before taking a big bite out of the droopy end. She was offended that So-and-so Dickhead Corbett had called her story idiotic. There must be a way to make the bottle story sound more legitimate. Or could she call herself a private investigator? Publisher's Clearing House? Some kind of market researcher? How about a lawyer? A lawyer, say, looking for a distant relative of someone who died without a will? She moved the pizza to her left hand and began scribbling in her note book. If she added enough details, people would think it had to be true.

Seven calls later, a man answered. El put a smile on her face before saying, "I'm with Watson Investigations and at the request of a client, we're looking for an April Corbett who might have been in British Columbia in the early seventies. Any chance she's a relative of yours?" After seven calls, she had started sounding pretty professional, if she did say so herself.

"You mean my sister?"

"That could very well be. The April Corbett I'm looking for stopped to help a woman search for her lost dog at a rest stop in the Fraser Canyon." She looked at Pete with a smug smile. "It was a little black dog, sort of like a Pomeranian. It had run off after a chipmunk and ended up falling off a ledge down a steep hill. The woman in question – her name was Edna, Edna Jenkins – was rather, uh, corpulent –," El glanced down at her own rather large thighs, "– and unable to get down the hill to retrieve the wayward dog. So April, perhaps the same April Corbett who is your sister, at no small personal risk to herself, slid down that hill to rescue little Blackie." Here she paused long enough for feedback.

"That sounds like something April would do."

Eureka! "So apparently Ms. Jenkins is ailing and wanting to include a little something for April in her will, but needs to find out where she is and how she can be contacted. First of all, was your sister in British Columbia – perhaps just passing through – in or around 1972?"

"Could be. She was somewhere in the west. I know she spent some time in the Canadian north. She was planning to go to Alaska but never made it there."

El could barely contain her excitement, but kept her voice as professional as she was able. "And where is April now?"

There was an uncomfortable pause, then, "I really don't like to give out that kind of information Ms…?"

El glanced at the cover of the Road King magazine under her left elbow. "Mack," she blurted out, but it didn't sound like a real name, so she quickly corrected herself, "Marilyn MacKenzie." She'd used MJ's last name for the dog lady, so why not use her first?

"I'll try to reach her myself, and have her get in touch with you. How's that?"

How indeed? Should she give out the Watson Transportation number, her cell number, or her home number? Not that it mattered much, since all her calls were forwarded when she wasn't in the office. What if this April called and got a voice message that had nothing to do with investigations or lawyers? What if this April knew very well that she had never rescued a small dog in the Fraser Canyon? Would she even call back at all? "That will be fine," she said, and recited the Watson 1-800 number. She knew from experience that a lot of people wait for someone to call them again rather than pay for a long distance call.

El hung up the phone and slouched back into her chair. After a big sigh and a couple of minutes staring at her phone, she looked over at Peterbilt and said, "What the hell did I tell him my name was?"

By the time Hunter had collected Sorry and their things from the lodge, being careful to stash their own belongings separate from Orville's, and Goldie had brought him a photo copy of her mother's note, they were late getting on the road. The drive to Whitehorse would take over eleven hours, but factoring in Sorry's meal breaks, there was no way they'd get to Whitehorse much before midnight. Hunter took the wheel from Eagle to Dawson City, and after lunch and a fuel stop, Sorry took over from there.

"It's just not me," said Sorry, slamming the door of the Blazer and jamming the key into the ignition. "She always said she loved me just the way I am, and now she wants me to be somebody else. It's not fuckin' fair." He peeled out of the parking spot and onto King Street, heading for Front Street and the Klondike Highway.

"Take it easy," Hunter said. "The riverboat's just up ahead. Watch out for foot traffic."

"Don't be such an old lady."

"What turned you so sour, all of a sudden?" Hunter frowned. "You want me to drive?"

Sorry slowed down as they neared the Keno, the big white riverboat with its orange paddlewheel, beached on the bank of the Yukon River in Dawson since 1960. A couple with two young kids stood on the river side of the road, waiting to cross Front Street to the shops on the other side. Sorry braked to a sudden stop to let them cross.

Hunter couldn't help noticing that the little girl and boy were roughly the same ages as Sorry's two kids, Sasha and Bruno. Sorry watched them cross, the little boy between the two parents, holding their hands, running ahead until he was airborne, then swinging back to the ground as they caught up with him. Sorry let out a long sigh.

"So I take it you were talking to Simone," said Hunter as the Blazer accelerated at a slower pace.

The big man nodded. "Some chick she met at Bruno's daycare –"

"Chick?"

"Another mother, okay? You're right, I'm in a fuckin' sour mood. Humor me, okay?" Sorry threw a scowl in Hunter's direction. "Anyway, Mo obviously was airing our dirty laundry to this *mother*, and the *mother* is some kind of do-gooder so she talked her husband into finding me a job, except said *mother* was talking about it to my *wife*, as if I was some kind of idiot who couldn't find my own job or be trusted to talk to this guy myself."

"That sounds promising. What kind of job?"

"Local deliveries. Some kind of distributor, plumbing I think. The guy's the manager or maybe the owner. "

"Making deliveries in the Lower Mainland? Day shift, I assume. Sounds perfect for a guy with two young kids. And sounds like Mo wants to keep you around after all."

Hunter let Sorry chew on the idea as he drove out of Dawson City. For miles along the highway, they could see tailings ponds and piles of gravel, evidence of man's historic and ongoing search for El Dorado. Dark green hills rose on either side, a pristine backdrop to the swiss cheese landscape.

Somewhat more subdued, after they passed the Dawson airport the big man said, "Can you see me reporting in to work every day with a smarmy smile on my face? Yes, boss. No, boss. Whatever you say, boss. Every day, forever?" He snorted. "When I have an opinion on something, I fuckin' say it out loud. That's the way I am. She knew that the first day she met me."

"You sound like a petulant teenager, Dan. You have a family to support. Suck it up, be a man, and do something worthwhile with your life."

"But –"

"Look. Abraham Lincoln said something like, people are as happy as they make up their minds to be. You haven't even started this new job, and you're already looking for excuses to quit. Why don't you start looking for excuses to like the job, and reasons to like the guy who's prepared to give it to you? You want to stick with Mo – or her to stick with you – then make up your mind to work at it, and enjoy the ride."

Sorry sulked for a few seconds, then said, "Look who's talking."

Hunter clenched his jaw and took a deep breath. He sure walked into that one. What had he done to save his marriage to Christine? In retrospect, he guessed he'd put blinders on. He figured her complaints weren't as serious as she made them out to be, trusted she would put up with his workaholic behavior because it went with his job and besides, she knew he was a Mountie before she said 'yes'. And then he thought about the nights he didn't make it home for dinner because he was at the bar with Ken, trying to keep his best friend sane.

"Our situation was complicated."

"Yeah, right."

"Our kids were older. And they were both girls. Bruno, especially, needs a good male role model."

"And you figure that's me?"

"Yes, Dan. I do."

By unspoken mutual agreement, they dropped the subject for the rest of the drive.

Hunter woke up feeling cold and stiff. He was in the reclined passenger seat of the Blazer; the jacket he'd covered his chest and shoulders with had slipped down to his waist. He blinked his eyes against the climbing sun, as the details of his arrival in Whitehorse some hours before came back to him, his memory gradually emerging from the fog of sleep.

It had been too late to go to Bart's, and he'd decided that what was left of the night wasn't worth paying for a hotel room, or even driving the streets of Whitehorse looking for a vacancy sign. They decided to drive to the mechanic's to see if the Blue Knight was outside so at least one of them could take advantage of the bunk in the Freightliner's sleeper. The mechanic's dog had raised a ruckus, rousing the mechanic, who was gracious enough not to swear out loud although he was none too pleased to see them. Hunter stupidly agreed to toss for the sleeper, and lost. So now Sorry was snoring peacefully on a mattress in the sleeper while he, the truck's owner, was unsuccessfully trying to get back to sleep in an uncomfortable and smelly SUV. You don't want to roll down the windows in the Yukon during mosquito season, which means pretty much all summer.

So Hunter was not feeling at all refreshed or energetic when he arrived at the RCMP detachment a few hours later. He was escorted to Bart's office, where he slouched in a chair waiting for Bart to come back from a meeting.

"So what have you got for me?"

Bart's voice jolted Hunter out of an involuntary snooze. He yawned and rubbed one eye.

"Keeping you up?"

"Sorry. Orville's belongings are locked in the back of your brother-in-law's Blazer, out in the parking lot. You want to get them now?"

Bart shook his head. "I don't know what to make of him."

"That's not like you. You've got an instinct for people."

"That's the problem. My instinct tells me he's a good man. Why would a good man stick a knife in an old friend?"

"They were friends?"

"The deceased, as it turns out, was using an alias. The man we knew in town as Colin Thompson, owner of Lost Mine strip club and bar, was born Charles Collins in Barrie, Ontario. A records search turned up a claim staked in 1984 by partners Charles Collins and Orville Barstow. Partners usually start out as friends, or at least trusting each other; maybe not so wise on Orville's part. Collins also had a police record: fraud and theft in Toronto in the 70s."

"So the partners had a falling out?"

"Kind of looks that way. Collins showed up in town the spring of '86 with a new name and enough money to buy that bar. That was just a couple years after they staked that claim. Changed his looks, too. I always wondered why a guy would go to the trouble of keeping his head shaved up here. Most mammals up here grow thick coats in the winter. I guess bald was part of his new identity."

"Did Orville admit to anything?"

"His line is pretty much 'Nothing personal, but I'm not talking to you. Charge me and I'll get a lawyer.' So he won't talk until he's charged and he won't talk if he is. I can't say I feel good about it, but given the circumstantial evidence, we've asked the Crown to approve a murder charge. Second degree. At least that way we can search his truck and belongings and have time to look for witnesses. Otherwise, since he'd already fled the country, I wouldn't expect him to stick around."

Just then a constable appeared at the door, piece of paper in hand. "Just got the Barstow warrant," he said. "You want to see him?"

"You bet," said Bart, then to Hunter, "I don't think this will take long. You want to wait here or in the canteen?"

"Any chance I could see the file?"

Bart frowned a second, then slapped a thick folder with his hand and said, "Don't let me catch you reading this." With a wink and a nod, he left the room.

It didn't take Hunter more than a minute or two to lose himself in the file. The gears turned a little slower than they used to, but his drive to investigate came back as strong as if he'd never left the force. He scanned the crime scene photos and the report by the first officers on the scene, then began to look for the witness interviews that had led to Orville being identified as a 'person of interest'.

There were several witness interviews, all of them either employees of Lost Mine or patrons who had been in the bar sometime during the evening prior to Collins' murder. What struck Hunter immediately was that Orville Barstow hadn't been alone, or at least, there had been another man present when Orville had first encountered Collins in the bar. It was Orville, however, who had spoken to Collins. The most detailed witness accounts came from two men who had evidently been sitting at the table next to the one occupied by Orville and his unidentified companion. Hunter read the transcript of each interview twice.

'Colin came up to talk to us –like we're regulars, eh? He sends us free beers sometimes, and sits down with us once in a while. I guess I mean used to. He was a nice guy and I feel real bad for his wife and kid that he's gone. So he was standing beside my buddy's chair and we were talkin', like, and then I see this old guy at the table behind Colin do a double take, like he can't believe what he's hearin'. Then he says, kind of low like, 'Colin's, isn't it?' and Colin freezes, without turning around even, and if you ever heard someone say the blood drained outa his face, well, that's exactly like it was. Like he saw a ghost or somethin'. But he keeps talkin' to us, like he didn't hear the guy. And then the guy says louder, You bleedin' bastard, like, the guy's English, eh? I mean from England.

'You left us for dead, you bastard, he said. You could see Colin start to sweat.' The witness went on to say that they didn't hear the younger man who was with Orville say anything, just Orville. 'But if looks could kill, Colin woulda been a dead man, right that minute.' The witness said Colin continued to pretend he hadn't heard anything, and began to walk away. Orville's companion made as if to get to his feet and follow, but Orville put his hand on the man's arm and said something like 'Now is not the time'. The two finished their drinks in silence – at least, they said nothing that the witnesses could hear – and left the bar. 'From the look on their faces, they were really pissed off at Colin.'

The second witness told the same story, with some critical information added. He walked out to the parking lot just a few minutes after Orville left. He saw Orville get in his truck and drive away, and was able to give the RCMP a fairly accurate description of the truck. Collins had been killed in the parking lot about two hours later. All of the witnesses were asked if they saw Orville's companion get into a vehicle, or if they had ever seen him before or since. None of them had.

Hunter had questions forming in his mind, questions that he would put to Bart. Did they have any additional information on Orville's companion? Did Collins' wife have any information on Collins' past? Did Collins speak to anyone at the bar about, or make any phone calls mentioning, the appearance of the two men? Were the RCMP able to locate anyone in Whitehorse who was previously acquainted with Orville Barstow?

He had to remind himself that he wasn't part of this investigation, that his job now was hauling freight and he still had a delivery to complete once his tractor was repaired. Yet, in spite of that, he felt a sense of frustration, almost a straining at the leash, about his inability to help Bart get to the truth about this man who had befriended an aging Alaskan bush woman and her granddaughter. He had yet to meet Orville, but had already developed a sense of his kindness and good nature.

Bart's return interrupted his musings.

"Damn!" Bart smacked a fist into his open palm. "We've arrested the old codger and he still won't say a damn thing to save himself. He's not the guy – I can feel it – but we can't get him to give us anything else to go on."

"His companion…," began Hunter.

Bart swung around and pointed a finger at him. "Exactly! Who was the guy, and what kind of misguided loyalty won't let Barstow give him up? It's not like they're gang bangers sticking to a club code of honor."

"Is he afraid of this other man?"

Bart shook his head, frowning. "I don't get that feeling. He's so damn calm, seems so open and friendly, almost unflappable. Yet he refuses to cooperate in any way with us."

Hunter rubbed his neck, then ran his hand over his eyes. He'd forgotten how tired he was.

"By the way, you look like hell," said Bart.

"I could use a few more hours of sleep," said Hunter. "Maybe eight or nine of them."

Bart looked thoughtful, stroking his chin as if he had a beard. Then he went still, his eyes went blank, one of those moments Hunter had seen him have before, when he seemed to go somewhere outside his body before coming up with an insight or idea. Was Bartholomew Sam a shaman, like his father? If he was, he didn't share that information with his RCMP colleagues. Hunter watched him closely but said nothing.

"I know what we'll do," said Bart, turning his eyes on Hunter.

Hunter barely noticed the 'we', but somehow knew that what was coming involved him.

"Hunter Rayne," said Bart, with a sly smile, "you are under arrest."

Elspeth was comfortably settled in the big recliner in her living room, sipping on a Coke and reading a secondhand Harlequin from the library book sale when the telephone rang. She groaned, thinking it was the driver she'd sent to Idaho calling for directions again. She had potatoes boiling and a pork chop in mushroom soup gravy simmering on the stove, and had hoped to be sitting down to dinner in about ten minutes. She cranked down the footrest on the recliner and got to her feet.

"Watson!" she said, without thinking. It was the way she always answered the phone.

"Is that the detective agency?" said an uncertain voice on the other end of the line.

El's mouth fell open. "Yes, it is," she said, hoping she didn't have to remember the names she'd given the fellow in Michigan. "Can I help you?"

"Someone there was looking for me, or for someone with the same name as me. My maiden name is Corbett. April Corbett."

El pumped her fist in the air. The fish was on the line. "Yes. Yes, we were."

"Something about rescuing a dog?"

"What I told your brother was that a woman whose dog you rescued wanted to reward you."

"I'm afraid I don't recall the incident. Where was this exactly?"

El took a deep breath. She felt uncomfortable continuing the charade with the woman herself. "Actually, I don't have all the details myself. My job was to locate you – get your phone number, essentially –so that the – uh – my client – could call you himself."

"Himself? It's a man? Who is it that's looking for me?" The voice on the phone had gone from pleasantly curious to suspicious and more than a little anxious.

El didn't want April Corbett to freak right out and refuse to give out her contact information, and she had promised Hunter – sort of – just to find a phone number, not to make the call. "Uh – he's a middleman himself, I guess you could say."

"Oh, my God. It's my daughter. Is it? Is it my daughter? Is she looking for me? Then she's alive?"

El was confused. This was going in a totally different direction from what she'd expected. "Your daughter?" April Corbett was supposed to be missing; Hunter said nothing about a daughter. "Are you the April Corbett who went to the Yukon in the early seventies?"

"Yes! Yes!"

El swallowed hard. She found it so interesting, helping Hunter out, and she would hate to screw up again. More than interesting, she felt so proud, so gratified, that he would let her play a role in something of such consequence, almost life and death. She really, really wanted to succeed this time. "I'm sorry, but I was never told anything about your daughter. But if you can leave your number with me –"

"What's going on? Has something happened to her? If it's not my daughter, who is it that's looking for me?"

El heard a man's voice in the background, although she couldn't make out what he was saying. For sure, she didn't want to give out Hunter's name. Before she could say anything, she heard April say, "I don't know, baby. They want my phone number but they won't tell me why."

Then a man's voice came on the line. "Who is this? Is this some kind of scam?"

What could she say that wouldn't dig her into a deeper hole? "No, sir. Believe me, it will be in her best interest –"

"In *your* best interest, no doubt. If you can't be up front about it, I can't see how it's in my wife's best interest."

"But –," El wished she could think fast enough to solve this before he hung up on her. "This is really important. I'm not at lib-…"

He interrupted her again. "There you go again. I'll be the one to decide if it's important. Just tell me exactly what it's about."

El hated to be interrupted. Many drivers had found that out the hard way. It was one of the few – well, maybe one of the many – ways to make her mad.

"Let me fuckin' finish, asshole!" she bellowed.

The man's response was a definitive 'click', followed by a dial tone.

"Did Orville ever see you?"

Hunter had never seen Orville, but the reverse might not necessarily be true. Orville had been around the first day he'd visited Betty Salmon's cabin; Hunter had seen his old Ford truck, if not the man himself. But had Orville seen him, or seen him well enough to recognize him again? "He might have, from a distance. I should scruffy myself up. Got anything I could wear?"

Bart looked him up and down. "You're not far off my brother-in-law's height and weight. You remember that stuff we took out of the back of his Blazer?"

Hunter wrinkled his nose as he recalled the filthy clothing, steeped in mud and what smelled like motor oil. "So what's my story?"

"You've got to have something in common with our Mr. Barstow, right?"

A few hours later, a disheveled, limping miner was escorted to a holding cell in the detachment lock-up. He wore a pair of cargo pants and a wrinkled olive drab shirt. One young constable unlocked the cell door, and another gave the miner a gentle shove with a pleasant, "Here you go, buddy. Make yourself at home."

The miner resisted with a, "But he deserved what he got. I'm not the bad guy here." He planted his feet outside the cell and grabbed one of the bars.

The constable gave him another shove – rougher this time – and said, "Tell it to the judge, buddy. No good talking to me."

Hunter stood looking after the two constables as they walked away. The detachment building had been only five years old when he'd been a young constable here in 1972, and it was beginning to show its age. It felt so familiar on the other side of the bars. This side was a different story. He grabbed two bars and leaned his head against the door for a minute or two before turning around to examine the cell and its only other occupant.

"Welcome," said a jovial looking older man sitting on a bench with his back against the wall. "It's not the Hilton, but it's clean and mosquito free."

"Damn," said Hunter, as if talking to himself. "I don't get it. I just came into town for a restaurant meal, a hotel shower and to see what was holding up our supplies and I end up here in the lock-up. I should've stayed out on the claim and waited until that son-of-a-bitch got back." He shook his head and exhaled loudly. "Assuming he was ever coming back."

"No use crying over spilt milk," said Orville, cheerfully. "Your partner screwed you over?"

"The SOB was supposed to buy supplies and be back within two weeks. Three weeks pass and I figure it's time to hike out and see if he's okay."

"And was he?"

Hunter's miner persona snorted. "He was happy as a pig in shit. He spent half the money on booze and broads – mostly booze from the smell of him – and probably would've spent the whole wad if I hadn't showed up." He shook his head. "You work your ass off and don't come out ahead."

"How did you end up in here?"

"I beat the crap out of him and took all the money he had left – *my* share of it, or maybe less – and then the drunken son-of-a-bitch has the nerve to call the cops and say he was robbed." Hunter rubbed a grimy sleeve across his nose and immediately regretted it. It took everything he had to keep from gagging at the smell. The shirt had obviously been rolled up dirty and wet, and now smelled like wet dog. He did his best to look sorry for himself for a couple of minutes, then walked over and sat beside Orville.

"How about you? What's a nice guy like you doing in a place like this? You remind me of Santa Claus."

Orville smiled, but didn't seem in a hurry to reply, and that gave Hunter a flash of concern that Orville had recognized him, so he glossed over his question by adding, "I hope when Mickey sobers up he'll get them to drop the charges. He's not a bad guy when he's sober."

"I'm sure you'll be out of here in no time," Orville said.

Hunter had to agree with Bart. Orville Barstow didn't strike him as a murderer, especially not one who would stick a knife under an old friend's ribs, unless he was an extraordinarily talented actor. So what about Orville's mystery companion? Who was he, and how could Hunter shift the conversation in a direction that would bring him into it?

"When he's sober, Mickey'd give me the shirt off his back. He'd even take a hit for me." Hunter began to rub at a black smudge on the bench between himself and Orville as a cover for watching the older man out of the corner of his eye. "Like he was my big brother, you know what I mean?"

"So he's a true friend, then," said Orville, in the same light and friendly tone. He, too, was idly watching Hunter's finger stroke the bench.

Hunter kept rubbing away at the smudge. "More than a friend, I mean." The witnesses said Orville's companion was a younger, taller man. They'd been asked to describe him further, but the witnesses didn't have much to add, except that he had the dark hair and sparse beard typical of a native. On a hunch, Hunter said, "Once he said I was like a son to him."

It was almost imperceptible, but Hunter had years of experience in recognizing tells. Orville's eyes flicked away from the bench and he raised his head slightly. He said nothing in response.

"I always wished I had a son myself," Hunter said. "Must be nice to know you've left a piece of you behind in the world, eh?" He stopped rubbing the bench and leaned closer to Orville. "Sorry, I don't know your name. Why are you in here, anyway? You seem like a real nice guy."

Orville smiled. Sadly, Hunter thought.

"My name is Orville Barstow." He took a breath and looked up, beyond the bars, into a distance that Hunter couldn't see. "And I guess one could say that I'm here in jail because I won't talk to the police."

"That's not a crime."

"No. I don't think it is."

"Then why are you really here?"

"Ultimately, I guess it's because I'm old and I've had a good life, and I wanted to protect someone dear to me."

"So you got into a fight over a woman, eh?"

"No, no. Nothing like that."

"Either I'm not very smart or you're deliberately trying to confuse me."

"I'm sorry. I guess I am being rather vague"

"So you want me to mind my own business. I can take a hint." Hunter tried to look hurt, gambling that Orville Barstow was sympathetic enough to fall for it.

Orville held up his hands, as if giving up. "I'm sorry," he said again. "It's not that, really. I guess I'm just uncomfortable with the idea that I've been arrested for murder."

Hunter lifted his eyebrows. "Murder? Wow! I never would have guessed you were in for killing somebody. You're just about the farthest thing from a murderer I've ever met."

The old man shrugged. "I never would have guessed I'd be arrested for murder myself. I'd rather cut my losses and walk away from trouble than do something like that."

"So you didn't do it, then."

"Of course I didn't do it."

"Then why did they arrest you?"

Orville seemed to be thinking it over. He leaned in close and spoke in almost a whisper.

"I don't want to incriminate anyone else, you see? I guess a witness gave them my description, because I did talk to the fellow who was killed that night. I don't know for sure what happened, other than what I heard on the radio the next day, but they seem to think it was either me or the fellow I was with. I don't want to make trouble for him, this other fellow."

"So you could get out of here if you gave up this other guy, but you're being noble and taking the fall? Are you crazy?"

"Maybe I am."

"Who is this other guy? Your brother?"

Orville shook his head. Otherwise, he didn't respond.

"Does he know that you're taking a fall for him, this other guy?"

"I'm sure he doesn't even know I'm here."

"Other than that, he wasn't very forthcoming about the crime," said Hunter. He was back in his own clothes, sitting in Bart's office, wishing he could wash the smell of motor oil and wet dog out of his nostrils. As previously arranged, one of the constables had come back to get him after an hour and a half with Orville, saying that the complainant had decided not to press charges. Before leaving, he shook Orville's hand and wished him well.

"I don't think he suspected I was a plant, necessarily. He just wasn't taking any chances."

Bart nodded slowly, obviously considering what Hunter had just told him. "I'll have our team do some more checking," he said. "If it's his son, like you suspect, I don't think there's any record of a marriage, but it's entirely possible that he fathered a child outside of wedlock. Or could it be a nephew? Did he say anything else of significance?"

Hunter leaned back in his chair, closed his eyes and dropped his chin to his chest. He was trying to concentrate on recalling details of his conversation with Orville, but he found himself fighting off the magnetic pull of sleep.

Bart frowned. "Are you okay?"

"I could sure use a coffee," said Hunter, running both hands down his face.

While Bart left his office to get coffee for them both, Hunter leaned forward, his elbows on his knees, eyes to the floor, and thought about his conversation with Orville Barstow. With the possible exception of that one comment about being old and protecting someone dear to him, Orville had kept his conversation upbeat and positive. He had told Hunter that he had done his time as a prospector, had a few small successes that lured him forward, "like some fool donkey following a carrot on a stick." He had seen the money come and go, and had eventually recognized that the excitement of the journey toward El Dorado was a reward in itself.

"I've loved the excitement and anticipation of searching for gold. I loved the sparkle of flakes at the bottom of the pan, being on the creeks and rivers with their dancing ripples and water music, the sight and sound of water running down the sluice box, the long active days under the summer sun and the challenge of wresting my living from this glorious land." Orville's eyes sparkled, much like the gold or the rippling water he spoke of, Hunter thought.

"I also found joy in the winter evenings by the stove, dreaming about how I'd spend next year's riches, and winter days snowshoeing through silent forests in the bracing cold. Now that I'm getting too old for the physical labor involved with prospecting or working a trapping concession, I can still make myself useful, one way or another." He seemed to look inward.

Useful to whom? Hunter wondered if he was thinking of Betty Salmon, or of his companion from the bar.

"I've managed to put away a little, perhaps enough to live frugally for a few more years, I'm fine with that," Orville had continued. "A simple life – in or out of jail – just enjoying the people I meet, appreciating the roof over my head, whether it's a tarp or some cold, concrete edifice. Either way, I'll make the best of whatever each day offers me." Hunter had tried to turn the conversation back to Orville's alleged crime, but the old man had said, "I don't like to dwell on it. I'm confident that things will work out for the best."

Bart returned with two mugs of coffee, handing one to Hunter.

Hunter took a cautious sip, then said, "You were asking about my conversation with Orville. We talked about the north, about gold, about our respective philosophies. I found him so engaging and downright agreeable, it was hard for me to stay in character as a disgruntled prisoner and unsuccessful fellow miner."

"You sure he didn't recognize you?"

Hunter sipped his coffee. It tasted like it had been sitting in the pot too long, but it was hot and strong and better than none at all. He shook his head. "Not a hundred percent. He's got a sort of mischievous look in his eyes that makes you wonder if he's stringing you along."

"I noticed."

"Why isn't he more concerned about the prospect of going to jail for the rest of his life? Could it be that's exactly what he wants? Maybe life in a jail cell with three square meals a day is his idea of a retirement plan. No more scrounging wood against forty below zero winter days, no more fighting off man-eating mosquitoes, no more skinning small rodents for stew and paying through the nose for wilted vegetables and canned milk."

"You think he actually might have killed Collins with that in mind?"

"No. I still don't think he did it. But why would he be protecting a murderer? The answer has got to be somewhere in Orville's past, so that's where you'll have to look." They both fell silent, as if there was no more to be said about Orville Barstow.

"Any news on my cold case from your end?" Hunter asked, setting his empty coffee mug on Bart's desk.

Bart pulled a file folder to the middle of his desk and opened it. "Let's see," he said, skimming pages of notes. "I told you about the note with the name of Grant Sanford. The fingerprints found in the cabin matched those of Sanford, and without a body or witness, we can only assume that was the real identity of the missing man."

"Can I see the photo?"

Bart handed him a faxed black and white photograph of a military ID card. If Hunter was expecting a flash of recognition, it didn't come. He had never met Martin Blake aka Grant Sanford, so that wasn't surprising. He was a little surprised that the man in the 1964 photo – military hair cut, serious demeanor – looked older than he imagined April's lover would be. He studied the photo for another moment, noting the darker skin across his cheeks indicating a ruddy complexion or a recent sunburn.

"How old was he in this photo?" he asked as he handed the photo back.

"Thirty-two."

"That would have made him over forty at the time of his death." April had been barely twenty. The man was at least twice April's age. That surprised him, and he had to remind himself that he'd never had the chance to get to know her well. "Did you find anything on the relatives of Sanford's murdered wife? Any suggestion that they might have tracked him down, looking for revenge?"

"We sent a request to the Louisiana State Police but it's not high on their priority list. Seems records from that time were transferred, along with jurisdiction, from one city to another about ten years ago and they've got more pressing things to worry about than searching for thirty year old files to help us investigate what may or may not have been a murder."

Hunter nodded. Even the RCMP weren't sure this was an actual homicide, given the evidence indicating there'd been a grizzly in the cabin. It would be hard to find a champion to devote time and effort to it, especially once they heard that April had survived. The RCMP might not be motivated to follow up the new leads, but Hunter was. He had to know for sure what had happened to April's lover in the cabin. He couldn't explain it. That's just how he was wired.

"There's a good chance that the woman is still alive," he said.

"What?"

"The missing woman, the one that trapper –Fred Klimmer – thought lived in the cabin with Blake, or Sanford, whatever his name is." He told Bart about meeting the young woman in Eagle who looked like April, about how her mother had been nursed back to health by a bush woman. "April left Betty Salmon a note indicating she was coming back for her baby. I'd like to compare her handwriting with the note about Sanford."

Bart sifted though the file and handed over a photo copy of the note that had been left at the detachment reception desk in 1973. Out of his back pocket, Hunter pulled the copy Goldie had taken of her mother's note on the back of the polaroid, unfolded it, and placed the copies side by side on Bart's desk.

"Not the same handwriting," said Bart.

Hunter frowned. It would take an expert to find similarities. The note on the back of the photo was in cursive script; the note with Sanford's name was in block letters, scrawled with no regard for the lines on the paper.

"Were you able to track down someone in Michigan who knows April?" he asked Bart.

Bart winced. "Not high on the detachment priority list. There's even less justification for me to put manpower on that now that you've told me she survived."

Hunter nodded; that was exactly what he had expected to hear. The RCMP wasn't going to follow up, but El had volunteered to make some calls, trying to track April down. She didn't have the skills, nor the clout of an RCMP investigator, but he had no doubt she would make the time. What were the chances of her coming up with something?

"One thing you might be interested to know, though," said Bart.

Hunter looked up from the two notes he'd been comparing. "What's that?"

"We did find Fred Klimmer. He suffered a stroke a few years back so now he doesn't get around well. He rents a couple of rooms in a private home here in town. I guess he's on social welfare or some kind of disability pension."

"Have you interviewed him?"

Bart shook his head and gave Hunter a lopsided smile. "I've got great respect for you, Hunter, but may I remind you, you're not my boss."

"Right. I guess I'm the one who's really interested in figuring out what happened back in 1972."

"Guilt? Unfinished business?"

"Pardon me?"

"You think you should have solved it yourself years ago, so now you want to finish what you started back in 1972?"

Hunter stood up and stretched. "I haven't tried to psycho-analyze myself, but you could be right. When does your brother-in-law get back?"

"Tomorrow. You ready to give his truck back?"

Hunter nodded. And fervently hoped that his own truck would be ready by then.

CHAPTER TWELVE

Betty Salmon stared after the taillights of the Merc as it headed away from the cabin; she stared without moving until the truck had disappeared behind the trees. Goldie had been restless since yesterday morning, unable to focus on her chores. Today she had decided to drive into Eagle to check for mail, then to Yukon Sally's well before she was due at work, in case there was a call from Hunter or – Goldie hadn't admitted it, but Betty knew it was on the child's mind – even from her mother.

Betty was working in the garden. She planted vegetables in June every year, so that's exactly what she was doing, but this year was not like every year. Something in her disciplined, routine life had shifted, like a log at the base of the woodpile, and her well-ordered world was wobbling, on the verge of collapse. Never mind that she'd known it would come some day. She'd known the child would grow up and want a life of her own, but she'd hoped against hope that it would happen when Goldie's departure would no longer affect her so strongly.

Hootie had lapped up his fill from the water bucket by the outdoor kitchen, and now came to flop down at the edge of the garden. Betty threw down her trowel and went to sit beside him, ruffling the fur on top of his head, then stroking the soft skin of his ear between two fingers. He sighed with contentment, his head resting between his front paws, and Betty sighed, too. Not with contentment, but with a mixture of worry and confusion.

"What do you think, Hootie? What's an old woman to do?" She hadn't realized it until sometime during her sleepless night, but in the short time she had known Orville, she had already come to expect him to be there for her when Goldie left. That funny old man had become a soft place for her to land, a protector and a friend. "Should I tell Goldie where to look for her mother?"

Maybe Goldie's mother wasn't where the letter from April had been postmarked twenty-three years ago. Maybe she had moved on. Maybe she had died. But possibly, the letter's return address would provide a clue to where she could be found. Betty wished now that she had read the letter before tucking it into that Blue Ribbon baking powder tin and hiding it beneath the floorboards of the old cabin in Hootalinqua. The letter might still be there. If she showed Goldie the letter, would the child forgive her for keeping it a secret? *At least now, even if Goldie moves away from Eagle, she will still love me. She will come to visit, she will send pictures and letters, she will sometimes bring her children to come play at my knee.* Could revealing the letter take that all away?

And what of Orville? Was the old man worth fighting for? If she decided he was, what could she do to make sure he came back to her? She didn't even know why he had been taken by the Mounties, whether they would release him and, if they did, whether he would come back to Eagle to stay with her. She had some decisions to make, and depending on what she decided, she would need ideas about how to make things happen.

"I've eaten next to nothing since they took Orville," she told Hootie. She'd had no appetite, and she became convinced that she'd been led to fast, led to seek help the way her mother had taught her, to seek advice from the spirits that had guided her in the past. Deliberate or not, fasting was easy for an old woman to do, and she'd begun to feel lightheaded already. It had been many, many years since she'd asked the spirits to guide her, but now would be the time.

Hootie looked up at her without moving his head from between his paws. "Will you come with me on this journey, old friend?" she asked.

His tail thumped on the dry earth, and she smiled. She got to her feet, steadied herself through a few seconds of dizziness, and walked toward the path that led to the river, confident that the spirits who had led her to fast would now guide her steps to where they awaited her.

Yukon Sally took pity on Goldie and let her start work early.

"You're driving me crazy, pacing around the kitchen," she said. "Two sets of guests have already checked out this morning, so you can get a head start and clean out those two cabins. Don't worry. I'll come and get you if anyone calls."

Goldie stripped the sheets in the first cabin, replaced them with the clean ones she had taken from the laundry room in the lodge. Dirty towels and a bath mat went into the hamper. She picked up the spray bottle and sponge to start cleaning the bathroom, but found herself seated on the side of the bathtub, imagining a telephone call.

First Yukon Sally would holler from the lodge, 'Goldie! Phone call!' and she would run to the lodge and pick up the receiver. 'Hello?' she would say, and a woman's voice on the other end would say, 'Goldie? Is that Golden Dawn?' and she would say, 'Yes. Who is this?' and the woman on the phone would start to cry, and say 'Oh, Goldie! I've been trying to find you for so many years. Goldie, this is your mother.' Then Goldie would start to cry, and tell her mother how much she wanted to see her.

At that point, she stopped imagining the phone call and began to imagine being sent a plane ticket to where her mother lived. Was she back in Michigan? Maybe she had moved to California. What if she lived in Santa Barbara, where Mark was from? What if Goldie could get a ride with Mark back to his home in California and he could take her right to her mother's house?

She heard someone approaching the cabin, so she hurriedly stood up and turned around to spray cleaning solution on the tub. She was on her knees beside the tub, industriously wiping at the enamel surface when footsteps stopped behind her, but no one spoke. She turned her head to see who it was.

"Don't stop. I'm enjoying the view." It was Mark.

Goldie tossed the sponge at him and got to her feet. "You brat," she said. "It's not nice to sneak up on people."

"Nothing sneaky about me, Goldie." He stomped his feet, his boots thudding on the plank floor. "Aunt Sally told me you were here, so I thought I'd see if you were ready for a break. I brought you a soda."

Goldie was flattered; she smiled at him, but not broadly enough to let on just how thrilled she was. "I've barely started, but I could use something cold. How about we go outside, though? I've never been keen on spending my breaks in a bathroom."

They wandered down to the bench beside the creek. He was so close that as they walked over the uneven ground, his arm bumped her shoulder now and then. She didn't move away. On the bench, he motioned her to sit down first, then sat so close to her that their thighs touched. She moved her leg away a little, as casually as she could.

"Did Sally tell you that I'm waiting for a phone call?"

"She did. About your mother, right? So you're not an orphan after all." He grinned and gave her a gentle poke in the ribs with his elbow.

She nudged him back, aware that they were both initiating physical contact, as if compelled to touch each other by some magnetic force. It both frightened and fascinated her. Frightened because she didn't want to be one of those pathetic girls who were used by an Outsider over the summer and who then never heard from their so-called boyfriends again; fascinated because she'd never liked a boy this much before, and the sensations he stirred in her were new and so exhilarating, she began to feel lightheaded, almost giddy. He moved a lock of hair off her face, his fingertips ever-so-softly tracing a line across her cheek, from the tip of her nose to the top of her ear. She could understand why those girls had given in. Could she ever.

His hand moved from her ear to her neck, gently but firmly pulling her face toward his. She couldn't make herself pull away. Then his lips were on hers and he kissed her tentatively, like an exploration, as if his lips were asking hers, *does this feel right to you?* She kissed him back softly, and in seconds they had their arms around each other, locking them face to face and lips to lips, and she felt his tongue part her lips and enter her mouth. She kissed him back, each taste of his mouth increasing her hunger for more.

"Goldie! Goldie, where are you?"

It was Sally's voice, shouting. Goldie pulled herself away, wriggled out of Mark's arms.

"Goldie! Your phone call! Can you hear me?"

She stood up and looked at Mark, offering him an uncertain smile, then turned away. "I hear you, Sally," she shouted back. "I'm on my way."

When she reached the lodge kitchen, she was almost breathless, and grateful that her red face could be attributed to running. Sally held out the receiver toward her and she grabbed it with both hands. "Hello?"

It was Hunter's voice, not her mother's, that answered back.

"We may have found your mother," he said.

Hunter had installed himself at a payphone in the lobby of the Klondike Inn where he could use his credit card to make some calls cheaper than on his cell phone. His first call was to Watson Transportation. He hoped El wasn't too busy to carry on a complete conversation without putting him on hold, but that was not to be. She put him on hold without even giving him time to identify himself.

"You back on the road?" was the first thing she said when she came back on the line.

He told her not yet.

"I thought you said the parts were due in today. You've been gone a whole frickin' week already. What's the hold up? What am I gonna tell the mine?"

"The mechanic says the parts arrived too late for the plane out of Edmonton; they might be here this afternoon, or maybe not until tomorrow."

She swore, but Hunter knew how to divert her attention. "Any luck tracking down April Corbett?"

"Oh, yeah!" she almost growled. "Watson Investigations, at your service." He heard her laugh, just a quick 'heh, heh'.

"Well?"

El paused long enough for Hunter to realize she wasn't going to be telling the whole truth. He sighed. "You called her, didn't you? Do you realize that by doing so, you may be interfering with the RCMP's investigation?"

"Whoa! You're the one who asked me to look for her."

"I asked you to look for a phone number."

"Give your head a shake, Hunter. If I hadn't made a bunch of calls – at my expense, I might add – right now you'd be writing down a list of thirty or forty phone numbers, and then having to call every one of them to see if they knew her. I saved you a lot of trouble. I tracked her down through her brother, and found her somewhere that you'd never have thought of looking for her. Her brother wouldn't give me her number, but he gave her mine and she was curious enough to call."

El was right. She had saved him a lot of trouble. He had no choice but to apologize.

"That's better. And before you ask, no, I didn't tell her who I was or who you were, or why you wanted to find her. I made up a story, and I came out looking like a total idiot, so her husband hung up on me. Lucky for you I have caller ID on my phone. Now you can bloody well call her yourself, and good luck to you."

He apologized again. "You did good, El. Thank you."

"It was a lot of work," she said, her voice petulant.

"And I appreciate it."

She finally gave him the number, and told him that it was an Oregon area code. Then she gave him another earful about the delay in delivering the load for the mine near Fairbanks. "Get on it, Hunter. I better not find out you've been holding up that shipment just to play detective with your friends up there."

"You know me better than that," he started to say, but she'd already hung up.

His next call was to the mechanic, who promised to call him on his cell phone as soon as there was an update on the repairs. Then it was time to make the call to Oregon. He leaned back in the chair, hands behind his head, eyes on the ceiling. He believed in planning ahead in situations like this, and it seemed especially important this time, with the possibility that his own emotions as well as April's could come into play.

What he didn't plan for was no answer, not even an answering machine. He tried a second time, just in case he'd hit the wrong numbers. Again, no answer.

When he called Goldie, as promised, he could only tell her that he had a good lead, but hadn't yet managed to reach the woman that could be her mother. He knew she depended on receiving his calls while she was at Yukon Sally's lodge. "Can they get a message to you if you go back home?"

"Yes," she said. "If you call after I've gone home, I'm sure Mark will come get me."

Hunter remembered the young man with the Jeep who'd been sharing a beer with Goldie, then pictured a young RCMP constable chatting up a dark haired waitress who looked just like her, some twenty odd years ago.

He smiled to himself as he hung up the phone.

Lost Mine was closed. The owner – whether he was Colin Thompson or Charles Collins – had obviously been the heart and soul of the place, and now there was no one to unlock the doors in the morning or close up for the night, no one to order the beer and liquor from the wholesaler, order the food and stock the freezer, no one to supervise the employees, hire and fire them or even pay them. There was a dark stain in the parking lot where the owner's blood had spread through the gravel. Hunter drove past it and parked close to the entrance.

He recognized the place. It was the same bar where he'd met April Corbett in the spring of 1972 soon after he arrived in Whitehorse at his first posting with the RCMP. He'd been there many a time with his friend Ken Marsh, but in those days it went by the name of the Sluice Box Pub. They used to serve good pub food like burgers and fries and beef dip sandwiches, the kind of food that Sorry was looking for right now.

"Just give me a minute," Hunter told him when Sorry said yet again how hungry he was. "I'd like to get the lay of the land."

He walked up to the front door and then along the narrow covered deck in front of the building, peering into the dark interior from the few windows, one of which sported a large CLOSED sign with bright red letters. He remembered that dark pubs and steak houses had been popular in the 70s, and the Sluice Box was no exception. Winter or summer, there was always the same comfortably dark interior with nubbled glass tea light holders throwing orange light in the middle of each table. He couldn't see much, but what he did see looked much the same. Heavy wooden tables and chairs. Plank floor. Long dark bar lined with stout stools. Dart board and pool table in the back.

He didn't know what he'd hoped to see here, but when he was a detective he always made a point of visiting crime scenes on his own, after the forensic unit had left. He wanted to get a feel for the site, try to imagine the 'before' picture as well as the 'after'. He turned away from the building and surveyed the parking lot. Sorry was lounging against the hood of the Blazer, smoking a cigarette. His head turned at the sound of a motorcycle engine, and two bikes came roaring into the lot, raising a light cloud of dust. Instead of parking in front, they drove around the side of the building. Hunter walked in the direction the bikes had disappeared. The plank deck continued around the corner, lined with a railing that looked like a hitching pole. The lot here wasn't wide enough for cars, but it was a perfect place to park a bike.

"Hello, there," he said. "You heard the place is closed?"

The two men had parked at an angle to the deck. They each stood beside a bike and were taking off their helmets.

"I wondered why the parking lot was so empty," said the older of the two. "Why's it closed?"

"Did you know the owner, Colin Thompson?"

"Maybe to see him. Not personally. Why?"

"He died last week. I expect the place will be up for sale."

The two men looked at each other. "Where to now?" the younger one asked. The owner's death obviously didn't interest him.

"Are you boys from around here?"

"Nope. Just pass through every year going to Dawson for the midnight sun."

"Were either of you here last week, by any chance?"

They hadn't been. "Not since last year," one said. Hunter thanked them and walked away.

"You done here? Let's go find someplace to eat." Sorry opened the door of the SUV and slid inside before Hunter could reply.

Seated in a nearby diner, stirring cream into his coffee, Hunter speculated aloud that the reason no one had seen Orville's companion get in his vehicle and drive away was because the man had parked around the side of the building, which meant he probably had a motorcycle. "That'd be an extravagance up here."

"What do you mean by that?" asked Sorry. He blew the paper off his straw and it flew across the table to land in Hunter's coffee.

Hunter raised an eyebrow as he lifted the paper out of his coffee and dropped it on a napkin. "A bike's not a good choice for transportation in the Yukon or Alaska. It's too cold for about nine months of the year. I figure that could indicate one of two things: either Orville's companion doesn't live in the north, or he owns both a motorcycle and another vehicle, probably a truck. He's paid – is still paying in insurance and upkeep – on his main transportation as well as his bike. That makes the bike an extravagance."

"Is that supposed to be some kind of clue?"

"If he was a local, or even from a smaller community in the north, they might know him in the local motorcycle shop."

"Yeah, right. 'Hey, buddy! You know a native-indian-looking dude with a beard who owns a motorcycle?' That's not going to get you very far. You got a picture?"

Hunter shook his head.

"Anything else that sets this guy apart from a couple thousand other guys with beards and a bike?"

"He was here in Whitehorse last Friday." Hunter realized that wasn't going to help. "He had grease under his fingernails, the witness said."

Sorry snorted derisively, and sat back as the waitress delivered their lunch.

"So if you found this friend of Orville's, you figure the cops have enough to arrest him?"

"I'd hope he's man enough to turn himself in once he finds out Orville's been arrested and is willing to take the rap for him. Collins had a rifle behind the seat of his truck. Good chance it could be construed as justifiable homicide or self-defense, maybe pled down to manslaughter."

Sorry's mouth was already full when he spoke. "Hope springs eternal¬ –"

Hunter knew the motorcycle wasn't nearly enough to go on, unless the RCMP turned up another witness who could identify the man. It looked more and more like Orville Barstow was the only lead to follow.

After Sorry's hunger had been satisfied, they dropped the Blazer off and Bart's wife opened the garage so they could retrieve Sorry's motorcycle. Then they went to visit the mechanic. The good news was that the parts had arrived. The bad news was that he wouldn't have it ready for the road until late in the day. "Good thing we've got your bike so we've got transportation until the truck's ready." Hunter noticed Sorry was looking at the ground. His mouth twitched and he kicked at a rock that was embedded in the dirt.

"Listen, bro," said Sorry, still working at the rock. "I'm heading back home this afternoon."

"You're quitting on me?"

The biker kind of shrugged. "It's just that if I want this job that Mo found for me, I've got to get back. The guy said come see him first thing Monday. You're the one who said I should do the right thing to get back with her."

"I didn't mean you should leave before the job's done here. It's a twelve hour drive – maybe more – to the site near Fairbanks from here. I need a co-driver or I'm parked an hour out of Fairbanks for almost half a day." Hunter clenched his jaw and glared at Sorry from under lowered brows. Unless he fudged his log book, the hours of service regulations wouldn't allow him to drive more than eleven hours at a stretch. And if he didn't get some sleep, he wouldn't be even capable of driving that length of time without the risk of falling asleep at the wheel.

The biker shot him a quick glance, then swung his eyes back to the rock at his feet. "It's my marriage we're talkin' about here, man. Your delivery's another day late, somebody loses a couple of bucks and everybody forgets about it next month. If I don't take this job and patch things up with Mo, I could lose my wife and my kids, then my whole fuckin' life is ruined."

Hunter shook his head, but had no argument against Sorry's reasoning. With Sorry gone, he'd have to be ready to hit the road as soon as the mechanic gave his truck the green light. He couldn't help but remember El's comment. *'I better not find out you've been holding up that shipment just to play detective with your friends up there.'* As much as he felt driven to pursue the mystery of April Corbett, as much as he felt compelled to get Orville Barstow out of jail, he wasn't a cop, he was a truck driver. His obligation to Watson Transportation had to come first.

His truck was being worked on, the Blazer was back at Bart's house, and once Sorry left with his motorcycle, Hunter had no means of transportation unless he sprang for a taxi. The truck repairs were already going to put him in the red this month, not to mention the extra expenses due to the delay – accommodation in Eagle and meals on the road, especially meals since he'd had to feed Sorry – so he might have to ask his landlord for an extension on his rent and tell his daughters he couldn't help out with their expenses this month. He shrugged, mentally and physically. *You do what you can with what you've got.*

"Do what you have to," he said. After Sorry was gone, Hunter managed to sweet talk the mechanic into letting him sleep on his couch. The mechanic's house was downright dirty, but exhaustion proved stronger than Hunter's aversion to dog hair and grease-stained upholstery – food grease rather than automotive, judging by the rancid smell – and greater than his rekindled drive to investigate crime. Soon he was deeply asleep.

Compared to all the drama surrounding the repairs and delay, the delivery itself was uneventful. The mine was more than happy to see him, but Hunter guessed that anyone doing business in remote parts of Alaska ¬– the mine site was quite a way from Fairbanks itself – had learned to expect transportation delays given the distances involved and the condition of many northern roads. The mine was open around the clock, so a crew was prepared to offload the machinery soon after he pulled his rig in at the site. He called Elspeth with the news as soon as he was somewhere with a decent cell signal, which meant near Fairbanks.

She told him she was still searching for a load home. "Fairbanks is a long shot. I'd head back to Whitehorse if I were you." Hunter understood. Chances were slim that she could find him a load from Fairbanks, so he might as well keep driving. That's exactly what he did.

CHAPTER THIRTEEN

"If you have no identification, how did you get across the border?" the female Mountie in Whitehorse had asked.

"I borrowed this from a friend." Goldie held out the driver's license that she had begged off her old school friend, Tessa Charlie. "But I was born in Canada, ma'am. Although my mother was – is – an American, I was born in Canada."

"Your father is Canadian?" The woman looked at her sideways, as if she wasn't prepared to believe Goldie's story, but her face was kind. They were seated across the table from each other in a small interview room at the Whitehorse detachment. Mark had driven Goldie here, with Sally's blessing, after Goldie had found her grandmother's obscure note.

"I don't know who my father is, ma'am." For some reason, saying it out loud made her feel ashamed. *That makes me a bastard*, she thought. Like she wasn't a legal person.

"Doesn't your mother know?"

Goldie looked at the floor between her feet. She wore tennis shoes that used to be white, but were now a grimy brown from walking miles on the dirt roads of Eagle. The female Mountie probably wasn't much older than she was, but she felt like a small child being grilled by her teacher. "I haven't seen my mother since I was a baby."

"Okay. Now, what was it you came here to report?"

"A missing person. My grandmother left our home in Eagle yesterday, and I think she was coming to our old cabin here in the Yukon." Goldie couldn't keep her voice from quaking.

"Where is this cabin?" asked the Mountie.

"It's either one not far from where the Stewart River joins the Yukon, or maybe it's one on the Yukon somewhere between Hootalinqua and Lake Laberge."

The Mountie was silent for a moment, as if trying to process what she'd just been told. "You realize that those locations are over a hundred and fifty miles apart and neither of them is accessible by road. Is that as accurate as you can be?" When Goldie nodded, the Mountie sighed. She picked up a pen and held it hovering above a pad on the table in front of her. "Your grandmother was driving a vehicle?"

"No. I'm pretty sure she took our boat. It's missing, along with the two cans of gas that we store for the generator."

"So she was travelling up the Yukon River by boat, then. What kind of boat?"

"An open aluminum boat with a motor. It can sit about six people."

"Big motor?"

"Big enough for fishing and towing in logs now and then. It's an Evinrude."

"She can't get very far upriver without fueling up. The water's still pretty high this time of year, and running pretty strong." She was frowning, looking almost as worried as Goldie herself. "How old is your grandmother?" she asked, with that sideways look again.

"She's about seventy."

"Is she –" The Mountie seemed to be searching for the right words. "– is your grandmother getting a little confused about things?"

Goldie thought about everything that had been happening lately, her grandmother's uncharacteristic behavior, how irritable she'd been before that and how Goldie herself had begun to be concerned about her grandmother's state of mind. "No. Yes. Maybe, but not definitely. She's been –." It was Goldie's turn to search for the right words. "I guess she's been acting a little strange."

"She hasn't been diagnosed with Alzheimer's or dementia?"

"Nothing like that."

"Technically, she's not a missing person. She's an adult; she's indicated to you that she was leaving, where she was going, and that she would be back."

"But she doesn't even have enough gas to reach Dawson, and that's the only place she could buy more fuel. Once she runs out of fuel, she'll have no choice but to continue on foot. I don't know what she was thinking. She's not as strong as she used to be, and the boat and the motor are old, too. Even though I'm young and strong and was brought up in the bush, I wouldn't want to start a trip like that all alone."

"So you're concerned that she won't be able to complete this journey safely, is that correct?"

Goldie nodded. Concerned? She was worried sick. As much as she wanted news of her mother, she would never have permitted her grandmother to risk her life to retrieve some old letter. If only Gran had waited to talk to her before she'd left, Goldie could have told her about the news that Hunter might have already located her mother.

The Mountie was nodding, as if to herself, and making notes on a pad of paper. Then she looked up and asked Goldie if she'd like a cup of coffee or something. When Goldie shook her head, the Mountie smiled, sadly somehow. "If you don't mind, just sit here and wait for a bit. I'll be sending someone in to talk to you."

At the door, she turned with that same sad smile. "This sounds more like a job for Search and Rescue, not the police."

Hunter preferred daylight driving, when there was more to see, over night driving, when he was less distracted by his surroundings and too inclined to think about the past. It suited him just fine that his trip to and from the mine took place at the summer solstice, which meant no matter what hour of the day it was, it was never dark. With the trailer empty, he made better time back to the Yukon. Around four a.m., he pulled into Beaver Creek, the location of the Canada Customs office some twenty miles away from the actual U.S.-Canada border on the Alaska Highway.

Commercial customs was closed, so he climbed into his bunk and slept until they opened at eight. Then he found a spot to park in Beaver Creek and had a big breakfast at one of the few restaurants in town. He walked around long enough to stretch his legs and reacquaint himself with the town, then napped in the truck's sleeper for another few hours.

Just before leaving, he picked up a roast beef sandwich and carton of milk at the 1202 Motor Inn, site of the only gas station in town. There was a busload of tourists milling about the little store, so he walked outside and leaned his butt on a log fence at the edge of the parking lot to eat his lunch. He watched a dusty Kenworth pull up next to the diesel pump. El's comment about playing detective kept coming back to him; he had spent many hours on the road to Fairbanks and back thinking about why he kept involving himself in investigations that really weren't any of his business. He found himself arguing back and forth.

I do it because people – friends, mostly – ask me for my help.

But you're a truck driver now. You quit the RCMP, remember?

Even the police ask me for my help.

Sure they do. After you've already butted into their investigations.

It's not like I seek out these crimes. Fate keeps bringing me face to face with them.

So turn around and look the other way.

It's only a couple of times a year.

One of these times, you'll come up against a bad guy with a weapon. You're an unarmed civilian without a backup. What then?

"I can't change who I am," he said aloud, crumpling up the wrapper from his sandwich before raising the carton of milk to his lips.

"I beg your pardon?" It was a short, middle aged woman in a purple tee shirt and denim shorts. She had a fanny pack around her waist and red Reeboks on her feet. The tee shirt read 'Calistoga'. She carried a can of Dr. Pepper in one hand and what looked like an oatmeal cookie wrapped in plastic wrap in the other.

"Sorry," he said. "Just talking to myself."

The woman proceeded to lean against the log rail a few feet away from him. She wasn't unattractive, but obviously wasn't trying to appeal to the opposite sex. "No need to apologize," she said. "I think out loud all the time myself. It's just I thought you were reading my mind. Are you from here? I don't mean Beaver Creek, specifically; I mean the north." She gestured at the sky with the arm holding the cookie.

He told her no.

His answer seemed to disappoint her. "It's my first time here," she said. "I got this Calvin and Hobbes book from my ex for Christmas. It's called 'Yukon Ho!' They set off for the Yukon, but they never got here. Calvin and Hobbes, I mean. I got the idea that this was the place to come if you were running away from something." She inhaled deeply, not quite a sigh. "Are you?" She took a bite of her cookie.

He looked at her with surprise. "Am I what?"

"Running away from something." When he didn't answer right away, she added, "Don't mind me. I'm just going through something myself. I've been considering a geographic cure, if you know what I mean."

He nodded. He did know what she meant. His ex-wife considered his choice of livelihood an attempt at a geographic cure. Cure for what? he'd sometimes wondered. Cure for being a bad husband? A negligent father? A failure as a friend? Or a cure for that paralyzing malaise that struck him after his best friend's camouflaged suicide and his own divorce?

"I know what you mean," he said.

She smiled uncertainly, then pushed herself off the fence, flicking cookie crumbs off her shorts. "Doesn't matter where you are or who you're with, I guess," she said. "If you're not happy with yourself, how can you expect anyone else to be happy with you?"

"So don't worry, be happy?" he said with a wry smile.

"Learn to be happy with who you are, warts and all. Speaking for myself, of course." Her smile blossomed and it seemed to light up her face. The sight of it made him feel good. "I'd better go. They've started loading my bus." She laughed. "A tour bus wasn't exactly the best choice of transportation for running away from everything, was it?" she said. "Thanks for listening."

"Thank *you*," he said, then watched her walk away. She had a little bounce in her step, like a child.

Now, who sent her? he wondered, and thought again how a coincidence could seem like anything but.

Almost exactly forty-eight hours after he left it, he was back in the city of Whitehorse looking for a place to park his truck and trailer, preferably somewhere he could grab a shower and a good meal. In spite of the time, which was just after eight in the evening, he ended up calling Bart.

"Am I glad to hear from you," said his old friend. He told Hunter where he could safely drop his trailer and suggested he bobtail over to the Klondike Inn. "I'll even buy you dinner."

"What's happened? Why do you sound so glad to hear from me?"

"It has to do with your friends from Eagle. I'll tell you when you I see you."

"Did you bring the note with you?" Hunter asked.

Goldie loosened the drawstring on a denim purse, and rummaged inside it for a few seconds. She brought out a leather billfold – it looked handmade, with stitching visible on the outside – and withdrew a piece of paper. "She can read okay, but she doesn't do much writing," she said, as if in apology.

Hunter pulled a pair of drugstore reading glasses from his shirt pocket and adjusted them on his nose so he could see over them if he had to. The printing on the note was heavy and uneven, some of the letters barely legible. At Hunter's best guess, the note read:

'I am sorry I hid your mother from you. That was wrong and now I must make it right. I left something at the old cabin that can help you find her. I will bring it to you. I love you more than my life.'

It was signed with a scrawled 'Betty Salmon'.

"Bart says you don't know exactly where this cabin is."

"I was just a child." Goldie Salmon sounded distressed; her eyes expressed her anguish. "She loaded me and two dogs and as many of our possessions as she could in the boat, and we headed down the river. I'd like to think I'd recognize one of the cabins, but I don't know for sure that I would."

"One of them?"

Bart broke in. "The original cabin was near Hootalinqua, where the Salmon woman was living when Goldie and her mother showed up. Evidently some time later she moved them to a second cabin on the Stewart River."

"You don't know which one she's referring to here?"

Goldie just lifted her shoulders in a helpless gesture.

"Would anyone else know?" Again the shrug. "Does your grandmother have any friends she might have told?"

"She's never been very friendly with the other women in Eagle," said Goldie. "Other than the buyers she did business with in Carmacks and Dawson, and now in Eagle, I've never known her to talk much to anyone. She's kind of a recluse, so it's not like she ever invites anyone over for tea." She frowned. "Until lately."

"And lately?" asked Bart.

Hunter looked over his glasses at Bart, then at the girl. He thought he could guess what was coming.

"Lately she's gotten very friendly with that man who's been staying at our place."

"And who might that be?" In spite of the question, Hunter could tell that Bart was thinking the same thing as he was.

"You know," she said, looking from one man to the other. "Orville. The man you picked up in Chicken."

Fighting the current upriver had been much more difficult than Betty had expected. Her fuel supply was soon exhausted, and she had no chance of reaching Dawson City for more. She was fortunate to be able to beach the boat in a sheltered cove on the east shore before the motor died, and she'd pulled it up the riverbank as far as she could. Hootie helped. She'd secured a loop of rope around his chest, and commanded him to "marche", while she pulled on a second rope. She didn't want to lose the boat. She'd have to get a ride here to pick it up when she got back from Hootalinqua.

She had sat for a while on the bank, chewing on a piece of moose jerky, watching the river. Dawson was about a hundred miles by river from Eagle. She had gone only about a quarter of the way, maybe less. It could take her a week and the rest of her supplies to get to Dawson, if she and Hootie were able to make their way following the river without any major obstacles. Once at Dawson, she would have no other choice than to beg a ride.

She tore off another piece of jerky with her teeth and chewed it slowly, considering her options. Had the spirits misled her, or had she misinterpreted their messages? Had what she considered their messages been nothing more than her own ill-considered impulses? She couldn't – or refused to – believe that she'd made such a stupid mistake, but there was no doubt that her mission was next to impossible. How would she be able to walk the seventy or eighty miles through wilderness to reach the ferry to Dawson City? Once there, she would have to ask a stranger for a ride to Carmacks, or maybe to the side of the highway just north of Lake Laberge, then walk again from there to the site of the old cabin near Hootalinqua. Was the cabin even there after some twenty years? If it was, was it uninhabited and would she be able to pry up the old board to find the tin that contained the letter?

Those questions were almost insignificant compared to the central question. Would she survive such a journey at her age? Since moving to Eagle, her excursions on foot had never lasted more than a day or two. Lately, two hours of splitting firewood tired her out. Her arthritis gave her trouble after a day in the garden, let alone a week of dodging tree limbs and scrambling over rocks and windfall. Why had the spirits misled her so? Was she being guided, not to retrieve the letter so Goldie could find her mother, but instead to free Goldie from the burden of caring for her aging Gran? Was she now on a journey to join her Gwich'in mother and their ancestors?

"No!" she cried aloud.

Hootie, who had been lying in a sunny patch on the beach, leapt to his feet and began to growl, unsure of what had alarmed his master but prepared to defend her.

"We're not running back home with our tails curled under our asses, Hootie," Betty said. "I may be old, but I'm not helpless. I've survived this land for over seventy years, and I'm still strong and in good health. This land, this river, they may be wild and rough, but unlike the men I've known, they've been fair with me. If the spirits have other plans for me and I'm meant to die on this journey, so be it. I'll fight to survive like I've always fought, right to my last breath."

Hootie was at her side, his tail wagging his approval. She knew he would give his life for her. She laid a hand on his head and massaged it with her knobby fingers. "You agree, don't you, ol' boy? One more big adventure for us both, eh?"

She sorted through the supplies in the boat, choosing only the most critical – an aluminum pot, a good knife, her tin plate and a few utensils, all of the food she'd brought for herself and Hootie, her bedroll and matches, a change of clothes, her rifle and some fishing gear – and fashioned two packs out of rope and a canvas tarp torn in strips and squares, a double one for Hootie and a backpack for herself. She unscrewed the motor, which weighed almost as much as she did, and with difficulty hoisted it off the back of the boat, then half dragged it ten feet across the rocky beach to maneuver it under a bush. She nodded with satisfaction, waited to get her breath back, then managed to flip the boat over on top of the empty jerry cans and the remaining supplies.

She secured Hootie's pack, one strap around his neck, the other around his ribcage, then hoisted her own on her back. She shrugged her shoulders once or twice to adjust the pack, happy to find it comfortable, or at least not terribly uncomfortable. Picking up her rifle, she smiled at Hootie and gave him a few sound pats on the rump. "Ready, my friend?"

Hootie wagged his tail, and the two of them set off briskly upriver, along the stony beach.

"If you lose him, you better find him again. Or don't come back." Bart pointed a stern finger at Hunter's face and then turned to the constable who was accompanying Hunter and Orville in the search for Betty Salmon. "That goes for you, too."

"Don't you worry, Sergeant," said Orville. "I wouldn't dream of making life difficult for these two fine men." His eyes narrowed as he looked at Hunter, and he shook his head.

Hunter got the message. Orville had recognized him as his fellow prisoner in the Whitehorse jail.

"Besides, if I ran off, you'd only hunt me down again. Don't you Mounties always get your man?" The twinkle in the old man's eyes made Hunter smile.

Bart had sent Goldie back home with her young friend Mark. "If your grandmother makes it back to your cabin in Eagle, you'll have to let us know right away," he told her. Mark promised that he and his Jeep would be at Goldie's disposal.

Bart told Hunter that his initial reluctance to involve the RCMP in a search for Betty Salmon had disappeared after talking to her granddaughter. "It was the RCMP's failure to locate April Corbett that set this potential tragedy in motion, beginning way back when. I can't just shrug this off as an old woman's foolishness and leave her to her fate."

He'd assigned a man from the detachment to accompany Hunter and Orville in their search for Betty Salmon. Although Search and Rescue was consulted, it was decided that sending an RCMP constable was the unavoidable choice, given that a prisoner in custody was included in the search party. They were driving up to Dawson City overnight in one of the detachment's Suburbans, where they would be given an eighteen foot flat-bottom RCMP boat to take downriver. "I'm told she'll cooperate with you and Orville," Bart told Hunter. "Her granddaughter says if we send searchers to find her without you, she's likely to hide from them, or at a minimum, refuse to go with them."

"I'm glad you didn't say 'rescue' her," Orville commented. "I've known a few old bush women like Betty over the years. In spite of her age, she's probably as capable of navigating the Yukon land and rivers on her own as any of you gentlemen might be. Nevertheless, I am as concerned – probably more concerned – for the good woman's welfare as any of you, and I would be proud to assist in locating her and making sure she gets home safely." He said that Betty had described the locations of her old cabins to him, and he was pretty sure he could find them, or what remained of them.

"I've seen her boat. There's no way she could even make it upriver to Dawson with that motor. It's a fifteen or twenty horsepower Evinrude. When we head downriver from Dawson, we'll be running with the current so should be able to make good time without using much fuel. I doubt that she even made it to the Fortymile so we can go full throttle over half the distance to Eagle before we need to look for any sign of her boat, or the good woman herself."

"And if we don't see her along the river?" said Hunter.

"If she can hear our boat, I have no doubt that she'll be watching us, but I don't expect we'll see her unless she wants us to. You and I will have to take turns calling her name, so she knows it's us." He paused, eyes downcast. "If we don't see any sign of her before we reach Eagle, well, I don't want to consider that possibility."

As they loaded gear and provisions into the RCMP Suburban, Hunter looked at the sky. "At least the weather's good," he said. The sky was blue, with a few benign-looking clouds along the horizon.

The constable assigned to accompany them, a sturdy round-faced man named Serge Boudreau, peered over at Hunter while he finished loading their gear into the back of the Suburban. "You didn't hear the forecast?"

Both Hunter and Orville turned to him. "No. Why?" Hunter asked.

"They say there's rain headed inland. It may be windy, wet and cold by the time we launch the boat at Dawson tomorrow morning."

They planned to drive the three hundred and something miles from Whitehorse to Dawson, then head downstream on the Yukon River toward the Alaska border. The river trip from Dawson to Eagle was about a hundred miles. Hunter sat in the back seat of the RCMP Suburban with Orville while Constable Boudreau drove. The constable had his elbow resting on the door frame, the window rolled down. Hunter could hear the loud hum of the tires, and felt confident that anything he and Orville said would not be overheard. He intended to bring up their first meeting, but the old man beat him to it.

"So you were a plant," said Orville.

"Are you surprised?"

"You were very convincing, although I did think your haircut was rather fine for someone who had been living in the bush. Are you disappointed that I didn't confess?"

"Not at all. Sergeant Sam didn't expect a confession from you. He hoped you would tell me who your friend was, the fellow at your table."

Orville shook his head. "I couldn't do that."

"You don't have to tell me his name. Just tell me, hypothetically, what kind of relationship would a man have to have with you to make you willing to let him to get away with murder?"

Orville turned to look at Hunter. He frowned but said nothing.

"Can't be good for a man's soul," Hunter continued, looking away. "Getting away with murder, I mean."

After a long moment of silence, "I must admit I hadn't thought of it that way," said Orville.

"If I had a son," said Hunter, "or a nephew, for example, and he committed a serious crime, I supposed I'd have to think long and hard about turning him in. I wouldn't want him to hate me for it." He leaned back against the seat and crossed his arms over his chest. "On the other hand, I would be disappointed if a young man I cared for wasn't prepared to take responsibility for what he'd done. You'd think committing a murder and not owning up to it would eat away at a man if he had any kind of conscience, make him unhappy in the long run. Wouldn't you say so?"

Orville's fingers were stroking his beard, as if he was deep in thought, but he didn't respond.

Hunter continued. "I can see a young man getting angry enough to hurt someone, do something on impulse that he'd never in a million years do if he'd had time to think about it. Heat of passion, they call it. If a young man, say, turned himself in, the courts might go easier on him. I've seen second degree murder pled down to manslaughter and a reduced sentence in situations like that."

"You have?" Orville was still stroking his beard. "I suppose you would, being a Mountie." He cocked his head to one side and said,

"You're the fellow who came to see Betty in Eagle, aren't you? Why? Were you looking for me then?"

Hunter shook his head. "Back in 1972, I was involved in a cold case that included the disappearance of April Corbett, Goldie's mother."

"So you went to Eagle to see Goldie?"

"No. We had no idea April ever had a child. I went to Eagle – uh, off duty, you might say – and saw a girl who looked just like April Corbett did in 1972." He shot Orville a wry smile. "Coincidence at play."

"Coincidence is God's way of remaining anonymous. Einstein said that, but I don't think he believed it."

"And you don't believe it either."

The old man shrugged. "If I knew for sure there was a god, I might believe it. On some level, almost everything unplanned could be called a coincidence. Is it a coincidence that you and I are sitting here talking right now?"

"It's certainly not something I expected to happen when I drove into town this morning." Whether or not Orville had done it intentionally, the conversation had shifted away from the Collins murder, so Hunter tried a different tack. "I'd like to know what would make a mother abandon her baby. The instinctive love of a parent for a child is as powerful as it gets. It amazed me the first time I held each of my two daughters." He tried to ignore the pang of guilt this admission brought, guilt over the failure of his marriage and how little time he had managed to spend with his daughters since. "Do you have children?"

Orville looked out the window. Hunter could see his shoulders rise and fall with a huge sigh. A moment later the old man turned back toward Hunter and nodded gently. "I'm very attached to the son of a woman I lived with for many years. She was a single mother – a Southern Tutchone from Aishihik Lake – who was swept off her feet by some idealistic back-to-the-land hippie. He fathered her child, then decided he'd had enough fun playing Indian and moved back to Toronto without leaving a forwarding address. She'd had a hard life – much like Betty – and I had great respect for her." He paused, his jaw working, eyes looking straight ahead but appearing not to see. "Her son began to call me his father." Orville sighed again. "She died when the young man was only twelve. Cancer. She knew she was dying, and made me promise to watch out for him. I was happy to; he truly was like a son to me. He lived with me until a few years ago."

They both paused to watch as Constable Boudreau accelerated the Suburban past a slow and dusty motorhome. The motorhome driver's hands were at ten and two, and his full attention was focused on the road ahead. He looked older than Orville.

"He's a good boy, but a little hot headed. And understandably bitter about the way his father deserted his mother and him, as if they were toys he'd grown tired of. I think that has made him resentful toward any non-native who tries to take advantage of him."

"Like Collins?"

Orville's mustache twitched, but he didn't elaborate. His expression was hard to read. Wistful? Reflective? Amused? Amused at Hunter's clumsy attempt to get information about his dark haired companion?

Before the conversation came to a halt, Hunter ventured to say, "What would his mother think of our hypothetical situation? I mean, let's say, suppose her son got away with murder."

The old man shook his head. Looking straight at Hunter his mustache twitched inscrutably again. "Speaking hypothetically? She wouldn't like it. She wouldn't like it at all."

CHAPTER FOURTEEN

Betty shrugged off her pack and dropped it on a rock-strewn mound covered with kinnikinnick , crushing what was left of its tiny, pink, urn-shaped flowers. She sank to her knees beside it. She and Hootie had been walking most of the past two days, stopping when they needed to rest, eat or sleep and came across suitably comfortable spots. They hiked along the shore when they could and when they couldn't, she tried to keep to anything that looked like a trail without losing track of the river. "What do we do now, Hootie?" she said, surveying the rushing water some forty feet ahead of them.

She had chosen the northeast side of the Yukon River to avoid its confluence with the Fortymile, but at this time of year even the smaller creeks could be difficult to cross. Now they had come up against just such a creek, and Betty considered her options. She couldn't wade across – the creek was too deep, the current too strong and the water too cold – but she might be able to fashion a raft to pole across at a shallower and calmer stretch. It was inevitable that the current would carry her at least part of the way downstream. With good luck, she would end up on the other side of the creek before it reached the river. With bad luck, she and Hootie would be carried out into the Yukon River and swept back downstream toward Eagle, and very likely, to their deaths from hypothermia and drowning.

Her other option was to make her way as far upstream as she could in the hopes of finding a spot where it was shallow and calm enough to wade across. That was a detour she could ill afford. It could take her hours to find such a spot, and she could end up miles up the creek. She tried to remember if she had ever been close to here with James Monroe, when she lived with him near Fortymile, but he had usually gone out hunting alone while she stayed at the cabin, and she couldn't recall crossing to this side of the river except in winter when ice turned the river into a solid road.

Either option required her to follow the creek upstream to find a suitable spot. She glanced over at her companion. The day's hike had been much more than Hootie was used to, and he had found a small depression filled with brown spruce needles to curl up in. Betty smiled sadly. She knew that Hootie would follow her until he could no longer walk and she loved him for it. "We'll make it, old friend," she said as she struggled to her feet. Her knees protested, and she massaged them for a moment before straightening up and picking up her pack and her walking stick.

They had been making their way, gently uphill, on a rough moose path for almost an hour. The light had changed. No longer were there bright patches of yellow light on the foliage ahead, so she knew before she could see them overhead that dark clouds had moved across the sun. The wind had picked up as well, whistling softly through the upper branches of the spruce and setting the aspen leaves trembling.

The creek, when she could see it from the path, was beginning to look less forbidding, and she felt hopeful that it would soon be shallow enough to ford if they could find a spot wide and level enough. Hootie, as always, walked about ten feet in front of her, picking his way over deadfall and past low-hanging spruce boughs. He paused now and then to look back, either to make sure she was following or that he was still heading the way she intended. His steps slowed, and his nose lifted, nostrils wide, as he caught a scent from up ahead. Betty heard him growl, low in his throat, a sound she knew all too well – his bear growl.

She stopped dead in her tracks and listened. This time of year, grizzly sows were out foraging along with the cubs that had been born inside their dens during winter hibernation. It wouldn't do to surprise a sow with cubs, or a bear feeding on the carcass of an elk or moose calf. From where she stood, she could see clusters of rose hips here and there through the foliage, still clinging to the twigs of last year's growth. It wouldn't surprise her if there was a bear foraging for them along the trail ahead. Should she turn back, or continue on?

"Hootie?" she whispered. She would let him decide.

Dan Sorenson felt kind of bad about leaving Hunter to finish the trip himself, but a man does what he has to do. He decided to make an effort to help Hunter by keeping an eye out on his way back home for a native guy with grease under his fingernails on a motorcycle, a guy who might have been in the Yukon the week before. He didn't hold out much hope, but at least he could say he tried.

Every time he came across some brothers on their bikes – he even went so far as to talk to guys on ricers when he happened to find himself parked beside their Hondas or Kawasakis – he would ask them where they'd been and depending on their answer, whether they'd seen a dude like the one Hunter was looking for. "What kind of ride?" they'd ask. "Dunno," is all he could say. Fat chance he'd find the Lost Mine dude with so little info.

So it surprised him when he seemed to come close. It was in Chilliwack, when he was less than an hour from home. He needed to eat, so he pulled off at the Tim Horton's just off the highway. There were a couple of guys outside, standing beside their bikes and smoking while they finished off their coffee in paper cups. Sorry almost didn't ask, figuring it was a lost cause this far from the Yukon, but he did a double take when he saw that one of them had Yukon plates on his big Yamaha. The other guy had a black BMW that reminded him of Darth Vader.

"You just down from up north? I just came from Whitehorse myself," he said as he slammed the kickstand down and dismounted his Harley beside them. He took off his helmet, then stretched his shoulders as they looked him up and down.

The bigger guy, who had blond hair so obviously wasn't the dude Hunter wanted to find, was standing beside the Yamaha with Yukon plates – Sorry had to admit that for a ricer it was a sweet looking ride, nicely chromed – and was the one to speak. "I went out for a joyride and forgot to turn around."

"Done that more than once myself. Nice ride," said Sorry, eyeing the bike. "You from Whitehorse?"

The guy nodded.

"Not many guys up there have bikes, eh?"

The guy nodded again, dropped his cigarette butt and ground it into the asphalt with his boot heel. "Summer's too short," he said.

"Any chance you know a native dude with a scruffy beard who lives up that way and rides a bike? Got a friend who asked me to look out for him, but I'm drawing a blank on the dude's name."

The guy shrugged. "What kind of bike?"

"He didn't say." Sorry felt like an idiot.

"I knew a native guy up there worked at the local bike shop awhile, moved down here a few years back. He still looks kind of scruffy, like he did when he'd just come out of the bush. I ran into him in downtown Whitehorse recently, said he was on vacation and decided to ride back up north for the hell of it."

Sorry figured that sounded promising, but he didn't want to show too much enthusiasm. "Down here? Like, where here? I wonder if that's him. You know his name?"

"Jimmy something. Never knew his last name."

"You know where he works?"

"Said he's still working as a bike mechanic. I think he said Surrey."

Sorry caught a whiff of Tim Horton's chili and slapped his back pocket to make sure he still had his wallet. "Thanks, eh?" he said, then as an afterthought, "You said you saw him recently?"

"Week or so, I guess."

Sorry nodded his thanks and headed for the entrance, already salivating at the thought of the chili. He could call and give that potentially useful piece of information to Hunter once he got home, or he could check out a couple of bike shops in Surrey, since that was his own home turf and he knew some of the guys . If he struck out, well then maybe Hunter could check out the motorcycle shop in Whitehorse. Might be as good a clue as any, he thought.

The girl behind the counter asked him what he wanted and he was about to ask for a double order of the chili when he realized that if all went well, he might be in bed with his lovely wife Mo a few hours later. She hated manly farts. He swallowed hard, then bravely ordered a bowl of soup, a cream cheese bagel, and three glazed donuts.

No way was he going to risk being banished to the couch his first night back.

Betty was debating whether to start making noise to alert the bear to her presence in the hope that it would hightail it in the opposite direction. Tired of carrying the rifle and finding her arthritic fingers cramping up, she had tucked it into her pack several hours earlier. She knew she couldn't pull it loose without taking off her pack, and it would take more time than she wished to spend to take the makeshift pack off her back and hoist it back on again.

Hootie growled low in his throat once more, then turned in the direction of the creek and began picking his way around the trees, across deadfall and the low-growing scrub. Betty sensed his caution and followed as quietly as she could, still wondering if it might not be wiser to alert the bear to human presence, but wanting to trust her dog's instinct to remain silent. A light breeze carried a rotten smell from the bear's direction. She wasn't sure if it was a carcass the bear had been feeding on, or a camouflage smell that the bear had picked up, and she didn't want to find out. From the same direction came a deep snuffling sound and the crack of a breaking branch. It sounded a little too close for comfort.

The creek came into view, and although there was a pretty steep bank that she would have to slide down, the water itself looked reasonably calm and shallow. If they could get across the creek, they would seem like less of a threat to the bear and it would reduce the danger of being charged. Hootie reached the bank, but instead of heading down to the creek, he made an about-face and stood stiff-legged with his ruff raised, his ears pricked in the direction of the moose path behind Betty.

She was only about eight feet from the bank and watching where she placed each foot when she heard Hootie snarl and he bounded past her so fast he was a blur of grey fur. Her adrenalin picked her up and carried her to the bank and down into the creek bed before she had any conscious thought of doing so. She was aware of the sounds of a brawl behind her – Hootie's deep bark and a bear's grating bellow accompanied by the violent rustling of undergrowth – and then she heard the sound she dreaded, a high-pitched yelp that told her Hootie had been hit.

Suddenly she was in the water, the cold of it slicing at her skin like a razor, her boots and pant legs suddenly heavy with the weight of it. It reached her knees, and suddenly her thighs; she felt the frigid water assault her crotch, then rise almost to her waist. One foot slipped on a rock and she couldn't move fast enough to regain her balance. She fell sideways into the icy water and the sudden cold around her arms and chest took her breath away. Gasping, she flailed around trying to get hold of the walking stick she'd dropped in the fall, but it floated out of reach in the current. As she struggled to find purchase with her feet, the current caught her pack and she felt herself being carried backwards down the creek. She had no choice but to shrug out of the heavy pack, heavier still as it began to absorb water. Still it took all of her strength to turn over, and she braced her legs and arms against anything in the creek bed they came in contact with, any rock or submerged and half buried branch or log. The water was deep enough to rush into her open mouth with every gasp, so she spat and coughed and gagged until she could keep her chin above the stream. She was only vaguely aware that her pack was floating steadily downstream; not drowning had become her only priority.

A few times, it seemed to her that the water would win, but she managed to struggle to her feet and take one agonizing step after another, her legs and feet almost numb, until she reached the other shore. Only then did her thoughts turn again to the bear, and to the possibility that her ordeal was just beginning. She crawled up the low bank, barely feeling the rocks under her hands and knees, and tried to conceal herself in some tall scrub under a white spruce about fifteen feet into the woods. She began shivering uncontrollably. The sensation of cold had morphed into pain from her face to her toes, and she could hear nothing but her own rasping breath and the thudding of her heart.

She lay exhausted, abandoning her body to convulsive shivering. As her breathing slowed, a delicious warmth slowly grew from somewhere under her ribcage, gradually displacing cold in her chest and hips, and then crept the length of each arm and each leg. The warmth and silence were so comforting and she felt so safe that there was no room for fear or pain, and alone in the bush a mile or more upstream from the Yukon River, Betty Salmon fell into an exhausted sleep.

"That's her boat." Orville was standing at the back of the RCMP patrol boat, pointing at the eastern bank of the Yukon River. An aluminum skiff with patchy red paint on its hull was visible on the beach. "Stop. Turn around. That's got to be her boat."

Hunter was relieved to see that the boat Orville referred to seemed to have been deliberately beached, rather than borne ashore by the current. Someone had pulled it away from the river's edge and turned it over. He hoped Orville was right, and he also hoped that it had been Betty herself who had beached the boat. He didn't see how she could have gone very far on foot, so if they turned around and followed the shoreline, they might have a good chance of finding her. On the way from Dawson they had been looking for any sign of her boat, scanning the banks on both sides of the river. Now they knew which side to look on, and which stretch of the river to begin searching.

Constable Serge Boudreau brought the patrol boat around. It was an open eighteen foot, flat-bottom boat with a hundred horsepower motor, more than adequate to fight the current. The wind had picked up and whitecaps had begun to form on the surface of the river. As the boat drew close to the bank, the constable cut the engine and Hunter jumped over the bow on to the shore, pulling the boat behind him until half of it was lodged on land. Orville jumped out behind him and hurried across the beach to the overturned skiff.

Underneath, they saw an assortment of items, including a couple of empty jerry cans, a length of rope and a heavy tarp, some kitchen items and a bundle of clothing. "Definitely Betty's," said Orville. He picked up a quilted jacket with a fur-lined hood. "I saw this hanging in her kitchen." He looked up at the heavy grey clouds overhead, then tucked the jacket under his arm. "She'll be sorry she left this behind. She might want it when we find her."

Hunter smiled sadly to himself at Orville's usc of 'when' instead of 'if', and hoped his optimism was justified. The old man had obviously grown very fond of Betty Salmon. Hunter had seen too many unhappy endings in his life and fervently wished for a positive outcome for both Betty's and Orville's sakes.

Hunter spoke to the constable, who had remained seated beside the motor in the back of the boat. "Let's take it slow heading upriver until we see anything to indicate she's been there. We can cut the engine from time to time so Orville can call her name if we're on a stretch where it's not possible to travel on foot within sight of the river." He nodded at the lanyard with a whistle around Boudreau's neck. "Her granddaughter says she took her dog. He might respond to your whistle."

They carried on upriver along the shoreline, Hunter occasionally lifting the binoculars that hung around his neck for a closer look at something. The constant wind was cool, but clouds had already started to thin in the west, holding out the promise of clear skies and the sun breaking through as it rose higher in the sky. They had been travelling slowly upriver for almost an hour and Hunter judged they were halfway to the abandoned townsite at Fortymile, where the Fortymile River entered the Yukon from thc west. There was a break in the trees lining the eastern bank. It was the wide mouth of a creek.

"She couldn't have made it across here." Hunter had to raise his voice for the others to hear him above the sound of the motor. He gestured at the wide mouth of a creek that emptied into the river. "Not here. She'd have had to hike upstream to find a better place to cross."

Boudreau nodded. "What do you want to do?" he hollered back.

"What's that?" Orville pointed to something floating in the water about fifty yards up the creek. "See that thing floating? Over there, about ten feet from that flat rock."

Hunter located the object through the binoculars. "Could be a piece of tarp. Looks like it might be caught up on something." He signaled to Boudreau to bring the boat closer.

It took some careful maneuvering to get close enough to grab the object without getting the boat hung up on a submerged log. To reach it, Hunter had to lean well out of the boat and stretch his arm out as far as he could. Orville shifted to the other side of the boat to counterbalance. It took two passes, but Hunter was finally able to unhook the object from the branch of the submerged log that had snagged it. He held it outside the boat as its folds released a steady stream of water.

"It's a pack," said Orville. "Look at the way the ropes are looped. It was meant to be carried on somebody's back." He reached for it, almost pulling it out of Hunter's hand. "Let me see it. Let me see what's in it."

For it to remain as intact as it was, Hunter knew it hadn't been in the water very long. He hesitated to speculate on how and why it had ended up floating down the creek, but it was hard not to imagine that the owner had once been in the water with it. If the current had carried the owner past it and into the Yukon River, it was highly unlikely that he – or she – had survived.

"Let's see how far upstream we can take the boat," Hunter shouted over the noise of the engine.

Boudreau nodded and pointed the boat's square nose upstream. Hunter stood near the bow, scanning both sides of the creek for any sign of the pack's owner, while Orville's fingers struggled with the knots in the wet rope as he tried to unwrap the contents of the tarp.

"It's hers! It's Betty's." Orville held up a faded red and gold tin labeled Red Rose Tea. "She wouldn't go anywhere without her tin of tea." He dropped the tin back onto the wet tarp and, like Hunter, began to look intently at the creek banks.

Hunter pointed to the bank on the right. "You concentrate on this side, I'll do the other," he said.

"Keep an eye out for rocks and logs near the surface," shouted the constable from the rear of the boat. "I don't want us all to end up in the river."

Just after he spoke, something thudded against the underside of the boat. Hunter sucked in his breath. The noise was too soft to have been something hard, like a rock or a log. They all turned to look behind the boat, to see if what they hit would surface behind the propeller. A spruce branch, needles intact, spun slowly away from the back of the boat.

The creek began to narrow, and up ahead they saw that the creek bed was steeper and less even, creating a stretch of white water. Boudreau steered the boat to a tiny bay with a gently sloping shoreline and shut off the engine so they could talk. Since they didn't know if Betty had made it across the creek, it was decided that they would split up. Boudreau, mindful of Orville's status as a prisoner, said he would drop Hunter on this side, which was the south side, while he accompanied Orville on the other.

"Let's call first," said Hunter, standing in the shallow water at the shore and holding the boat's bow rope. "Call or whistle in case she's within hailing distance." And able to hear, he thought.

Orville began to call Betty's name, but Boudreau held up a hand to silence him, then with his hands framing the sides of his mouth, he let out a yell that Hunter found astonishingly loud. "Hallooooo!"

The three of them listened intently for an answering sound, then the constable yelled again, even louder. No response.

"Meet back here if we don't connect upstream?" asked Hunter. When Boudreau nodded, Hunter grabbed a pack out of the boat – one of three Search and Rescue Packs that they had brought – then gave the boat a shove back into the current. He watched them until they'd found a suitable spot about forty yards downstream and had pulled the boat securely up onto the bank before he began to walk upstream along the shoreline.

Without the sound of the motor and away from his companions, Hunter became aware of how loud and constant the rush and tumble of the water could be as it hurried over and around the rocks of the creek bed. Even Constable Boudreau's loudest call would be easily eclipsed by the noise of the creek wherever there was white water. He had to admit that it gave him scant hope. Finding her pack in the water had been an ominous sign.

He could go only so far along the bank before he was forced to detour around a rocky outcropping. This took him far enough into the trees that the sound of the creek faded to a whisper. There wasn't anything you could call a trail. He followed the proverbial path of least resistance, wherever he could see an opening, sometimes forced to scramble over or duck under wind-fallen trees, often removing his pack to do so. He peered through the underbrush and tree boughs that surrounded him, looking for any sign that Betty might have passed this way, but realized that in many places he could be within ten feet of her – or anything, living or dead – and remain completely unaware.

He began to whistle. It started out as a series of random notes as he walked, a five second tune at most. He paused mid-step to listen, and heard only the sound of the creek, muted by distance. Five seconds, and a pause. Five more seconds, and a pause. Random notes coalesced into a familiar melody, dredged up from somewhere in his past, and the words started to sing themselves in his head.

Darling, I am growing old,
Silver threads among the gold,
Shine upon my brow today,
Life is fading fast away.

The last line of the chorus seemed a little ominous, but it was just a framework for the noise he was making, after all. If Betty hadn't been swept into the Yukon River, she might hear a human whistle and answer back, or her dog might bark. The song recalled winter evenings in his parents' home with his father on the old upright piano and himself on the violin. His mother would stand with one hand on his father's shoulder, leaning close enough to read the words in the music book, her voice a clear soprano. He felt an unexpected twinge of nostalgia.

Another verse came to mind as he kept whistling, and considering Orville's obvious fondness for Betty, he wondered if perhaps the song was fitting in more ways than one.

Love is always young and fair,
What to us is silver hair,
Faded cheeks or steps grown slow,
To the hearts that beat below?

What was that? He strained to listen, not sure if he had actually heard something more than a chickadee's call or a raven's squawk. When he heard nothing further, he stuck four fingers in his mouth and whistled as loud as he could, then listened again. Nothing.

He kept going.

CHAPTER FIFTEEN

Dan Sorenson stopped at the Dell Hotel on the King George Highway in Surrey, less than ten minutes from home. He parked his Harley outside the lounge, grabbed a beat-up leather pouch from his saddle bag and headed inside. He paused a moment at the door, letting his eyes adjust to the low light. The bartender was a guy he knew, and a few bikers he used to drink with were bellied up to the bar.

He had planned to just hit the men's can and leave, but Twitcher had turned around and seen him.

"Hey, man," the guy said, and more heads turned toward him. "Long time, no see. How you doin'?"

Sorry nodded. "Good, Twitch. How 'bout you?"

Doughboy invited him to come sit down. "I'll buy you a beer." He gestured to the bartender. "Pour him a beer, man."

Sorry felt stuck between a rock and a hard place. Now that he'd been seen, he couldn't very well just use the john and walk out, but if he arrived back home with beer on his breath, he'd be up shit creek with Mo.

"Give me a sec, okay," he said and ducked into the hallway that led to the john. Once inside, he relieved himself, then went to the sink and splashed water on his face. He had a toothbrush and a nearly empty tube of toothpaste in his pouch, along with a comb and razor. He decided the shave could wait till he got home, but gave his teeth a good brushing and combed his hair. Then he took a deep breath and headed back into the pub.

The beer was sitting there with his name on it. The glass was frosty and the beer had just the right amount of head. He could smell it from where he stood beside Doughboy, and it smelled damn good. He made a little small talk with Doughboy and Twitcher; he knew they'd rib him if he told them the truth.

As offhand as he could make it, Sorry asked them if they'd run across a bike mechanic in town who looked like a Yukon native.

"A native what?" asked Doughboy.

"Indian, what else?"

"A Yukon native is anybody who was born in the Yukon, bro," said Twitch, and started telling a story about his own trip to the Yukon, back in '84. Sorry stood there nodding, eyeing the beer as his mind replayed that conversation with Hunter, the one where Hunter had said 'At this moment, drinking that one beer is more important to you than making your boss happy and keeping your job', but right at this moment the stakes were even higher. It was about making Mo happy and keeping his family together.

When Twitch finished his story, Sorry clapped a hand on Doughboy's shoulder and – as much as it hurt to give it up – slid that frosty beer glass down the bar toward him. "Thanks, man, but the fact is I haven't seen my woman for almost two weeks and I'm kind of in a hurry, if you know what I mean. I want to greet her with minty breath." He exhaled pointedly in Doughboy's direction, then pulled the last of his folding money out of his jeans pocket and slapped five bucks on the bar. "The beer's on me."

Doughboy made a face, but he didn't refuse the beer or the five bucks.

Sorry headed out the door feeling pretty proud of himself, but by the time he'd peeled out of the parking lot onto King George, he had a sinking feeling in his gut. Was Mo going to be happy to see him? Was she even going to be home? Or had he given up the beer and a fiver he could ill afford for nothing?

Hunter had been bushwhacking his way through the Yukon wilderness for almost an hour and was at a point close to the riverbank, judging by the noise level of the creek.

He wasn't sure if Orville and Constable Boudreau had kept pace with him on the other side, and had begun to wonder how far up the creek they should go looking for traces of Betty Salmon when he heard a faint rustling in the underbrush about fifteen feet ahead. He froze. An unarmed man was not at the top of the food chain in this part of the world, and he couldn't control the rush of adrenaline that prepared him for a fight. Flight was out of the question. There's no way he could outrun a predator, or even an angry moose, in this terrain.

A tangle of leaves parted, he saw the black nose and white muzzle of a dog. "Hootie?"

Betty Salmon's dog emerged from the foliage. His coat was disheveled and he had two canvas bundles hanging lopsided on his back, the ropes holding them creasing the fur from his chest to his shoulders, yet he seemed happy to see Hunter. Hunter dropped to one knee and said, "Hey, fella. Good boy." As the dog approached, Hunter could see that the fur on his left shoulder was matted with blood, and he could see a jagged tear in the tarp on that same side. Either the dog had fallen hard and scraped the tarp and his shoulder on something sharp, or it had been a blow from a hoof or claw. The dog was still able to walk; there was no time to investigate the injury.

"Good boy," he said again. "Where's Betty?"

He knew he would soon have an answer. If Betty was on land, Hootie would have stayed by her side. In that case, she would be nearby, and he was certain the dog would return to her. If she'd disappeared in the water, Hootie would feel lost and wait to follow Hunter's lead. "Where's Betty?" he repeated, as if the dog could understand.

The dog stood looking at Hunter for a few seconds, then turned and took a few steps in the direction he had come. He stopped and glanced back at Hunter, as if to ask him, "Are you coming with me?"

"Good boy, Hootie," he said. "Let's go find your mom."

He didn't have to follow far. Moments later he saw Betty Salmon's body lying on its side, the legs bent in a semi-fetal position, and half hidden by bushy undergrowth at the base of a small spruce. She wasn't far from the bank of the creek, but he wouldn't have spotted her without the dog's help. Hunter went down on his knees beside her, shrugging the SAR pack off his shoulders as he did so. He called her name, but she didn't stir, so he leaned in close to feel for a pulse at her carotid artery. Although her skin was cool, it wasn't cold. When he didn't feel the pulse right away, he adjusted his position and eventually felt a light throb beneath his fingertips. He held the back of his hand close to her nostrils, and was able to feel soft but even breaths.

Her clothes were damp but not wet, so he judged that she'd been out of the water for at least a couple of hours. The broken stems and crushed foliage in front of her chest and abdomen hinted that her best friend had been lying next to her, sharing his body warmth, and possibly keeping her alive. As if to confirm, Hootie emerged through the scrub and stood in the same spot, his eyes moving from Betty to Hunter and back again.

Hunter's first move was to open his SAR pack and find the thermal blanket. He ripped the plastic package open and tucked the blanket close around Betty's body. He then stood up and worked at the wet knots to remove the pack from Hootie's back. As the ropes loosened, the pack fell to the ground and Hunter moved it out of the way. The dog immediately went down for a good long roll, then shook the dead leaves and spruce needles out of his fur. When Hunter lifted the edge of the Mylar blanket and invited the dog to lie down next to the unconscious woman, Hootie seemed to understand what he was asking and curled up next to her.

Hunter's next move was to signal to Orville and Constable Boudreau to cross the creek and join him so they could transport Betty out to the boat. He told Hootie to stay, hoping the dog would understand, and made his way down the low bank to the edge of the creek. It looked shallow enough to cross, even more so a few hundred feet upstream, so he felt hopeful they could access the creek bank and make the crossing without too much difficulty. He yelled and whistled in case they were close enough to hear. When there was no immediate response, he searched in his pack for emergency flares.

He found a smoke flare, as well as an emergency whistle. He used the whistle a few times while he figured out how to activate the flare.

While the flare sent up a stream of white smoke, he set about gathering dry twigs and branches to light a fire. If Betty Salmon became conscious enough, with a fire he could heat up some water to make a tea or broth. Not only that, if the other two were bushwhacking in an area surrounded by trees, they might not see the smoke before the signal flare went out. He might need the fire to create a more long-lasting smoke signal, if the flare didn't do the trick.

It didn't take him long to find out.

At first Betty was confused. She opened her eyes and saw something silver, a silver sheet – she felt something like plastic against her cheek – and beyond that she saw green leaves. The silver plastic was disorienting. It wasn't natural. What was it doing here in the bush? Her entire body ached. She tried to move her left arm, but it was tucked up against her chest, its movement blocked by something heavy pressed up against her. She moved her fingers, and realized that what she was feeling was animal fur, and then she remembered the bear. She froze, afraid to reveal to the bear that she was still alive, but it was too late. The animal moved, and she felt the loss of its warmth against her chest, and then she felt its warm breath and saw its black nose.

"Oh, my friend, my sweet, sweet friend." She sobbed with relief when she saw the worried eyes of her dog searching her own, and she reached up to draw his head to hers. "You didn't leave me, Hootie. You're okay." She struggled to raise herself onto her elbow and hugged Hootie's neck with the other arm, but almost immediately fell back. 'I'm weak as a kitten,' she thought to herself, confused again.

She couldn't keep her eyes from closing and immediately drifted back to sleep.

"How did you get her to the nursing station in Dawson?"

Hunter was in a reception area cum waiting room at the nursing station, essentially a public clinic, in Dawson City. He was on the phone with Bart, giving him an update on the search for Betty Salmon. "She refused to lie down on the stretcher, so we mickey-moused a travois of sorts that she could sit on," he told Bart. "We had to threaten to tie her down at first, she was determined to walk out under her own steam."

"Independent old gal, eh? Sounds a lot like my grandmother," said Bart. "So taking her to the nursing station was just a precaution?"

"No. The spirit was willing, but the flesh was weak. She did try to walk, but her legs gave out before she took two steps. Hypothermia and exhaustion. It's lucky the day was warming up instead of cooling down when she fell in the creek, or there's a good chance she wouldn't have survived. Her clothes were soaked, but her dog – a big old Malamute – had been lying beside her and kept her from getting colder. When Orville showed up with her warm jacket, he literally gave her the shirt off his back so she'd have something dry against her skin. While your man and I built the travois, Orville undressed her, gave her his dry shirt and wrapped her in thermal blankets. He hung the rest of her clothes in the sun and made her some kind of hot broth – whatever those cubes in the SAR pack are – so by the time we hauled her out of there she had warmed up quite a bit.

"Constable Boudreau had to hike down the north side of the creek to pick up the boat, so Orville and I took turns, one of us dragging the travois and the other following behind to hoist it over obstacles – not an easy job with all the deadfall – until we reached the beach we'd started from. The nurse who got her settled in bed thinks she's out of the woods, but they want her to stay here overnight for observation."

"I'll call her granddaughter. I assume she and her boyfriend will pick the old girl up and take her back to Eagle. I'll suggest they pick her up in the morning. You're coming back tonight with Serge and the prisoner?"

Hunter hesitated. Orville had been by Betty's side since they found her. He knew the old man wouldn't want to leave Betty Salmon until Goldie showed up, and neither did Hunter, but he doubted that Bart would allow his officer to stay in Dawson just to let a prisoner keep his lady friend company.

"For sure. I'd like to have a little more time with Orville," he told Bart. "I spent some time talking to him on the drive up, and I might be close to getting him to reveal the identity of our other suspect."

"Did you say 'our' suspect?"

"I'm tired, chief. Slip of the tongue." Was that what people referred to as a Freudian slip? El's comment about him playing cop came back to him. "We're all tired. Before we head back, we could all use a few hours sleep, at least. Boudreau's been doing most of the driving. I doubt if he managed to nap more than an hour or two in the last thirty-two, and we did some rather strenuous bushwhacking."

"I thought Serge was game to start back almost right away. What if you two spell each other off on the driving?"

"I'm as tired as he is. Either one of us would be likely to fall asleep at the wheel." He ran a hand down his face, his three day beard rough beneath his palm. He felt in no condition to drive, and was sure the constable would feel the same."I'll talk to the staff here. Maybe they'll let us sleep on a couch or a couple of spare cots here at the nursing station so we can crash until the granddaughter arrives."

A couple of hours later, after sharing a pizza, Hunter and Boudreau were asleep in the nursing station. Hunter was slouched on the couch in the waiting area; the constable had arranged for a cot to be placed just outside the room where Betty Salmon slept. Boudreau had bought a small bag of dog food for Hootie, who had eaten ravenously. The nurses turned a blind eye when Hunter brought him into Betty's room, and he was now asleep on the floor under her bed. Orville was dozing in a chair beside the bed, handcuffed to the bedrail while Boudreau caught some sleep.

Hunter was awakened by the sound of a woman's voice.

"Excuse me. I'm sorry to wake you, but there's no one at the reception desk. I'm looking for someone and I was told she might be here."

He opened his eyes, and saw a woman standing in front of him. She had short blond hair and was dressed in jeans and a denim vest over a white long-sleeved shirt, and a large leather purse was hanging on one shoulder. She was frowning slightly.

Before he could answer, she said, "You look familiar to me."

Her face was familiar to him, too. She looked about his age. Someone he'd known years ago when he'd lived in the Yukon?

"Do you know if there's a woman named Betty Salmon here?"

His mouth fell open as he tried to reconcile the woman's tired face, mature figure and blond hair with the slender, dark-haired, free spirited girl he'd last seen almost twenty five years before. "April?"

Her frown deepened. "You remember me from Whitehorse? I'm sorry–"

"Hunter Rayne. I used to spend time at the Sluice Box when you worked there."

"One of the Mounties," she said, still frowning as if trying to place him. Then she nodded. "I had a crush on one of you guys. His name was Ken something. You were his friend, right?"

Hunter offered a crooked smile. "Yes, Ken was my friend." It had happened to him more than once. Hunter had never been considered a bad-looking guy, but he'd found out early in their friendship that he couldn't compete with Ken's dashing good looks and outgoing personality. He wondered, if he *had* asked her out, way back when, if she would have even gone out with him, or would she have held out for an invitation from Ken. He didn't really want to know. "He passed away a few years ago."

She put a hand to her mouth before saying, "I'm sorry." Her lips couldn't seem to hold the apologetic smile for more than half a second. "Look, I've got a lot on my mind right now. I had a call from a number in Whitehorse and I know that someone in the Yukon is looking for me. It has to be something important, and I thought Betty Salmon –" She stopped in mid-sentence, as if debating how much to say to him.

"That someone was me. I've been looking for you since 1972." He smiled in sympathy at her confusion and motioned for her to sit down beside him.

She sat on the edge of the couch, both hands gripping her purse. The question 'Why?' was evident in her eyes.

Hunter paused a moment, trying to decide just where to start his story. He chose to answer what he knew was her most pressing question first. "Your daughter wants to meet you."

"Oh, my God. I hoped so much. Oh, my God. Where is she? Is she here?"

He shook his head. "That's not why I've been looking for you, at least not the original reason. I want to know what happened in Blake Martin's cabin in October of 1972."

The woman froze. An expression Hunter couldn't read crossed her face, and the hands that held her purse began to clench and unclench, as if she were kneading the leather bag.

Before he asked her any questions, he knew he should answer some of hers. He told her where her daughter had been living, and how Betty Salmon had only just revealed to Goldie the truth about her mother and the way April had arrived at Betty's cabin near Hootalinqua with her as a baby.

"She didn't tell my daughter about me before last week?" As she digested that fact, the expression on April's face progressed from puzzled to angry. "She stole my baby. Betty Salmon stole my baby."

Hunter's heart sank. He'd guessed there was a chance Betty Salmon could be prosecuted for abducting Goldie, but he wanted to believe it wouldn't happen. It would be a complicated and costly proceeding, given the involvement of both the Canadian and American legal systems, and the amount of time that had passed. Putting Betty in prison for any length of time would no doubt be worse than death for a woman who'd always been so fiercely independent and reclusive. He nodded at April, but held up one hand to caution her.

"You told Betty you'd come back for your daughter. Did you ever come looking for her?"

"I wanted to. She was just a baby. It wasn't her fault –"

"Did you come back?"

"I wrote to Betty. I needed to know where she was, if she was still in the same place. I didn't even know for sure I could find my way back there again. I thought maybe I'd arrange for her to bring the baby to me in Whitehorse or somewhere."

"And did you come back to the Yukon?"

Hunter had his answer when April looked at the floor.

"Why didn't you come back for her?"

April closed her eyes and swallowed before replying in a quiet voice, "I needed to make a new life for myself, find a little more security, before I came back for my baby." She straightened her shoulders and raised her eyes to Hunter's. "Betty never answered my letters. I sent them to Carmacks General Delivery and all but one of them were returned by the post office."

Hunter shook his head. "Goldie has grown up believing herself to be Betty's granddaughter. Betty is the only family she's ever known. Who will win if you accuse her of abducting Goldie?" He paused. "More importantly, who will lose? All three of you will be hurt, and badly."

"I want to talk to Betty."

Hunter shook his head again. He tried to imagine what Betty's reaction would be. She was in no condition to receive a shock like that. "Wait for your daughter. She's on her way here from Eagle. Let her break the news to Betty."

He suggested April go back to her hotel and get some sleep, but she informed him she had flown up to Dawson from Whitehorse without even booking a place to stay. "Besides, I couldn't sleep now anyway."

Hunter looked at his watch. It was almost eleven o'clock. He'd already managed to sleep a couple of hours, and doubted he would be able to get back to sleep himself. "Then how about we go find somewhere we can get something to eat? I still have some questions for you, remember?"

Dan Sorenson was sitting in the big armchair in front of the television pushing buttons on the remote. He was flipping from one channel to another, but there was nothing on TV that he wanted to watch. Hell, he didn't want to be watching TV at all, but he was too wired to even try to sleep.

At first, coming home felt wonderful. The kids and the dog were out the front door and dancing around him before he'd even swung his leg over the Harley. Sasha jumped into his arms and Bruno hugged his leg, and Doobie was wiggling his butt so hard he almost fell over, all the while showing his teeth in that goofy Doberman grin.

He couldn't stop grinning himself. He bent down and gave Doobie's neck a good scratch, then headed for the house with a kid perched on each hip, both kids chattering non-stop.

Mo stood in the doorway, smiling. He leaned forward to kiss her and she kissed him back, just a superficial smack, but it was a good start. He'd arrived just in time to barbecue the hamburgers, she told him.

"We're having hamburgers and fries, just like McDonald's only more healthy," said Sasha. "Isn't that right, Mama?"

"Oui, cherie," Mo said, "More healthy and they taste better, too. The buns are fresh and won't be all soggy."

Sorry couldn't resist saying, "Your mom's buns are the freshest and best I've ever tasted."

Mo's smile vanished and she looked away. He decided he'd better not push his luck, and tried to be on his best behavior, but somehow things still managed to go downhill from there.

He helped with the dishes after dinner, then played with the kids so Mo could have some time to herself for a long bath. Later he read stories to the kids and put them to bed. He even cleaned off the barbecue grill and picked up all the kids' toys from the patio.

It was a bad sign when Mo sat in the recliner reading one of her French novels and left him sitting by himself on the couch to watch a rerun of NYPD Blue. He kept trying to catch her eye, and when she did finally glance up at him, all he got in exchange for his sexiest come-hither expression was about two seconds of a rather chilly smile.

"C'mon, Mo," he said with a wink. "Didn't you miss me, just a little?"

She didn't look up from her book again, only shrugged.

He was doing exactly what she told him to do, he was treating her like a queen, and still she was treating him like shit. With every minute, his resentment grew. Why should he put up with a woman who didn't appreciate him? He began to work his jaw, trying to keep from saying anything that might make things worse. *Pussy whipped!* He made a conscious effort to see things from her point of view, to figure out if there was any justification for her behavior, but the phrase his fellow bikers would use if they could see him now kept repeating itself in his brain. *Pussy whipped!*

Next time she glanced in his direction, he was glaring at her. He looked away and began to scratch at a corner of his mustache. Out of the corner of his eye, he saw her put her book down on the end table and get up from the recliner. Without speaking, she left the room and came back a minute later with a blanket and a pillow.

"You can't be serious," he said, enunciating each word slowly.

He was on the verge of an angry explosion when she put her hands on his shoulders – as soft and gentle as kitten paws – and he felt the warmth of them through his teeshirt. She leaned in and kissed him on the lips, a tender kiss, lingering just a delicious few seconds. "I do love you, mon cher. But I was hurt and sadly disappointed one time too much. I am afraid to trust you, cherie." Her eyes searched his, for an answer or for forgiveness, he couldn't tell which. "I hope you understand me, and please – please, Daniel – give me time to trust you again."

She turned and walked away. At the hallway leading to the bedrooms, she stopped and turned back to him. "I will set my alarm clock and wake you in time," she said. "Good night, mon coco." With a little wave and a smaller smile, she was gone.

So now Sorry sat on the couch. The biker side of him kept arguing with the husband and father side of him; the biker side sneered and chanted 'pussy whipped!' while the husband and father side told him to give her time, she was worth it. The kids were worth it. Then the biker would say 'Fuck her!' and call Mo a bitch. Sorry was caught in the middle, feeling so unsettled he couldn't rest.

Doobie wandered in from the kitchen, his nails clicking on the linoleum tiles until he reached the carpet. He laid his head on Sorry's knee, looking up at him with woeful brown eyes. Were those eyes expressing sympathy for Sorry's circumstances, or did the dog just have to pee?

"Okay, pal," said Sorry, rubbing the dog's head. "Let's go pee."

He walked out the back door behind the dog. Doobie trotted over to a well-watered lilac bush while Sorry stood in the middle of the weedy lawn and unzipped his fly. As he pissed, he looked up at the night sky. There was a waning moon, still big and bright enough to make soft shadows as his eyes adjusted to the dark. He heard a soft snuffle from Bruno's open window and a feeling of contentment seeded itself somewhere in his chest.

"Welcome home, Sorenson," he whispered to himself. The husband and father side of him repeated the earlier messages: 'Give her time, she's worth it, the kids are worth it', and surprised him a little by adding one more line.

'And you, Daniel Henrik Sorenson, you're worth it, too.'

CHAPTER SIXTEEN

They sat in a corner booth at the first open bar they came to by walking the unpaved streets of Dawson. On the table between them an unappetizing plate of nachos was cooling off and two bottles of Corona beer were warming up. The soft yellow light of the fixture hanging above the table was kinder to April than the white light of the nurses' station had been. In spite of the bleached hair, he could more clearly see in her the young woman he had been attracted to so many years ago. He had no illusions about how much his own face had aged, nor did he feel attracted to her now, or wish she was attracted to him. He'd never really known her, he realized, never thought of her as the kind of woman who would willfully abandon her child.

At his request, April explained to Hunter why she had suddenly decided to come back to the Yukon. She had received some mysterious calls and felt sure that they had something to do with her daughter.

"A woman from some detective agency had managed to track me down, but she wouldn't say why. I knew it had to be about my daughter. Then when I saw two calls from a Whitehorse payphone on my caller ID, I decided I had to come. I flew into Whitehorse just this afternoon and immediately went to talk to the RCMP to ask if they knew the whereabouts of Betty Salmon or my daughter. She was born at Martin's cabin so her birth was never recorded. She didn't have an official last name, except maybe my own maiden name, so the only name I had for her was Golden Dawn. They told me Betty was missing, and that the report had been made by her granddaughter, a girl named Goldie. I can't tell you how that made me feel, knowing Goldie was alive and I would get to see her."

She blinked rapidly, then closed her eyes a moment before continuing. "I was still at the detachment when news came in that Betty had been found and taken to Dawson, and that Goldie would be notified to come for her, so I arranged a flight here."

"Your daughter's twenty-five years old." Hunter softened the inherent reproach with a sad smile.

"You're asking me why I waited this long to come looking for her." April looked down at her lap, and seemed in no hurry to explain.

Since learning that April was alive, Hunter had wondered if she had ever made an effort to find her daughter. Had Betty's relocation to a remote village in Alaska made it impossible for her to find Goldie? Or was there another reason, possibly a reason related to the bloody cabin near Johnson's Crossing? There was no statute of limitations on murder. Had she been afraid that she was on the suspect list?

"What were you afraid of?"

She took a deep breath. "It took a lot for me to come here," she said. "My husband – he's a psychologist who does counseling for army vets – he says I have PTSD. Do you know what that is?"

Hunter nodded. Reasoning that the police and the military weren't all that far apart, he'd researched combat stress when Ken was struggling with depression, before his suicide. He didn't want to apply the term to his own situation, but in the back of his mind he knew that seeing Ken's body had been some kind of trigger – the proverbial last straw – the event that began his own descent into apathy and enervation at work, that feeling of burnout that eventually led him to resign from the force.

She closed her eyes again. "I'm on Prozac now," she said. "But up until recently, just the thought of returning to Michigan or the Yukon would have me curled up in a fetal position in a dark room."

"I'm sorry."

"My husband wanted to come with me, but I told him it was something I had to do on my own. Facing my demons, I guess."

They were both silent for a moment. Hunter picked at the nachos and April took a couple of sips of beer.

"Tell me about Martin Blake."

Even in the soft light he saw the color drain from her face.

"Martin was a kind man. He knew I was pregnant and had nowhere else to go, and he took me in."

Hunter was confused. That wasn't what he expected to hear.

"So what happened?"

"He's dead, isn't he?" Her face displayed her sorrow.

"I can't confirm that. The day you left, what happened?"

Instead of answering, she said, "That wasn't his real name, you know. He confessed to me once – I guess he felt safe telling me because I was kind of a deserter myself, in a way – he confessed that he was a deserter from the army. That's why he kept such a low profile. Well, one reason. He wasn't a sociable man. He didn't share much information about his past, even with me."

"You mean from the U.S. Army, right? So he told you that was why he didn't use his real name?" They'd been right in identifying him as Grant Sanford, he thought.

"That's right," she said. "He'd been in Vietnam, and when he came back to the States on compassionate leave – his dad suffered a heart attack – he knew he couldn't go back. He said he'd killed a man in Vietnam. He said he was very young, almost a boy. He saw the boy's face when he was hit; he looked so surprised that he'd been shot, and Martin watched him die. He didn't ever want to have to do it again."

"But he killed his wife," said Hunter, thinking Blake must have lied to April about when and why he'd deserted.

"No," she said, sounding and looking horrified. "Why are you saying that? Martin was never even married, and if he was, he never would have hurt a woman. If he couldn't face killing another soldier in Vietnam, how could he be capable of killing anyone at home?"

Had Martin been able to hide his dark side from April? That wouldn't be at all unusual, given how short a time they'd been together. "Betty Salmon said you'd been badly beaten when she found you beside the river."

April shuddered. "Yes," she said. Her eyes seemed to lose their focus, and she seemed to be holding her breath.

"Can you talk about it?" he prompted gently. "Did he hurt you that day?"

She let out her breath and shook her head. "No. That wasn't Martin." Her eyes sought out Hunter's, and he saw a sudden realization in them, or perhaps a plea. "He did kill Martin, didn't he? All that blood. I knew he couldn't have survived."

"Tell me what happened." He reached across the table and squeezed her hand.

She took a deep breath and squared her shoulders, as if steeling herself. "I think it was the man Martin told me about a few weeks before. Martin said he recognized a man from army training in Louisiana, and he was worried the guy might have recognized him and might turn him in. Whoever he was, I never saw him before, and I prayed to God I would never see his face again."

She took a couple more deep breaths before continuing, her eyes again somehow unfocused as she spoke. "I was in bed with the baby. Napping. Martin had taken the canoe out fishing. I heard the dogs bark, then someone entered the cabin. I assumed it was Martin, so I called out. Just hello or something, to let him know I was awake, then I dozed off again." She frowned, as if straining to remember. "Next thing I knew, someone pulled back the quilt, held me by the throat and ripped off my shirt, and there was a heavy, foul-smelling man on top of me. I was afraid for the baby; I couldn't feel her beside me but I heard her crying. Her cries were muffled, and I worried she was smothering."

She was staring into a distance well beyond the walls of the room. "I screamed and tried to push him off, and he hit me with his fist, again and again until I stopped fighting. Even when I stopped, he punched me in the head and called me a sanctimonious bitch. I know he raped me, I was hurt and bleeding there later, but I think I passed out because I don't exactly remember it, and I don't remember Martin coming back. He must have, though, because when I woke up, Martin was lying face down on the bed across my legs. He wasn't moving and there was so much blood." She stopped speaking, as if she was out of breath.

Hunter squeezed her hand, hoping it would ground her, but she pulled her hand away and put it in her lap.

"The man who hurt you, can you describe him?"

She shook her head. "His face is a blur. He was big and he had a beard like Martin's. I think so, anyway. I hate to think about it, him killing Martin when Martin was probably trying to protect me."

"He didn't hurt the baby." Hunter tried to nudge her in a more positive direction.

"He pushed the baby off the bed. I found her all tangled up in the quilt, so I guess it cushioned her fall."

"Did you check to see if Martin was still breathing?"

She shook her head. "He wasn't moving and there was so much blood. I just had a sense that he was dead." She looked at Hunter as if imploring him to tell her she wasn't negligent. "I couldn't bear to touch him, and I couldn't have helped him if I stayed. I don't even know first aid. I just wanted to get the baby away from there in case he came back, so I gathered up a bundle of stuff I thought I'd need and ran."

"You took the canoe." Hunter remembered Betty Salmon's story.

"Yes. I was going to go to Whitehorse. I was going to go to the police." She offered a wan smile. "It was the only thing I could do, although if I had been thinking straight, I'd have known I didn't have a chance to get there. I guess I was half dead, or more, when Betty found me. I was struggling just to stay awake and hold on to little Golden. After I recovered, any idea of getting to Whitehorse just evaporated."

"You got there eventually. When you left the Yukon the next October, you dropped that anonymous note off at the RCMP detachment, the note giving us Martin's real name."

April frowned and shook her head. "A note? What note? I don't remember going to the RCMP in Whitehorse. I hitched a ride from Carmacks, where I'd gone with Betty. She went to sell her furs and beadwork and stock up on supplies for the winter. I hitched a ride down the highway to pick up my car. I drove south from there and never went back."

"You didn't leave a note about Grant Sanford? It mentioned him being from a military base in Leesville, Louisiana."

"Grant Sanford?" She shook her head again. "I don't remember a Grant Sanford. Who is he?"

"That wasn't Martin Blake's real name?"

"I wouldn't know. He didn't tell me. He said it was better that I not know."

Hunter tried to make sense of what she'd just said. The fingerprints had belonged to someone named Grant Sanford who was an army deserter, but Martin Blake had never given that name to April.

They had assumed that the fingerprints they'd found in the cabin belonged to Martin Blake. If they weren't Martin's prints, Hunter wondered, who was Grant Sanford and what was he doing in that cabin? "Did Martin have regular visitors at the cabin, friends or people he did business with?"

She shook her head. "None while I was there."

Maybe April could ID the photo of Grant Sanford as the man she knew as Martin. "Tell me more about this man Martin said he recognized from army training."

"I don't know anything more."

"Can you remember anything else he told you? Where did he run into the man?"

She chewed her lower lip, frowning, before she spoke again. "Teslin, I guess. He usually went to Teslin, I think. When he got back, he told me about this guy he'd seen there. He said he pretended not to know the guy, but they'd been somewhere in the army together and he was afraid he'd been recognized." She picked up a chip from the plate of nachos, examined it with a worried expression on her face, then put it down again. "Up until then, I always thought Martin was a draft dodger. That was when he told me he was afraid the man would turn him in as a deserter. I remember wondering what I would do if somebody came for Martin. The baby was due in a few weeks. I was pretty reckless in those days, but not reckless enough to have my baby all by myself in a cabin, miles away from any other human, let alone a doctor. I decided that if somebody came to get Martin, I'd ask them to at least take me back up the highway for my car."

She looked at her watch. "When do you think my daughter will arrive in Dawson? Shouldn't we go see if she's at the clinic yet?"

Goldie stole a glance at Mark's profile. He looked serious and competent and self-assured. She would have liked to stare at him, but the occasional quick glance would have to do. Riding with Mark felt different in Sally's big F250, not like it had in Mark's sporty red Jeep. It felt right, somehow, sitting here beside him in the big Ford crew cab pickup, almost like they were – she was afraid to think it – married or something. He couldn't know what she was feeling, but she felt embarrassed just the same; when he caught her looking at him, she started to blush.

"What?" he asked.

She pressed her lips together, suppressing a nervous giggle. "I was just thinking about Gran," she lied.

"She'll be okay."

"I know that's what they said. She'll be *physically* okay." Goldie sighed. "I'm more worried about her –" Goldie paused. Was she worried about her mental state or her emotional state? It was odd to think about Gran having emotions; she'd always been so strong and stoic and didn't show much emotion one way or another. Irritation sometimes. More rarely, enjoyment. Gran was like a rock or a tree, impassive and restrained. "I don't know what this experience will do to her."

"Meaning?"

"Failing at what she set out to do. Having to be rescued. She's not used to that. She's been living life on her terms, being a survivor. Now suddenly she won't know how to think of herself."

"Everybody gets old. Why should she expect to be different?"

Goldie looked out her window. They were on the Top of the World Highway, heading for Dawson City for the second time in just three days. The expansive view in every direction was no longer new, but seeing the sun drop behind the hills just after midnight and watching its progress just under the horizon – its fire flowing like molten gold along the hilltops under the twilight sky – was. It truly felt like they were travelling along the top of the planet.

"You get old and then you die," Mark said with a shrug, as if it were something trivial.

Somehow Mark's comment seemed unkind, and she wanted to argue against it. "That's not very nice," was all she said.

He shrugged again. "It's not my fault that life's a bitch."

She let it go. They were both tired, and she was feeling stressed. About Gran. About maybe finding her mother. Even about her relationship – or lack of one, she didn't really know where she stood – with Mark. A twilight gloom settled into the cab of the truck. Goldie told herself things weren't that bad. Gran would be okay. She was closer to finding her mother than she'd ever been. Mark cared enough for her to drive her to Dawson. It was no good. Her inborn optimism still eluded her.

But as the sun stopped its teasing and yellow light burst over the hills and into the truck, Mark reached over and squeezed her hand. She turned to him, and couldn't help but smile at his broad, ingenuous grin.

"Golden," he said, squeezing her hand again. "Just like you."

They arrived in Dawson just after three in the morning. In spite of the hour, there were several people wandering up and down Front Street, probably tourists enjoying the novelty of twenty-four hours of natural light. Mark eased the big pickup to a stop beside a group of teenagers to ask for directions to the clinic. A Kurt Cobain look-alike said he'd been there so he knew where it was. He told them to turn left down Church Street and look for a yellowish building on the right. A minute later they pulled up in front of a building with a Yukon government sign that read 'Dawson City Health Centre'.

Goldie climbed the stairs with butterflies in her stomach. It seemed all wrong. Gran didn't belong here. Sally had told her the nurse was sure Gran would be okay, but what was 'okay'? Was the nurse's 'okay' going to be okay enough for Gran. At the top of the stairs, she took a deep breath, then opened the heavy doors.

She was aware of a couple of people seated in the waiting room, but went directly to the nurse at a reception desk.

"I'm here to see Betty Salmon," she whispered. "I'm her granddaughter."

The nurse nodded and smiled, whispering back. "Have a seat. I'll go see if she's awake."

Goldie turned around. She realized that one of the people in the waiting area was Hunter Rayne. He remained seated but raised a hand to say hello. The blond woman beside him was on her feet, looking uncertainly at Goldie.

"Golden?" the woman said hesitantly. "Are you Golden?" The woman's naked angst loaded the simple question with an overwhelming significance.

Goldie froze. Her first crazy impulse was to run. In all her dreams about meeting her mother, she had never imagined an ordinary-looking woman – this slightly plump woman clutching a big leather handbag could be a tourist from anywhere Outside – approaching her unannounced. She wasn't prepared for this meeting. She wasn't prepared for that woman.

Goldie opened her mouth but nothing came out.

"Golden?" the woman repeated. She was an inch or two shorter than Goldie, something else that was completely unexpected. Hunter had said how much Goldie looked like her mother. She couldn't see herself in this stranger at all. The woman let her handbag fall to the floor and reached out with both hands toward Goldie, her eyes searching Goldie's face. A look of pain flooded the woman's features.

Could this stranger be her mother? In turn, Goldie studied the face in front of her and caught something familiar, something of herself reflected in the nose, in the chin. Almost involuntarily, almost convulsively, she wrapped her arms around the woman in a fierce hug, and felt the woman's fingers stroking her hair, her breath warm against her neck. Was it real? Was she really, finally hugging and being hugged by her mother? Goldie felt almost dizzy with the thought.

As they stepped back from each other, the woman seemed to Goldie once again a stranger. Everything she'd rehearsed to say evaded her, and Goldie found herself saying, "Have you seen Betty? How is she?" and watching the woman's lips tremble as she shook her head. A single tear ran down the woman's cheek as she once again reached out, taking hold of Goldie's hand. "I'm sorry," Goldie said. "I wasn't expecting –." She swallowed. "I mean, I don't know what to say. All the way here I've been so worried about Gran."

"Orville is with her. And Hootie as well." It was Hunter Rayne speaking. "She was completely exhausted when we found her, and she may well be asleep."

"Miss?"

Goldie spun around, relieved at the interruption. She gave her mother's hand a little squeeze before letting go.

"She's awake."

The nurse led her down a short hallway to a door. A uniformed Mountie was standing by the door, looking grumpy and a little disheveled. He nodded to her as the nurse ushered her inside, then entered the room right behind her.

Orville Barstow sat in a chair beside the bed, one hand grasping the rail of the hospital bed. As he lifted his hand, Goldie realized he was handcuffed to the rail. The Mountie slipped past her and undid the handcuff.

"Come on, Orville," he said. "Let's give these ladies a little privacy."

Goldie approached the bed, surprised that her grandmother hadn't said a word in greeting. Her eyes had opened and closed, but her head hadn't moved. Hootie came out from underneath the bed and licked Goldie's hand. She let her hand rest on his head as she stared down at her grandmother's face. She looked frail, and somehow smaller than Goldie had ever seen her look before.

"Gran?" she whispered.

"Take me home," said Gran. Her voice belied the frailty of her appearance. Still, she didn't try to sit up.

"The nurse says you need more rest." Gran had never been very demonstrative, but Goldie felt a need to touch her. She bent in to kiss her cheek.

"The nurse doesn't know what she's talking about." Gran waved a dismissive hand in front of Goldie's face. "I'll sleep better at home anyway."

Goldie's concern for the old woman evaporated and was replaced by an unexpected anger. "What were you thinking?" she said. "Do you know how worried I've been? You could have died. How could you possibly think you could travel that far alone?"

Gran propped herself up on one elbow and glared at her. "Ever think that I wasn't meant to come back? Maybe I can't choose the way I live anymore, but I can damn well die the way I want to!"

"What are you saying? How can you be so selfish?"

"Selfish? What's so selfish about it? You made me feel selfish for keeping you from knowing who your mother was so you wouldn't leave me and go looking for her. You called me selfish for making you feel guilty so you'd stay and keep me company in my old age." She spoke with surprising force, and a small clump of saliva bubbled at the corner of her mouth. "I thought selfish was never letting you make a life for yourself Outside. Did it occur to you that this time I was trying to do you a favor?" She fell back on her pillow and turned her face away.

Goldie's jaw dropped, her anger evaporated like snowflakes on a hot stove. She grabbed her grandmother's shoulders and shook her gently. "No, Gran. No. You're wrong. I wouldn't have traded my life, my growing up with you for anything."

When Gran finally spoke again, her voice had softened. "You are being kind to an old woman. I know how bad you always wanted me to tell you about your mother."

"Oh, Gran." Goldie eyes stung, and she felt a hot tear leave a cool track down one cheek. "Mark and I will take you home as soon as they say it's okay for you to leave."

"Mark brought you?"

Goldie nodded. She sensed the old woman's worry. Perhaps she thought Mark, too, would take her place in Goldie's affections. Gran seemed to be resigned to Goldie leaving, going Outside, going away with her mother. "Have you seen her?"

The old woman stiffened visibly. "Have I seen who?" she asked.

Goldie felt her stomach drop. So Gran didn't know that her mother was here. Goldie wasn't going to tell her. Not now. "The nurse," Goldie lied. "Have you asked her when it will be okay for you to leave?"

Her grandmother's eyes narrowed, but before she could speak there was a knock at the door.

"Is everything okay in there?" It was the nurse.

"Yes, fine. We were just wondering when I could take her home."

The nurse asked for a few minutes to check Gran's vital signs so she could complete her paperwork.

Gran asked where Orville was and Goldie left to go look for him while the nurse was wrapping Gran's arm in a blood pressure cuff. There was no one in the reception room except the woman who was her mother. The woman sat with her eyes closed and her shoulders slumped, the big handbag in her lap. Goldie crossed the room and sat down beside her.

"I'm sorry," she said again. Her mother smiled uncertainly. "Too much is happening all at once. I –" Goldie shook her head. "You caught me totally by surprise and I've just been so worried about Gran."

"It's okay." Her mother sighed and said, "Four a.m. in a clinic in Dawson City wasn't exactly the best time for us to meet, was it?" followed by a wan smile.

Goldie looked away, down at the floor. "Gran wants me to find Orville – the elderly man with a beard. Did you see where he went?"

Her mother nodded toward the front door. Goldie opened it just in time to see an RCMP Suburban pulling away from a parking spot in front of the building. "They can't be leaving," she said. "Hunter, too? They're just leaving us here like this?"

"The older fellow with the beard wanted to stay and say goodbye to Betty, but the Mountie said he had been told to leave Dawson as soon as you arrived. The other Mountie – Hunter, I guess – tried to make him change his mind, but he wouldn't budge."

It was all Goldie could do not to cry. She sat down and buried her face in her hands. She couldn't just leave her mother and take Gran back to Eagle. She also couldn't just leave Gran here at the clinic while she spent time getting to know her mother. She was caught in the middle, with Mark waiting outside in the truck. It was ironic, she thought, that here she was with a mother she didn't know and the woman who had been like a mother to her ever since she could remember, and yet she felt that she – the child – would have to be the one looking out for both of them. Now. This morning. No time outs. How could she keep one or both of them from being badly hurt?

She sensed her mother's presence beside her, and felt her mother's hand rub her back and her mother's arm come to rest across her shoulders.

"It'll be okay, sweetheart. It'll be okay."

Once again, Hunter sat in the back seat with Orville. The old man was visibly upset about their abrupt departure from the clinic, and he assumed that Betty Salmon would be even more so. Hunter had been on the verge of telling Constable Boudreau to go ahead without him, just so he could be there long enough to explain to Betty why Orville had to leave without saying goodbye. *Not my job to fix all the injustice in the world,* he told himself. *I'm not some Roy Rogers or Lone Ranger.*

At least he'd found out from April that she lived in Salem, Oregon and that her married name was Tranter, and he'd extracted a promise from her to contact Bart Sam at the Whitehorse RCMP detachment before she left the Yukon. He wished he'd had more time to talk to her himself, and found himself hoping that El wouldn't find a load for him until he'd had more time here. Her admonition came back to him again.

"You might be right."

Surprised by the sudden comment, Hunter turned to look at Orville. The old man was sitting with his arms crossed over his chest, chin down and eyes closed. At first Hunter wondered if he was talking in his sleep.

"I've been thinking about what you said." Orville's turned his head slightly, his right eye just a slit.

Hunter raised his eyebrows but didn't speak.

"It's a very hard decision for me, you know. The fact is, I don't know who killed Charles Collins. I didn't see it happen. I wasn't there. All I could be witness to is that I was at his bar with a companion, and that companion was angry at Collins, as was I. You people have no evidence against me, either, other than that I was there and had reason to be angry with Collins."

You people. Once again, Hunter didn't bother correcting him. Sometimes it was easier to let people think he was still in law enforcement.

"But you did know about the murder, correct?"

"Tinkerbell – my truck – still has a working radio, so yes, I heard about the murder, along with everyone else in Whitehorse who listened to the radio that morning."

"And you didn't feel you should come forward as a witness?"

"A witness to what? I told you, I wasn't there when the man was killed. Why would I want to throw my companion under the bus to save my own skin, when I don't know if he's any guiltier than I am? Besides, chances are I won't be found guilty of anything anyway."

"And if he did kill Charles Collins?"

Orville sighed. "That's where the difficulty comes in. If he did kill Collins, it wouldn't be good to let him get off scot-free. It wouldn't be good for him, it wouldn't please his mother – may she rest in peace – and it certainly wouldn't be good for me if I do end up being convicted of murder. You see my dilemma?"

"I do." Hunter shrugged. "But it's a decision you'll have to make on your own."

Orville looked puzzled. "Aren't you going to pressure me to reveal his name? Isn't that what you people do?"

"Not me," said Hunter. "Not anymore."

"Where are my clothes? Let me out of this thing." Betty pulled and pushed at the bars on either side of the bed, but they wouldn't go down. Being confined to a bed was starting to annoy her. The nurse laughed, which irritated her even more.

"Just a minute. I'll send your daughter in to help you get dressed."

"I don't need help to get dressed. I just need my clothes."

The nurse, a rosy cheeked young woman who smelled of baby powder, winked at her as she walked out the door.

"Besides, she's not my daughter." Betty dropped her voice. "She's not even my real granddaughter." She immediately regretted saying it aloud, even though there was no one in the room to hear. She eased herself back down onto the pillow. She wished Goldie would hurry back. Or having Orville there again would be fine, too.

The sheets were so stiff and the mattress so firm, it made her feel as if she were lying on crusty snow, without the cold. Alone. Being alone wasn't the same here as it was in the bush, she thought. Alone would be okay back home at the cabin, but here – She sensed a movement to her right, and two big paws dented the edge of the mattress, then a black nose was thrust between the bars to touch her hand.

"Hootie. Good boy." Betty, reached over the bars to lay her hand on her dog's broad head, just as the door opened and Goldie walked in. She came up to the bed and grabbed the bedrail with both hands, but didn't speak.

"You're crying, child. Why?"

The girl took a deep breath before she spoke. "I have something to tell you, Gran." She threw her head back and closed her eyes, in obvious distress. "I wish–. If only–. Oh, Gran, the timing is so wrong." She looked away and paused so long that Betty's mind had time to imagine half a dozen scenarios. The nurse had told Goldie that her grandmother was dying, or that she wouldn't be able to leave the clinic. Or maybe the cabin had burned down. Orville had suffered a fatal heart attack in the waiting room. Goldie herself was dying, or perhaps the child was pregnant.

"My mother is here."

It took a moment for the meaning of her words to sink in. "Your mother? April? April is here?"

The girl nodded.

"Here, in Dawson? Now?"

"I'm sorry, Gran. I know you're not feeling very strong right now after your ordeal, and you're in a hurry to get back to the Eagle. And that's what I expected to do, take you back home and look after you until you're feeling better. But now that my mother's here–" Her voice trailed off, and another tear coursed down her cheek.

Betty reached up and wiped it away with her thumb. She was still trying to work out the significance of Goldie's news. Had her mother come to take her away? If so, would Goldie agree to go? What were the chances her mother would just come to Eagle for a visit and then go away?

Hootie had gone over to Goldie as soon as she entered and now sat beside her, looking up expectantly at her face, his tail thumping softly against the floor. Betty knew he wanted to go outside, or perhaps, just like Betty, he was anxious to get back home. What did Goldie expect her to do? Lie in this damned bed for days?

"Get me out of here." Betty rattled the bedrails again. "Hootie needs to get out of here and so do I."

"And then what, Gran?"

"Take me home. You and your young friend came to take me back to Eagle, didn't you?"

"You don't understand, do you?" There were no tears now. Goldie spoke to her as if she were a moron or a whining child. "My mother is here. I need to spend some time with her. I can't just rush back to Eagle with you now."

Betty set her jaw. She did understand. She understood, but she more than wanted to go home, she needed to get out of Dawson, back to the solitude of her cabin, back to the routine of life at her little homestead outside of Eagle Village. "You can't just leave me here. Where's Orville?"

"Gone. They've taken him back to Whitehorse."

"Then *you* have to take me home. I can't stand to be here a minute longer."

"You did this to yourself, Gran. You're the one who left on that – that crazy stupid journey down the Yukon River. You're the one who kept my mother a secret from me almost all my life. You're the one who – oh, never mind." With that, the girl threw up her hands and whirled around, almost running to the door and jerking it open so hard that it hit Hootie, who had scampered along beside her.

Betty and her dog watched the door close, then looked at each other, both powerless to escape from the room, let alone from Dawson City, without her help.

Once outside in the hallway, Goldie paused. She didn't want to go back and face Gran, nor did she want to explain things to the woman who claimed to be her mother. Goldie wished she could just run away from the whole situation. It wasn't right. It wasn't fair to make her choose between her mother and Gran, especially to make the choice here and now. Her first impulse was to sneak out the back door and climb into the truck with Mark, slam the door and tell him to drive, just drive. Drive south, out of the Yukon, away from Alaska, out on the open road.

That line from the poetry book left behind by her mother – the mother of her imagination, not the woman in the waiting room – came back to her. *Afoot and lighthearted, I take to the open road. Healthy, free, the world before me, the long brown path before me leading wherever I choose.* Gran had wronged her, but so had her mother. Her mother had left her as an infant, and never come back for her until today. Now they both expected her to love them. They both felt they had some kind of claim on her.

Her situation reminded her of that bible story she'd learned in school, the story of the judgment of King Solomon, when two women were fighting over a baby and the king picked up a sword and said he would divide the baby in two. One woman said she would rather give the baby away than see it killed, and the king thought this was the real mother. But what did '*real mother*' mean to King Solomon? Was it the *biological* mother, or instead, the woman who was the most concerned for the baby's welfare, or the *best* mother. So far, had either of the mother figures in her life acted in her best interests, rather than their own? She thought not.

I can't, she decided. *I can't just run away.* There was no King Solomon to make a judgment for her, so she would have to do it herself. She squared her shoulders, turned around and walked back into her grandmother's room.

CHAPTER SEVENTEEN

While Boudreau piloted the RCMP Suburban down the Klondike Highway to Whitehorse, Hunter waited for Orville to resume their earlier conversation, but aside from the occasional comment on something outside the windows of the Suburban – a moose and her calf trotting down the shoulder, a broken-down semi in the northbound lane, or a convoy of identical RVs from California – Orville pretty much kept his thoughts to himself. As did Hunter.

His brief interview with April had him re-examining the entire bloody cabin case from day one, as near as he could remember it. He reviewed all the possible suspects and tried to determine which of them could be unequivocally eliminated. Until April's eyewitness account had confirmed Blake's death at another man's hands, one of the prime suspects had always been a grizzly. Hunter was now certain that the grizzly had just been an opportunistic scavenger who was attracted by the smell of blood and dragged a dead or dying Blake out of the cabin. The man who had called the RCMP to investigate the abandoned cabin, Fred Klimmer, couldn't be entirely ruled out, since there was no way to get a good alibi for a trapper living alone in the bush, but other than the fact that he'd made the initial call, there was no reason to consider him a suspect.

April hadn't come back for her baby. Was that because she was afraid of being arrested for the murder, whether self-defense or not? He knew he carried a bias toward her innocence, and had since the beginning. If she hadn't planned on coming back to the Yukon, why had she left her baby behind? Could it have something to do with the baby's father? Was he involved? If April was lying about what happened in the cabin, what could compel her to tell the truth?

With the identification of Martin Blake as Grant Sanford, a new possibility arose. Was it possible that Sanford had been tracked down by relatives of his wife and her brother – the two people he'd murdered in Louisiana – and they had come seeking revenge? Or was it someone obsessed with punishing the men who had deserted their fellow soldiers in Vietnam? If a customs officer at the Yukon-Alaska border still had strong feelings against draft dodgers now, in 1997, how had recently returned Vietnam veterans felt in 1972?

Maybe April had been the intended target that day. Blake could have walked in on a man who had nothing against him, but had come to sexually assault the attractive young woman. Could it have been a man who had first seen her at The Sluice Box? Hunter was sure he wasn't the only one who wanted to get to know her better that summer. Maybe the carefree hippie chick had laughed off the man's advances and he'd been enraged by the rejection and jealous of Blake?

It was also possible that Blake had been in a dispute with another trapper in the area. Hunter tried to recall other instances of territorial disputes between trappers or prospectors. He was convinced that in some cases, these disputes had never come to light. Men in those dangerous, solitary occupations in remote wilderness areas might disappear for any number of reasons and not be missed for months or years, if ever. Bodies in the river, or scavenged and scattered by animals, buried in snow or decaying in a remote part of the wilderness, never seen again. How many missing people in Alaska and the Canadian north had been searched for and never found, and how many more had never even been reported missing? He guessed there had been many.

"Orville?" The old man's eyes were closed, but his features were not relaxed enough to suggest he was asleep, although his head swayed slightly with the movement of the vehicle. "You awake?"

One eye opened and the beard bobbed in a nod. "I am."

"Did you ever get into a territory dispute with another trapper?"

The old man's whiskers spread in a smile and he shook his head. "Come now, officer. Your cover was blown, or have you forgotten?"

"It's not what you think. I've given up on getting a confession out of you." Hunter returned the smile. "Here's what I'm after. A man disappeared from his cabin back in 1972. Looked like his body had been dragged out of the cabin by a grizzly, but indications are that he was either gravely injured or already dead before the grizzly showed up. We never found a body so we have no way of knowing what the cause of death might have been, but we have reason to believe that he was killed by another man. Why would another man have come to a trapper's base camp inside his concession with intent to harm?"

Orville nodded three or four times, slowly. "I see."

"One of the possible theories is that a trap line dispute ended in murder. Based on your experience as a trapper, does that sound plausible to you?"

"Most men in the north abide by an unwritten code of ethics, so to speak. But there are thieves and scoundrels in every line of work, I expect, and you've probably seen your share."

Hunter nodded.

"If it were me, and I found another man's traps in my concession, I'd spring the trap and hang it on a nearby tree. If he's put the trap there by mistake – as you can imagine, it's easy to get confused about concession boundaries, especially when you're new to the area – then he'd just pack up his trap and move it back to where it belongs. If he figured he was in the right, he'd reset his trap and we'd have to have a discussion at some point. Now, if some crook were actually stealing fur out of my traps, that would be a different matter entirely. That's like taking cash out of my pocket, and I'd track the fellow down and make him give me my fur back or else, if you'll pardon the pun, fur would fly."

"You'd report him?"

"Some men might go that route." From the wrinkles in the corners of Orville's eyes, Hunter assumed a sly smile hid behind the beard. "I prefer a little backwoods diplomacy."

"So it's possible such a dispute might escalate to murder."

"You're the policeman. You tell me."

When Hunter didn't respond immediately, the old man said, "Well?"

"Depends entirely on the men involved, doesn't it?"

Orville nodded. Again that sly smile. "Would you, sir, if you were a trapper instead of a Mountie?"

"Would I what?"

"Murder someone over money, or its equivalent?"

Hunter didn't have to think about it. It was a topic that he had discussed with fellow Mounties many times in the past over a beer or two or three. "No."

"You sound pretty sure of that. When would you? Murder someone, I mean?"

"I don't think murder is the right word. I would kill someone if it was necessary in order to keep him from taking someone else's life. If someone dear to me was in immediate danger –" He imagined one of his daughters, Janice or Lesley, being threatened or attacked and his muscles tensed at the mere thought. "– I wouldn't hesitate to kill." He took a deep breath and tried to relax. It took him a few seconds to ask, "How about you?"

"We're much the same, you and I. But I think your question really should be, if someone did come to the trapper's cabin with intent to harm, as you put it, was there something more at stake than a few furs on a trap line?"

"Could be." Hunter nodded his head thoughtfully. Something more at stake. Funny how he used to tell himself that April's welfare was what caused the mystery of the bloody cabin to gnaw at him over the years. Here she was, alive and well, and he still hadn't lost his obsession to solve the case.

Betty was a little unsteady on her feet, but she figured it was from being confined in bed, not to mention lack of decent food since she left Eagle. She shook off Goldie's arm as soon as she got her balance. "I'm not crippled," she said, and added,"–just hungry. I could use a mug of tea and a good breakfast."

Goldie stood in front of the door, blocking her way out of the room. Betty and Hootie both stood facing her, itching to get out. "I have to tell you something, Gran."

"Well, what is it? I don't want to hang around here any longer than I have to."

The girl jerked her head in the direction of the outer door. "My mother is out there. I need you to sit down with her – with us – and I want you and her to answer my questions. You both owe it to me, and whichever one of you refuses to give me the answers I'm entitled to –." She chewed on her lip before continuing. "Well, let's just say I'll know which one of you cares about me and which one just cares about herself."

Betty felt her anger rising and was on the verge of saying, 'After all I've done for you,' but thought better of it. Her mouth went dry. Whatever was meant to happen would happen. The child deserved to know.

"Step away, child." As Betty pushed past Goldie, she motioned toward Hootie. "Take him out the back door so he can do what he needs. Maybe your young friend can look after him. They don't want dogs in here."

When Goldie didn't move right away, she added, "Go. Go on. Take the dog out the back." She watched the girl grab the dog's ruff and lead him toward the back exit, then she turned and, steadying herself on the wall, walked out to the waiting room.

"April," she said.

The woman stood up as Betty entered the room. Her immediate appearance was quite unlike the way she'd looked last time Betty saw her, as if April had returned disguised as an older woman, but there was no mistaking that face and its similarity to her daughter's.

"So, how are you now?" Betty asked.

"I'm well, Betty. How are you?"

"No. I said, how are you *now*? What kind of mother are you? Last time we met, you were not a good mother."

"What are you talking about? I've always been a good mother. I have three other children besides Goldie. I've raised them well and we're a very close family."

"Maybe now you are a good mother. You weren't for Goldie. Not then."

April's face clouded. "That's not how I remember it. You're trying to excuse what you did. Why didn't you answer my letters?"

Betty softened her voice and stepped closer to the woman, looking deep into her eyes. Her eyes were troubled, not just angry. Betty reached for April's cheek as if to lay her hand against it, but slowly drew it away again. "I'm not putting blame on you. You weren't fit for life in the north. You weren't strong enough. You never got over being beaten, and you didn't like the hard work it takes to survive in the bush." She shook her head. "You were a flower child, not a bush woman."

"I should have taken her with me."

Betty shook her head again. "I made it hard for you. No. I made it *easy* for you *not* to take her. You were glad when I said I'd keep her."

"Glad for her sake, maybe. I didn't know if my car would still be where I left it, or how hard the trip would be on her, or even for sure where I was going."

"That's what you want to believe. The truth is that your nerves were bad and you had no patience with her."

There was a sudden hard edge to April's voice. "I know very well what the truth is. You wanted a baby of your own so you kept her. You've had her to yourself for almost twenty-four years and I will not – I will *not* – discourage her from coming home to Oregon with me."

Betty glanced at the front door. "She'll be here soon." She took a deep breath and stood as tall as her aching body would allow. "I will not fight you for her. She is a grown woman now and she can choose what to do with her life. Just promise me you will make this day easy for her, whatever she chooses."

The door opened, and they both turned to see Goldie enter the room. Goldie's worried eyes moved from Betty to her mother and back again, but no one spoke. They heard voices from outside, then behind Goldie a young couple with two small children entered the clinic. All three women stayed silent as they watched the young mother settle her children on either side of her chair while the young father rang the bell at the reception desk.

Goldie directed a small, uncertain smile at April, then at Betty, and said, "We better go find someplace else to talk."

"Call me Al, Danny."

Big Al was Sorry's new boss. He was a beefy, clean-looking dude with round pink cheeks and an early Beatles hair style. Using the name Danny was, in Sorry's opinion, the first strike against him. Other than that, so far Dan Sorenson liked his new boss, but it was only his first day on the job. It was easy to like a guy who seemed to like you back, he thought. *I guess I haven't fucked up yet.*

Sorry made the effort to arrive on time. Mo had barely said a word, but she was watching him closely as he got ready to leave, even made him scrambled eggs and toast and handed him a bag lunch. When he got to the warehouse in Newton, the boss invited him into his office and offered him a fresh coffee. The guy had made him fill out some paperwork, just so it was official that Sorry was on the payroll and could drive the company truck, then Al had quickly gone over what he expected from his driver. Stuff like he should dress professionally – Sorry's clean jeans and new blue tee shirt seemed to meet the criteria – be on time for work, be polite to the customers, obey traffic regulations. All the usual bullshit.

The preliminaries were over quickly because there was work to be done, deliveries to make. Sorry's new employer was a plumbing, heating and electrical supplies wholesaler that distributed wholesale orders to contractors and retailers all around the Lower Mainland of Vancouver.

Big Al said, "Damn, I'm glad you were free to start right away. We've had to use two or three delivery outfits since we lost our last driver. Besides the extra cost, you can't just get on the blower and talk to a driver to find out when he'll get there, or divert him to pick up a hot shipment that's just landed at the airport or whatever." They were standing at the back of a loaded truck and Big Al was gesturing at the cartons and crates stacked inside its box. Today's load contained everything from small tools and parts to bathtubs, shower stalls and furnaces.

"Everything including the kitchen sink," the boss joked.

Sorry rewarded Al's stupid joke with a genuine laugh, at least he hoped it sounded genuine, and assured him that he knew the city well and was good with paperwork. He'd have no trouble keeping track of what to deliver where and when, and returning all of the signed receipts at the end of the day.

Big Al handed him a cell phone in some kind of leather holster. "You'll need this. Put your belt through this loop. Speed dial number one to reach me, not for personal calls and whatever you do, don't leave it in your truck when you're making a delivery, okay. And make sure you lock the doors – the cab and the roll up –anytime the truck's outa your sight. Last guy wasn't always careful with that."

Sorry was on the verge of asking him what happened to the last guy when a speaker on the ceiling came to life. "Al. Call on line two. Al. Call on line two, please."

Big Al slapped Sorry on the shoulder and said, "Gotta get that. Got any questions, just get on the blower." As he walked away, he pointed at the cell phone in Sorry's hand. "Only stupid question is the one you don't ask. Better ask a dozen stupid questions than make one mistake. Got it?"

Sorry nodded and held up his right hand to signal that he got it, then lit a cigarette and started leafing through his paperwork and checking the orders against the load on the truck. A forklift ground to a halt behind him and a middle-aged man in coveralls swung out from behind the wheel. Sorry noticed the name on the coveralls was Tito.

"You're the new guy, eh?" said Tito. "Better put that coffin nail out before the boss sees ya. He's allergic, eh?" The man looked Sorry up and down as Sorry took a last deep drag, then shook his head. "Don't expect you'll be around long," he added, stressing the 'you'.

Sorry was half inclined to mash the cigarette out in Tito's face, but that wouldn't have been a very good start to their relationship so he ground it out on the warehouse floor, then picked up the butt and tucked it in his back pocket.

"Al must've forgot to mention that," he said, then stuck out his big mitt. "Hey, Tito." It was all he could do to keep from calling him Titty. "My name's Dan Sorenson. Nice to meet you, and I appreciate the tip." *If only Hunter could see me now,* he thought. "You the one who loaded my truck?"

"Yes. Usually me and the driver do it together, so I can load the stuff in the order you want, if you got a plan for your route, eh?" Tito squinted at Sorry, waiting for a reaction.

Sorry gave him what he wanted. "You did a good job on your own, man. I appreciate it. I had to fill out some paperwork for Al this morning, but tomorrow I'll come right in here and we can do the load together." Sorry worked real hard and dredged up a smile. "Take it easy on me, okay? I'm the new guy, and you know I'm gonna make some mistakes. I'm sure as the senior employee you'll be patient until I learn the ropes." Sorry could hardly believe what was coming out of his mouth. *I'm lying like a rug.* Hunter was right. It sure comes easy and I think it's gonna pay off.

He checked his wristwatch as he pulled out of the yard. His first stop was about twenty minutes away. As he accelerated down Highway 10 toward Cloverdale, he reached into the lunch bag Mo had packed and felt around. There was a sandwich and an apple, and his fingers identified a plastic-wrapped object that felt like cookies. Perfect. Just a little something to tide him over until lunch.

Goldie looked over at Yukon Sally's pickup and saw Mark with his seat reclined and his head back. She knew he needed the sleep after driving through the night, so the three women bypassed the truck in silence and headed for a small green space across the lane from the clinic, adjacent to the Dawson City Museum in the Old Territorial Administration Building. Out of nowhere it seemed, Hootie appeared and trotted just ahead of them. "Are you up to walking, Gran?" asked Goldie. "There must be a bench around here somewhere."

Betty nodded, but this time she let Goldie take her arm and Goldie felt her grandmother lean against her, ever so slightly. "The nurse said you should take it easy for a couple of days, so don't push yourself."

They found a bench in the sun, facing a little garden in the center of the lawn. Goldie motioned to her mother to sit, then sat down herself in the middle of the bench and waited for Betty to settle herself on her right.

"I'd like to –," began April.

Goldie raised a hand to stop her and shook her head. "Wait. Before you speak, let me say what I need to say. Please."

Two young boys on bicycles raced down the path that bisected the little park, one yelling over his shoulder to the other to hurry up. Goldie watched until they disappeared around the back of the big wooden building that housed the museum. She took a deep breath and blew it out again. Where to start?

"This is a very emotional day for me. I've been crazy worried about Gran – Betty," she added for her mother's benefit, "– and suddenly seeing my mother for the first time is kind of an overload." She paused, her eyes closed and her lips pressed together. "I don't want to hurt either one of you, but somehow I think that today, it has to be about me. It may not be intentional on your part – on either of your parts – but I feel like I'm in the middle of a tug-of-war. I'm not responsible for what happened twenty-four years ago, so it's not fair to make me responsible for what's happening today. Do you understand what I'm saying?" She looked first at Betty, and then at April.

Betty nodded, a solemn expression on her weathered face. April blinked her eyes and looked at the dirt between her feet, as if she'd been scolded.

Goldie kept her eyes on her mother as she said, "The way I see it, you made life very difficult for me. I'm a nobody. It's lucky they let me go to school in Eagle, and it's lucky my friend Tessa gave me her driver's license to cross the border today, because I have no legal name and no legal country. And Gran, you did nothing to fix that. You just took me somewhere you knew it wouldn't matter so much. I need that fixed. I need to have a legal identity so I can have a life, wherever I go.

"I've grown up not really knowing who I am. I always thought, because of the color of my hair and because Gran is part Gwich'in, that I was part Gwich'in myself. My native heritage has been a proud part of my identity, and since I found out about you," she nodded at her mother, "that's been taken away from me.

"It's not that I'm angry about that – being angry won't solve anything –but it's made me feel kind of lost and I'm impatient to discover who I really am. Me. Alone. Myself, standing on my own two feet, going where I want and not where either of you think I should go. Or stay."As she spoke, she scuffed her foot repeatedly on the ground in front of the bench, creating a small depression in the brown dirt. *Afoot and lighthearted, I take to the open road.*

"Gran, I need to leave Eagle. Not today, not tomorrow, but soon." She turned to her mother. "I will come visit you in Oregon, but I won't stay." *Healthy, free, the world before me.* "I want to go to college, get a job, see as much of the world as I can afford to see before I decide where to spend the rest of my life." *The long brown path before me leading wherever I choose.* "Do you understand?"

This time it was April who nodded. "I hope you do a better job of discovering yourself than I did, and I wish you luck. I hope you're taking into account that this wasn't an easy trip for me to make. I had to …"

Betty raised both her hands and motioned for April to wait. "Let me speak first," she said. "I will not take part in any tug-of-war. I will miss you very much, but you will go with my blessing. I'm an old woman, and I don't have much time left so ..."

"No! Don't do that to me again!" Goldie sprang up from the bench and turned to face her grandmother. "Everybody gets old, everybody dies. It's not my fault! And I can't put my life on hold waiting for you to die." She immediately regretted her outburst and went down on one knee before the old woman, taking one of her grandmother's hands in both of hers. "I'm sorry, Gran. It's not that I don't care. I do care, and it hurts me. I hope you live to be a hundred and that my children are lucky enough to get to know you, but I'll never get to have any children if you don't let me go."

Gran closed her eyes tight, her mouth twisted as if she were in pain. She nodded and patted Goldie's hand.

April cleared her throat, and Goldie turned to look at her. "I would have called or written if I'd known how to reach you, either one of you. Look, I know my timing was bad. I've accomplished what I came for. I've met you –" She smiled at Goldie. "– and I'm sure you'll let me know how to reach you again. I only ask one thing, for now, and then I'll go."

Goldie stood and stepped back from the bench. She used her right hand to shield her eyes against the brightness of the sun. "Yes?"

"A promise that you'll spend some time with me, that you will come to visit me in Oregon, or let me come to visit you, whether it's here in the north or somewhere else." She directed her gaze to the ground as she continued. "I can't change the past. Maybe it was for the best that I left you behind with Betty. You seem to me to be a wonderful young woman, strong and kind and beautiful." Her eyes were wet as she raised them to Goldie's and smiled. "I'm sorry. I'm sorry if I've hurt you in any way."

April stood up and stepped forward to hug her. Relieved that the tug-of-war she'd anticipated hadn't materialized, Goldie hugged her back and whispered the same words back to her. "I'm sorry, too. I didn't want to hurt you today." She looked at Gran over April's shoulder. "Either of you."

"If you don't want to hurt me, why are you letting me starve? I need something to eat, and a mug of strong tea, or I'm not getting up off this bench." Gran made shooing motions with her hands. There was no sign of a smile on her face. "Go. Go for a walk, both of you. Find me something to eat. Let me be alone with my dog for awhile. We feel a need to warm our bones here in the sun and your sappy babble is more than we can stomach. Right, Hootie?" At his name, the dog stood and laid his head on the old woman's lap, his tail wagging.

When Goldie hesitated, Gran spoke again, louder and more insistent. "I said go. Go away and don't come back unless you plan to feed me." She wrapped her arms around the dog's neck and laid her cheek against the top of his head.

April smiled. "Same old Betty." She nodded at Goldie and reached for her arm. As Goldie and her mother walked away, they heard the old woman speaking softly to her dog.

"I guess you saved my life again, didn't you, boy? Thank you, old friend."

Hunter decided he'd only stay one more day and promised himself that by the next afternoon, he'd fuel up the Freightliner and head back to B.C. where he had a greater chance of scoring a southbound load. He knew he should call El to see if she had found anything for him yet, but decided to put it off. He had persuaded Bart to let him look through the case files related to the bloody cabin. There had to be something there, something that hadn't seemed important at the time, but now with the new information – or misinformation? – from April, he could review it from a fresh perspective.

Bart left for a meeting, and Hunter turned to the documents in front of him, determined to find something that would help him unravel the mystery of Martin Blake's death. Seeing the original notes regarding the case hit him hard. Reading his own and Ken's words from 1972 pulled him back in time and it was all he could do to concentrate on their meaning instead of losing himself in personal memories of those first heady years in the RCMP. Back then as young recruits they were motivated and stimulated and cared so deeply about what they were doing. It was a far cry from the last years before Ken's death. By that time, both of them – Ken more so than Hunter – had become jaded and disillusioned by the justice system, so often a revolving door that failed to keep brutal criminals off the street.

He pulled himself back to the present and went over some of Ken's notes, trying to read between the lines. He remembered Ken telling him that he'd spoken to Blake once in Whitehorse, before April left her job. He said the guy seemed okay but not very sociable. That was understandable for an army deserter trying to keep his distance from any kind of law enforcement.

Hunter himself had submitted notes on an interview with Fred Klimmer. The man had told him he'd moved to the Yukon several years earlier from northern Manitoba. His story corresponded to provincial records. He'd had no history of run-ins with law enforcement in Manitoba or the Yukon. Investigators had more or less eliminated him as a suspect based on his past history and lack of a motive.

Although not homicide investigators at the time, Hunter and Ken had both done some of the leg work on the case, and he remembered interviewing some of the residents of Johnson's Crossing and Teslin, the settlements closest to Blake's cabin, soon after Blake's disappearance. It never came to light that Blake was a deserter, nor that he was on the run after the murders in Louisiana. Both Johnson's Crossing and Teslin were on the Alaska Highway but by November, when the main tourist season was over, any strangers spending time in town or asking about Martin Blake should have attracted attention and come up in their interviews.

As far as Hunter could remember from his own inquiries, most comments about Blake mirrored Ken's impression of the man. He was not overtly friendly, but hadn't made any obvious enemies. There had been no reports of strangers asking for directions to his cabin, nor were most of the locals certain of the exact location. Out of the total population of not much more than a dozen, the few residents they spoke to in Johnson's Crossing didn't have any consistent theory about the disappearance of Martin Blake.

"I seen it before," said one old timer. "It's a hard life. Guy gets fed up. Not worth packing up stuff. Just high tails it out and leaves everything behind."

But the dogs? "Takes a real asshole to leave the dogs chained up. Say, did you find his boat? Maybe the fella was out on the river and drowned and the body is half way to Dawson by now."

But the blood? "Yep. Coulda been a grizz."

Teslin was a larger settlement – population a little over one hundred – and not many of the people they talked to even knew Blake's name, let alone cared. That's where the post office was located, and Ken had asked about mail for Martin Blake. Did he get any? Did he send any? In the early days of the investigation, the answer had been yes, he'd mailed the occasional letter to an address in Ontario, and sent for and received several mail-order items over the three years he'd been living in the area. He'd purchased the goods using postal money orders, paid for in cash. How about letters? The clerk said no.

Did he make any phone calls while he was in town? The clerk didn't know. How did he get to town? Pickup truck. What kind? Beater of an old Ford. Yet there was no record of a registration under his name and Blake's truck was never found. Had the killer stolen it? Or had Blake somehow made it out alive?

"Oh, yeah," the clerk had said. "Just thought of something. One time last summer I saw his truck – I'm pretty sure it was his – turn off toward Tagish at Jake's Corner. He might've known somebody up the road to Tagish."

Before he'd had time to look into that, a homicide investigator had taken over the case and Hunter was back to his routine patrol. Hunter didn't see anything else about Tagish or Jake's Corner in the case file, nor had he ever heard those locations mentioned again. He wondered whether someone around Jake's Corner might be able to shed light on the mystery surrounding Martin Blake. Before the case went cold, the name of Grant Sanford hadn't been mentioned. The anonymous note had made its way into the file a year later without any fanfare and it had been years before someone finally matched the prints taken from the cabin to those of the murder suspect and deserter who had once gone by that name.

CHAPTER EIGHTEEN

Hunter had almost finished reviewing the file and was wondering why Bart hadn't returned from his meeting yet when he heard voices in the hall outside. He pushed the file to the center of Bart's desk and stood up to stretch. His muscles had been taxed by the unaccustomed exertions of pulling Betty Salmon's travois through the Yukon bush. After napping in a chair at the clinic and then sitting so long in the RCMP vehicle, and now spending a couple of hours hunched over the case file, his neck and back had stiffened up.

The door opened to admit April, followed by Bart. Hunter nodded his greeting, relieved that she had shown up as promised, and surprised that she had arrived so soon.

"How did you get here so fast?"

"I just picked her up from the airport. She called the detachment just as I got out of my meeting." Bart moved a chair next to Hunter's, so she could sit in front of his desk.

"You aren't going to Eagle?" asked Hunter.

She shook her head as she took the seat Bart had offered. "I'll be sending Goldie a ticket to Portland. She's promised to come for a good long visit." Her face clouded with an uncertain frown. "Soon, I hope."

Hunter glanced at Bart. The Staff Sergeant's dark eyes were focused on him, as if waiting for him to make the first move. "Okay if I ask her a few questions?"

Bart nodded and settled himself behind his desk.

"Your car," began Hunter. "You left your car somewhere. Where?"

Her face was blank. Hunter guessed she was thinking of her current vehicle, so he prompted her. "Where was your Volkswagen while you were living in the cabin with Martin Blake?"

"Sorry," she said, shaking her head as if just waking up. "Tired, I guess. Martin had me park it at a friend of his. He had a small homestead just off the Road to Tagish. Lived alone. He and Martin were friends, sort of. I don't think Martin had any other friends up here."

"You remember the friend's name?"

"I only knew him as Tag. He seemed nice enough. Quite sociable, compared to Martin." She shook her head. "Martin was pretty secretive about his past."

"Why did you leave your car there and not take it to the cabin?"

"Martin said I'd probably get it stuck or damaged if I tried to go off road with it. He said it would be safe at Tag's place. His truck was a real beater and had lots of clearance, so we used it to get to the cabin."

"Kind of trapped you there, then," interjected Bart.

The same thing had occurred to Hunter. He wondered again if she was lying about Blake's character and her relationship with the man, maybe to herself as much as to others.

"Look. I didn't feel trapped. He took me with him to town for supplies a few times."

"Where was his truck the day you were attacked? Why didn't you take it to escape?"

Her face went blank for a few seconds, then she frowned with the effort of remembering. "It was gone," she said, seeming confused. "I don't remember seeing it. Maybe that man took it. Maybe Martin left it somewhere. I don't know. I don't know why it wasn't there."

"So your car was left with Martin's friend on the Tagish Road for over a year. I don't suppose you have an address?" Simultaneously, Bart and April gave a short laugh. Hunter smiled. "Didn't think so. Would you remember how to find this homestead?"

"I think so."

She said she planned to book a flight out the following afternoon, so she would be free until then to show Hunter where Tag's place was.

"Great. But while we're here." Hunter motioned toward the case file on the desk, looking at Bart as he said, "If I'm not mistaken, Staff Sergeant Sam would like to show you a photograph of the man we believe to be Martin Blake."

Bart found the photo of Grant Sanford in the file and slid it across the desk in Hunter's direction. "It would help the investigation if you could confirm this is Martin Blake. It's a military photo so was taken before Blake deserted and well before you met him, so take your time."

Hunter picked up the photo and looked at it again before holding it up for April.

"May I?" she asked, reaching for the photo. She took a hard look, glanced up at Bart and Hunter in turn, then sighed and concentrated on the photo again. Finally she shook her head. "I'm sorry, but it really doesn't look like him. I know men look different without facial hair, and I never saw Martin without a beard, but there's nothing familiar about this face." She was about to put the photo back on the desk, but hesitated and said, "I never saw him without long hair and a beard. I can't swear to it that it's not him in this picture, but if I had to come down on one side or the other, I'd say it's not him."

Hunter exchanged glances with Bart. He hoped the shaman's son would have one of his famous insights, but no such luck. "If it's not Martin Blake, then who is this man?" said Bart.

"More to the point," said Hunter, "then who was Martin Blake?"

Fifteen minutes later, Hunter helped April climb into the passenger seat of his Freightliner tractor for the hour and a half drive to Tagish.

Bart's eyes were laughing when he told Hunter to go ahead and take April to see if they could find the mysterious Tag. "You do the leg work. Tell me what you find out and if I think it's worth it, I'll take over when you leave the Yukon." He shrugged and looked sideways at Hunter, adding "If you ever do leave, that is."

Hunter shot him a dirty look before climbing into the cab.

"Why do you drive a semi?" asked April as he fired up the engine.

"Real men like big trucks." He hadn't told her that he wasn't still a member of the RCMP. At this point, there was no reason for her to know. "Besides, I left my car at home," he added.

As he drove through the streets of Whitehorse on the way to the Alaska Highway, Hunter asked April about her meeting with Goldie. She explained that Goldie had brought her and Betty together so they could understand the difficult position she was in, having to decide on the spot which one of them to spend time with. She had them help her make that decision. "Betty's need for her was more immediate. I could see that. I had my visit with her and said 'so long'." With a wry laugh she added, "Age before beauty. Isn't that the rule?"

"She's a smart girl," said Hunter, braking to a stop before a left turn.

"I like to think she takes after me."

Hunter wondered who else the girl might take after. It was possible her father had some bearing on Martin Blake's disappearance, whether or not April knew or was willing to admit it. He remembered what Betty had said about April leaving Michigan because of the baby's father.

"Does her father know about her?"

The smile fell from April's face. She was silent until Hunter had turned onto the highway.

"I doubt that he cares."

"You didn't answer my question."

"Why does it matter?"

"Why did you leave Michigan?"

"What's that got to do with anything?"

He tried to make his voice playful as he said, "I should warn you that homicide investigators never know where to draw the line when it comes to getting information from witnesses." His attempt at humor fell flat. He saw her tense up as she stared out the passenger side window. "Well?"

"I didn't want my ex-boyfriend to know. I left in a hurry as soon as I found out I was pregnant."

"Was he abusive?"

"What makes you think that?"

"You said the thought of returning to Michigan made you curl up in a fetal position in a dark room, remember?"

Her answer was expressionless. "He wasn't my idea of a life partner." But after she spoke she shivered as if she were cold. Hunter's grandmother would have told her that someone had just walked over her grave.

"Did he come looking for you?"

"If he did, he didn't find me."

Hunter decided it was time to change the subject. He nodded and let a few moments of silence ease the tension. "So, how did you meet Martin?"

"Are all investigators so nosy?"

"You don't like to talk about him?"

"Just giving you a hard time." She chewed on her lip a few seconds before saying, "The Sluice Box. Just like you and your lady killer of a partner."

Her sudden flippant mention of Ken was like a jab in the ribs.

"I knew people were going to start noticing my pregnancy, in spite of the loose smocks and dresses I used to wear. He seemed like a nice enough guy and he had a cabin in the woods. He was in town for a few days waiting for a guy to arrive from up north with a new dog so we had dinner together a couple of nights and hit it off. He invited me out to see his cabin. I said sure, on the condition that I could stay until spring, and that was that. I was pretty naïve. Thought I was some kind of earth mother. Who in their right mind moves far away from doctors and hospitals to have a baby?" She sighed. "If only I'd known how it would change my life, I wouldn't have made the decision so lightly."

"How did it change your life?"

She gave an exasperated grunt. "What do you think? Raped. Beaten. Almost killed. Almost died of exposure with my baby. Separated from my baby for twenty-four years. Pick one."

Hunter apologized and concentrated on his driving.

"Martin was paranoid," April said suddenly ten minutes later. "And he had nightmares about Vietnam. I should have mentioned that before, when I told you he'd seen a man from the army and was worried about being recognized."

"You're saying he might have only imagined he knew the man?"

She shrugged. "I don't know. Maybe."

"Did it affect his behavior in other ways?"

"Like I said before, he didn't share too much about his past. He had those nightmares though."

She fell silent again, then "I need to get a birth certificate for Golden."

"You're the mother. If anyone can obtain a delayed birth certificate for her, it would be you. You might need Betty to corroborate, but go talk to the Vital Statistics office and find out. It's downtown beside the high-rise log cabin. I'll take you there tomorrow morning if you want."

She went on as if she hadn't heard him. "I guess I was pretty screwed up back then, to think it wasn't important. My head was somewhere else in those days. Sometimes it's more important not to have a record of your existence, you know what I mean?"

Hunter glanced at her, but she had tilted her head back and closed her eyes. He let her sleep until they reached the Tagish Road.

Even after twenty-four years, April was able to recognize the turnoff to the homestead by its location after a sharp curve, but she said the hand lettered wooden sign that read "Wolf Creek Cabins" was new. The man she'd known as Tag was still living there, a fact that she found surprising but that Hunter did not. During his years in the Yukon he'd met many diehard residents who claimed to have found the perfect spot to live out their years and declared their intention to die there as well.

The man called Tag must have been in his sixties. He was fit and wiry, dressed in blue jeans and hiking boots, a plaid shirt left open over a faded navy tee shirt and a Blue Jays ball cap. He had been pushing a wheelbarrow full of split logs when they arrived. Hunter noticed a woman working in a garden between two small log cabins.

Three dogs of assorted breeds came bounding up to investigate their arrival, sniffing first around the tires of the Freightliner tractor, then around Hunter's and April's legs.

"You looking to rent a cabin?" The man slapped a mosquito off his neck as he addressed Hunter.

Hunter shook his head and motioned toward April, glad he'd remembered to apply Deet before he and April had left the detachment.

"Remember me?" asked April. When the man cocked his head and looked sheepish, as if he'd forgotten, she added, "I came here with Martin Blake, and I left my car here. You weren't here when I came to get it but I left you a note, remember?"

"Aha! The hippie chick with the flowers on her Beetle." He scratched the stubble on his chin. "My god, that has to have been over twenty years ago. Never saw Blake again. What'd you do with the poor bugger?" He laughed as if it were a joke.

Hunter caught April's horrified expression and answered for her. "He disappeared the year before April picked up her car. It was in the news at the time."

"Never heard about it. I moved out to the bush to get away from the news." He laughed. "Doesn't everybody?"

"We were wondering if you'd heard from him since then. We're trying to solve the mystery of where he went."

"Can't help you there. Like I said, I never saw him again. My brother dropped off a couple more letters for him, but when he never came by to get them, I told him to send the letters back."

Tag explained that he'd been introduced to Blake by his brother, who had met Blake in Ontario when he'd first arrived in Canada. In fact, Tag's brother was the one who had brought Blake up to the Yukon and Tag had helped him find a place to live and get set up as a trapper. "My brother drove truck, so he'd get up here now and again, two or three times a year, and come stay with me when he did." He shook his head. "That Blake was an odd duck. Paranoid as hell. I guess he didn't want anybody to know his whereabouts, so he had mail from home sent care of my brother's place in the Soo."

"The Sioux?" April looked puzzled.

"Sault Ste. Marie. That's where I grew up. They call it the Soo." He explained that on the rare occasions that Tag's brother got a letter for him at his home in Sault Ste. Marie, he'd bring it with him on his next trip to Whitehorse.

"Not exactly express mail," said Hunter. "Where were the letters from? Any return address?"

Tag took off his ball cap and ran a sleeve across his forehead before putting it back on. "If I remember right, they came from somewhere in Ohio. Salinas, I think. No, that's not it."

"Maybe your brother would know. How can we get in touch with him?"

"Passed away ten years ago. Colon cancer." He nodded his thanks for Hunter's apology, then added, "If it's any help, the letters must have been from a relative, because they had the same last name. His real last name, that is." He snapped his fingers. "Salineville. That was it. Salt town, I guess."

"His real name wasn't Blake, was it?" Hunter thought that this might finally confirm Martin Blake's true identity as Grant Sanford.

"Blake was his real name, alright, but not his last name." Tag bent down and scratched one of the dogs, which appeared to be part golden retriever, behind the ears. "Blake was his first name. His last name was Michaels."

Sorry noticed the fuel gauge on his old mustard colored Volvo was hovering around empty and cursed himself for wasting that five dollar bill on Doughboy's beer. He checked all his pockets, then the glove box and was relieved to find a crumpled twenty and some coins he'd carelessly stashed there before he'd lost his last job. He was happy to have made it through the day without being fired. It wasn't like it was a common occurrence, but he'd been fired on the first day before. If he wanted to keep Mo happy, he'd have to stick this job out for a long time, maybe even a couple of years unless something better came along.

He wasn't much given to introspection, but for some reason, he wasn't feeling in a hurry to get home. He hated to admit it, but he was scared. Scared of how Mo would behave toward him today, and scared of how he would behave toward her if the atmosphere was as chilly as it had been last night. "Keep your eyes on the prize," he muttered to himself.

He bought ten bucks worth of gas on King George Highway and figured he might as well stop in at a nearby bike shop to follow up on that guy Hunter was looking for. The owner was an old friend of his, from back when the Black Cobras first started out. His name was Paul but they called him Winston because he had jowls like Winston Churchill's.

"Hey, Winnie, how's it hangin', man?"

They shot the shit for a couple of minutes, covering mutual friends who were now dead or in jail, before Sorry asked him if he knew of any mechanics in town who grew up in the Yukon.

"Damn right. Guy was looking for work here a couple years back, and I sent him down the road." Winston pointed with his right hand. It seemed to Sorry that he was pointing at a naked woman on a calendar that hung on the wall behind the cash register.

"You told him to fuck off? Why?"

Winston shook his head and rolled his eyes. "Down the road, man. The ricer shop a couple a blocks that way." He hawked and spit into a greasy rag, then stuffed the end of it into his back pocket. "He's still there, comes in from time to time to get parts for his Harley."

It was almost closing time so Sorry didn't waste any time going down the road to a shop with Yamaha and Suzuki banners plastered all over its front window.

"You mean Jimmy?" asked the sales guy manning the counter.

The guy ushered him into the back of the shop, where a native-looking dude was kneeling, working on an old Honda CB350, a classic Jap bike that even Sorry could recognize.

"You Jimmy?" he asked.

The guy glanced up at Sorry and took his time answering. "Yeah. What can I help you with?"

"You from Whitehorse?"

The guy wiped his hands on the greasy coveralls he wore and slowly got to his feet, looking Sorry up and down. Jimmy was about five ten, wiry and strong. Sorry was taller, broader and outweighed him by at least fifty pounds. "I don't believe I know you," Jimmy said.

"I got a message for you, Jimmy." Sorry laid a hand on the guy's shoulder, and the guy pushed it off. Sorry smiled. He considered it his hardass smile. "About an old dude looks like Santa Claus."

The guy's face clouded. Sorry knew he had the right man.

"What about him?"

"You know he's in jail, eh? Old Orville."

"Jail? For what?"

"What do you think?"

Sorry was pretty sure it was fear that flashed across Jimmy's face. He wondered if Jimmy took him for a cop.

"How the fuck am I supposed to know?"

Another hardass smile.

"You know–?" Sorry began, then sniffed, stroked his mustache and sniffed again. "I wouldn't have much respect for a brother who would let another brother take the rap for him, let alone an asshole who would let his old man take a fall for him. You know what I mean, Jimmy?"

"He's not my old man," Jimmy replied.

"If it walks like a duck and quacks like a duck –"

"What the fuck is that supposed to mean? Besides, what's it to you? Who the fuck are you, anyway?"

"Give your head a shake, Jimmy. You got a chance to do the right thing here." He noticed Jimmy's hand reach around to slide a wrench off the workbench behind him. "And that ain't it," he said as he grabbed the guy's shoulder and spun him around with one hand, got him in a headlock with the other. When Jimmy tried to cow kick him, Sorry lifted him off the ground and thrust a hand under the guy's crotch to grab his balls. "You ain't gonna win here, pal. Let's just talk nice, okay?" He started to squeeze.

The guy squirmed a few seconds and then gave up."Let go of me," he managed to choke out, then as Sorry loosened his grasp, "Okay, okay. Let's talk nice."

Sorry heard the sales guy open the door behind him. "What's going on in here? You okay, Jimmy?"

Sorry glared at Jimmy until he answered. "Yeah. I'm fine, Mike. Thanks." He was straightening out his coveralls as he spoke.

When the sales guy had gone, Sorry hustled Jimmy out the back door of the shop into an alley. He held Jimmy up against the wall with one hand while he fished a cigarette out of his tee shirt and put it between his lips. "You gonna be a good little injun now, James?"

Jimmy sneered and spat on the ground but he didn't try to leave.

Sorry lit his cigarette and took a deep drag. "So what is it you want out of life, Jimmy? Money? Fame? A good woman? Kids? A happy family? Where do you see yourself in five years, ten years, best case scenario?" Jimmy looked at him like he was crazy. "Dig deep, man. This is heavy shit. I wish somebody had made me take a close look at myself when I was your age." In fact, somebody had. Sorry had been on a fast track to doing hard time when he'd had the good fortune to be arrested for assault by Hunter Rayne about a dozen years earlier. A cop who cared about him as a person. Who knew?

He grabbed Jimmy by the collar. "Speak up, dude. This is fucking important."

"I don't know what you want me to say, man."

Sorry took a pull on his cigarette and blew the smoke in Jimmy's face. "Easy question, just answer it. Okay, look at it this way. Who's your hero? Who or what do you want to be when you grow up? If you don't give a shit, you might as well jump off a bridge. If you do give a shit, then you're the one who's got to make it happen. You can't sit on your ass waiting for it to be handed to you on a silver platter." Sorry gave him a couple of minutes to think it over.

"I like to work on bikes. I like to ride. That's my life. That's all I want to do. I work on bikes at the shop, I rebuild bikes in my garage, I eat take out, I watch TV and fall asleep. What else does a guy like me have to aim for?"

"What do you mean, a guy like you? "

"I'm a half breed with a grade eight education. What do you expect me to do?"

"You shithead. Nobody gives a fuck if you're a half breed unless you wear it on your shoulder and dare the world to knock it off."

"Nobody gives a fuck about me, period." The guy kicked at a stone, pouting. Sorry almost laughed, the guy reminded him so much of little Bruno when he'd been scolded for sneaking the green vegetables off his plate and feeding them to Doobie. He hoped Bruno would never feel the way this Jimmy guy felt. He never would, if Sorry could help it. Come to think of it, Orville must be worried the same way about Jimmy.

"Nobody? What do you call the old man who's willing to take a murder rap for you?"

Sullen silence.

"Look, you got a choice here. You can do the right thing and feel good about yourself for the rest of your life, or you can keep on making excuses why you'll never be a real man and never amount to anything. If that's the case, I suggest you go find yourself a bridge." Sorry dropped his cigarette butt and smashed it with the toe of his boot. "Your choice, man." It sounded a lot like what Hunter had said to him, way back when.

"And what? Spend the rest of my life in jail?"

Sorry snorted. "Give your head a shake. This is Canada, man. You plead to voluntary manslaughter, self-defense or whatever, you're put away in medium – Matsqui, maybe – with three squares a day, gym time and an education program for a few years, then you're back out with a high school diploma and maybe even a cute social worker hanging on your arm."

Jimmy looked puzzled. "What's it to you? Who are you, anyway?"

Sorry couldn't resist saying, "Who was that masked man?" This struck him as so funny that he burst out laughing, a big belly laugh that made Jimmy wince. "Never thought of myself as the Lone Ranger type." He noticed the guy wasn't laughing. "You never watched the Lone Ranger as a kid?"

The guy just glowered at him. "That doesn't answer my question."

"So I'm doing a favor for a friend, or maybe you could say, a friend of a friend. Where I come from, we don't like to snitch to the cops. I still haven't decided whether I'll be telling my friend where to find you. You want to live looking over your shoulder, go ahead. But if I was you, I'd go bail out the old man and get my life back on the rails."

With that, Sorry grabbed Jimmy by the scruff of the neck and pushed him back inside.

April had been able to book a room at the Edgewater for the night. "I hate eating alone in restaurants," she said as Hunter helped her down from the passenger seat of the Blue Knight. "You hungry?"

Hunter hesitated a moment. The place would bring back memories, but then again, so did being with April. Maybe it was fitting that he and April spend this last night in Whitehorse at a place that had been special to the one friend they'd had in common back then. "Sure," he said.

The place looked somehow different enough, or perhaps he'd been away long enough, that it didn't feel as familiar as he expected. There was a free table by the window, so they sat down and soon had ordered drinks and dinner. There were a few unanswered questions about April that had been nagging at him, and as soon as their drinks were delivered ¬– red wine for her and a beer for him – and he saw her start to relax, he took advantage of the opportunity to satisfy his curiosity.

"So how did you end up in Oregon?"

She let out a long breath. "I was looking for a safe place." She took a sip of her wine and set it down, staring at the stem of the glass as she spun it gently on the polished surface of the table. "There was a straight kind of guy from high school, a friend of my brother's, who had a crush on me. I knew he was studying at Portland State and I thought I'd look him up."

"You didn't go back to see your parents?"

She shrugged. "They were divorced. My mom ran off with the Fuller Brush salesman when I was just fourteen and my dad was a mean drunk. I left home as soon as I finished school. No reason to go back." She took another sip of wine, swallowed it and stuck out her jaw defiantly. "Ever."

He was struck by how her cheerful, easy going nature back in 1972 had belied what she must have been through before she left her home in Michigan. Abusive father. Abusive boyfriend. It made him sad. "You found the man you were looking for?"

"He's my rock." She smiled wryly. "We have three kids and a dog, just your typical middle class Pacific Northwest family. One kid is away at college, two still at home. How about you?"

"Two girls. Young adults, really." He had more questions for her, but before he could speak again, she interrupted his train of thought.

"What about your friend? You said he passed away. What happened? Cancer?"

Hunter looked down at his hands. He didn't want to answer, but he felt he had to say something. "Accidental discharge of a firearm." He managed a pained smile.

She nodded, her expression sad.

"Do you remember the date of the attack on you and Martin?"

She lifted her shoulders and showed her palms in a helpless shrug.

"We had no way of knowing for sure when it happened," he told her, "except that it was before the snowfall. I was hoping you could help." He locked his eyes on hers. "Didn't you ever wonder what happened at the cabin after you left?"

She averted her eyes and the wine glass stopped halfway to her lips. "I didn't want to think about it. I still don't. Do you feel you have to tell me?"

"Do you know a man named Fred Klimmer? He apparently had one of the trapline concessions adjacent to Martin's. He was originally from northern Manitoba and had moved to the Yukon just a few years earlier."

She shook her head. "A few men stopped in at the cabin while I was there, but he never invited them inside, that's for sure. Like I told you, and like Tag said, Martin was pretty paranoid and kept to himself mostly. My husband says that's another symptom of PTSD. He certainly never introduced me to any trappers in the area. I'm sure I would have remembered. Why?"

"He's the one who called us in. He said he'd seen that some of Martin's traps hadn't been tended in a long time, so he decided to swing by on his snow sled and check on him. He found the cabin abandoned, the door open. The dogs were still there, chained to their shelters, and hungry, as if they hadn't been fed for days."

"But Martin wasn't there? Or his body?" She shivered. "I don't remember there being snow. Do we have to talk about this?"

"Just a couple more questions. I'd rather not have to ask you to come back to the detachment, although that will be Staff Sergeant Sam's call."

"Look, I was a victim. I was almost killed. Why should the RCMP care after twenty-five years if I don't?" She still wouldn't meet his eyes.

His voice softened, even though he wasn't sure of her motive for not cooperating. He was well aware, even if she wasn't, that he had no legitimate reason to be questioning her. "I'm sorry."

She finally looked straight at him and even managed a small smile.

"I just wanted you to try again to remember what your attacker looked like. Anything that might help identify him. A tattoo. A scar. A mole or a birthmark."

She tilted her head back and closed her eyes. He wondered whether she was making an effort to visualize the man in the cabin, or to think up a plausible description that would get Hunter off her back.

"Brown eyes, I think. A heavy, dark beard that hid his mouth and chin. An unwashed smell." Her facial expression showed her disgust. "He snarled at me." Her eyes opened and sought out his. "He snarled at me," she repeated. "He snarled at me and his lips curled back and I saw his teeth. Crooked teeth. I remember his crooked teeth."

"Crooked in what way? Can you describe them?"

She closed her eyes again to concentrate, but soon shook her head. "No. If I try too hard to picture them, I get confused. I just remember crooked teeth. Evil teeth." She shivered. "No. It's been too long. I can't describe them, but I might recognize them if I saw them again."

He shrugged. "Well, it's one more thing to look for," he said.

"As much as I want to forget that day and never think of it again, I will come back to testify if you find him," she said, picking up her wine glass and raising it toward him. "Here's to you guys catching the fucking bastard."

Hunter raised his glass. "I'll drink to that."

Goldie could tell that Betty was asleep by the slow cadence of her breathing. Braving the evening mosquitoes , she left the cabin. She felt a need to walk down the path to the river. On the long drive back to Eagle from Dawson City, her head had been spinning with thoughts of her mother, and Betty, and Mark – all the sudden changes in her life. She tried to calm that inner turmoil as she walked the familiar path between the trees, Hootie trotting along ahead.

Her grandmother had been asleep when they went through U.S. Customs. Mark handed over his own driver's license and the one that Tessa had loaned to Goldie. The customs officer had peered in at Gran, and asked if she, too, was a U.S. citizen. Goldie stammered out something about Gran not having a driver's license. When Mark whispered, "She's a native. She's her granny," pointing to Goldie, the officer had shrugged and waved them on.

Goldie assumed that Betty had no government ID either, but it was something she hadn't given much thought to before today. It was no wonder that Gran had never made any effort to get a birth certificate for her, since she probably didn't have one herself. That compounded her worry about what would happen to Gran if Goldie weren't around and she could no longer support or take care of herself. If she wasn't officially a citizen of either Canada or the U.S., would there be any government assistance for her?

Goldie wanted to leave Eagle so bad that it hurt. She wanted to move on and experience life outside, see as much of the world as she could, meet new people, learn new things. As much as she loved Gran, she just couldn't let Gran's welfare be her primary objective in life. It wasn't fair. The decision she faced caused an almost physical knot in her chest. Either she gave up her freedom for Gran's sake or she suffered the guilt of deserting the woman who had raised her. It wasn't fair for Gran to make her do that. Maybe it wasn't fair either way. What was it she'd heard Mark say, flippantly, at his own complaints? *Life's a bitch and then you die.*

At the thought of Mark, she felt a warmth in her chest and a restless sensation between her legs. When he'd dropped them off at their cabin, he waited outside in the summer kitchen, drinking a can of pop he'd bought in Dawson, until she'd got Betty into bed. When she came out to join him, he motioned her to sit beside him, put his arm around her shoulders and offered her a sip of his Pepsi. He gave her shoulders a squeeze and she felt his breath on her neck as he leaned close to plant a soft kiss on her cheek.

No clumsy adolescent groping like the boys from school. He was gentle and respectful and she felt lightheaded with love. Love? The very word scared her, but what else could it be? She felt a great tenderness for him and it made her want to be so close to him that their bodies would merge into one, somehow. But the fear of losing herself to that feeling made her stiffen against it. He hugged her again and stood up.

"You're tired. We both are. I'll tell Aunt Sally that you might not be back at work tomorrow." With that, he had climbed back in Yukon Sally's big pickup and driven away. She stood to watch him go, but she was too wired to sit still or go to bed, so here she was.

She reached the bank of the Yukon and sank cross-legged on a patch of long grass overlooking the river. Never had she felt her life so beyond her control. It was exciting and at the same time she missed the familiarity of the grueling but predictable life she'd been living when it was just her and Gran. They always knew what they had to do each month to make sure they would have enough to feed themselves and Hootie from season to season, and enough wood for the stove. Now the next month and the next season were uncertain. Would she visit her mother in Oregon and end up staying there, going to college perhaps, or getting a job? Would Mark ask her to go with him to California?

The Yukon flowed past her vantage point, the smooth malleability of its surface disguising the power of the currents beneath. She knew it would let her punch her puny fist deep into its face, but it wouldn't let her break free of its icy grip if it chose to pull her down. Like Alaska herself, it gave so generously and yet could take so cruelly away. No, not cruelly. Indifferently. She sighed. The river always helped put things in perspective. She had faith that, when the time came, she would know what to do.

She would miss the river.

CHAPTER NINETEEN

Hunter lay awake in the sleeper of his Freightliner. Now that it was approaching time to leave the Yukon, he felt under pressure to solve the riddle of the bloody cabin. After today's revelation about Martin Blake/Blake Michaels' identity, he felt the key could lie with Grant Sanford. Why would someone leave that note at the RCMP detachment in Whitehorse tying Grant Sanford to the bloody cabin? Who stood to benefit from that misinformation? Maybe, given the trauma April seemed to have suffered that day, she was wrong in identifying the dead man in the cabin as Martin Blake.

Could it be that the paranoid Blake Michaels had killed April's attacker, panicked, and once again gone on the run? Is that why his vehicle was never found? And what about the man Blake had seen and worried could identify him? Was that just PTSD paranoia, or was there a good reason for Blake to leave the southern end of the Yukon without his dogs and never even return to the area for his mail?

If Grant Sanford, army deserter and murderer, wanted the world to think him dead, identifying the missing and presumed dead trapper as Grant Sanford was a good way to do it. That led to two possibilities: either Grant Sanford killed Martin Blake, or he recognized an opportunity and took advantage of it. The trapper's disappearance had made the local news and would have spread in the region by word of mouth, indicating Sanford probably lived in the

Yukon. Was he the man Blake had seen in Teslin and worried he'd been recognized by?

The sun had set and risen again, sunlight streaked in via gaps in the curtain, and Hunter was still awake. He turned over, punched his pillow and turned his face to the back wall of the bunk. The note had turned up in October of 1973, so whoever left the note about Grant Sanford had been in Whitehorse almost a year after the attack on April. Could he still be in the Yukon?

So he had new questions, questions that he knew April couldn't answer. One person he could think of who might be able to shed some light on the case was the trapper who had been concerned about Martin Blake's untended traps, the man who had alerted the RCMP to the abandoned cabin. Was there anything he hadn't told them about Blake back in 1972? Hunter had given himself until the afternoon before he left Whitehorse in search of a load home. He decided to see if he could talk to Fred Klimmer before he headed south.

That decision was enough to let his imagination rest and he was soon asleep.

"That was twenty-five years ago, man. If I couldn't help you then, what makes you think I can help you now?"

The man lowered himself into a well-used recliner, propped his cane against the right side armrest. Greasy crumbs, presumably from his breakfast, clung to the front of his shabby argyle pullover. His speech was slow. The stroke had affected his left side, giving his face a lopsided appearance. Hunter would have had trouble recognizing him. Fred Klimmer was a withered version of the robust man Hunter remembered; his face sported grey stubble instead of a full dark beard and his nose was red and misshapen. The man couldn't have been any older than Orville, but the two retired trappers couldn't have been more different. Where Orville radiated joy and optimism, this man was dismal and sullen. Hunter felt sympathy for Klimmer, in spite of his previous dislike for the man.

The man's present home was two rooms in a large and rundown private house. The flooring was thin parquet tiles, chipped in places, and the walls were in need of fresh paint. On one side of the main room was a laminate counter, fridge and hotplate with a small wooden table and a single wooden chair. Hunter sat on a lumpy sofa next to Klimmer's recliner, both facing a small but recent model television against the opposite wall. The room was untidy, and smelled of old garbage and burned bacon. Klimmer's world had shrunk from the vast Yukon wilderness to this stuffy apartment. A waiting room for death.

"Just covering all the bases," Hunter said. "Maybe you later remembered something you didn't mention at the time. Maybe you came across something while you were hunting or working your traps?" The man just stared at him, but his right hand toyed with the TV remote control that lay on a metal TV tray beside his chair. "Did you ever come across Blake's truck, for example?"

The man shook his head, more with irritation, it seemed, than as an answer. "Why this interest all of a sudden? Just leave it alone."

Klimmer's attitude struck Hunter as odd. Most elderly people welcomed distractions like this from their normal routine. He didn't remember the man as being unfriendly, just unlikeable. Now he sounded downright hostile. Maybe it came with the stroke. Or maybe not.

"Do you have any family back home?" he asked.

"If I had family, do you think I'd be living here in this godforsaken frozen country with no money for booze and nothing to do but watch soap operas and sitcoms?"

"Manitoba's weather isn't much better than here, maybe worse."

Hunter caught the slight jerk of the man's head before Klimmer grunted, "Right."

"My mother and father are both from Winnipeg. Where in Manitoba are you from?"

The man's right eye narrowed. "Enough questions, okay?"

"Just trying to be friendly, chief." If this was his last shot at solving the case, he really wanted to get Klimmer talking, loosen him up. "Look, I still feel like I owe you one. You didn't have to go check on your neighbor; you didn't have to do the right thing and call us in on it. I'd feel better if I made your day today, at least. You say you've got no money for booze? What's your poison? I'll get you a forty pounder to cheer you up."

Klimmer's right eyebrow shot up and he offered half a smile. "I wouldn't turn down a bottle of Jack Daniels," he said, "if you can get it."

Hunter told Klimmer he had a couple of errands to run but he'd be back in an hour or two. He called Bart as soon as he was out the door, told him about his visit to Klimmer and asked for a favor. "Can you turn something up on him? Place of birth, where he grew up, next of kin – anything you can find in a hurry. The case file says he's from northern Manitoba and has no prior criminal record there, but I've got a funny feeling that he's not being totally straight with me."

He could hear Bart Sam sigh before he replied, "Grasping at straws, Hunter? He was ruled out as a suspect twenty-five years ago, wasn't he?"

"Yes. Fred Klimmer was ruled out."

"What are you getting at then?"

"Fred Klimmer was ruled out but Grant Sanford wasn't."

"Grant Sanford? He's the dead man, isn't he?"

"Look, we don't have much time. Our only witness will be on a flight out of Whitehorse this afternoon. And another thing, we found out yesterday that Martin Blake's real name was Blake Michaels from a place called Salineville in Ohio. Can you get something on him? Find out if Blake Michaels was a deserter from the US military and if he has any relatives who can confirm that he hasn't made contact with them in the last twenty-five years?"

There were a few seconds of silence. Hunter heard Bart say, "You're not the boss of me." With that, the line went dead.

Hunter didn't waste any time getting to the detachment.

"He's expecting you," said the woman at the front desk and showed him into Bart's office.

"What took you so long?" Bart was sitting at his desk, making notes on a document of some kind. He barely looked up.

"You ever try to park a Freightliner?" Hunter didn't bother sitting down. "Are you looking into Klimmer and Michaels or not?"

"Give me a break. It takes time to find someone who'll do a database search." When Bart looked up, he was grinning like the Cheshire cat. "Got some news for you," he said.

Hunter raised his eyebrows.

"Had a call this morning from a fellow named Jimmy Moses. He wants to turn himself in, was wondering if he could go to the detachment in Surrey, save himself the cost of a drive north."

"Orville's stepson?"

"It looks that way. He needs someone to look after his things first, he says. He's got a motorcycle he doesn't want to lose."

"How did he hear about Orville?"

"Your biking Viking friend, evidently."

"Way to go, Dan." Sorry might not display a lot of finesse, but he could still manage to get the job done. Sometimes. The thought made Hunter smile. "Have you told Orville yet?"

"No." He shot Hunter an amused glance. "And, yes, you can go talk to Orville."

Hunter rolled his eyes. "There you go, reading my mind again. When are you going to turn in your badge and get your shaman's license?"

"I've already got it, and if you can do two things at once, so can I." As Hunter headed out the door, Bart added, "And I called your witness at her hotel. She'll be standing by this morning until she leaves for the airport in case she's needed."

Orville looked none the worse for being back in jail. He still had a twinkle in his eye and a smile on his face when he was shown into the room. His first question was, "How's Betty? Have you heard from her granddaughter?"

Hunter was sorry to disappoint him, but not sorry to say what he'd come to say. "Jimmy's going to turn himself in."

Orville's face fell. "Oh, dear. I was desperately hoping it wasn't him. What's next?"

"They'll bring him here." He smiled sympathetically. "You won't be able to see him."

Orville stared down at his hands. His thick fingers were calloused, but the nails neatly trimmed and clean. "How can I help him?"

"He needs a lawyer. Now, before he says something he shouldn't."

The old man shook his head sadly. "He won't trust a lawyer, believe me. I'm afraid for him. He'll be his own worst enemy in this, the way he always fights authority."

"I know a good lawyer, one that he'll feel comfortable with."

"How do you know? You don't even know Jimmy."

"I don't know Jimmy, but I know my friend. His name is Joe Solomon, and he's known around the east side of Vancouver as Legal Joe. If anyone can help Jimmy out of this, it's Legal Joe."

Orville looked puzzled. Hunter felt he could almost read the old man's mind.

"I'm a truck driver, not a law enforcement officer. I used to be a member of the RCMP, and Staff Sergeant Sam has been good enough to let me talk to you, but I am not speaking on his behalf, or on behalf of the force."

"I see, I think." The old man didn't sound so sure.

"I don't know what happened in the Lost Mine parking lot, but I know you, Orville. I'd like to see you keep out of prison, and if you truly believe that Jimmy is innocent of premeditated murder, I'd like to see him get a light sentence, for your sake, if not for his."

Orville frowned and shook his head. "This Legal Joe, why would you think Jimmy's going to trust him? The only people Jimmy really seems to feel comfortable with are bikers."

Hunter smiled. "I'll send my biker friend back to see him, then, before he turns himself in."

"Look what the cat dragged in." Elspeth Watson hung up the phone and threw down her pen. "You've got your nerve, Sorenson, coming in here after leaving my driver in the lurch up north last week."

Sorry flipped her a bird. He was standing at the front counter, eyeing the empty pizza box on her desk. "Hold your tongue, woman! Here I was all set to buy you lunch and you treat me like this."

"You? Buy me lunch?" She depressed the intercom button and hollered, "Wally! Look outside, will ya. See any flying pigs?" She hoisted herself out of her big captain's chair, stretched her back and shoulders, and walked over to the counter opposite Sorenson. "What are you doing here, anyway? Come to apologize, I hope."

He stroked his mustache. "Nope. I was making a delivery just down the road here and I'm hungry so I decided to go to Edna's for lunch. Wanna come?"

The door from the warehouse opened and Wally stuck his head around. "Huh? Flying Pigs? Is that a new trucking company or something?"

El waved him away and turned back to the biker, who was picking his teeth with one of her business cards from the little plastic cardholder she kept on the front counter. "Already ate," she told him. "As if you didn't know that."

"So let me use your phone, then," he said.

She rolled her eyes. "Why? You got a phone on your belt there."

"I can't make personal calls on it, at least, not my first week on the job."

"Another new job?"

He didn't answer. "I need to talk to Hunter Rayne. Can you get him for me?"

She shook her head. "Not unless it's on Watson Transportation business."

"It's important. He's been looking for this guy and I've got to tell Hunter that I found him."

El took a deep breath and glared at him. "No fuckin' way. Your friend has been spending way too much time looking for whoever he's looking for and not taking care of business. I tried to call him half a dozen times over the past two days and he doesn't even answer his goddamn phone. I had a load for him out of Fort St. John and because he was busy running around on one of his investigations, we lost it and – I –am – pissed – off! I wasted more than half a day trying to find the load, and had to offer the shipper a sweet deal on it, then the asshole never even called me back." She punctuated the last phrase by slamming her fist three times on the counter.

Sorenson scratched his ear. "How do you really feel?" he said. Then, with an exaggerated smile and fluttering eyelashes, he asked her again to get Hunter on the phone. "Look, I left my truck unlocked and I need to get back out there. Call him now, okay? Right now. I'm sure he'll pay you back."

"And I'm sure he won't answer. Again." But she went back to her desk, picked up the phone and dialed Hunter's cell. To her surprise, he answered on the second ring. "Where the hell have you been? Didn't you get my messages?" she bellowed into the phone. "I'm not busting my ass to get you another load, Rayne. I lost the last one because you were out playing detective again so you can damn well drive back empty. You're going back to the bottom of the roster and you won't get a load from me until I'm good and ready to give you another chance. Find your own fuckin' load back outa there or drive home empty."

There were a few seconds of silence on the other end of the line and El wasn't sure if he was still there. "You hear me?" she added, her voice a little softer.

"I apologize," came Hunter's calm voice. The guy never seemed to get upset about anything. "I got involved in an emergency search and rescue. An elderly woman was lost somewhere along the Yukon River and because she knew me and trusted me, I volunteered to take part in the search. Fortunately, we found her and she's now getting medical care. Unfortunately, I knew I was going to be out of cell range almost the entire time so I left my phone in Whitehorse and I haven't been back in town long." She heard him take a breath. "I'm very sorry. You say you've already lost that load for me?"

"You're damn right." El felt he'd taken most of the wind out of her sails, but she wasn't ready to forgive him. "You should've called before you left."

He agreed with her and apologized again. There wasn't much else left for her to say.

"Hey! Let me talk to him." Sorry was standing by her desk, his big grimy hand with wiggling fingers reaching for the receiver.

Another line began to buzz. "Don't touch my phone. Go use the phone on the counter," she said and punched a few buttons to transfer Hunter's call to the extension.

"And Sorenson, you better make it quick," she added, just before she answered the other line.

"Good work, Dan."

"Huh?"

"Finding Jimmy Moses." He'd been about to head over to the Edgewater to pick up April when his cell phone rang, and he was still digesting what El had told him. If she wasn't going to find him a load, unless he got incredibly lucky, he'd be heading home empty. And broke. "How did you convince him to turn himself in?" Hunter asked, although he wasn't sure he wanted to know.

"Just my charm," said Sorry, followed by one of those booming laughs that made Hunter pull the phone away from his ear. "No kidding, he already turned himself in?"

"Not exactly. He needs someone to take care of his things. You know where he lives?"

"I know where he works. That's almost the same thing. What kind of things?"

"You'll have to ask him. A bike for one thing."

"What am I, a storage locker? I'll go see him but I can't help the guy."

"Put him in touch with Legal Joe, okay?"

"Look, I don't have much time here. I still have to eat and you know I can't work on an empty stomach." Hunter heard El say something in the background, then Sorry said a rushed, "Gotta go, boss. Talk to you later."

"Legal Joe, okay?" said Hunter, but his only answer was a dial tone.

"Door's not locked. Come on in."

Hunter eased open the door to Fred Klimmer's suite and stepped inside. "I'm back," he said, holding a brown bag containing a bottle of Jack Daniels out in front of him. "Hope you don't mind, but I brought my wife in with me. She's tired of waiting in the car. Mind if we join you? We brought our own drinks."

He looked back at April and winked. They'd discussed it beforehand. He was pretty confident Klimmer wouldn't recognize

April, but wanted to be sure the man had no reason to even suspect who she was. "Susan, this is Mr. Klimmer."

"Fred," Klimmer said gruffly, not getting out of his recliner. "I hate people calling me 'mister'." He reached for the brown bag with his good arm, set it on his knee and let the paper fall to the floor as he pulled out the bottle. He motioned to a shelf above the counter. "Get me a glass."

Hunter went to get the glass while April settled herself on the loveseat. She pulled a can of cider and a can of beer out of her big handbag.

"Have you always lived in Whitehorse, Mr. – uh, Fred?" asked April, popping the top on her cider.

"No." He held the glass between his knees and poured himself a double, then tucked the bottle on the chair beside him. He finished the glass of bourbon in three swallows, then closed his eyes and sighed. "Damn. It's been awhile."

Hunter lowered himself to the loveseat beside April and she handed him the beer. "Fred's originally from Northern Manitoba. When I first met him, he was working a trapline north of the Canol Road." He knew he'd have to stroke Klimmer's ego or, in spite of the free bourbon, the man would probably ask them to leave. "He's one of the real Yukoners, tough as they come."

Klimmer glanced sideways at him, the right side of his face barely moving in the semblance of a smile, then poured himself another double.

"Living here in the Yukon so long, you must have some good stories to tell, Fred." April was playing her part well. "Some humorous ones, too, I'll bet."

He shot her a dismissive glance and took a slug of bourbon.

Hunter and April took turns trying to entertain him, trying to cajole him into a smile, but instead of lifting his spirits, the more he drank, the more sullen and hostile the man became. So much for catching a fly with honey, thought Hunter. Time to give vinegar a try.

He cleared his throat loudly and got to his feet, then helped April to hers and guided her over to stand directly in front of Klimmer. "Well, Susan. I guess we made a mistake thinking we could cheer up *Mister* –" He stressed the word, adding a touch of derision. "– Freddie

Klimmer. The son of a bitch is totally lacking in social skills and obviously not worth our time."

The right side of Klimmer's upper lip lifted in a snarl, enough to partially expose his upper teeth. A glance at April's face told Hunter that she'd seen enough.

Klimmer struggled to lower the footrest of his recliner, but by the time he did, Hunter had hustled April to the door. As April headed outside, Hunter turned and smiled broadly at Klimmer, baring his own teeth. "Have a great day!" he said, and shut the door.

Hunter was about to help April into the passenger side of the Freightliner when he realized she was shaking. Instinctively, he wrapped his arms around her. She tucked her forehead into the curve of his neck.

"It's okay," he said. "He can't hurt you now."

She drew back and wiped a tear from her eye with the back of her hand. "I know. It's a twenty-five year old hurt that's never gone away." She sniffed and wiped away another tear. "I'll testify. By God, I'll testify. I'll be back here to testify whenever they need me if I have to walk all the way from Oregon."

CHAPTER TWENTY

"You were right." Bart motioned Hunter to a chair, then took a seat behind his desk. "We found a relative of Fred Klimmer's in Thompson, Manitoba. A nephew. Evidently Uncle Fred was a bit of a loner. He used to trap around Thompson, but had a falling out with the nephew's father, thumbed his nose at the whole family and set off for the Yukon. They never heard from him again, didn't know exactly where he'd gone, but figured he'd get in touch with them when he was ready."

Hunter leaned forward, eager for more information. His theory was taking shape. "Any photos?"

"They're going to see if they can find some old family snapshots and fax one over to me. I did get a description, however. Klimmer was short and stocky with dark hair, and last they saw him, he had a full beard."

Hunter nodded. "How short?"

"Five seven or eight, he thought."

"That son of a bitch," said Hunter, shaking his head.

"Klimmer?"

"No, Sanford." He pulled his chair closer to Bart's desk. "This is my theory. Sanford somehow met up with Klimmer on his way north. Could have been anywhere between Thompson and the Yukon, maybe even after Klimmer was living here. Sanford might have been hitchhiking, and could even have targeted Klimmer because of the facial resemblance. He killed Klimmer, disposed of his body and took on his identity. He might look similar, but he's four or five inches taller."

Bart was frowning. "So you're saying Sanford became Klimmer, not Martin Blake, or Blake Michaels." He grunted. "Let's just call him Blake, okay? How'd you get to this theory?"

"It was the note," said Hunter. "Who stood to gain by leaving that note identifying the fatality in the bloody cabin as Sanford? The only person who stood to gain was Sanford himself, trying to put law enforcement off his trail, once and for all. With no body, there was no way to prove who had actually died in that cabin."

"Did Sanford kill Blake, then?"

"Just half an hour ago, April recognized Klimmer as the man who attacked her, so yes, I'd say he killed Blake. Unless he tells us, which is highly unlikely, we'll just have to make that assumption."

"Because Blake caught him raping the woman?"

"If I had to guess, I'd say raping April was a crime of opportunity. He came to eliminate Blake because Blake had recognized him. They knew each other from Fort Polk in Louisiana, although I doubt that Blake knew about the murders Sanford had committed before he fled the States. Blake told April he was worried that Sanford would turn *him* in."

"How does everything else tie in? The missing truck, for example."

Hunter shrugged. "You know as well as I do that it's easy to make things disappear in the Yukon. He could have driven it away from the cabin and run it into the river. I'd say if the bear hadn't gotten to Blake, he'd have ended up in the river, too, and anyone looking for him would assume he'd deserted his trapline. In fact, maybe what was left of him did end up in the river. I remember Klimmer looking for something at the edge of the clearing around the cabin. Maybe he was checking to make sure he hadn't left anything behind."

"If you're right, then all we have to do is compare this so-called Klimmer's fingerprints to the Sanford prints sent to us from the US military. They'll want to get their hands on him, too."

"Right. I'm kicking myself for not suggesting we get Klimmer fingerprinted in the first place. We just assumed, because the clear fingerprint we got was on Blake's laminated drivers' license, that it was Blake's. I'll bet Klimmer pulled out Blake's license to confirm his identity. That was a lucky break for him."

Bart cocked his head. "Or very smart. Maybe that was his strategy all along. Kill two birds with one stone. Get rid of a potential snitch, and get himself declared missing and presumed dead at the same time."

"You could be right." Hunter took a deep breath and exhaled slowly. He didn't have a role in this anymore. It was up to the RCMP to wrap up the investigation and make an arrest. "Over to you, then, chief." It was a bittersweet feeling. The case was more or less solved. Hunter should have felt satisfied, and he did, but somehow sad and deflated at the same time.

His smile reflected how he felt as he held his hand out to say goodbye to his old friend, the shaman's son.

As always, Bart seemed to read his mind. With the same wan smile, he said, "Thank you. Your work here is done."

Big Al was standing at the exit door with his arms folded across his chest and a very sour expression on his face when Sorry got back to the warehouse. Sorry blew out a lungful of air and rolled his eyes as he picked up the clipboard with the day's signed receipts and made his way toward his boss.

"Afternoon, boss," he said, with what he hoped was an ingenuous smile. "Got a minute to talk?" He'd learned long ago that the best defense was a good offense.

Big Al sighed and motioned for Sorry to follow him inside.

"About today," Sorry began, settling his butt into one of the chairs opposite Big Al's desk. He used two fingers to straighten his mustache. "It's about that call you got from the cops."

"The police called me, yes."

"Fortunately, no one was badly hurt."

Big Al sat forward with his elbows on the desk, his lips pressed tight together, his hands playing with a pen. "Okay, give me your side of it, Danny. The police implied that you started it."

Sorry lowered his voice, trying to sound serious and sincere. "What I did was for your sake, boss. I was trying to do my best for you and the company."

"Explain, please."

Sorry took a breath and began the spiel he'd rehearsed on his way back to the warehouse. "Okay, I'd stopped in at this freight warehouse on Annacis to use the phone 'cause I didn't want to tie up your company cell phone with a personal call. I just wanted to touch base with my lovely wife to see if the kids were okay. So, I'm at this freight warehouse. A friend of mine owns the place –." El Watson was a friend, wasn't she? More or less. "– and I've got to take responsibility here. I thought because it was a private yard and I knew the place, that my truck – *your* truck – would be safe unlocked for a couple of minutes, then suddenly the warehouse guy comes in sayin' some dude was trying to get into my truck – *our* truck, the company truck, that is."

Big Al was seriously frowning, but Sorry wasn't worried.

"So I dropped the phone and ran out there to see this dude's ass sticking out of the driver's side of the truck. The keys weren't in it, of course, but I didn't want him stealing anything or doing any damage to *our* truck, so I grabbed him by the legs and yanked him outa there backwards so fast I accidentally kinda slammed his face into the dirt. Then the guy gets up and wants to fight me, so I had to let him know I wouldn't hesitate to defend myself." Sorry's brain did a replay of the guy spitting blood into the gravel after his teeth went through his tongue as his chin hit the ground. He'd given the guy a bloody nose, too, but he figured it was best not to go into that much detail.

After a what-can-you-do shrug, Sorry continued. "The dude overreacted and called the cops. I'd barely gone two blocks when a cop car pulled me over and made me turn around and go back to Watson – er, the place it happened. When I explained why I'd roughed the guy up a little, seems there was some agreement all around that it was an unfortunate incident but no need to press charges either way. You know what I mean?"

Big Al took a moment, chewing on his lower lip while his wheels were turning, before saying, "Roughed him up, you say. A little, you say. In self-defense. You look just like you did when you left this morning. Where did he hit you?"

Sorry put on an innocent face. "Can I help it if I've got faster reflexes than him? He would've hit me if I hadn't nailed him first."

"Why would he call the police if he was trying to steal the truck?"

"Think about it. He's going to admit to the police he was trying to steal the truck?" Sorry frowned. "He made up some bullshit story about me leaving the lights on and he was just trying to do me a favor."

"Did you?"

"Huh?"

"Did you leave the truck's lights on?"

"That's not the point, is it, boss? Would we even be talking about that if it weren't for the idiot who tried to steal the truck – your truck? The cops only called you to verify that I work for you, right?"

Big Al pressed his lips tight together again, inhaled and exhaled. "You know, Danny, this was only your second day on the job and already you've created trouble for me and the company. I'm really not sure you're the right man for this job."

Sorry's gut sank. If he got fired, he was fucked as far as Mo was concerned. "Look, I'm sorry, boss. I really, really, wanted to do the right thing for you and the company, but I guess I got carried away. You won't regret keeping me on. Nothing like that will happen again. I promise."

Inside, he was saying, *If you fire me, I'll kick your fat ass across the parking lot and toss your balls to a junk-yard dog.* He impressed himself with his ability to brown nose. It wasn't hard at all if you just stayed calm and didn't let your temper reach your big mouth.

Big Al kept playing with that pen, either thinking it over or trying to make Sorry sweat.

Sorry was just about to lose it on him when Big Al finally spoke.

"Okay. I'll give you another chance."

Big Al put his arm on Sorry's shoulder as they walked back out to the warehouse together. "I like you, Danny," he said with an emphatic nod. "You're a little rough around the edges, but deep down, I think you're a stand up guy."

Sorry showed his teeth in the obligatory genuine smile. "I like you, too, boss," is what he said, giving Big Al a playful tap on the arm with his fist.

I don't give a shit what you think, you big turd, is what went through his mind.

After almost three weeks on the road, most of it sleeping in the tin box behind the seats in his truck, it felt glorious to be waking up in his own bed. His window was open to the scents of cedar and grass and lilac that took turns drifting in on the occasional current of warm summer air. Hunter stretched his limbs under the sheets, then again as he stood beside his bed. Luxurious. His one bedroom suite in the basement of a private house on a south facing slope in North Vancouver was humble, almost Spartan, by most standards, but compared to being on the road, it truly was a luxury.

He pulled on a pair of shorts and walked barefoot to his back door, stepped out onto the concrete patio, smooth and cool in the shade of the sundeck overhead. He could hear his landlord's voice from the deck above, a one sided conversation in that deep, gentle voice. Gord was a good man. Although Hunter had only known him since coming to live there after his divorce, Gord felt more like family, sometimes, than Hunter's own father, who lived half an ocean away in Hawaii.

"Bye, Toots," he heard Gord say, then the soft beep of the call ending, and a louder, "Good morning, stranger. Coffee's on."

Hunter grinned as he took the wooden stairs to the deck two at a time. Dressed only in shorts with his hair still tousled from sleep, he wasn't surprised to find his landlord in exactly the same condition, except for the coffee in his hand. In spite of his age, Gord's chest evidenced his active life of golfing and gardening; his tan attested to the hours he spent outdoors in the sun. Hunter helped himself to a mug of coffee in the kitchen and came back out to join the retired doctor. The two of them sat at opposite sides of the table, both of their chairs facing south toward the tall cedars at the base of the property and the view of Burrard Inlet behind them.

"Nice to have you back. How are you?"

"Just tickety boo," said Hunter, raising his coffee mug in Gord's direction as a thank you. "And you?"

"The same. How was the Yukon?"

Hunter felt two scrawny velvet paws wrap around his ankle, the prick of claws and a quick nip at the bottom of his calf. "Ow!" He lifted that leg to inspect for damage as the perpetrator scrambled across the sundeck and into the house through the open kitchen door. "No blood."

"She must like you," said Gord, deadpan, showing off a set of parallel scratches on his left arm. The Siamese cat had been a gift from one of his daughters, and crazy as it was, was good company for the widowed senior.

"The Yukon was great. Alaska, too." The two men sat drinking their coffee as Hunter gave his landlord a brief travelogue from his trip north. "I've got today and Tuesday morning off to do my laundry and banking, but I'm back on the road again tomorrow afternoon." He sighed. "The only reason I've got today off is because it's a national holiday and the shipper is closed. By the way, happy Canada Day."

"You, too. Heading north again?"

"South this time. Back to Southern California, my usual run."

"You'll be able to celebrate Independence Day while you're there."

"Sure thing." Hunter snorted as he considered the prospect. "I'll be at a truck stop in San Bernadino celebrating yet another unpaid day."

Gord raised his eyebrows. "You don't sound too happy. That's not like you. Are you becoming disillusioned with your job?"

Hunter sipped at his coffee while he thought about how to answer his landlord's question. El had relented and found him half a load at least from Prince George back to Vancouver, but with the truck repairs, the down time and the empty miles, overall he'd lost money on the trip north. He tried to picture himself doing something else. Local deliveries, like Sorry, so he'd be home every night. An office job, sitting behind a desk. Something in retail, or even getting into corporate security or insurance investigations. Wearing a suit and tie.

"No," he said, drawing out the word. "I still like what I do." Being home alone every night wasn't something he was ready for. Somehow it was more therapeutic being alone on the road. He relished the hours of solitude, the change of scenery, the feel of hundreds of horsepower under his control, the loose camaraderie with other drivers.

"You're a highway cowboy."

"Highway cowboy." Hunter nodded, a smile playing across his face. "Good one, Gord."

The next day Hunter parked his Pontiac sedan against the fence at the Watson Transportation yard, pulled his duffle bag out of the back seat and transferred it to the cab of his Freightliner. He planned to give the Blue Knight a quick wash and close inspection before he was scheduled to hook up a loaded trailer of hot tubs to haul across the border. As he started a preliminary walk around the tractor, a five ton truck barreled into the yard, sounding its horn. It made him jump, and he turned around to glare at the driver.

"You're back," bellowed Sorry from the cab of the truck. "Want to go get some lunch?"

Five minutes later they were seated at a window table in Edna's Kitchen as Susan, one half of the Chinese couple who owned and operated the restaurant, was memorizing their orders. A burger and fries for Sorry, a Denver sandwich with fries for Hunter. Edna's coffee left something to be desired, so they both ordered Cokes.

Susan turned away and yelled something unintelligible to her husband Walter, then she turned back and pointed at Sorry with a finger. "You have dessert. Apple pie? Sticky bun? Jello? What?" Before he could answer, she turned to Hunter and repeated her questions, adding, "How 'bout you like nice lychee ice cream on hot day like today?"

Feeling under pressure, they both ordered the apple pie and Susan bustled off to another table, her Reeboks squeaking on the tile floor.

"So how are things between you and Simone?" asked Hunter, straightening the cutlery in front of him. "Has she forgiven you?"

With an exaggerated nod, Sorry said, "Coming along. New York wasn't built in a day, you know what I mean? I have to bite my tongue a lot in this new job, though, but it's getting easier every day." He leaned forward and lowered his voice. "I've learned to lie like a carpet. The payoff is Mo finally let me back in our bedroom on Friday." This was followed by one of his big laughs, causing customers at several other tables to turn around and stare. He leaned back and stroked his mustache, looking smug.

"I heard from Bart that Orville's stepson turned himself in. Thanks for that," said Hunter.

Susan rushed up to the table, deposited their two sodas, and moved on. Hunter's napkin fluttered to the floor in her wake. Sorry called to her retreating back, "Hey! Where's my straw?"

"You a grown man. You don't need straw," she shouted back without turning around.

"Yeah, I did like you said. I told him Legal Joe was cool, and that the two of them spoke the same language, you know what I mean? He wasn't sure, said he hates lawyers, but then he called me later to say thanks. Legal Joe told him he could get him off with a light sentence in medium security. Self defense, did he tell you that?"

Hunter was just about to take a sip of Coke but he shook his head.

"Jimmy Moses said he waited for this Collins guy to come out after he closed up the place, and they got into an argument. The prick owed him and Orville a pile of cash, and Moses wanted him to pay it back. Collins tells him no way and fuck off, so Jimmy loses it and takes a swing at him. Collins holds him off and roars like a bear, then reaches inside his truck. Moses sees him feeling around for a rifle, so he pulls his hunting knife off his belt and sticks the fucker with it. Wouldn't have done it if it weren't for the gun, he said. Sounds like a righteous move to me."

Susan plunked down their lunch plates and raced away.

The man at the table behind Sorry had evidently been listening in on the Jimmy Moses story and shot Sorry an appalled sideways glance as he passed their table on his way to the exit.

"So I guess you won't be free to ride with me for quite a while," said Hunter as they left Edna's. "Sounds like this job of yours is going to be more or less permanent."

"Yeah," said Sorry, scratching his belly. "More or less permanent. As long as Mo is happy." He frowned in concentration and ran a finger back and forth under his nose. "Until something better comes along, anyway."

Hunter stood watching Sorry as he started up the delivery truck, rolled down the window and lit up a cigarette. Blowing smoke out of his nostrils, Sorry raised a hand in goodbye and drove away.

CHAPTER TWENTY-ONE

It was the end of August when Hunter got a call on his cell phone from Mark, the young man he'd met in Eagle at Yukon Sally's lodge. Mark said he would be arriving in Vancouver in a couple of days on his way home from Alaska and was wondering if Hunter knew of a cheap place to stay. Hunter told him he was in luck if he wanted to crash on his couch. "I'm usually on the road, but I've got a couple of days off this week, if you don't mind a detour to North Vancouver."

It had been a hot day, and Hunter was relaxing in the evening sun on his small patio, reading a Tom Clancy novel between sips out of a can of Labatt's Blue and the occasional bite of a pepperoni stick. He heard footsteps above him and then his landlord's voice over the railing. "Are you there, Hunter? You've got guests. I'll send them round back."

Guests? Guests were a rarity. Even his daughters usually met him at a restaurant somewhere, and he'd just had dinner with the girls the day before.

Seconds later, the sight of a dark-haired young woman rounding the corner of the house made him catch his breath. It was Goldie. She rushed up to him and gave him a hug. "I don't know how I can ever thank you for everything you've done for us," she said.

Mark appeared behind her, just nodding his hello.

"Glad I could help, but I've only got one couch."

Goldie's blush was immediate.

"We'll manage," said Mark. "I've got a foamy and a sleeping bag."

Hunter smiled at the way the young man had come to her rescue. He was obviously a good kid. He proved it once again when he saw Gord struggling down the stairs with a folded lawn chair in each hand and hurried up to help him.

"Thought you could use these," said the old man, and declined Hunter's invitation to join them. "Got to get back to my show. I'm watching a biography of Patsy Cline," he said and disappeared back up the stairs.

Moments later the three of them were seated on the patch of lawn beyond Hunter's patio, Hunter and Mark enjoying their beer, Goldie waiting for the kettle to boil for tea. The sun was low in the sky, spreading a wash of deep yellow over the trees and grass in front of them and casting the shadows of the big cedars almost as far as their chairs. Hunter asked them what they'd been up to and where they were going.

Goldie's excitement was almost palpable. "Mark is on his way home to Santa Barbara, and he's going to drop me off at my mother's place on the way through Oregon. I'm hoping I can get into college, if I can find a part-time job." Her broad smile was replaced by a look of surprise. "What a lovely cat! It's a Siamese. Look beside you, Mark."

"Don't –." Hunter's warning came too late. Mark snatched his hand back as if he'd been bitten, and he had.

"Did it break the skin?"

Mark examined his hand and told them that he'd survive.

Hunter asked the question he'd been wanting to ask since they'd arrived. "How's Betty?"

Goldie half shrugged. "She wasn't real happy to see me go, but she understands. I told her I'd be back to see her next summer, or maybe even send her a ticket to come visit me wherever I end up." She stole a quick glance at Mark, who couldn't hide a smile. "I have trouble imagining her in a city, so I'm not too hopeful. Oh, there's the kettle." She got up to go make her tea.

The next morning Hunter made them a big breakfast of bacon and eggs and toast, then he followed them to the driveway in front of the house to see them off. The Jeep was covered in road dust, so

Mark used Gord's garden hose and an old towel to give it a quick cleaning as they said their goodbyes. Goldie gave Hunter another quick hug and made him promise to stop in next time he drove through Oregon.

"Salem's right on the I-5, you know." She rolled her eyes at her own stupidity. "Of course you know. You drive through it often enough."

Hunter watched the Jeep head up the driveway and turn toward the highway, then headed back to join Gord and the cat on the sundeck for another coffee. They spoke of being young and getting old and never knowing where life would lead them next and making the very best of every day, whatever that meant.

"Wish you were young again?" Hunter asked. In spite of a sense that something was missing in his life, that constant vague yearning for something – or someone – to fulfill him, right at this moment he had a feeling of contentment, of being right where he was supposed to be.

The old man shook his head. "Being young was too much work. Look at me now." He gestured wide, taking in the sundeck, the garden, the view of the inlet and across to the skyline of Vancouver beyond, even including Hunter and the cat. He wiggled his bare toes, leaned back with a satisfied sigh, and picked up his mug of fresh coffee.

Hunter smiled, kicked off his moccasins, and did the same.

CHAPTER TWENTY-TWO

It was the first snow of the season. Betty Salmon had just tromped through it to the outhouse and back, missing the presence of Hootie at her heels. He always used to be there to keep her company on the path to the outhouse in the morning. She closed the cabin door against the icy flurries and opened the woodstove, stirred the ashes to expose the glowing orange coals, and loaded half a dozen fresh splits. The water on the stove was hot enough to make tea, so she did, letting it steep until it was good and strong.

She sat in her chair facing the woodstove, her hands wrapped around the hot stoneware mug. The heat eased the ache in her fingers that the cold weather always seemed to bring. She thought about Goldie, wondering where the child was now, and what she was doing, and if she was happy. She worried aloud whether there would be a letter from her at the post office this week. She had promised to send pictures of California.

"Whether there is or not, we'll give her a call from town on Sunday morning." The voice came from behind her.

Betty felt the cold draft from the open cabin door as Orville and Hootie entered, the old man stomping the snow off his boots before prying them off his feet. Hootie, tail wagging and tongue lolling happily to one side, came to greet her. "Fire's stoked and the tea's ready," she said over her shoulder. "Get anything?"

"We got a nice fat rabbit," he said, standing next to her and giving her a quick hug and kiss before she had time to push him away. "Didn't we, Hootie?"

Hootie's tail wagged in response.

"You little traitor," said Betty, stroking the Malamute's broad forehead. Then to Orville, "I still can't believe how he's taken to you."

"He's only taken to me because you have, too," he said with a wink. "Haven't you, my little ptarmigan?"

"Go on with you. Drink your tea." Betty scowled at him, but inside she was smiling.

She had no doubt that Orville knew it, too.

THE END